THE BLOOD RUNE

THE RONAN RYAN ODYSSEY - BOOK ONE

MARK KLEINSCHMIDT

ASTREBLA PUBLISHING

For Delia, who is everything.

PROLOGUE

I t was before time ... before the Norse, before their ancestors ... before the gods.

The northern lands were the realm of sabre-tooth tigers and woolly mammoths, huge wolves and fleet-footed deer. Their land was alternately in the icy grip of winter, when the sun barely made an appearance, or basking with relief in a brief summer. During those long, balmy days, the earth devoured the sun's warmth like a starving child. Fertile soil, released from the clutches of snow, powered frantic plant growth, abundant food for mammoth and deer alike. And tigers and wolves feasted on their fattened flesh.

In the gathering dusk, a small herd of mammoth cows and calves grazed under the watchful eye of the dominant female, their supple trunks twisting off great tufts of sedge, coiling them up to gaping mouths. Downwind, a tiger left the trees, melting through the grass, eyes fixed on the closest baby.

As the tiger leapt, the matriarch shrieked, her scything tusks arcing toward the great cat's exposed belly. Locked in deadly combat, neither noticed a fireball streaking toward them, swamping the twilight with blazing, white-hot light.

The earth trembled. The air exploded. Tiger and prey vaporised in an instant.

A blazing slab of rock, smaller than a mammoth's head, seared through their midst, fizzing off flaming shards as it struck the earth. It slashed a deepening gash along the valley floor, pushing up a wall of soil before coming to a hissing halt. A thunderous reverberation of solid sound rolled across the landscape, shattering trees, laying them flat like grass before a tempest. It surged, unrelenting, before shattering on the mountainous flanks of the valley, dislodging boulders, collapsing caves. Thrown back on itself, it choked on its own dying echoes.

All that remained was empty silence ... obliterated landscape ... inscrutable stars.

A sprinkling of rounded, glassy flakes lay scattered along a trail of destruction. And there, beneath Earth's soft flesh, a rock from another world lay cooling in the embrace of its new home.

PART I

THE WAKENING

1

THE ARCHER

The archer was part of the forest, as silent and unmoving as a tree. Through a small gap between the trunks, he could make out his prey. He judged the distance—perhaps thirty metres. Easing his bow up, arrow already in place, he drew the string taut to his chin, eyes trained on the target.

It was a small gap, close to a hand-span—enough to see a sliver of the man's shadowed silhouette, right above the heart; enough for an arrow fired true.

Thirty metres? After years of practice, skewering lemons on fence posts at that distance was a cinch, but this shot wasn't a piece of fruit.

A breath of air feathered his right cheek; he adjusted his aim ... not much ... enough. Not an easy shot, but far from impossible. As the last of his breath slid away, he pictured his arrow flying true, and relaxed his fingers. The taut string zinged off calloused fingertips.

Skimming between the trees, the arrow flew like a missile, locked onto its target.

The shadowed head spun, eyes gleaming with animal cunning, torso swaying from the arrow's path. A leather-gloved hand struck like a cobra, plucking the speeding shaft from the air, and in one continuous motion, reversed the arrow, flicking it on a return flight, twice as fast.

And the archer watched it coming, through that small gap between the trees, sunlight glinting from the razor-sharp head with every revolution of the shaft. As if in slow motion, it drew ever closer, aimed at his heart. But he was frozen.

His arrow, made by *his* hands, was almost upon him. He'd failed again; the man had won, like always ... the arrow ... the man.

Ronan Ryan woke with a small cry, bolt upright in his dark bedroom, sucking in quick breaths. Sweat soaked his tee-shirt and plastered sandy hair to his forehead.

It was always the same: the opportunity, the shot ... the failure. The scenarios changed, but the outcome didn't. And the shadowed man—Ronan could never see the face, but the menacing bulk and the fluid movements were unmistakable—was always his stepfather.

The dream first appeared when Bruno Masters smashed Ronan's original bow in a vindictive rage. Ever since, it was the final element of every humiliation at the hands of the man. Were Masters to know about it, he would've taken great delight, viewing it as a bonus, the ultimate indignity of whatever punishment he'd meted out.

Whether the assault was verbal or physical, Ronan would take his seething heart or aching body away into the bush, anywhere away from his stepfather. More often than not, he would head across the creek from his mother's house, and up the bush-cloaked hillside to an ancient gum tree hollowed by centuries of termites and bush fires. After collecting his hidden bow, quiver and arm guard, he would loose arrows at a distant target until, fingers bloodied and arms burning, he no longer had the strength to draw the string, and the helpless tears of frustration and anger had dried, unseen, on his cheeks.

The dream hadn't troubled Ronan since Grandpa Paddy came to stay. Over the ensuing year, Bruno Masters became a tightly coiled spring. Ronan saw it in the man's face, in the eyes. Yet, for all those glorious months, the old Irishman's presence controlled Masters. Now, Grandpa Paddy was gone and, while the dream had returned, the actual violence hadn't ... not yet.

However, after twelve months of swallowing the rage that drove the attacks, Masters was a barely dormant volcano, giving off increasing warning rumbles.

Ronan's stomach turned at the prospect of a return to what came before. The hurtful words or scathing looks behind his mother's back were bad enough, but the man's crushing grip as he pounded Ronan's flesh was like being buried under a landslide, a mountain of suffocating helplessness. Yet far worse was the constant dread hanging like a great weight round his neck: that venomous threat of retribution on his mother and half-brother if Ronan ever dared breathe a word.

So, he had remained silent, absorbing the assaults with dogged determination, taking grim satisfaction that he never gave his stepfather any reason to fulfil the threat. Now, with no Grandpa Paddy, a whole blissful year of no beatings was about to end, Ronan felt it in his bones. And the mere suggestion stirred the dormant worm of fear in the bottom of his gut.

The worm writhed; the archer had returned.

2

THE AMBUSH

Three days after the archer returned to his dreams, a despondent Ronan stared from his bedroom window. Beyond the garden gate, the ground disappeared, plunging to the nearby creek with its guardian she-oaks—he didn't notice their drooping crowns or hear the song of the wind in their needle-like leaves. That watercourse, and the eucalypt bushland rising on the other side, was normally a magnet to him but, today, he was lethargic, hollow and lost. Ronan didn't want to do anything—not eat, go to school or practice with his bow—he only wanted the hurt and fear to stop, the ache to leave his heart and, most of all, he wanted Grandpa Paddy to walk through the door and reassure him that everything would be fine.

But dead is dead. The peaceful, pasty face lying in the open coffin was undeniable, a crushing reality on top of a truck-load of grief.

On the sombre drive back from the Killarney cemetery, Ronan was oblivious to the stately gums flashing by; all he could think of was how things could've been different.

There wouldn't have been a funeral if Grandpa Paddy had only worn a respirator when he'd mixed the chemicals to mend the leaking water tank; if only he hadn't climbed into that confined space alone.

The irony haunted Ronan. The family spent the whole of last year worrying the old man might catch the virus, yet he still died—in a freak accident. Grandpa Paddy would've called it fate, or destiny; Ronan called it cruel, unfair. And overriding that irony, and pushing hard behind the heartache, was the cold clutching hand of fear ... fear of what lay ahead.

The real beatings began when Ronan was twelve. Masters' latest sure-fire business deal had evaporated, along with his money, and he had tried to drown his financial sorrows with excessive alcohol, taking his frustrations out on Ronan.

Until a couple of months before Grandpa Paddy's unexpected arrival at the farm, Masters had been away most of the time, so the attacks were few and far between ... almost bearable. But each time the man returned, his demeanour was worse. Eventually, he no longer went away, but stayed in his study, brooding and drinking ... until the next inevitable explosion.

When Ronan saw the warning signs, he would subtly bait Masters to ensure the drunken rages didn't go near his mother and younger brother. But, for a whole glorious year, there was never a raised hand. It was a sublime twelve months where Ronan and his grandfather had worked, played and laughed together. Ronan learnt to charm with clever words and fight with sharp ones. The assaults faded into the past.

Now, with Grandpa Paddy gone, it was, once again, up to Ronan to look out for his family. Already Masters was revelling in the loss of restraint, shooting sharp words under his breath toward Ronan, care-lessly cuffing an ear when no one was looking, and his new favourite, pinching a chunk of flesh and giving a painful twist. However, the major eruption might be delayed now Masters had let off steam.

Earlier, immediately after the funeral service, the mourners had gathered at the pub for light refreshments, a wake of sorts.

Masters, heavy shoulders hunched, beefy hands smothering a frosted beer glass, sat at the bar with Roley Evans, a drinking mate. They were perched beside the doorway leading to the toilets and, with several glasses of fruit punch under his belt, Ronan had no choice but to run the gauntlet. He waited until Masters' back turned before making a dash for it, and as he passed, he caught the words, "... good riddance to that bloody interfering old mick."

Ronan jerked to a halt as if Masters had grabbed his collar; caution fled. "He was twice the man you'll ever be," he snarled, voice quivering with rage.

Masters turned, a sneer distorting his slash of a mouth. "Well, if it isn't the smart-mouthed little bastard. Like father, like son."

"Yeah, well, Ruddi is damned lucky he doesn't take after you!" Even in his fury, Ronan recognised Grandpa Paddy's influence in his sharp words. And while the blood was still rushing to Masters' face, Ronan disappeared toward the toilets.

When Ronan walked from the cubicle, Roley Evans and his expectant smirk were nonchalantly leaning against the entry door. Ronan's gut fluttered, his eyes darted.

Masters stepped from another stall. "Looking for me, bastard?"

Head down, Ronan tried to walk past, but Masters shot out a hand, throwing a vise grip round Ronan's upper arm, jerking hard. The force spun him into his stepfather's beery breath. Ronan glared defiantly as Masters' free fingers locked onto a chunk of Ronan's chest, through his shirt. It was a hot coal searing into his skin, and although gasping under his breath, he gritted his teeth, not making a sound.

"Tough little nut, ain't he?" Evans observed, as if commenting on a positive trait of a working dog.

"Not as tough as he thinks," Masters hissed, walking stubby pincer fingers across Ronan's chest, down his stomach, beneath his arms, across his back—grip and twist, grip and twist. Each time those cruel nippers found a fresh piece of flesh, a tiny spot-fire ignited, hot enough to leave a scorch mark on Ronan's white funeral shirt.

Ronan couldn't escape—Masters always had one hand locked on flesh, besides, there was nowhere to go. So he stood and took it, trying not to flinch as each fresh ignition sizzled into his brain.

The torment was ended by urgent knocking on the door behind the grinning Roley Evans. Masters gave a final twist and nodded at his friend. As they strode out the door, Evans mumbled, "Sorry, mate, the door stuck."

Ronan threw his face into the sink, hiding his pain, sluicing water over simmering skin, and didn't look up until the footsteps passed and the cubicle door closed. The face that greeted him in the mirror appeared close to normal, if still a little flushed, but his previously crisp shirt was now covered in funky flower bud puckers. And hidden behind each was a full blossom of blistering pain.

Neither water, rubbing nor wishful thinking would smooth the upheavals to the shirt. His mother must never know, but they may as well have been painted red. Then he remembered the spare white sport shirt sitting in his cricket kit bag—it would have to do. As he wound a circuitous, mother-avoiding route to the car, he formulated a cover story of spilling food and having to wash it off.

It had started—as he knew it would—and his hands were aching for the curve of his bow, fingertips tingling for the touch of the bowstring. With a fresh shirt on, he trudged back to the wake, swallowing the bitterness pooling in his mouth. The assault in the pub toilet was a mere taste of what was in store.

3

THE VISITOR

On the day after the funeral, David Dalziel and his briefcase turned up. Smoky, the ageing, one-eyed homestead mongrel, announced the stranger's arrival with deep-throated woofing.

It was mid-morning, and yesterday's assault still smouldered in Ronan's memory and flesh. "That'll do, Smoke," he chided, squinting at a squat silver car wallowing up the uneven track to the house. It came to a halt beneath the spreading branches of the gum tree by the garden gate, heat shimmers rising from its shiny metal skin. The driver was not from the bush: he opened his door before giving the dust time to settle —it coated the car's plush interior despite the driver's futile hand-waving. Defeated, he uncoiled his lanky, business-suited frame from behind the steering wheel.

"Good morning, young man," he said, words clipped and precise, all rough edges meticulously filed off. As he pushed through the gate, he gave a final, fruitless swipe at the swirling cloud.

"Hello," Ronan replied uncertainly. Some of the eddying dust followed the man onto the wide verandah; with a fastidious flick he tried to stop it blemishing his stiff grey suit. Smoky, despite having barked a danger warning, felt there was more to do; sniffing a tyre, he cocked a leg, washing rivulets of dust from the black rubber.

The man held out a slack hand that had seen little sun and even less manual labour. "David Dalziel."

Ronan looked at it as though it might be coated with virus, but his manners prevailed. "Ronan Ryan," he said, returning the grip hesitantly. "Pleased to meet you." Which seemed a ridiculous thing to say when you didn't know the person, but his mother always used those words—along with her magical smile—when meeting people for the first time, and people always appeared pleased to meet her.

"Indeed," Dalziel said.

Unsure what that meant, or if he should reply, Ronan said nothing.

David Dalziel shifted a small, brown leather briefcase from one hand to the other, sniffing his skinny nostrils closed. "Ronan Padraig Ryan?" He pronounced Ronan's middle name as it was spelt.

"Paw-rick," Ronan corrected without thinking.

"Indeed."

"So, are you Ronan Pawdrig Ryan?" Dalziel repeated, still failing with the second name.

"Yes," Ronan replied slowly. "How do you know?"

"I am a lawyer ... from Brisbane," Dalziel said, as if it explained everything.

Ronan held the man's gaze, barricading the doorway with his sprouting teenage frame and widening shoulders.

"Who is it, Ronan?" his mother called from the kitchen.

"A bloke from Brisbane," he said over his shoulder, eyes never leaving the stranger.

His mother glided up the hall, wiping flour-covered hands down her apron front. "Oh." She lifted her apron, wiping her fingers harder. By the time she reached Ronan's side, the hand was clean and extended, and she was beaming. "I'm Maureen Masters."

The briefcase swapped back to the left hand, nostrils sniffing closed again. "David Dalziel of Dempsey, Darcy and Dalziel."

"Pleased to meet you, Mr Dalziel," she said, shaking the offered hand without hesitation. "How can I help you?"

"I am here in accordance with the wishes of the late Padraig Ryan," he said, mispronouncing it again.

Ronan fought the sting of rising tears, but could do nothing about the engulfing tide of grief. "It's Paw-rick."

"Ronan!"

He raised a questioning eyebrow at his mother.

Dalziel sniffed. "Perfectly alright. I do apologise."

Maureen smiled her own apology. "Won't you please come in?"

He could be an axe-murderer! Ronan thought, reluctantly stepping aside—such a thing would never cross his mother's mind; she always thought the best of everyone.

David Dalziel hesitated.

Maureen smiled again, motioning along the hallway. "Please, come in. Would you like some smoko? I'm about to take scones out of the oven ... and we have homemade strawberry jam and cream."

"Sounds splendid," he said, stepping into the cool interior, smoothing his blue-striped tie as the fly-screen door bumped closed behind him.

"Ronan, would you tell Bruno and Ruddi that we have a visitor, please?"

Reluctantly, Ronan left her with the unannounced stranger.

4

THE MENACE

Bruno Masters sat at his office desk, dark eyes flicking across rows of numbers on the computer screen, half-full glass of whiskey at his elbow. *Probably another money-losing scheme,* Ronan thought, his heart bubbling into fear and resentment at the sight of the man. Suddenly unable to speak, he hurried past the open door and into the bathroom, where he sluiced the agitation away with cold water.

Masters hadn't always been brutal: Ronan's early memories were of a fitter, leaner stepfather who treated him with tolerance, and his mother with a degree of affection and respect. But a change came over the man, and even the arrival of his own son failed to reverse the slide. Any pleasure he derived from Ruddi's arrival soon turned sour, along with his finances—he had inherited a small fortune and quickly turned it into an even smaller one.

The good part about Masters' dwindling inheritance was that he was generally away trying to work out where his late parents' wealth was disappearing to, or chasing the latest get-rich-quick scheme, which had the opposite effect.

Eventually, with the last of the fortune squandered, all the man had left was a resented wife, a resentful son, and a loathed stepson. That's when Ronan wished the money hadn't run out, for he no longer had his mother, Ruddi and Doyle Farm to himself.

With the man permanently in residence, the previous sprinkling of beratement, menace and abuse became an almost constant barrage. Ronan ignored the verbal assaults as best he could, meticulously hiding the bruises from the man's vise-like grip and heavy blows. His dogged refusal to show pain helped hide the harsh truth from his mother, and it took the sharp eyes of an old Irishman to discover the truth from the other side of the world.

Ronan remembered it well: it was a Saturday evening, his mother had taken Ruddi off to a guitar lesson while Masters sat behind the closed office door, swilling whiskey and brooding. It had been the perfect opportunity for Ronan to chat with his grandfather in County Donegal.

While waiting for the call to connect, Ronan reached out to adjust the web cam. As he did, his short shirt sleeve rode high up his arm.

"And what sort of scrap have you been getting yourself into, lad?" Grandpa Paddy's words burst across the internet; Ronan jumped like a startled rabbit, eyes darting toward the office before realising he was wearing headphones.

"Howya, Grandpa."

"Howya yourself, lad. How are things in the land of upside down?"

"All the blood is rushing to my head and making my brain grow big," Ronan said with a smile. He always looked forward to the banter with his grandfather; it was fun, and frivolous, and never failed to give his day a lift. Now, and more importantly, it was diverting attention from the bruises on his arm.

"Ach, and you'll soon be smarter than me ... but you're not there yet, lad."

"Am I close?" Ronan asked hopefully.

"Not yet awhile," the old man said, shaking his head and smiling, before sobering. "Spill it."

Ronan cast a furtive glance at the door before leaning close to the camera. "Masters," was all he said. But that one word released the dam of pent-up anger and fear, and the story tumbled out in whispered urgency.

At the end of the call, Grandpa Paddy said, "Keep your mouth shut and your head down, lad. You hear me?"

A week later, Grandpa Paddy arrived at Doyle Farm, bringing with him a reprieve—the bruising stopped, even if the drinking and seething resentment didn't.

Now, calming himself in the bathroom, Ronan threw a final handful of water over his face, towelling it dry, checking the mirror for normality. Satisfied, he left. "Smoko," he said without expression as he passed the office door, disappearing before Masters could turn his shaved dome.

Ruddi was in the lounge room, eyes glued to bounding and scampering figures on the large television screen, fingers frenetically working the buttons of the gaming controller between his hands.

"What level, bro?" Ronan asked, only to be met by silence. More than six years younger than Ronan, Ruddi had his father's dark hair and solid build, but his mother's gentle eyes and easy smile. Despite their occasional differences, they'd been best mates since ... forever.

"Earth calling Ruddi."

"Huh?" Ruddi's head never turned.

"What level are you?" Ronan vaulted over the back of the couch, flopping beside the younger boy.

"Aw, twenty-three, but I can't get past this last monster."

Ronan reached for the controller. "Here, let me show you."

Ruddi swung it away. "No. I want to do it. Just tell me how."

"Alright, no need to get stroppy." Ronan studied the screen. "Give me a look at your inventory." Ruddi pressed, flicked and clicked. "Okay, now let's have a look ..."

Recently turned sixteen, Ronan towered over the soon-to-be-ten Ruddi, but in their preferred gamerscause slump, their tousled heads were almost level. Immersed in the game, they didn't hear the heavy tread behind them.

"Turn that infernal thing off and get out there for smoko," Masters growled, cuffing Ronan's ear, sending his head slamming into Ruddi's.

"Ow!" Ruddi yelped, rubbing his ear, shooting his father a sour glare. Ronan said nothing, he wouldn't give his stepfather the satisfaction of knowing it hurt. He simply stood and turned, defiantly facing the man across the couch. The intervening air carried whiskey breath and menace like a static charge.

5

THE STANDOFF

Ronan's eyes never wavered from Masters. "Hurry up, Ruddi," he said from the side of his mouth. Ruddi feverishly pressed buttons to save the game. With each passing second, the colour of Masters' face deepened. Ronan watched the massive fists curling into bludgeons.

With a recent teenage growth bringing him almost level with his stepfather's gaze, Ronan sensed the looming height equality added to Masters' resentment. He stood there in defiance, silently buying Ruddi a few precious seconds, making himself the focus of the man's ire. The explosion, when it came, would be directed at Ronan and not Ruddi. It always was; it had to be. And despite yesterday's fracas in the pub toilet, there was clearly more to come.

The worst, full-blown eruption, so far, was inked across Ronan's memory like a tattoo. It happened several years ago, and he'd thought he'd breathed his last.

———

It was a warm afternoon; both boys were playing in the backyard.

Ronan fired arrows at lemons stuck into the side of a huge, round bale of hay his mother was using for garden mulch. Every time an arrowhead sliced through the target, he glowed with satisfaction—seven without missing. Meanwhile, Ruddi, one of his father's rusty golf clubs in hand, swung lustily at fallen lemons under the tree, whooping with delight at the spray of juice whenever he made contact.

Masters was not long home from a lengthy business trip to somewhere or other, and he rumbled onto the verandah, half-tumbler of whiskey in his hand, unbuttoned cuffs dangling. He saw his son and roared, "Ruddi! How many times have I told you not to touch my clubs? Get up here!"

Masters' temper radiated across the yard like a bonfire.

"But, Dad," Ruddi protested, "it's an old one you don't use anymore." He held up the juice-spattered club stained with rust and laced with cobwebs.

"Don't touch means don't touch! Get up here! Now!"

Shoulders slumped, Ruddi dropped the club on the grass and dragged his feet to the steps. Masters met him at the top, placing his glass on the verandah rail, grabbing his son by the scruff of the neck. With a jerk, he pulled Ruddi upward, bumping him against the railing. The glass teetered and fell, shattering in the garden. Masters swore. "Now look what you've done." Spittle flecked his lips.

Ruddi's face drained, his legs sagged. "But ... I ... I ..."

Masters screwed a massive fist tighter into Ruddi's collar, frog-marching him across the verandah to the wall-mounted hat rack. It was a long row of hooks fashioned from worn horse shoes, and hanging from the farthest hook was a broad leather strap. Masters called it The Persuader. Far too often, Ronan and Ruddi felt it across their backsides or legs; far too often, it was unwarranted. Ronan fumed as his stepfather reached for the strap.

Without thinking, he let fly a well-aimed arrow. It zinged from the bowstring in the instant Masters' fist encircled The Persuader and lifted it off the hook. The arrowhead sliced through the centre of the strap, pinning it to the backing board of the hat rack.

Masters recoiled as if from a snake strike. Ronan was instantly paralysed—the enormity of what he'd done turned his muscles to concrete. Masters didn't say a word; he seemed to swell, jaw working, face darkening. Discarding Ruddi, he came down the half-dozen steps like an avalanche. Ronan hesitated for a fateful second before dropping the bow and bolting. But Masters, deceptively fast despite his increasing girth, caught him in a handful of quick strides. With his fist twisting Ronan's collar into a choking noose, Masters dragged him backward. Ronan flailed his arms, trying to land a blow to loosen the man's grip and let air through.

"You psychopathic little bastard," hissed into Ronan's buzzing ear. He tried to yell but could barely gasp. Ruddi's screamed plea to his father was lost in the swirl of darkness rolling across Ronan's vision. He slumped against Masters' restraint, further restricting the flow of air and blood.

As though from beneath a heavy blanket, Ronan heard his mother clattering down the steps, shrieking, "Bruno! Stop!" She launched herself like a mother cat.

Masters swatted her to the ground, losing his grasp on Ronan's collar in the process. The brute stood over his wife and stepson, jaw clenched, fists bunched, legs splayed, chest heaving.

Sobbing, Maureen cradled Ronan's head, glaring up at her husband, screaming, "You could've killed him!"

"The little bastard tried to kill *me*," Masters shot back between short breaths.

"He did not!" Ruddi yelled from the verandah where he'd been rooted to the spot for the past frantic seconds.

Ronan blinked at the harsh sunlight. "Oh, Ronan ... Ronan," Maureen sobbed, rocking his head in her lap. "Can you hear me? Are you okay?"

He nodded groggily, massaging the red welt across his throat, revelling in the air flowing to his lungs. "I'm fine, Mum." It was little more than a croak.

"Thank goodness!" she cried, rocking harder. She let out a huge sigh of relief before glaring at her husband with open hostility. "What the hell is going on?"

Masters was still huffing with fury. "I told you, he tried to shoot me with this bloody thing." He bent, gathering the discarded bow and quiver of arrows.

Ronan levered himself onto his haunches, shaking his head.

Masters ignored him. "He tried to kill me ... but he missed."

"I hit what I aimed for," Ronan said defiantly.

Masters snorted, lips curling. "You can't wriggle out of this, boy."

Ronan helped his mother to her feet and stood facing his tormentor, mutiny quivering in every fibre of his body. He pointed at the seven arrow-skewered lemons in the side of the hay bale. "Look for yourself," he said, with more bravado than he felt. "I hit exactly what I aimed for."

"He did," Ruddi confirmed. "Ro never misses, Mum."

The pride in his half-brother's tone warmed Ronan, but the apprehension in the boy's eyes rekindled Ronan's anger with his stepfather.

Masters snorted again. "And where did this super power suddenly come from?"

"As if you care," Ronan sneered.

Maureen put her hand on his arm. "Ronan," she said softly.

"It's true, Mum." There was a time when Ronan craved the approval of his stepfather, and tried many things to get it, but nothing he did was ever enough—he worked hard for good school grades ... no response; practised relentlessly at cricket, becoming the best all-rounder in the district ... no response; even took up karate after his stepfather lauded the prowess of a professional fighter ... no response. While none of the activities cut through with Masters, Ronan continued them because he enjoyed the challenge, and excelled. "He wouldn't have a clue what I do or what I like," he added, long past caring what the man thought.

Masters harrumphed with disdain.

"And I still do miss ... sometimes," Ronan admitted. "But never from this distance." Inspired by a book about Robin Hood, he'd scrimped and saved his pocket money for his treasured archery set, then honed a natural talent into considerable skill. "Here, I'll show you." He held out his hand.

"Not likely!" Masters swung the bow away. "And that's the last time you'll ever do anything like that again." He smashed the bow and arrows across a lifted knee before stalking off, discarding the splintered remains in his wake.

———

Now, facing his stepfather across the couch while Ruddi saved his video game, Ronan recalled his fury at the man for destroying what brought him so much joy and satisfaction. Well, he'd made himself another bow and fashioned a quiver full of arrows, hiding them where Masters would never find them.

"Boys," Maureen called from the kitchen, her voice lilting upward through the word. The tension between the two broke; Masters' welling rage subsided. He turned and, despite his weight and lack of fitness, strode fluidly toward the kitchen.

6

THE SHOWDOWN

Ronan and Ruddi looked at each other in silent acknowledgement of danger passed ... for now. Brothers in arms, they reluctantly trailed the lingering aura of hostility to the kitchen, where they encountered awkward silence. Masters had plonked himself at one end of the large table, arms crossed, an impatient scowl doing nothing for his face. David Dalziel sat to one side in aloof professionalism. At the opposite end, Maureen looked up from pouring the tea. "Ah, there you are, boys."

They took their customary places either side of her—symbolic guardians—and about as far away from Masters as they could get. Ronan had the further comfort of having the lawyer in between.

"Milk and sugar, Mr Dalziel?"

"Milk only, thank you."

With everyone served, Maureen settled serenely, hands clasped in her lap. "Please start."

The boys needed no second bidding, diving into the pile of steaming scones. Bruno Masters' sour face announced he'd prefer to be elsewhere, and David Dalziel popped a morsel into his mouth, chewing as though identifying individual ingredients.

"Delightful scone, Mrs Masters," he said after swallowing.

"Please, call me Maureen. And thank you, it's my mother's recipe."

"My compliments to your mother, then."

Ronan and Ruddi looked at each other, faces blank.

"I'm afraid we lost Mum and Dad some years ago." Maureen's eyes moistened.

"Ah, yes, I was terribly sorry to hear that," said Dalziel and, without missing a beat, "I am sure she would be proud of the way you are treating her recipe."

Maureen smiled weakly, nodding; Masters' thin lips compressed.

"Now, Mr Dalziel, you said this was about Paddy." Maureen offered him another scone.

Dalziel held up a hand, shaking his head at the food. "That is correct, Mrs Masters ... I will keep things formal, if you do not mind." He lifted his briefcase to the table, popped the catch and extracted a sheaf of papers. "I'm here to advise you of the wishes of the late Mr Padraig Ryan, better known as Paddy, of Doyle Farm—"

Masters' face reddened. "He bloody-well wasn't from here!"

"Bruno, please?" Maureen's voice was tired. She was always pleading with him lately, to moderate his language, his drinking, his sullen disposition, his outbursts. As always, he was having none of it.

"Bloody interfering old mick should've stayed in Ireland where he belonged."

"Mr Masters, whether you feel Mr Ryan belonged here or not, is immaterial." The lawyer's tone was dry. "This was his address of record, and that is all that matters."

The air between the two men crackled with tension.

"Now." Dalziel paused, pulling his mobile phone from a pocket, and placing it on the table beside the papers. "Before we start, I must get your approval to live-stream this conversation to my chambers, where it will be stored in accordance with the wishes of Mr Ryan."

"No bloody way!" The colour in Masters' face deepened.

Ronan peered eagerly from one to the other.

Maureen's brow furrowed. "Is that necessary?"

"Is it legal?" snapped Masters, slapping the table, rattling plates, making the lawyer's phone shimmy.

"Unusual, to be sure," Dalziel said, adjusting the phone, "but, as an officer of the court, I can assure you it is perfectly legal."

"No way," Masters snorted.

"However," said the lawyer, "if you do not wish to be recorded, you forfeit the right to be present, and to receive what was left to you by the late Mr Ryan."

Masters snorted again. "He won't have left anything for me, that's for sure."

"Oh, but he has, Mr Masters."

By the faces round the table, David Dalziel was the only one who could countenance such a thing.

"But why does it need to be recorded?" Masters snarled.

"While not usual, it is quite acceptable to make a record-of-meeting for such things, and the late Mr Ryan insisted that this be a live-streamed recording for reasons that I am not at liberty to divulge."

"I'm sure," Masters sneered.

"So," the lawyer said, sliding a single sheet of paper and a pen across the table to each person, "I need everyone to sign this acceptance of conditions, and we can proceed with the formalities."

"I'm in," said Ronan enthusiastically.

Ruddi's eyes sparkled. "Me too."

"I see no problem," said Maureen, elegantly penning her name onto the page.

Masters didn't move, glowering at Ronan as though his stepson was causing his worsening mood.

"Respectfully, Mr Masters," said Dalziel, each syllable an exercise in precision, "if you are not comfortable with the arrangements, it is your prerogative to withhold your assent. However, in the absence of your signed agreement, I must ask that you remove yourself from this gathering so we can proceed with the wishes of the deceased."

Masters' face bypassed scarlet and went straight to turkey-red, his agitation increasing with every word the lawyer uttered. He slammed a beefy fist onto the table top, rattling the crockery again. David Dalziel didn't bat an eyelid.

"Are you telling me I can't stay in my own home?" Masters roared.

"Absolutely not, Mr Masters. We can conduct these formalities in my chambers in Brisbane if that suits better. I am merely carrying out the wishes of—"

"The late Mr Paddy bloody Ryan," Masters snarled. "Yeah, I get the bloody message."

Ronan glanced at his mother's colouring cheeks.

"Bruno, please?" It came out as weary resignation rather than a plea. Masters looked like his blood was trying to burst through the skin of his face and neck.

"It was at Mr Ryan's insistence, and considerable expense, that I came here to do this in your own home. He felt it would lead to a more convivial ... ah ... pleasant atmosphere than our chambers in Brisbane."

Ronan smirked.

"Bruno, please?" Maureen said again. "What harm can it do ... it's what Paddy wanted."

"Well, that's the point, isn't it?" Spittle sprayed. "Always poking his nose in where it wasn't wanted, and he's still doing it from the grave."

Ronan lunged to his feet, toppling his chair. "He was worth two of you!" he yelled, not caring about the consequences.

"Ronan, please ...?"

Masters' malevolence was naked and loud. "He was an interfering old bastard! Good riddance!"

"At least he never raised his hand to a woman," Ronan said, using his agile tongue to hit the man where it hurt. Boy, would he cop it when the lawyer left, but he no longer cared. For good measure, he threw some of Grandpa Paddy's words at his tormentor. "You're a bully and a coward!"

The air drained from the room. Masters froze momentarily before slowly rising. "Why ... you ... ungrateful ... little ... mongrel. I took you in when no one wanted you, or your soiled mother."

Maureen gasped, face blanching, lips trembling as tears sprang to her eyes. A tremulous "Bruno" was all she could manage, a choked plea; she seemed to shrivel in her chair.

Ronan flew at Masters, but the lawyer's arm flashed out. Like most farm boys, Ronan was fit and wiry, muscles honed by shovel, rake and axe, and hours spent running in the bush. In addition, he was adding weight to his lean frame, but the soft-looking city lawyer stopped him in his tracks.

"Enough!" Dalziel's voice was a whip crack of authority in the hostile air. "Mr Masters, please sit down or forfeit your bequest."

Masters' jaw knotted, clenching and unclenching as if chewing gum, and his eyes, burning with enmity, were locked unwaveringly on Ronan. "Go to hell!" he snapped. "The lot of you can all go to hell!" He stormed from the room, hurling the screen door closed, stomping down the front steps. The slamming car door, roaring engine and crunching of spinning tyres on gravel was like an electric charge in the morning air.

7

THE MESSAGE

A welcome calm descended on the house as the vehicle's roar faded. Ronan glimpsed it through the window, dragging billowing dust round a distant bend before melting into a heat-shimmer. Dalziel tut-tutted. "My goodness," he said, not looking at all perturbed, his arm still encircling Ronan's chest. Embarrassed, Ronan twisted away.

Ruddi was hugging his mother as though attempting to draw comfort as much as deliver it. Maureen's head was bowed, her shoulders shaking. Ronan hugged them both, murmuring, "It'll be alright, Mum." But he didn't know how it could possibly be so.

"Mrs Masters, if I may?" Dalziel passed across a pressed linen handkerchief.

The small act of kindness triggered a low howl of anguish from Maureen. Ronan pulled her head into his chest, awkwardly stroking her dishevelled hair, humming an Irish tune he'd learnt from his grandfather, and after a moment, Ruddi joined in. Dalziel, with no sign of discomfort, quietly collected his mobile phone and withdrew to the verandah.

Ronan's first memory of Grandpa Paddy was of an old man on the computer screen talking with a funny accent to Maureen about Ronan's 'da', and singing songs of Ireland. From when he was old enough to sit still for five minutes, Ruddi was part of every call, chattering away and singing along with gusto.

Accompanying Grandpa Paddy to Australia last year was a tattered photograph of two young boys, ten and four, laughing into a webcam. Only one was a blood relative, but the old man was Grandpa Paddy to both.

Whether from the soothing tune or just the passage of time, their mother's misery eventually eased. "Thank you, boys," she said, blowing her nose delicately, dabbing puffy eyes, straightening her hair. She gave them both a squeeze and a weak smile. "I don't know what I'd do without you pair." Taking a deep breath and a sip of tea, she called, "Please come in, Mr Dalziel." While the lawyer resumed his seat, she pressed the handkerchief one more time to the corner of her eye. "I'm terribly sorry about that," she sighed.

"Not at all, Mrs Masters." Delving into his briefcase, he pulled out three letters and two small parcels. "Would you mind all sitting opposite me so I can guide you through what we need to do, please?"

As they arranged themselves along the other side of the table, Maureen said, "Don't you need to record this?"

"Only if Mr Masters is present," Dalziel said, extending a courtesy to Masters that Ronan felt was undeserved. "But now that he has left, there is no need to continue recording."

"You were already recording?" Maureen asked with a hint of accusation.

Ronan and Ruddi threw questioning looks at each other.

"I shall explain," Dalziel said, holding up a placating hand and sniffing. "Mr Ryan came to me several months ago, asking for my assistance." Dalziel laid out more papers. "Mr Ryan was concerned for the family's harmony, should he not be around to ensure it."

Ronan knew he was referring to Masters' menace. He looked at his mother, but she averted her eyes. Why she hadn't kicked Masters out years ago, he couldn't understand, or, more to the point, why she married him in the first place.

Dalziel continued, "Mr Ryan was one very canny gentleman and, to date, his strategy has been quite effective, if somewhat unorthodox. He said he could never trust Mr Masters to abide by any agreement, so we decided that making live-streaming a condition of remaining in the room was a good way to ensure Mr Masters was not present."

Ronan, Maureen and Ruddi looked from one to the other, each reflecting the others' puzzlement.

"Mr Ryan was concerned that what he was leaving for each of you would cause Mr Masters to become even more difficult. I think Mr Ryan was very shrewd."

The lawyer's words kindled an ache of pride in Ronan. Even though his grandfather now lay in the ground more than twenty kilometres away, Ronan felt his firm presence at the kitchen table.

"Now, it was perfectly legal for me to make that recording earlier, as I was participating in the conversation," Dalziel explained. "However, I cannot give it to anyone who was not present. But"—his voice descended into courtroom gravity—"it may be used as evidence in legal proceedings."

Three sets of eyes widened. Maureen blanched. "Legal proceedings?"

"An absolute last resort, let me assure you," Dalziel said, shaking his head, "but, should Mr Masters claim unfair treatment, that recording is proof otherwise." He selected three sheets of paper. "Now, before we go any further, I need you all to sign these individual acknowledgements of receipt for what I am about to give you." He pushed a one-page form in front of each of them.

Ronan scrawled his name on the indicated line; chicken scratch, Ruddi called it, like Grandpa Paddy's. Ruddi's penmanship was more like his father's upright, standing-to-attention lettering that reminded Ronan of a row of soldiers on parade.

A pensive Maureen looked up from her page. "But Paddy knew what Bruno was like. Why he would want to bait him?"

"I think Grandpa Paddy knew he'd blow a valve and want no part of it," Ronan said, "which is just as well, because Grandpa wouldn't have left anything for him anyway."

Dalziel gave a single nod. "Partly correct, young man."

"Well, I knew you were only bluffing when you said Grandpa Paddy left something for him." Ronan smiled at the idea.

"Oh, but he did indeed leave something for Mr Masters."

Ronan gaped.

The lawyer nodded again. "I was to give Mr Masters the simple message, 'Better men than you'."

Maureen and Ruddi looked puzzled, but Ronan knew exactly what it meant. Not long after Grandpa Paddy had arrived from Ireland, Ronan heard him and Masters arguing in the hay shed. Peering through a gap between loose sheets of corrugated iron, Ronan had seen the two men standing toe to toe.

Paddy poked a stiff forefinger into Masters' chest, saying, "You raise a hand to them, or threaten any of them ever again, and you'll wish you'd never been born."

Masters bared his teeth like a snarling dog. "What're you going to do about it, old man, talk me to death?"

The defeated sag of his grandfather's shoulders sent a wave of disappointment through Ronan. It turned to fear as the old man began turning away—he wouldn't be able to stop Masters after all. But Paddy had pivoted like a professional boxer, driving his work-hardened right fist wrist-deep into the younger man's bulging gut.

It was one of Ronan's most unforgettable memories—Masters' breath had exploded from him in a great whoosh. Face ashen, eyes wide in astonishment, mouth gaping like a stranded fish, his legs buckled, but Grandpa Paddy had held him up for a long, glorious, effortless moment.

"I've put better men than you on the canvas," Paddy hissed into Masters' ear as he teetered in agony. "Better men than you." The old man relaxed his grip, turned in disdain and walked from the shed as if going for a relaxing stroll. Behind him, Masters had collapsed in a gasping heap among the horse dung, flies and stale hay.

The recollection brought a warm glow to Ronan. "I wish he would've stayed just so I could see his face when you gave him the message."

"Ronan!"

"Mum, you know what he's like. He's mean and cruel, but he was bearable while Grandpa Paddy was here, wasn't he?" Ronan blinked hard against angry tears. What he actually meant was, Masters never *hit* him while Grandpa Paddy was around, but there were still plenty of verbal strikes—'ungrateful little cur', 'smart-mouthed little bastard', 'cheeky mongrel', and even, 'worthless piece of crap'. At one time, those words would've cut through Ronan's sense of self like a knife slash, but they no longer had any impact. Grandpa Paddy had told him that those ugly words reflected on Masters, not him.

Ronan so wanted to reveal all to his mother, and the lawyer, but the bowel-loosening fear of retribution crushed the desire. The only thing protecting his mother and brother was his silence. There was no telling what Masters would do if he suspected the full extent of his abuse was known.

Instead, Ronan said, "You know he flogs Ruddi and me with that big strap, and he hit you that day he broke my bow."

Ruddi looked ill. Maureen dabbed her eyes, staring into her plate, shaking her head. "He wasn't always like this," she said, almost to herself.

"But he *is* like this now, Mrs Masters," Dalziel said, "which is why Mr Ryan went to such lengths to ensure your ongoing safety."

"But how?" she asked, twisting the tear-dampened handkerchief in agitation.

"Well, all three of you should read what Mr Ryan left you," Dalziel said, replacing each signed form with a single, plain envelope. "You will need some time to digest the material, so I shall wait outside."

"The lounge room will be much more comfortable, Mr Dalziel," Maureen said, smiling weakly and reaching for her envelope, "... cooler, and no flies."

Ronan glanced at his mother. *Even now, she thinks of others.*

8

THE LETTERS

R onan turned the envelope. It was long and thin, and nestled in the top, left-hand corner of the front, as discreet and unobtrusive as Dalziel himself, was the return address of his law firm. But the bold scrawl inked across the centre of the envelope was what caught Ronan's attention: *Ronan Padraig Ryan*. Each spiky letter, unmistakably Grandpa Paddy's scratching, sent another tiny dagger to Ronan's heart. He ran his fingertips across the lettering, tracing the abrupt changes of direction, trying to will more from them than was there. Coming so soon after the old man's death, the memories they stirred brought a fresh burn to his eyes.

As though desperate to get closer to a vanishing wisp of smoke, Ronan tore open the envelope. Disappointment sagged through his body as he flattened the pages and saw the type-written words. Tears seeped past his best resistance, blurring his vision, dropping onto the page into blossoms of dissolved printer ink.

Surreptitiously swiping the moisture away, Ronan shot an embarrassed glance along the table—Ruddi was absorbed, mouthing words as he read his own letter; his mother was also reading, eyes red, handkerchief balled in her fist.

Ronan rifled through the pages, his heart surging when he found the third and final page covered with familiar scrawl.

Ronan, you know I'm not much for writing, I'd much rather talk, but that's no longer possible, which is why you've received this letter. It's up to you now to be the man on the farm, there is no other. Look after your mother and brother, and don't let Masters grind you down.

I've tried to ensure you all remain safe long after I'm gone. Trust David Dalziel, he's as dependable as the day is long. And trust Fergal Gallagher, he's family and will not let you down.

Be true to yourself, lad. You have your da's spirit and your ma's grace, and no one can ever take that from you unless you let them. But remember, Ronan, you've got to do your own growing, no matter how tall your father was.

Your ma is proud of you, your da would have been, and I surely am.

Stay true, stay strong, Ronan, and may the wind be always at your back.

Grandpa Paddy

Ronan blinked hard at his grandfather's words. Only yesterday they'd farewelled the old man, burying him in the little Killarney cemetery with its view across the town toward the mountains and Doyle Farm. Now, reading his words rekindled the pain of watching the dirt thud onto the coffin.

This morning, he'd wanted nothing more than for Grandpa Paddy to walk through the door again, and reassure him that everything would be fine, but the letter was the next best thing, it would have to be.

Ronan went back to the first page—sharp black printing on crisp, white paper.

Dear Mr Ronan Ryan

This letter is in accordance with arrangements made with our office by your late grandfather, Mr Padraig Ryan, hereafter referred to as Mr Ryan.

First, allow me to express, on behalf of the team at Dempsey, Darcy and Dalziel, our deepest condolences for your recent sad loss. Your grandfather was an outstanding individual with great commitment to family.

This letter includes the details of Mr Ryan's arrangements with this office, as well as a hand-written, personal letter to you, along with a typed transcript of same.

As explained to us by Mr Ryan, his presence at Doyle Farm over the past year exerted a steadying influence on a rather volatile member of the family, and helped ensure a more harmonious household.

Mr Ryan expressed concern that, were he no longer present, the harmony would be disrupted. Consequently, he instructed us to organise and pay for flights for one Fergal Seamus Gallagher, the third grandson of his mother's brother, to come to Australia and work on Doyle Farm until your 18th birthday, after which he would be free of his agreement with Mr Ryan.

There is also a small parcel that Mr Ryan left for you.

If there is ever anything you need, please do not hesitate to contact me on the number at the head of this letter. If I am not available, Mr Sebastian Dempsey or Mr Peter Darcy can be relied on to act in your best interests.

I wish you all the very best for the future.

Yours sincerely

David Dalziel

Ronan flipped to the next page, handing the first to his mother. The second page was a typed copy of his grandfather's hand-written letter, easier to read, but sterile compared to the inked scrawl. He looked up to find his mother watching him, eyes still red, cheeks flushed.

"What, Mum?"

Ruddi's head pivoted from one to the other.

Maureen smiled—part sadness, part pride. "I was just thinking how much you look like your father."

Ronan didn't know how to respond; she hadn't said that in ages. Looking at photos of his father was a bit like looking in a mirror, but not quite—same unruly sandy hair, nose and chin, but his mother's mouth and green eyes. Regardless, a glow of pride warmed him.

When his mother returned to the letter, Ronan shot a curious glance at her. If she was disturbed that Grandpa Paddy felt the need to organise someone to keep them safe from her husband, she gave no sign. Maybe she had accepted that Masters was inherently violent. "How will this Fergal Gallagher get here with the pandemic?" he asked.

"He'll have to have tests and do quarantine, I expect."

"We don't want him bringing Covid here." Ronan recalled it affecting older people more, and he wasn't having his mother endangered. "Are you sure it's safe?"

"They won't let him come if there's a risk, love."

Whoever *they* were, Ronan hoped they knew what they were doing.

"I think we should invite Mr Dalziel back in," she said. "Ruddi, could you get him, please?"

As Ruddi left the room, Ronan said in a low voice, "What's going on, Mum?"

"I don't know, love, but I hope we find out soon ..." Her words faded as Ruddi returned with the sniffing lawyer in his wake.

"Would you like another cup of tea, Mr Dalziel?" The teapot was already in her hand, suggesting a negative answer wasn't a consideration.

"Thank you, Mrs Masters, that would be lovely."

"Can you please explain what my letter means?" she asked, sliding the refilled cup across the table.

"I apologise if it was not clear—"

"It's clear enough; I just don't understand. It says I don't own Doyle Farm ... I thought I did. And besides, how do you know about the farm?"

Ronan stiffened at his mother's words. "Of course you own the farm, Mum."

Dalziel held up a soft hand. "It is complicated," he said, taking a precise sip of tea.

"How?" Ronan and his mother asked in unison. Ruddi looked puzzled.

"Well, apparently," Dalziel said, directing his attention to Maureen, "Mr Ryan advised your parents on their wills which, by the way, were drawn up by my colleague, Mr Peter Darcy."

"Oh, of course, I hadn't made that connection."

"Perfectly understandable, Mrs Masters."

Ronan didn't want to be diverted. "But what's this about Mum not owning the farm?"

"Like I said, it is complicated." He turned to Maureen. "The farm is actually held in a protective trust for you and your boys, and while you can run it however you wish, it can only ever benefit you three."

"Why wasn't I told?" Annoyance bubbled beneath her words.

"I can understand your disquiet, Mrs Masters, but your parents decided not to tell you because they thought it would upset your husband if he found out."

"But why?" Her brow creased.

"Quite by accident, they discovered your husband had the farm valued, and were afraid he might try to sell it, or use it as security to borrow money. They saw a significant risk that you and the boys might end up with nothing."

Maureen shook her head, more to ward off the words than deny their truth; Ruddi gaped; Ronan thanked the stars for a canny Irishman, sceptical grandparents and competent lawyers.

Dalziel continued. "Apparently, they sought Mr Ryan's advice as to whether they were overreacting. When he told them that he did not think they were, they engaged Mr Darcy to ensure Doyle Farm was secure for you and your boys."

"But why not tell me?" Maureen asked, shaking her head in disbelief.

"According to a discussion I had with Mr Ryan several months ago, your parents wrote to tell him they were feeling guilty about all the secrecy, and had decided to tell you after all. But, before they could, there was the ... ah ... unfortunate accident." Dalziel's voice trailed off.

That's an understatement, Ronan thought—his grandparents died when their car ran off the road and into the gorge below Deadman's Gap.

"Mr Ryan also said they initially hoped they were wrong about your husband. They wanted to spare you any potential hurt or family rift. But be assured," he added, "they acted out of love and concern."

Maureen smiled weakly, then frowned. "I'm still not sure I understand what it all means."

"I understand your confusion, Mrs Masters"—he lifted the briefcase onto his lap, withdrawing a large, buff envelope—"which is why I prepared this package of information." Handing the envelope across, he said, "This should explain everything. It includes the correspondence on the subject from your parents to Mr Ryan, as well as Mr Ryan's recollections of what he wrote to them. We don't have the actual letters Mr Ryan wrote to your parents, but you may have found them in their personal effects."

"I don't recall anything," Maureen said, loose golden strands of hair catching the light.

Dalziel nodded, gave another habitual sniff and drew two small parcels from the briefcase, both wrapped in plain brown paper and tied with string. Ronan felt an immediate fizz of excitement and curiosity: he recognised Grandpa Paddy's handiwork, he even wrapped Christmas presents that way—'no use wasting good money on fancy paper ... doesn't change what's inside'. Three pairs of eyes followed the parcels—one larger than the other—as the lawyer set them on the table.

"And this," he said, pulling a second, large envelope from the bag, "is the last thing I have to deliver." He placed it in the middle of the table. It was addressed to Masters.

"I thought you said Grandpa Paddy only left him a message?" Ronan said, unable to utter his stepfather's name.

"Ah, but this is not from your grandfather," Dalziel said, declining to elaborate. "But this is for you and you," he said, sliding the larger parcel to Ronan, and the smaller to Ruddi. "And that is my final duty for today." He clipped his briefcase closed and stood. "Thank you for your hospitality, Mrs Masters. I trust my appearance has not unduly distressed you."

"Not at all, Mr Dalziel. Thank you for your time."

Ronan didn't need to glance at his mother to know she wasn't being truthful.

"Please call me if you have any questions once you have gone through your material," the lawyer said, pushing in his chair. "And I would be grateful if you could ensure Mr Masters receives his letter." Dalziel smoothed his tie and, with a dip of his head, sniffed his way from the house.

9

THE NOTEBOOKS

Ronan looked across at his mother, hands folded on top of her envelope, as though willing the contents into what she needed —something to make sense of all she'd just learnt, to correct her upended world. By the time the dust from the lawyer's receding car settled back to the sun-baked road, Ronan's patience had expired. "I wonder what's in that?" he said, inclining his head toward the large envelope addressed to his stepfather.

"I have no idea, love."

"But it'd be good to know." They were Ruddi's first words in quite a while; they both looked at him as if he'd been temporarily forgotten.

Ronan was first to recover. He reached for the envelope, saying, "We could steam it open and have a quick look." Ruddi's eyes sparkled with excitement.

"Ronan!"

His hand snapped back like she'd slapped it.

"It's none of our business."

"But if it's about the farm, it affects us all, which *makes* it our business," Ronan said. "Doesn't it?"

"I suppose so." Maureen sounded defeated. "But it's addressed to Bruno, so it's up to him to share it with us if he wants. Besides, I'm sure

Mr Dalziel has included everything we need to know in what he's given us."

While curiosity niggled him like an elusive itch, Ronan couldn't argue with her logic. Instead, he sighed, turning his attention to his brown-paper-wrapped parcel. Ruddi had already torn into his, exposing a simple leather-covered notebook with a circular design in the centre. Ronan felt a jolt of surprise—its twin was sitting in Masters' locked office drawer.

Ronan had only seen it once, but he would never forget that day, a Saturday—years ago—his mother and Ruddi were in town shopping for school shoes. Masters had been at his office desk all morning, and whenever Ronan passed, the man was concentrating on either the computer screen or a notebook. The last time Ronan passed the open door, the chair was empty and the notebook, brown leather cover beckoning, lay closed beside the keyboard. The clinking from the kitchen suggested Masters was making a coffee.

With a furtive glance toward the sounds, Ronan slipped into the office. He was a moth, the leather notebook, the flame. Electric excitement shimmered through his trembling fingers as he reached out. The leather cover seemed alive, the rest of the world ceased to exist. He traced tingling fingertips across the intriguing embossed pattern—a small, circular cluster of swirling lines doing a random dance behind two raised, slanting and almost touching letters, a lowercase *d* and a capital *T*. Whatever it stood for, it looked very elegant. And, cradled in the bottom of the design, were the tiny letters, SK. As if worried it might bite, he lifted the notebook from the desktop. It unleashed a monster.

Masters strode into the room, coffee cup in hand, fury igniting in his eyes. He reefed the notebook from Ronan's hands, slamming it across the side of his stepson's face.

"Never touch my things again, boy," he hissed through clenched teeth.

That was the first time Masters hit Ronan. His ears rang and his vision blurred, and he ran from the room, eyes watering, as much from shock and confusion as pain. Taking his smarting face down to the creek behind the house, he sat on a log, absently tossing stones into the water, trying to make sense of the aggression. Masters didn't care for him, that much had been obvious for years, but Ronan couldn't understand the man's simmering hostility or outbursts of rage. Regardless, he knew that notebook was important, and couldn't help but wonder what it contained. But there were no further opportunities to find out—from that day, Masters kept it locked away whenever he left the room.

"Ro," his brother repeated.

Ronan snapped out of his reverie. "Huh?"

"I said, what do you reckon?" Ruddi held the notebook out for Ronan's closer inspection.

"It's wicked, Ruddi," he said with enthusiasm.

"Yeah, and Grandpa Paddy has written in it"—Ruddi ran his fingers down the page—"wow."

Ronan leant across so he could read the slanting scrawl, so like his own.

Hey Big Lad, now that you're almost a man, I thought it was time you had your very own Deetee notebook - if you need another, you'll have to visit the grand town of Killybegs in County Donegal, and buy a pair of Deetees, the best boots in all of Ireland, better even than Dubarrys, and that's saying something. Buying a pair of Deetees is the only way to get a Deetee notebook. Use it wisely, take care of your ma, be wary of your da, and stick close to your bro.

May the wind be always at your back, Big Lad.

With all the love of the Irish.

Grandpa Paddy

Ruddi swiped a hand across a damp cheek, carried the notebook to his mother, and squeezed onto her lap, forcing her chair away from the table. He placed the notebook on top of her letter, twining his arms round her neck, hugging tight, a little boy again.

"Why did Grandpa Paddy have to die?" Ruddi's words, muffled against her collar, were almost a sob.

Maureen pulled her son's head tighter to her shoulder, stroking his dark hair. "I wish I knew, love," she breathed. "I wish I knew."

Ronan, fighting the burn behind his eyes, turned to his own parcel.

It was much larger than Ruddi's and when he opened it, he found not one, but three Deetee notebooks. None were new like Ruddi's—they were worn, water-stained, streaked with dirt and blotched by grubby fingerprints. Yet each carried the intriguing dT symbol on its cover. Ronan brushed his fingers across the topmost, instantly feeling the same curious sensation he had when touching Master's notebook. And, tucked in the curve of the lower-most swirl, the tiny SK. Beneath the three grimy notebooks was a crisp, white, hand-written page.

Ronan, I have a huge and heartfelt apology to make. Seventeen years ago, I was given a box of your da's belongings. It was soon after he died and I was too heartbroken and maudlin to go through them, so I put them in the cupboard under the stairs where they lay forgotten all these years.

When I was cleaning up to come to Australia, I found the box and these notebooks. I wanted to wait and give these to you as an eighteenth birthday present from your da. I'm truly sorry for the hurt I've caused if you're reading this letter - it means you're not yet eighteen, and I'm no longer around to give them to you.

These were very important to your da, and he would have wanted you to have them and to appreciate their contents. None of it makes much sense to me, but it's all about his field work, what he discovered and what it all meant. I hope as you get older, these words give you an idea of what a clever and good man your da was. He would have been so proud of you, as I am. I know that, in time, you will be able to make sense of it all.

Stay true; stay strong, Ronan, and may the wind be always at your back.
Grandpa Paddy

Ronan struggled to finish the letter. Grief caught in the base of his throat like half-chewed, stale cake. He wiped at his eyes, embarrassed and annoyed ... Masters couldn't make him cry, but a letter from Grandpa Paddy could.

"What is it, Ronan?" His mother frowned.

"It's another letter from Grandpa Paddy," Ronan forced out, pushing it along the table to her outstretched hand.

"Oh," she said, after reading it. Eyes swimming with yearning, she gazed at the notebooks of her long-ago, lost love.

10

THE KEY

It was the end of a tumultuous day—Dalziel's arrival, Masters' departure, the letters, the notebooks, the emotion, the exhaustion. Maureen had told them about the contents of her letter from the lawyer explaining the special trust that owned Doyle Farm, why her parents did it, and why Fergal Gallagher was coming. Apparently, Grandpa Paddy hoped Masters could be kept in check for Ronan's sake, and the family held together for Maureen's and Ruddi's sakes.

Ronan had serious doubts.

He sat on his bed, pondering the notebooks, ignoring the night insects flitting past his face, crawling in his hair—in his frustration with his father's code, he'd forgotten to close the sliding screen on the window. The handwriting, eerily like his own, was easy to read, but the meaning was baffling. Quite apart from the expected archaeological terminology, his father's own peculiar shorthand created a fog in Ronan's head.

Like a shape forming in a cloud, an idea slipped together—he would compare his father's notebooks with his stepfather's. Because Masters' notebook was the same, Ronan hoped it might contain similar material from when the two men worked together on digs. And, if Masters' writing was plain English rather than secret code, he might be able to cross reference the two, unlocking the meaning of his father's words.

Masters hadn't yet returned after storming out of the morning's meeting, so there would never be a better time. But ever since that day when Ronan dared touch the unattended notebook, the man kept it locked in the desk drawer. Even so, Ronan had an idea where Masters hid the key—many times, he'd seen the man turn left on entering the office, reappearing within seconds to walk behind his desk and unlock the drawer. Ronan was betting on the bookshelves.

Head torch in place, he ghosted past his mother's closed bedroom door—avoiding the creaky floorboards he knew so well—and into his stepfather's forbidden territory. Easing the door closed, he froze at the hinges' dry squeal.

"Is that you, Bruno?" his mother called from the bedroom. Ronan dared not breath. The patter of bare feet in the hallway sent him darting behind the half-closed door. Maureen popped her head into the room, flicked the light on, gave a soft harrumph as if scolding herself for imagining noises, before killing the light and pulling the squeaky door closed with a loud click.

Ronan exhaled. Once he heard the bedroom door close, he clicked on his head torch and ran both hands along the top of all the books within two strides of the door. After several fruitless minutes, he realised the key must be on the very top of the bookcase, but Ronan didn't know how Masters could reach it if he, himself, couldn't.

Reluctantly admitting that perhaps he wasn't quite as tall as he liked to think, Ronan slid half-a-dozen books from the bottom shelf, making two neat stacks, side by side. Standing on the book towers, he inspected the top of the bookcase with his fingertips. All he got was a nose-full of dust and an almost irresistible urge to sneeze.

As he swung his head away in frustration, a fleeting glint caught his eye. He repeated the movement and there it was again, a tiny reflection at the top of the picture frame hanging between the bookcase and the door. After spiriting the book stacks across under the large, aerial photograph of Doyle Farm, Ronan stepped up, running his fingers along the frame in a fruitless exercise. Wait! They backtracked, stopping at an imperfection on the rear edge.

Ronan's fingertips inspected the irregularity, identifying a key shape; it was firmly attached; he pulled harder. The frame swung out and back, hitting the wall with a muted bump that sounded like a knuckle-rap in the night's silence. Immobile, Ronan held his breath, ears straining toward the bedroom, but there was no reaction. Steadying the frame with his left hand, he poked and prodded, but the shape wouldn't budge. He hooked his fingernails beneath the key, gritted his teeth and, with his thumb levering on top of the frame, dragged upward. Despite stubborn resistance, the key finally slid free. *Clever, a small magnet in the back of the frame.*

Seated at the desk, key poised, Ronan hesitated—excitement and unease, curiosity and guilt all tussled in his gut. Curiosity won. He aimed the key at the brass lock, but missed—his hand had jumped when Smoky gave a low growl outside the office window. The dog growled again, further away, toward the front of the house, then broke into full-throated barking, somewhere out near where David Dalziel had parked that morning. Between the woofing, Ronan heard the rumble of an engine. Masters was coming home!

As his frantic fingers searched the rear of the frame for the right spot, first one way, then the other, he almost toppled off the pile of books. At last, he felt a gentle tug, then relief, as the magnet sucked the key from his fingers, capturing it with a soft click.

The growl of the engine was lifting almost as fast as Ronan's heartbeat; Masters was coming up the last small rise toward the house. The man's heavy frame would soon fill the hallway.

With panicked hands, he killed the head torch, returning the books to the shelf by feel, fumbling them into any available gap, hoping they were up the right way. By the time the last slid into place, the tyres of Masters' four-wheel-drive were pulverising the gravel as they brought the large vehicle to a halt.

Under the cover of the slamming car door, and Smoky's continued barking, Ronan slipped from the room, pulling the door closed behind him. Barely had his hand left the doorknob than his mother's bedroom door clicked open. Eye-stabbing glare flooded the hallway as he darted into the adjacent guest bedroom, flattening himself against the wall, trying to blend into the pale paint.

The dog's animosity lifted with the squeal of the garden gate hinges, but an alcohol-thickened 'shut up, you mongrel!' punctuated by a meaty thwack, ended Smoky's plucky resistance. With an injured whine, he crawled under the house. Ronan's fists bunched; he knew exactly how the poor dog felt.

Maureen passed on the other side of the wall, and her uncertain 'Bruno?' greeted heavy footsteps on the verandah.

"What?" Masters slurred.

"I was worried about you." The retreat in her voice inflamed Ronan's anger.

Masters snorted. "That's a change."

"Don't be stupid. You know I worry when you're out late."

And drinking. They moved down the hallway past the guest room. Ronan shrank further into the paint.

"You weren't too worried about me when you invited that interfering old mick to stay."

"I couldn't say no, Bruno, he'd come halfway round the world to help us."

"Help us?" Masters growled. "He was nothing but trouble."

Masters halted beyond the open door of the guest room, swaying and squinting as if trying to pull the office door into focus. A half-turn of his head and he'd be looking into Ronan's eyes.

"Why's this closed?" he slurred. "That boy of yours better not be snooping again." Ever since he'd caught Ronan with his notebook, Masters kept the door open so he could check inside whenever he walked past—the room contained the family library, and Maureen wouldn't allow him to lock it.

"Why do you blame Ronan for everything?" she said, voice rising.

"Because," Masters retorted, "he's a typical bloody smart-mouthed snoop, just like his grandfather."

"In your eyes," she snapped, looking past her husband's shoulder, straight at Ronan. "I pulled it closed earlier so the breeze wouldn't catch it," she added tartly. "Open it if you want; I'm going to bed." With that, she stalked off.

Masters took a final, unsteady, questioning look at the closed door before rumbling after her.

11

THE PROMISE

Notebooks and their contents kept Ronan's slumber at bay. In particular, it was Masters' notebook and the secrets he was sure it would unlock, that filled his head. There was no doubt in Ronan's mind the notebook was key to deciphering his father's notes. He had to get his hands on it. Visions of his unknown father's hands scratching a pencil across the pages swirled with intertwined dTs, secret keys, locked drawers and closed doors. Eventually, sleep drew its restive curtain on his day.

It was a troubled, dream-littered sleep, but a long one. When Ruddi shook Ronan's shoulder next morning, the short rectangle of sunlight on the bedroom floor indicated it was way past time to be up. A magpie carolled from the lower branch of the gum tree, and down by the creek, kookaburras cackled in discord.

Ten minutes later Ronan breezed through the kitchen, tossing a cheery 'morning Mum' toward her turned back, scooping up a piece of buttered toast in passing, heading for the verandah. While in a hurry to get outside with Ruddi, he also didn't want to face his mother about last night. There's no way she hadn't guessed he'd been in the office after seeing him in the spare room, yet she said nothing at the time—Masters would've gone ballistic.

"Thanks, Mum," he called over his shoulder, more for last night than the slice of toast. She turned and smiled. Ronan's spirits soared as he pushed past the fly-screen door—with his mother on side, what he had in mind would be easier.

But the door hadn't even swung shut before she called. "What?" he said, halting at the top of the verandah steps. As the word popped from his mouth, Ronan cringed.

"I beg your pardon?"

Without turning, he knew her hands were on her hips. Instantly, he was a small boy again.

"Sorry. Yes, Mum?"

"Can you come here for a minute, please?"

His shoulders had been braced, ready for the day, but they slumped as he re-entered. *Here it comes.*

"You need to eat more than that for breakfast, my boy."

Ronan sighed with relief. "I'll have something else when I've done my chores." His second attempt to leave was no more successful.

"Ruddi has already done them," she said, besting him at every turn.

"Oh." A weight settled in Ronan's stomach. "I didn't take anything ... I just wanted to look at his notebook. There was no point asking, you know he'd never let me"—his justifications tumbled over each other in their urgency—"I didn't hurt anything. I just want to understand my dad's notes and—"

Maureen held up a hand. "Ronan ... stop."

"But—" The censure in her gaze cut him off, his eyes dropped.

"Talk to me." She made it sound like an invitation; it wasn't. Search as he did for a good excuse, he ended up going with the truth.

"I can't understand a lot of the stuff in my notebooks," Ronan began, looking her in the eye, "and I thought *his* might help ... sort of ... decode it."

"How do you even know about Bruno's notebook?" Maureen's eyes narrowed. "He won't even let me read it."

"I saw it once," Ronan said, reluctant to tell his mother how, "and it's the same as mine ... Dad's." Now that he'd referred to the dead father he'd never known as 'Dad', it felt so right. When he was small, he'd called Masters 'Dad' and, despite learning who his real father was, Ronan persisted—with his mother's encouragement. But he came

48

to realise the man didn't deserve the title, or the respect that went with it.

Eventually, and much to his mother's disappointment, Ronan dropped 'Dad' in favour of 'Stepfather', or even 'Mr Masters'. However, as the man's enmity grew, Ronan couldn't bring himself to use either of them. Now, if he had to refer to his stepfather at all, it was simply 'Masters', 'that man' or 'him'.

"They're yours now, Ronan." She gave a sad, half-smile. "It's what your dad would have wanted."

"That's what Grandpa Paddy said ... wrote. And that's why I had to see *his* notebook ... to help make sense of Dad's."

"Well, you can't. It's Bruno's, and he'll never let you near it. Besides, I doubt his notebook would be any use; in fact, I'm surprised he even kept one ... never showed much interest in that side of things, so I don't think his notebook will have anything useful. Anyway, he keeps it locked in his desk drawer, and I have no idea where the key is."

"Oh," was all Ronan said, hoping his elation didn't show. "Can't you at least ask him?"

"I could, love, but it would only make matters worse, especially after yesterday."

Ronan's last ember of hope snuffed out; his shoulders drooped. "I'll never be able to work out what it all means."

"We'll work it out together," his mother said brightly. "I was your father's assistant on the Sliabh Liag dig, you know, and I understand the way he recorded his notes."

"What's Sleeve League?" Ronan asked, puzzled.

"Sliabh Liag is Gaelic for Grey Mountain ... in northwest Ireland ... County Donegal ... sheer cliffs ... hundreds of metres straight up out of the sea ..." The brief spark of enthusiasm faded from her eyes, and her voice withered. "It's where your father fell."

It was as if someone poked a stiff finger into his stomach. All Ronan knew of his father's death was that he'd fallen off a cliff while excavating Viking artefacts in a cave. While conscious of his mother's current distress, an overwhelming desperation to learn all he could about his real father, consumed Ronan. "Can you tell me about it, please?"

"I should have told you sooner"—she nodded sombrely—"but it

never seemed like the right time ... perhaps now is." She brightened a little. "Why don't you grab your notebooks? We can talk about it while we read."

When Ronan returned, his mother had settled into a chair and was dabbing at tears with the corner of her apron. For some time after he dropped the notebooks on the table, she sat staring at them, stroking the stained leather, as though trying to rekindle old memories. After a wistful sigh, she began flicking through the pages as she might a photo album, stopping occasionally to read a passage, or smile at a fond recollection. "I remember now why your dad wrote his notes so cryptically," she said. Ronan's eyes gleamed. "Around that time, there was quite a trade in stolen Viking artefacts ... still is, I think ... and because your dad was so good at discovering them, he invented this code to protect his field notes"—the thrill of mystery zinged about Ronan's head—"just in case they fell into the wrong hands."

A shiver of excitement rippled through him. "So, it was dangerous?"

Maureen chuckled. "No, nothing like that, but he had a notebook stolen once." She shook her head at the memory. "Oh, it made him laugh ... it was a new one he hadn't started using yet ... the luck of the Irish, he called it ... but after that, he made his code even harder to understand."

"But you can understand it ... can't you?"

"Most of it ..." Words on the page stole her attention, and she returned to working through the notes.

Ronan watched in fascination, splitting his focus between her hands and her face. Her graceful fingers appeared reluctant to leave the page, skimming along before the sweep of her eyes. Every time she came to a significant part, the fingers paused, which was Ronan's cue to switch his gaze to her face to catch the result of the memory. Mostly, he saw happiness and delight, but there was a sprinkling of puzzlement—perhaps from lack of recall or impossible code—and, now and then, the shadow of melancholy.

Eventually, she finished. "Okay," she said, "these two are from our dig at Jarlshofon in The Shetlands." She pushed them aside and picked up the third. "And this"—her voice dropped to a whisper—"is from

Sliabh Liag." Her thumbs caressed the edge stitching. Ronan's eyes locked on the dT symbol in the centre of the leather cover.

"Now," she began, her sober tone dragging Ronan's attention from the notebook, "before we start, I want you to promise me"—her green eyes locked onto his—"you won't go near Bruno's desk again."

"But—"

"Ronan." It was his mother's this-is-not-a-negotiation voice.

Ronan had hoped to mount a satisfactory case against calling it '*his* desk'—it had belonged to Granddad Doyle—but her face told him to forget it. "Okay," he said, already constructing an argument in his head that saying 'okay' wasn't as binding as saying the words, 'I promise'. Fortunately, on this occasion, his mother couldn't read his mind.

"Right," she said, opening the notebook to the first page.

Bit by bit, the story of that final, fatal dig eased from his mother's memory, prompted by those scrawled notes and his own gentle prodding.

12

THE DIG

I t had been a typical Sliabh Liag morning—dizzying cliff, drizzling rain and gusts coming off icebergs. After unfettered passage across the wild North Atlantic, the wind threw itself against the dour sea cliffs, turning raindrops into flying needles, spearing them into exposed skin.

Three figures, bent beneath bulging backpacks, traversed the sheer rock face, heading toward their work site. The only way in—except for spiders and birds—was via a narrow ledge, rocks slick with moisture and lichen. Over two hundred metres below, heaving waves smashed themselves in a futile assault on the mountain's foundation, with nothing but streaming rocks and a raft of foam to mark the sacrifice.

Two sets of hands grasped a newly installed safety rope anchored to the raw rock face—Paidin Ryan ignored it. With a sureness of foot from running round similar Donegal mountains since he was a small child, he stepped confidently along the precipice. "Come on, you pair"—he grinned over his shoulder—"it'll be supper time before we get there."

His fiancé, Maureen Doyle pulled a face. "It's alright for you, Mr Smarty Pants, you're half mountain goat ... all that's missing is the good looks and the engaging personality."

"Ouch, but you have a sharp tongue, Maise," Paidin said, eyes twinkling, and using the Irish name for beauty that he'd affectionately given her.

"Sharp but true," Bruno Masters quipped from the back of the line, walking his hands along the rope.

Paidin shook his head in mock disbelief. "Even me mate has turned against me." And with a grin, he strode ahead, disappearing into the grey rock.

The story of a mysterious Norse woman of magic—a seeress—who appeared out of the Sliabh Liag rock a thousand years ago, had intrigued Paidin when he was a lad. Her robe was said to have been as grey as the rock that spawned her, and hemmed with wooden disks, each inscribed with a letter of the runic alphabet. With waist-length red hair plaited forward over her shoulder, she had floated across the cliff face toward the unsuspecting local man who saw her appear. Gaelic fields were never as green as her gemstone eyes, and flickering firelight nowhere near as hypnotic. When she held out her hands and smiled, he became hers forever.

It was only a story, but it fired Paidin's passion for the past. During his studies, he'd specialised in the Viking influence on Ireland, obsessing over the legend of the seeress. Now, convinced he'd found the cliff cave where the legend began, he was keen to investigate.

Maureen and Bruno finally caught up with Paidin deep inside the belly of the mountain. Crouched in a bright pool of lantern light, lost in thought, he was picking through rubble like a curious chicken.

"Paidin!" Maureen said.

"Huh?" He looked up with distant eyes.

"I said, what would you like us to start on?"

"Oh," Paidin said, pausing in his examination of centuries of debris. "If yesterday's find was part of a pouch, then its contents should be somewhere here." He swept his hand above a section of floor. A paper cup weighted with pebbles marked the spot where they found the remnant of desiccated leather, late the previous day.

"So, we're going to sift through this area?" Maureen prompted when Paidin resumed his chicken imitation.

In anticipation, Bruno laid a rough square of bright yellow cord round the cup, and began picking through the rocky debris within its bounds. "Already on it," he said, rattling pebbles into a discard bucket.

Paidin ignored him, attention only for the woman he was going to marry, halo of red hair glowing in the light bouncing off the cave roof. He gave her his special smile and whispered, "Find." It was their signal for a notable discovery.

Maureen's face, alight with the compliment, faded as she realised he was looking past her. She turned to follow his gaze and went still.

"Do you have goose bumps?" he asked.

"Yes." She croaked.

"Oh, for God's sake." Keeping his head buried in his work, Bruno hurled another handful of rubble into the bucket.

"Find!" Paidin and Maureen said in unison.

Their tone cut through Bruno's annoyance. He glanced up to see them both arching their backs, staring at the roof of the cave. There, close above their heads, was a pattern of etchings in the rock. "Is that what I think it is?"

"Depends what you think it is," Paidin quipped, peering upward.

"Do you always have to be such a smart arse?" Bruno retorted.

"Play nicely, boys," Maureen said, not taking her eyes off the cave ceiling.

Still scowling, Bruno ventured, "Is it one of the futharks?"

Paidin seemed mesmerised; he replied as if in a church. "Sure is."

"Wow," Maureen uttered.

Chiselled across the rock ceiling, in a long line from one side to the other, was a single row of angular runic symbols.

Bruno ran his eyes along the row of jagged grooves. "Interesting," he said without enthusiasm, "but, what's it all mean?"

The others appeared not to hear. He harrumphed and resumed sorting.

13

THE RUNES

Paidin's pencil was a blur. With his leather-bound notebook held above his head, he glanced from the runes, to the page where he was copying them, and back again. His obsession with the Viking influence on Ireland had delivered another triumph, further vindicating a difficult decision to pass up an opportunity in professional cricket. The runic inscription had him quaking with excitement.

Maureen recorded it with her camera—out wide for an overview, in close to capture the detail of individual runes—working the lens, ensuring sharp focus. Hands shaking, she clicked away, glancing across at her fiancé between shots.

She paused, frowning, then reached up and placed her hand over his, halting his frenetic pencil strokes. "Paidin, slow down," she said. "They're not going anywhere." Haphazard, spiky lines covered the page, a rough approximation of the groupings of symbols etched into the ceiling. Beneath the sketches, Paidin had already scrawled some notes and English translations; above, he'd written two words: Younger Futhark. "And your notes"—she shook her head—"no one will understand them."

Paidin lowered his arms, turning to his fiancé, excitement still dancing in his eyes, a smile on his lips. "Ah, but there's the method in my madness ... not worth stealing if it's illegible, now is it?"

"And *I* can't transcribe them."

"Find."

Maureen and Paidin spun at Bruno's tone, crowding close—it wasn't like him to show enthusiasm, let alone excitement. With the cautious strokes of his grubby paintbrush, a small cluster of unusual stones emerged from centuries of dust. They were all roughly round, flat and a similar size, and clumped together in a tiny pile. More detail appeared as Bruno worked his bristles, and the one that captured all their attention was the angular carving on the face of each disk—the same symbols as those chiselled into the rock above.

"I think these are runes," Bruno said, frowning.

"Spot on, Bruno, but, don't get carried away with your conclusions," Paidin said with a wry grin. "You don't want to ruin your reputation."

Bruno was the first to acknowledged that archaeology didn't excite him—he'd studied business—but he maintained he liked the field trips for the open air and company. However, he found Paidin's observations boring, analysis tedious and conclusions mystical.

Maureen took a wide shot before kneeling, leaning on elbows, hair falling forward as she focused the lens for several close shots. Bruno brushed yet more dust away, and the carved lines on each of the small stone disks became clearer. Dropping the camera from her eye, Maureen pointed to a twist of something that was definitely not stone. "Hold on, Bruno; is that more leather?"

Both men leant closer. "Looks like it," Paidin said. Bruno brushed away dirt.

After further inspection, Paidin stood, notebook in hand. "Maise, can you record this for Bruno, please? I want to make a better copy of the inscription."

"Whatever for?" she said with a mock roll of her green eyes.

By the time they paused for a late lunch, Maureen and Bruno had unearthed and recorded eight etched runes, as well as what remained of the leather pouch that once held them. Paidin had completed his second, slower and more precise copy of the runic symbols, and had retired to the cave mouth to work on the translation. When Maureen and Bruno joined him for a stale sandwich and a warm cup of tea, he was sitting against the cave wall, eyes closed, open notebook on his lap.

"All the excitement too much for you?" Bruno teased.

"Definitely," Paidin agreed, not bothering to open his eyes.

Maureen looked at the open notebook. "Any progress?" she said, nudging his leg with a toe.

Paidin lazily lifted one eyelid. "Something about stone, gods, power and wealth ... don't yet know exactly what."

"Well, keep at it," Bruno said round a mouthful. "We'll continue with the real work."

While they ate, Maureen scrolled through the images on the camera's display, checking them for quality, deleting the poor ones and showing Paidin any of particular interest.

"This is the last remnant of leather Bruno found, after all the runes came out," she said, turning the camera screen toward Paidin.

He stopped chewing, teacup halfway to his lips. "Can you zoom in on that bit there?" he asked, pointing with the corner of crust.

Maureen pressed buttons until the spot in question filled the tiny screen.

"Looks like a second layer of leather," Paidin said past half-chewed sandwich.

"Show me!" Bruno reached for the camera.

"Another pouch?" Maureen asked.

Paidin shrugged, cup still hovering out of reach of his lips. "Perhaps there was a second pouch beneath the first, and the two became stuck together."

"And," Maureen added, "we may have only just taken the top off the second?"

"More to find," Paidin said, inclining his mop of fair hair into the cave, finally taking a sip of tea.

When they returned to the site, Bruno attacked the dust in the depression that had cradled the rune pouch for ten centuries. It was his find, so it was his spot, but the others leant close. Within a few strokes, he'd uncovered another small stone. "Find," he called needlessly as he continued brushing. "That's weird," he said, watching the dust flow like water round the brush bristles before reattaching to the surface of the find.

"Looks magnetic," Maureen said.

"Really strong," Paidin agreed with a puzzled frown.

Bruno reached for it. "Gloves," Maureen and Paidin said in unison.

They snapped on latex gloves like surgeons preparing to operate. At Paidin's nod, Bruno grasped the stone and began rolling it between his fingers. "Just another stone," he said, losing interest, passing it to Paidin.

After scrutinising it, Paidin handed it on to Maureen. "Does it feel warm to you, Maise?"

She cupped it in her palm, staring at it like it was a rare gem. "Yes."

"Give me a look," Bruno demanded. Maureen dropped it into his outstretched hand. It appeared to darken as it left her touch. "You're both daft," he said, "it's as cold as ice."

"How would you describe it, then?" Paidin said, challenging his friend, as always, to be interested in more than just the fresh air and companionship of a dig.

Bruno peered at it, holding it up to the light and hefting it the way he'd often watched Paidin do. "Slightly oblong," he began as he placed it on his ruler. "About twenty-one millimetres by eighteen, and five thick, maybe three at the edges; very heavy for its size; doesn't look local; could be polished, but hard to tell with all this dust sticking to it; no markings that I can see. Possibly a token of some sort; maybe a pendant stone." He tossed it back to his friend. "What do you reckon?"

"Very puzzling," Paidin said, pulling a soft cloth from a pocket, and cleaning the dust from the magnetic stone as easily as drying a plate. "I've never seen anything this highly polished, or as black." He frowned. "I have no idea what it is; perhaps some form of concentrated magnetite, probably Scandinavian, and of high cultural value."

"How do you work that out?" Bruno said, unable to keep the trace of annoyance from his voice.

"Well," Paidin replied, "while these runes are extremely valuable historical artefacts, they would have been relatively worthless when they were buried, likewise the magnetite. But they were deliberately hidden in this rubble, in a very inaccessible place." He poked a splayed hand at the small pile of rocks beside where Bruno sat on his haunches, before sweeping it the length of the cave. "So, that tells us several things: whoever hid them didn't want them discovered by chance; this" —he held out the polished stone in his open palm—"was the most valued, unless there's something buried deeper; the runes themselves held some value, otherwise, why hide them at all; and, finally, they did want them found eventually."

"Otherwise, why go to all that effort to put up a signpost?" said Maureen nodded, staring at the runic lettering arcing above.

Frowning at the inscription, Bruno said, "But you didn't even know that was there when you started scratching round here." He pointed to the disturbed pile of rubble.

"You're right, Bruno," Paidin said. "It was just a hunch ... something about this spot didn't seem quite natural."

Bruno harrumphed.

"So," Maureen said, switching the focus of the discussion, "who hid it and why?" Then she added with a teasing smile, "Who would be silly enough to walk that ledge by choice?"

Paidin cocked an eye at her and grinned; Bruno returned his attention to the rubble-strewn floor. "So, there's something valuable buried here?" he said, eyes gleaming with excitement.

"Perhaps," Paidin replied, holding the stone up between thumb and forefinger, "you've already found it."

14

THE STONES

Next morning, they returned to the cave; this time in sunshine, with only an occasional breeze. Paidin had already switched on the powerful lanterns, and was busy at work before his companions had negotiated half of the dizzying ledge. When they arrived, he was lying on his back on the rough floor, hands cupped under his head, open notebook inverted on his chest, staring at the illuminated ceiling.

"Slacking already?" Bruno said dryly, walking into the circle of light.

"Any chance I get," came the quick reply.

"What *are* you doing, Paidin?" Maureen said.

"Reading, Maise, reading."

"Do share." She sat beside him, joining his upward gaze.

"Well, there's five things I find really interesting." He gestured to the chiselled inscription arcing above.

"I'm surprised there's only five."

He wrinkled his nose at her. "Number one: while it's written as a single line from one side of the ceiling to the other, I think it's a poem. Two: I've almost finished translating it, but still have no idea what it means. Three: there were only eight runes in the stash Bruno found yesterday, but there are sixteen in the Younger Futhark alphabet. Four: they were buried directly under the end of the inscription on the ceiling." He paused.

"What's number five?" Bruno said.

Paidin rolled his head to the side, saying, "There's another pile of rock over there, under the beginning of the inscription."

"I'll be damned," Bruno breathed, turning his attention to the rubble. "I'd better get to it, then."

Meanwhile, Paidin went back to studying the inscription, making copious notes, stopping often to contemplate; Maureen catalogued the dimensions of the runic letters and took additional photographs.

By mid-morning, Bruno found another leather pouch containing the eight missing runes; soon after, he uncovered a twin to yesterday's glossy find. Not even bothering to examine it, he tossed it to Paidin, then stood and said, with an air of disappointment, "I'm going to stretch my legs and get some sun."

A gloved-up Paidin cleaned the latest discovery, hefting it in his palm, feeling its warmth and watching its blackness fade.

"Look," he said to Maureen. "It's definitely getting lighter."

"That's really weird," she said.

"Sure is. Where's the other one?"

"Here in the tray."

"Can you pass it over, please?"

Maureen picked up yesterday's find and shaped to hand it across, but suddenly clenched her fist round it, recoiling. Paidin did the same. Immobile, they gaped at each other.

"It tried to jump out of my hand!" said Maureen.

"Same here," Paidin said in awe, easing his grip on the glossy disk.

They stared at each other as if they'd witnessed a magician pull a fiddle-playing leprechaun from a hat. In slow-motion unison, they lowered their eyes to the stones in trance-like wonder.

Paidin broke the spell. "Hold it tight, Maise ... see if it happens again." Grasping their stones even more firmly, they edged closer. "Can you feel that?"

"Wow, that's strong."

They withdrew their fists until the stones no longer tugged, and Paidin frowned. "I've never heard of that level of magnetism in a natural substance. I doubt we'd get them apart if they touched."

"Maybe that's why they were hidden on separate sides of the cave," said Maureen.

"Quite likely," Paidin said, taking out his notebook and scratching some quick, cryptic words.

"What's it all mean?"

"I don't know, but my translation makes a bit more sense now ... see what you think: 'The one who holds the living stone will always have companionship and the protection of the gods, as long as they remain loyal. The rune lightens and its power burns when it's coated with blood, and it will bring great wealth to a special person with a right mind and good heart'."

Maureen frowned. "It's a rune?"

"If I got the translation right."

She teased him with a doubtful humph.

Paidin ignored her. "But it's even better in Norse, and it's definitely a poem ... listen to this: 'The bearer of the living stone, in solitude is ne'er alone; the gods shall let no ill befall its keeper with eternal thrall. Its power burns if blood enfold the lightening rune, and wealth untold awaits the one who stands apart as true of mind and pure of heart'."

There was a protracted silence after Paidin finished, as they pondered those words written so long ago.

Maureen broke the trance. "It *is* way better in Norse ... sounds like something straight out of the sagas ... what do you reckon it means?"

"I suspect this is the 'living stone'," Paidin replied, hefting his smooth, warm disk. "And whoever wrote this poem believed it possessed magical powers to protect."

"Probably because they were overawed by the magnetism," Maureen said.

"Possibly. But it's a cool verse, don't you think?"

"Very cool. Let me take a photo."

Paidin held it up for her, then glanced over the poem once more before closing the notebook. "You coming out for some air?"

Maureen shook her head. "You go. I'll finish the last few measurements of the etchings, then I'll be out."

He touched her arm as she turned to grab the tape measure. "Make sure you bring that stone so we can show Bruno."

Her eyes narrowed. "You're going to play a trick on him, aren't you?"

Paidin grinned.

"Well, go easy ... he seems a bit testy today ... something is bothering him."

Paidin shrugged, giving her a quick peck on the lips.

"Off you go then," she said, eyes sparkling in the lantern light.

15

THE VOID

Ronan watched as anguish cast a shadow across his mother's face. At a loss what to say, or do, he awkwardly rubbed her shoulders.

Maureen sniffed. "That was the last time I saw him." Her words descended into quiet sobs. Lips compressed in determination, she reached for the corner of her apron again. "'Off you go then' was the last thing I said to him." The words caught in her throat, her face sagged, she dabbed at her eyes.

"What happened?" Ronan said.

There was a long pause before Maureen spoke again. "Bruno said your dad was talking about the stones, standing too close to the edge, and when he turned, his foot slipped ..." There was another long silence. "And before Bruno could do anything, Paidin was gone." Her face crumpled again.

Not knowing what to say, Ronan kept rubbing.

Eventually, Maureen continued. "Poor Bruno was distraught. He blamed himself ... said he should have told Paidin to move away from the edge. But it was so like your father ... fearless, surefooted, and so confident on that mountain." She gave a weak smile at the memory. "Your father loved Sliabh Liag."

Her story hollowed out Ronan's gut. *Why wasn't Masters the one who fell?* Then a sudden horror swamped him. "Mum, what if he survived?"

Maureen shook her head. "That's what I wanted to believe, but the Police said it was impossible. They said fifty metres was borderline ... your dad fell from over two hundred."

"Oh." Ronan felt a guilty surge of relief—a quick, if terrifying death would've been far more humane than floating, badly injured, until fatigue and pain had drained the last of his resistance.

"They searched for three days, but couldn't find him ... said the strong currents probably dragged him to the bottom of the ocean." Her shoulders shuddered. "We didn't have ... anything to ... bury"—she pushed the words out between heaving sobs—"nothing ... to say ... goodbye to."

Ronan hugged her to his chest. "It'll be alright, Mum."

A huge shudder ran through her; she sniffed hard, wiping again with the apron. "I know it will," she said, easing him away to access her pocket, "but, at the time, I remember thinking I was going to die." Maureen paused as though regretting the admission. "After that dig, we were coming back to Australia to be married ... suddenly, my whole world ended." Pulling out a handkerchief, she blew vigorously. "Thanks, love." She touched his arm, giving him a puffy-eyed, watery smile.

Ronan always marvelled at the special energy that seemed to flow from her touch, or smile. No matter how down or hurt he was, either one would instantly put things right.

"I know you find this hard to believe, but Bruno was a good man back then." She held up a hand, blocking the cutting remark that jumped to Ronan's lips. "And I know he has become difficult—"

"Difficult, Mum? Really?" Ronan wanted to yank his shirt up, point to the blotched patchwork of varying shades of red, purple and blue, and yell, "This is what he does!" Instead, he reminded her of the choking, the continuous hurtful remarks—the ones she knew about—and the unnecessary punishments with that horrible strip of leather hanging on the hat rack by the back door, the monstrosity both he and Ruddi had to endure.

"But he wasn't always like this," she said, shaking her head against his words. "If it hadn't been for Bruno, I don't know how I would have survived losing your father. I almost wanted to follow him off the cliff."

That admission numbed Ronan; he stared at his mother.

"It was like someone took a big spoon and scooped out my insides. I couldn't breathe, I couldn't eat ... I was full of emptiness ... a huge void. And Bruno was there to support me, help me get through it. He was so kind ... I'll always be so grateful." Maureen sighed. "I can't understand why he's changed so much."

"I don't think he's changed very much," Ronan said, rougher than he intended.

Maureen sighed again. "I know he broke your bow, but I honestly thought that was only a one-off thing from all the stress he was under."

Ronan shook his head. "For as long as I can remember, he's never liked me. It just got gradually worse until Grandpa Paddy came, then it was fine ... until he died."

"I can see that now, love ... just don't know why I didn't see it before."

"Because you always think the best of people, Mum."

"A fat lot of good that's done," she said, her misery palpable. During the long silence that followed, Maureen studied Ronan's face as if committing every pore to memory, or searching for a silver lining to the dark cloud she found herself under. At last, she said, "Anyway, Fergal Gallagher arrives soon ... hopefully Bruno will be better then."

"I hope you're right, Mum ... I really do."

Before his mother could respond, a hen started a self-congratulatory cackle beneath the floorboards. It was such a mundane sound, but it made them smile.

"There's another egg for you boys to collect."

Ronan sobered as his mind returned to his mother's story. "What happened to the stones?"

"Your dad had one ..." She paused, as though weighing whether to say it was at the bottom of the sea. "The other one was in my pocket... I gave it to Bruno when I left Ireland. Bruno cleaned up the dig and reported back to the university that funded the work ... that's where it will be."

"Oh," said Ronan, disappointed he would never see the intriguing magnetic stone that had so excited his parents on that fateful day.

"To be honest," Maureen said, "I never gave them another thought."

16

THE THIEF

It was late the day after David Dalziel's visit. Maureen had taken Ruddi into town for his regular guitar lesson; Masters was still away drinking somewhere; and Ronan was lying on his bed, reading, the last of the day's light struggling to illuminate the pages of his father's notebook. On the last page was the hasty copy Paidin made the morning they found the inscription; in the margins, the occasional translated word or phrase. But they were only fragments of the poem his mother recited earlier—she'd carried a photo of it for years, her constant reminder of the fun and exciting parts of their last day together.

But that notebook was at the bottom of the Atlantic. Now, all Ronan remembered was the tantalising 'living stone'. It gnawed at him. The more he stared at the strange symbols and the fragments of translation, the more desperately he wanted the rest of it. His mother and Ruddi wouldn't be home for an eternity—at least another hour and a half.

Ronan's mind flew to Masters' notebook. The man would be away for ages, and would never know; neither would his mother. Besides, 'okay' wasn't 'I promise'.

The clock echoed through Masters' office. Ronan's eyes flicked to the doorway several times before he slid the key into the drawer lock. The image of his mother stepping through the door momentarily froze him—her quiet disappointment always hurt more than her husband's backhanders.

Ronan paused. It wasn't too late to abort and simply wait for her to come home to recite the rest of the verse. He thought of the living stone, recalled the odd familiarity when he touched Masters' notebook, imagined his mother's censure, pictured the man's outrage ... he turned the key.

Again, he hesitated. Silent seconds slid by. To prolong the flutter of trepidation, Ronan eased the drawer open, millimetres at a time. There, in a nest of assorted pens, paper clips and discarded credit card receipts, sat a Deetee notebook—not worn and grimy like Ronan's three, but with the same leather cover and dT symbol in the nest of swirls. And, sitting across the edge of the symbol was a small, stone disk, as black and shiny as lawyers' shoes.

A procession of chills tap-danced down Ronan's spine—it must be the one his mother had in the cave; Masters hadn't sent it to the university after all. The chills went into overdrive; everything else ceased to exist; his hand gravitated to the stone. At his touch, the stone lightened and warmed, a tingle shot through his fingers and up his arm. Ronan snapped his hand away. The stone nestled back onto the notebook's embossed design, returning to its original, dense black.

Again, Ronan touched a finger to it; again, it lightened—hairs lifted all over his body. Several more times he touched and withdrew; each time, the colour faded and returned. Emboldened, he picked it up, held it in his palm; it was strangely comforting, as if it belonged. His fingers curled round it.

Feeling more relaxed, he sat in the chair, withdrew the Deetee notebook and laid it on the desk.

The outside world blasted across Ronan's awareness—Smoky barking up a storm, a roaring engine, squealing brakes, crunching tyres on gravel. Masters!

Panic barely ignited in Ronan's gut when it was quelled by an overwhelming calm flowing from his left palm. He had both the stone and the notebook; there was nothing Masters could do about it. Slipping the notebook into his pocket, he decided to lock the drawer and return the key, then study the notebook and stone in his room, before returning them while the man slept off his drunkenness. No one would ever know.

The squeal of gate hinges and a drunken curse preceded a bone-cracking thump. Smoky let out a sickening yelp. There was a meaty thud and the whimpering dog crawled to safety under the house.

Ronan's calmness evaporated. He whipped the drawer closed, spun the key. Masters' boot heels thudded on the steps. Ronan clambered onto the pile of books; the key jumped from his fingers, snapping onto the magnet. Heavy footsteps were echoing in the hall! The tower of books collapsed under Ronan's haste. His hand caught the frame as he stumbled; it thudded to the floor, glass shattering asunder.

Ronan shot out the door, notebook peeping from his pocket, right in front of Masters' astonished eyes. In a fear-driven flurry, he darted along the hallway and into his bedroom, slamming the door, frantically turning the key. It wouldn't delay Masters for long.

Almost immediately, the latch rattled. "Thieving little bastard!" ricocheted through the closed door. Thump, thump. As solid as it was, the door groaned under the assault of the man's beefy shoulder. At the first sound of splintering, Ronan dived out the window, into the middle of his mother's flowers—another transgression to pay for. He kicked free of broken gerbera stalks and rolled under the house, cowering. *You and me, Smoke.*

With a shattering crash, the bedroom door burst wide, slamming back against the wall. Ronan winced. Clomping boots ... getting closer. They stopped above him; heart pounding, he held his breath.

"You interfering little mongrel!" Masters roared through the open window, his fury rattling the panes and fizzing into the twilight. "You'll pay for this!"

Hunkered down, Ronan felt another surge of beguiling calm. All he had to do was stay clear until his mother returned, then try to explain his misdeeds, ask for forgiveness—his gut tumbled at the prospect. More clomping, receding into the office. A moment's silence, then metallic scraping followed by a thumping clang. *The gun safe?* Indecision anchored him—surely Masters wouldn't.

Thudding footsteps in the hallway activated Ronan's flight instinct.

The only option for survival was down to the creek and into the bush; Masters would never find him there.

Ronan tore across the lawn and out through the back gate, stone clasped in one hand, Deetee notebook in the other. The departed sun was still throwing a tinge of pink across the sky as he sprinted into the gathering gloom.

The metallic 'snick, snick' of the rabbit-shooting rifle being loaded spurred him on—the only farm job Masters shone at was shooting rabbits. Ronan hoped the man was too drunk to aim straight. Regardless, he jagged left. An angry, lead hornet burned through the air he'd vacated; hard on its heels, the crack of the rifle shot slapped echoes up and down the creek.

"Thieving little mongrel!"

Fear surged through Ronan's veins, supercharging his sprint.

Snick, snick!

Arms pumping, lungs burning, he feinted to the right, but cut left again. Again, the too-close zing of death, again, the echoing rifle report in his ears.

A sharp decline loomed ... five more strides and he'd be out of sight ... snick, snick ... two more strides ... one ... legs gathered to drop to safety. The ground before him disappeared as it pitched into the shimmer of water below. He'd made it! As he drew in a victory breath, a giant hammer blow struck him between the shoulder blades. It punched the air from his lungs and his world into oblivion.

PART II

THE MEETING

17

THE GIRL

Ferocious turbulence consumed Ronan. Thrashed backward and forward in a tangle of limbs, he tried to cry out, but it was as though an enormous hand was clamped over his face. An instant terror that Masters had taped his mouth and stuffed his blood-soaked body into the washing machine, threatened to choke him. Without warning, the agitation became a diabolical spin, flinging the air from his lungs, taking him to the point of suffocation. Abruptly, it ceased; welcome calm descended. A heartbeat later, vigorous shaking engulfed him.

As his awareness solidified, Ronan realised he was shivering fiercely, and lying on the wet, cold grass. Not the coarse scratchy stalks of Doyle Farm, but a thick velvet softness, heavy with morning moisture, scented like fresh-mown hay ... a dream. Warm air wafted across him; he opened an eye, recoiling at the moist nose of a cow sniffing his forehead. At his sudden movement, she snorted a cloud of foggy breath and spray across his face, bouncing sideways as if on springs. After trotting off a short distance, she spun and fixed large, dark eyeballs on the intruder.

Ronan shut his eyes. The dream was so real; and his churning gut ... like a super dose of motion-sickness.

When he was a kid, Granddad and Grandma Doyle took him on their favourite drive, winding through the hunched ridges to the top of

Deadman's Gap, before twisting and turning down the other side to the flat land near Killarney. It was an agonising outing punctuated by Granddad's staccato braking, jerky acceleration and jabbing turns. Slumped on the back seat of the old Land Rover, Ronan had watched the tree tops sliding past, bracing himself against the next unpredictable change of direction that would set his insides swirling. He lost count of the number of times Granddad pulled over so he could vomit into the grass.

The memory was too much for his nauseous stomach. A spasm started deep in his gut, gurgling upward with undeniable urgency; the remnants of lunch burst from his mouth in an acid spray. While it was instant relief, it was only a matter of time before the pressure rebuilt.

A new sun eased above the nearby hills, sending a golden wash across the landscape, but there was no warmth in the rays angling onto Ronan's body. Although shivering, he wasn't cold. The grass was wet, the sun weak, the breeze cool, but there was a strong warmth radiating through him. He opened both eyes. Between green stalks, he saw the cow standing, head low, peering at him, her slimy mucous clinging to his face. With a fistful of damp grass, he wiped most of it away. As a farm boy, he'd copped far worse, but that's what pants were for—hand wiping. Only there were no pants!

Ronan sat bolt upright. It was a mistake. He groaned and hunched over, head spinning, stomach agitating for another release; it would make him feel better, but it refused to come. Tentatively, he swivelled his head. He was sitting in a small field of the most luxuriant pasture he'd ever seen—thick and green and succulent—it looked good enough to eat; his stomach gave another unproductive heave. Cow snot covered his face and ... he was stark naked! The fingers of his left hand still gripped the stone, its warmth spreading up his arm, flowing through him like a fireside glow. What a weird dream; he'd wake up soon enough.

Gathering another bundle of long grass, Ronan climbed gingerly to his feet, taking stock of his surroundings. The cow, black and white coat shining with good health in the early morning sun, stood her ground, sniffing the air for the intruder's scent. Behind her, an ancient stone fence marked the edge of her domain; lichen and moss clung to the grey rock like randomly thrown blobs of camouflage paint. Its centuries-spanning permanence gave way to round wooden posts and square wire mesh that dropped from sight down the hillside where a steep, grey-tiled roof thrust upward. Beyond it, a patchwork of fields and woods spread like a travel rug across a broad valley surrounded by impossibly green hills. To the north, the land rose to the foothills of a grey mountain whose hulking shape blended with the clouds shrouding its peak. Dotted about the landscape were houses, cottages and barns, some in natural stone, but many painted stark white, or soft pastel shades, much like one of Grandpa Paddy's Irish postcards— pleasant dream, apart from the motion-sickness.

Not wanting to be caught naked, even if only in his head, Ronan set off in search of clothes, heading toward the building, hunched against the nausea, fistful of grass clasped in front.

The roof belonged to a large stone barn hunkered beyond the fence. Balancing with his warm left fist on the top of a sturdy post, Ronan clambered awkwardly over the barrier, using the wire mesh like a ladder. As he swung his trailing leg up and over, the heel caught, ruining an already fragile equilibrium. He dropped the grass loincloth to clutch at the post, but his body spun and toppled. It was an awkward landing.

Ronan lay on the wet ground, sucking air into lungs reluctant to expand. A fierce stinging on his lower leg was attempting to out-compete another surge of nausea—the latter was winning.

As his breath returned, Ronan heard the rhythmic striking of iron horseshoes approaching from beyond the barn. Fear sent his hand scrabbling for a fresh bundle of grass; he rolled to his feet, floundering into the building through a doorway wide enough for a horse truck. Seven heads turned, ears picked, large dark eyes curious; the familiar, acrid bite of horse urine cut at his nostrils. Ronan was in an expansive central aisle, a line of four horse stalls along either side, all but one occupied.

Trotting hoofbeats, growing louder, echoed through the cavernous building. Bare feet skidding to a halt in the deep layer of prickly sawdust, Ronan spun in panic. Two closed side-doors at the far end were out of reach; the horse was nearing the stables, its hoof tempo easing to a walk. The only viable option, apart from retreating outside, was the second stall on the left with the horse rug draped over the open half-door. He dived through the opening at the instant the clip-clop softened on the sawdust.

"Oi! I know you're in there; I saw your leg." It was a girl's voice, and as Irish as Grandpa Paddy's. "Come out, or I'm calling the guards."

The horseshoes struck pavement again as the rider backed her horse from the stables. Ronan couldn't blame her; he could be an axe murderer. Yet her voice held no fear, only calm competence edged with annoyance.

"I've warned you," she said. The melodious beeping of a dialled phone drifted to Ronan.

"Alright," he said, "I'm coming out." He exposed an arm to grab the rug, wrapped the horse-sweat-infused prickliness round himself, and stepped from the stall. Even though his body shivered beneath the rug, his face warmed.

"You're only a boy!" The girl sat astride a tall, grey gelding as though born to it, relaxed but in command, reins loose in one hand, mobile phone in the other.

"I'm sixteen!" More heat burst into Ronan's face.

"Like I said, only a boy." Eyes the colour of summer honey sparkled with mischief and satisfaction.

"And you're only a girl," Ronan shot back, attempting balance.

The rider stiffened, her lips a straight line. "Girl enough." She nudged the words toward him with a little shimmy of her head, raising her phone a second time. The horse gave a snort of impatience, pawing at the ground. He had done his work, delivered her home, and now wanted to be rid of both rider and saddle.

Ronan needed help, not a fight. "I'm sorry," he said reluctantly. "I didn't mean to be rude."

Both her posture and lips softened; the phone lowered. "You're Australian," she said, a statement, not a question.

What else would I be? he almost said. Instead, he nodded. "Can you help me ... please?" He paused as a fresh wave of nausea bubbled upward. "Someone stole my clothes and"—he glanced round—"... where am I?"

"Raven's Roost."

"Where's Raven's—"

"Have you been taking drugs?"

Ronan stiffened. "No!"

"Well then, how did you end up naked?"

"I told you, someone—"

"Stole your clothes," she cut in. "Yeah, I know, but how did they get them?"

Ronan looked at her as if she spoke a foreign language. "I don't know," he said, voice shrinking.

"You're bleeding."

"What?" His head was spinning enough as it was without a conversation jumping about like a cricket.

"Your leg ... it's bleeding."

"It's only a scratch"—Ronan's eyes tracked the warm red trail snaking down to his heel—"... must have caught it when I climbed over the fence."

"Ever tried gates?"

Ronan's face reddened. "I ..." He saw her playful smile; his rising irritation faded.

"Come on, let's get you some clothes and clean that leg."

The girl slid from the back of her mount, bouncing onto her toes.

Even though snug, Ronan wanted nothing more than to ditch the smelly, itchy horse blanket, yet he hesitated.

"What's wrong?" she said. "Don't you trust me?" There was that smile again.

"Of course. It's just ... er ... why—"

"Would I trust you?" she said, removing her riding helmet, shaking loose a golden-brown mane that mesmerised Ronan as it fell below her shoulder blades. "Apparently, I'm a good judge of character"—she unbuckled the girth—"but, I have to tend to my horse first." After those two matter-of-fact statements, she pulled the saddle off the tall grey, set it against the wall, and began grooming him with a large brush.

"I'd help you but ..." Ronan pointed his chin at his horse rug cloak that needed both hands to keep it wrapped tight. Besides, judging by her practised strokes, she didn't need anyone's help.

"Do you know horses?" she said, tone bordering on disinterest.

"A bit," he said, thinking of tending the cattle on Doyle Farm. "Nice stables," he added.

The girl kept brushing as if she hadn't heard. Ronan shrugged, turning his attention to the adjacent tack room. There were neat shelves of grooming equipment and bottles of leather care and horse health potions, hooks for bridles, and a row of saddle pegs, one of which was empty. Ronan stared at the undecipherable string of letters on the adjacent name-plate: S-a-o-i-r-s-e. "Is that your name?" No way he would attempt pronunciation and risk censure, irritation or ridicule from this spirited girl.

Without lifting turning, she said, "Sur-sha ... like inertia," in an expressionless, automatic way born of much repetition. "Saoirse Kelly ... what's your name?"

"Ronan Ryan."

"Now that's a fine Irish name, but you're not Irish."

Ronan swallowed. *It's an Irish dream?* "No, but my da was," he said, adopting Grandpa Paddy's term.

"Where are you from then, Ronan Ryan?" Saoirse's back remained turned while she groomed.

"Near Killarney, Queensland."

"Well, Killarney is a fine Irish name as well, but what's Queensland?"

A sharp retort jumped to Ronan's lips, but he swallowed it before it could escape. Instead, he replied, "The north-eastern state of Australia."

"Oh," she said with disinterest. "What are you doing in Ireland, then?"

Well, that's settled then. "I ... I'm not sure." The words were barely out before another heave wracked his body.

"Are you sick?"

As feeble as he felt, Ronan found himself fascinated by her lips. Even when serious, they held the hint of a smile, the corners upturned like a tiny recurve bow lying on its side. "No, just car-sick ... ah, motion-sickness."

"I know what car-sick means." Saoirse made the faintest eye roll. "What's wrong with your hand?"

"Huh?"

"Your left hand, it's been clenched the whole time."

Ronan spread his stiff fingers to show the glossy disk. They'd been clamped shut for so long he had trouble unwinding them. "It's my father's ... I've no pockets." He shrugged.

Saoirse glanced at it before leading the grey to the empty stall, turning him loose with an affectionate rub of the shoulder. "It must mean a lot."

"Why do you say that?"

"Well, you lost everything else, but you kept hold of a wee pebble." Both her voice and her eyes held the teasing twinkle of a smile.

"It's special," Ronan said, annoyance evaporating.

"Which is what I just said," Saoirse responded dryly, beckoning for him to follow as she strode from the stables. "We need to get you into some clothes ... Viking wants his rug back."

18

THE SHOWER

Saoirse led the way across the yard to a white-painted cottage. Its green door matched the trim round the windows and eaves; chimney sprouting from a grey-tiled roof like the stables. She pointed to a small external room whose low roof jutted down at a steep angle from the end wall of the cottage. "That's the mudroom," she informed him. "You'll find a fresh towel on the shelf." Saoirse spun in a swirl of brown locks, leaving Ronan's 'thank you' hanging in empty, shampoo-scented air.

The heavy door swung inward, hinges squealing a shrill protest. A cluster of dirty overcoats and rain jackets hung immediately inside; there was a chipped mirror, a couple of rolled towels on a small shelf, a toilet and a stained handbasin. The walls felt closer and the roof lower than they looked from the outside. Tucked into the far corner was an open shower with ancient brass taps, a rose the size of a dinner plate hanging from the ceiling, and a loaded wire soap rack. Ronan engaged the latch but there was no lock, so he dropped Viking's rug onto the rough stone floor, wedging it against the back of the door.

The water was hot and soothing, the soap scented and the shampoo sudsy, but as good as it was, it did nothing for the nausea. Despite swallowing air and burping several times, he still wanted to vomit. Ronan was halfway through drying himself when the door squealed ajar against the bundled horse rug. Pulling the towel close, he watched a long, pale arm with a fist-full of assorted clothes poke through the gap. "Try these, Ronan Ryan," Saoirse said. "They should fit. And pass out Viking's rug ... I'll throw it on while you get dressed."

Ronan grabbed the clothes and, not wanting to get too far behind in the verbal jousting, said, "Thank you, Saoirse Kelly."

After bundling the rug through the chink of open door, he pulled on baggy trousers and a loose shirt, neither of which extended to the extremities of his limbs. The coat, however, was a perfect fit. It was bright red, long in the sleeves and thick in its warmth. Standing in front of the mirror, he finger-combed his unruly hair in a vain attempt to restore order, eventually giving up with a resigned shrug.

The black stone wouldn't budge from the wire rack where he'd put it to shower. In exasperation, Ronan gave a hearty tug. The rack popped off its hook, clattering to the wet floor, sending soap and shampoo in disarray. Alarmed by the carnage, he jumped back, landing on the scatter of soap. Both feet shot backward, pitching him face-first. He threw out a desperate hand, snagging a tap in passing, flicking it on and slowing momentum, but to one side of his body only. His torso spun and he landed on his shoulder, cracking his skull against the stone floor.

Ronan's world turned black for the second time that day.

As consciousness seeped into his brain like the first hint of dawn, he was aware of rain—slow, steady and cold. And while he was, once again, on the point of shivering, at least he wasn't naked, but his clothes were soaked, his head hurt and his ear was full of water. He needed shelter.

A metallic squeal cut across Ronan's thoughts, then a startled exclamation: "Jaysis, boy, what have you done?" Saoirse leant across and turned off the cold-water tap.

Through chinks in his eyelids, Ronan saw a pair of long, denim-clad legs planted like saplings in tan boots darkened by the falling rain, a *dT* in swirls decorating their sides. "Oh, shit," he said, remembering what happened—*not rain at all!*

"Are you always this destructive?" For some strange reason, she was smiling.

Ronan lifted his head, wincing at the thumping behind his eyes. *Are dreams this painful? ... and realistic?* As he gingerly pushed into a sitting position against the wall, the girl's smile evaporated.

"You're hurt," she said, leaning close.

"More pride than anything," he said, annoyed at his uncharacteristic clumsiness.

"No, there's blood." Saoirse touched fingertips to the goose-egg swelling above his left ear—they came away red. As soft as it was, the contact made him take a sharp breath.

"Sorry," she said.

"*I* should be apologising," Ronan said wryly, glancing at the havoc —rack, soap, shampoo, soaked clothes.

Saoirse followed his gaze and laughed. In spite of himself, Ronan managed a chuckle.

"Don't worry about it," she said once her mirth had subsided. "Dad's always sending that old rack for a tumble." She extended a hand to Ronan, pulling him to his feet.

Gasping at the pain searing through his skull, Ronan clamped his eyes tight in a futile attempt to shut it out.

Saoirse grabbed his arm. "You're not going to faint on me, are you?"

"No," Ronan replied, "I just need to sit down until my head clears."

"Here." With a firm hand on his arm, she led him across to a bench below the mirror. "Wait here while I grab some more clothes," Saoirse said, rolling her eyes and leaving in another swirl of hair.

Ignoring the subtle gibe, Ronan settled onto the hard wooden surface, closing his eyes, leaning back gratefully, shallow-breathing against the pain, oblivious to the mirror's edge pressing against his spine. He needed to clean up his mess, and prise the living stone from the soap rack, but any movement sent fresh shards of fire searing through his head. So he sat. And waited. And breathed.

At last, Saoirse returned with a pair of fashionable long pants. Ronan barely opened an eye.

"I didn't think you'd need a shirt," she said. "If my best hiking jacket can't keep you dry, you're in trouble."

Despite the dampness down his left side telling him he was, indeed, in strife, Ronan said nothing. Even his vague head tilt of thanks was an effort and intensified the throbbing.

Dropping the trousers on his lap, Saoirse placed a gentle hand on his shoulder like a comforting nurse. "If you need help, I'll be right outside."

Ronan would rather die than let her, or anyone else, change his pants; the way he felt, death didn't seem so far away.

It took a while, but he managed to wrestle the saturated trousers off and the dry ones on without having to stand. They were thick, warm and full of pockets, although loose at the waist and short in the legs.

"You finished in there?" Saoirse called.

A weak, "Yeah," was all he managed before she breezed back into the shower room.

"Good, because we should call your parents. They'll be worried."

Ronan waved her words away feebly. "Mum won't miss me until she gets home late tonight ... my stepfather would be happy to never see me again," he said.

"All right then. But in the meantime, we need to get you fixed ... you're very pasty."

He gave a fragile nod; his head seemed ready to explode.

"With a bowl of broth," she continued, "a couple of Panadol and a good sleep, you'll be right as rain."

Too unsteady to resist, Ronan let Saoirse drape his arm round her neck, assisting him like a wounded comrade. At a slow shuffle, they left the scene of carnage.

19

THE MIRROR

I t was not a large cottage. Fifteen healthy strides would easily cover the distance from the mudroom to the entry. With Ronan's groggy meander, it took twice as many to get past a couple of curtain-hung windows, and arrive at a plain green door with a shiny brass knocker and matching letter flap. The door opened into a small living room, its welcoming couch the only thing Ronan had eyes for.

Once Saoirse eased him onto the broad cushions, she fetched two white tablets and a glass of water. "Be back in a sec," she said, disappearing past the protruding corner of a rust-stained refrigerator in the adjacent room.

On a sideboard to the left of the kitchen doorway sat a box-like television set, its bulbous screen a gigantic opaque grey eye staring blindly into the room. It reminded Ronan of watching The Wiggles at Grandma Doyle's when he'd barely started school—*Hot potato, hot potato ...*

Above it hung a family portrait of a gap-toothed Saoirse, and a much younger boy with the same eyes, seated on the laps of a smiling man and woman. On a threadbare rug between the couch and the television, squatted a low coffee table strewn with out-of-date horse magazines, high school textbooks and circular mug-stains. A motley collection of hanging coats, paired footwear and a tarnished metal umbrella stand cluttered round the front door, a gaggle of pets eager to escape. While tiny and cramped compared to the homestead at Doyle Farm, the cottage smelt of warmth, comfort and people. But there were no motherly knickknacks and photographs, and certainly none of the rubble and chaos that a preteen boy leaves in his wake.

Returning with a bowl of steaming water and a small first aid kit, Saoirse proceeded to bathe and dress his wounds. "I think you'll live," she said, her voice lilting with brightness as she applied sharp-smelling ointment to the wire scratch.

Ronan was inclined to believe her—the pain-killers were beginning to pacify his thumping head. "Thank you, Saoirse," he said with feeling. "If this is how you treat a stranger, your friends are fortunate indeed."

Saoirse glanced up as she finished taping a dressing on his leg. "Well, you've kissed the Blarney Stone, haven't you?"

Fresh heat flushed through Ronan's face; he hated how that always happened. "It's something my grandpa often says ... said, and I thought ... it seemed fitting."

"Why thank you, Ronan Ryan," she said, dipping her head. "He must have been a lovely man." It was her turn for cheek colour.

"He was." Ronan could say no more as his throat constricted.

Saoirse must have sensed the rawness of his loss. "When did he die?" she asked gently.

"A few weeks ago."

"I'm so sorry."

Ronan nodded his thanks, but was keen for a different subject—he didn't trust his tear ducts. After a brief silence, he found it. "So, why's this place needs guards? ... looks like a normal farm."

Saoirse gave him a sideways look. "You haven't been in Ireland long, have you?" she said. "Guards, Garda, Police ... all the same thing."

"Oh." Ronan shivered with unease as his brain screamed, 'Impossible!' There was no way he was actually *in* Ireland—unless he was drugged and transported. But that didn't make any sense either, and neither did the logical alternative. "Am I dreaming?"

Saoirse rose, hooking hair behind an ear. "Do you think you are?" she said playfully as she left the room.

"I must be."

"Why do you say that?" Her words faded as she moved further into the cottage.

"Because nothing else makes sense," Ronan said, peeling off the hiking coat in response to the building's warmth. The mere effort of raising his voice to make it carry had his head thumping afresh.

"And why's that?" Saoirse swept back into the room, giving Ronan a mild start.

"The last thing I remember, before waking up in your field, was being ... chased." He'd almost said 'shot at', which would have destroyed his fragile credibility.

"Who by?"

"I ... I can't remember." Again, caution overrode honesty.

"Maybe you're drugged," she suggested, a tiny smile playing at the corner of her mouth. "Or dead."

"If I'm dead, then so are you."

"Perhaps I am."

Ronan closed his eyes and leant back on the couch, exasperated, too feeble to continue the verbal jousting.

"Sorry," Saoirse said, smile fading. "Dad always says I have a smart mouth."

"Exactly what my stepfather tells me."

Saoirse's eyes softened; Ronan's hardened.

"Anyway," she said, "if you think you're in a dream, look in the mirror ... if you're not distorted, it's no dream."

Ronan blanched—his reflection had been crystal clear in the mudroom mirror earlier.

"Do you need a bucket?" Saoirse asked quickly.

"No, I'm fine, thanks," he replied, thoughts in turmoil. He took a calming breath. "I think I need a good sleep."

"Your shirt's wet," she said abruptly.

"It's not much."

"Well, you're not going to bed with a wet shirt," Saoirse insisted, leaving the room, returning with a red-checked flannel shirt that she dropped on his lap in passing. "I'll heat some broth."

Absently unbuttoning, Ronan paused with the shirt half off his shoulders, his mind in a flurry, trying to make sense of what was—yet couldn't be—happening.

"Would you like bread with your ...?" Saoirse had popped her head round the corner, her words evaporating at the sight of the yellowing patchwork of bruises mottling Ronan's torso.

"Jaysis," she breathed. "What happened to you?"

20

THE BULLY

Saoirse's presence snapped Ronan from his thoughts. He shrugged, letting the damp shirt fall from broadening shoulders—he was past caring about hiding the bruises, and past caring about being embarrassed by this strange Irish girl.

"Jaysis," Saoirse said again, almost to herself. "Who did this?" Her voice rose. "Bloody monster! We have to call the guards!"

Ronan caught himself before disputing that he was in Ireland. He didn't want to antagonise her; he needed all the help he could get while he worked out what the heck was happening. Maybe it was all hallucinations—perhaps Masters had caught and drugged him, and he couldn't remember any of it.

"Do you hear me, Ronan Ryan? We have to put the guards onto the bastard?"

Given how quickly she'd gone from 'jaysis' to 'bastard', Ronan wondered what was coming next. He dragged on the fresh shirt as a barrier to further discussion on the issue, but Saoirse was insistent. "The guards?"

Ronan shook his head, dropping his gaze. "I can't remember what happened." Hoping it wouldn't count as a second lie, he added, "I'd tell you if I could."

Saoirse peered at him in silence, eyebrows sceptical. Squirming under her scrutiny and desperate to change the subject, he mumbled, "I just need to lie down and get rid of this headache."

After considering him for a moment longer, she nodded. "But first, you need food." Once more, she disappeared into the kitchen.

Ronan's fingers were fumbling with the last button when Saoirse reappeared carrying a small tray laden with a bowl of steaming broth, an age-tarnished spoon and a single slice of dark bread under a thick smear of creamy butter. No sooner had she set it on his lap, then there was a sharp knock on the door. Saoirse went still, lips compressing. There was another rap, more insistent than the first.

Saoirse looked at the door, chewing her lower lip—it was the first hint of uncertainty. "I'm sorry," she said, although for what, Ronan had no clue.

A fresh assault on the door reverberated round the tiny cottage. "Saoirse, open the bloody door!"

As Saoirse lifted the latch, the door flung open, almost knocking her off balance. Ronan glared at the large lad who burst into the room.

"What took so damn long?" he growled, pushing past her. He looked about eighteen, not as tall as Saoirse, but with a build hinting at inactivity, the whitest hair Ronan had ever seen, and a pale face wearing haughty superiority as a birthright. He halted when he saw Ronan. "Who's this then?" he sneered.

"A friend," Saoirse said without expression.

The youth took in Ronan's haggard pallor and the food tray, saying, "Feeling poorly, friend?" The words were laced with sarcasm; Ronan ignored them. "Can't the poor wee thing talk?" the intruder taunted, directed more at Saoirse than Ronan.

Ronan's jaw muscles worked; the white-haired boy reminded him of Masters. Bitter experience had shown him that the best way to deal with a bully, if they couldn't be avoided, was to show no fear.

Saoirse's face darkened as she stepped between them. "Leave him alone," she snapped.

"My, very protective, aren't we?"

Saoirse didn't move. "What do you want, Fionn?" Her teeth were clenched.

"Just wanted to see me, girl," he said jauntily, looking past her at Ronan.

"I'm not your girl, or anyone else's girl." She spat the words at him.

The lad smirked. He was baiting them both, but his pale blue eyes never left Ronan, who had no strength for anything but to stare back.

"Putting on a show, are we?" he said, as much to Ronan as to Saoirse.

"Whatever you reckon," Saoirse said with disdain. Ronan held the bully's gaze, trying to convey contempt.

After a long, silent duel, the youth finally dropped his eyes. As though attempting to cover the surrender, he said, "Any more of that fine broth, Saoirse?"

The tension drained from Ronan; relief surging in its place. Saoirse remained resolutely between them, face set. "No, that's the last," she said.

"Well, perhaps your friend will share?" He went to move past, but she stepped into his path.

For a fleeting second, Ronan considered it, but he knew better. First the broth, then the bread, then the couch or something else. Bullies were never satisfied; he'd learnt that the hard way.

The youth searched for another opening. "Does your silent friend have a name, Saoirse?"

"Why would you want to know?" she said. "You won't remember it tomorrow."

"I might surprise you," he sneered.

"Just leave us alone, Fionn."

"Oh, it's *us* then, is it?" While his tone suggested delight at the opening he'd found, his eyes held annoyance, or something darker.

"Why are you here?" she snapped, surprising Ronan with her ferocity.

"I'm going down to Killybegs ... I want some company." It wasn't a request.

Ronan had heard enough of the smug sod. Setting the untouched tray aside, he stood with a grimace, and moved to Saoirse's side, extending his right hand. "Ronan Ryan," he said.

The bully gleefully took the offered hand in his own version of a vise-like grip. "Ronan Ryan, eh? Fionn Egan."

Saoirse's eyes flicked from one to the other.

"Finnegan is a name I'll remember," Ronan said, his quick tongue at play.

Fire ignited in the other's eyes. "It's Fionn ... Egan," he snarled. Gripping Ronan's hand tighter, Egan jerked him forward. Ronan pretended to teeter, took a quick half-step to increase momentum, and dropped his chin. The top of his forehead crunched into Egan's unsuspecting face. Something cracked; the bully howled in pain, released Ronan's hand and clutched his nose.

Ronan threw one hand to his head, holding the other up in apology. "Geez, mate, I'm sorry ... you pulled me off balance."

Egan squinted at them, confusion, anger and pain swirling in his eyes. Blood gushed between his fingers, dripping to the floor from wrist and elbow.

"That looks painful," Saoirse said, pulling Ronan's hand from his forehead, and saying with exaggerated concern, "Do you need some ice?"

Growling malevolently, Egan stalked out, rattling the door in his wake.

21

THE HEADACHE

S oft evening light filtered through the faded curtains of the tiny bedroom, falling across Ronan's face. His eyelids flickered, then eased open. Panic gripped him—he was in a strange room, disorientated. Then, out of the swirling mists of his memory came a gunshot, great turbulence, a cow, a girl, a shower and a white-haired bully. None of it made sense. One instant he was running for his life from his enraged stepfather, the next he was naked on the grass, apparently in Ireland.

Ronan's churning thoughts kept circling back to one thing—the living stone. If that chaotic turbulence wasn't some mysterious power of the stone, then he'd been drugged, and was now living a weird, chemically induced dream; however, the mirror appeared to rule that out. Of his current experiences, as unbelievable as they all were, the most outrageous, by far, was the location. Which brought Ronan back to the stone. If it had transported him to Ireland, it could take him home ... couldn't it?

Alarm rattled through him as he realised there was no warmth in his palm. His sleep-fogged mind dragged him to where he'd last seen the stone, stuck to the wire soap rack on the floor of the shower. Anxiety drained the lethargy from his bones and the drowsiness from his brain. Ronan had to have it back in his hand; it was his only connection to home. Without it, he would never see his mother, or Ruddi, again.

He sprang upright onto the edge of the bed—bad move. The jackhammer in his head kicked into overdrive, his vision swam, and the horrible swirl in his gut suggested he was about to taste Saoirse's broth for a second time. Immobile, he willed both head and stomach to settle. Subdued voices drifted beneath the closed bedroom door—one reverberated, too deep to be the bully, the other was Saoirse.

Earlier, after Egan had carried his smashed nose and mangled pride back to wherever he came from, Saoirse had asked Ronan, "That wasn't an accident, was it?"

"What do you mean?" he'd responded with wide-eyed innocence.

Saoirse had considered Ronan with a raised eyebrow, before saying with a smile, "Accident or not, it was priceless. Now eat your broth." Afterwards, she'd rolled him into the bed, pulling the door closed behind her.

Judging by the light, Ronan guessed he had slept for a good eight hours—he needed it. But what he craved more than anything was the warmth of the stone. He stood, but couldn't straighten; the crippling torment in his skull pushed all thought of the living stone to one side. Hunched like an old man, he slow-walked toward the door and the voices beyond.

The click of the latch cut the conversation like a switch. Squinting through the pain, Ronan saw Saoirse and a middle-aged man studying him as he shuffled from the bedroom. The man was an older version of the one in the photograph above the television—a bit more grey in the hair, a few more wrinkles in the face.

Ronan must have looked as bad as he felt, for they both rushed to his side.

"What are you doing out of bed?" Saoirse scolded, taking an arm, guiding him to the couch.

"Need something for this head." Ronan grimaced, then sank onto the lounge with a sigh, leaning back, closing his eyes against the throbbing.

"That is some lump, lad," the man said in wonder, eyeing the goose egg above Ronan's ear.

"And he's been beaten pretty badly," Saoirse said. "There are bruises all over his body." She reddened when her father considered her with a raised eyebrow. "I ... the ... he was changing his shirt ..." Her face glowed brighter.

But the man appeared not to notice. "Who set upon you, lad?"

"I don't know," Ronan responded.

"He thinks he's in a dream," Saoirse whispered. "I think his brain's addled."

"I'm right here," Ronan said, not bothering to open his eyes.

Saoirse ignored him. Instead, she said to her father, "Do you think we should call the doctor?"

"We should at least call his parents to let them know he's okay," the man said.

"All I need is some more Panadol ... please?"

Saoirse glanced at her father, who, after scrutinising Ronan, nodded. "Okay then," she said, leaving the room.

The elder Kelly put a large, work-roughened hand on Ronan's shoulder. "Are you sure you're okay, lad?"

Ronan opened his eyes. "Yeah ... thanks." Belatedly remembering his manners, he extended a hand, saying, "I'm Ronan, by the way, Ronan Ryan."

"Darragh Kelly," the man said, giving Ronan's hand a friendly shake. "Saoirse's da," he added unnecessarily.

"Pleased to meet you, Mr Kelly," Ronan murmured.

Saoirse returned with a glass of water and a couple of tablets and, seeing the handshake, said, "Well, now your friends outnumber your enemies two to one."

Ronan managed an unsteady smile and washed the pills down.

"For later ... if you need it," she said, placing another lot on the low table beside the couch.

"Thanks."

Saoirse frowned at her father. "Do you think he's okay?"

"I just need to sleep," Ronan insisted, settling back with a muted sigh.

"And you're more than welcome to lay your head here, my friend,"

Darragh told him. "But first, what's your parents' number ... they must be fretting."

Ronan sat forward, feeling like he'd been caught with contraband. In his mind, he cast about wildly, unsure which way to turn, or what to say. To buy thinking time, he pulled on his best mask of confusion. Looking from one to the other, he said in a distressed voice, "I ... I can't remember." And he dropped his face into his hands, as much to hide his shame as to aid in the deception.

The Kellys exchanged glances; Saoirse shrugged her shoulders. "Maybe he'll remember in the morning."

Not if I can help it, Ronan thought as he leant back again. Closing his eyes, he concentrated on breathing, trying to shut out the pain, ignoring the murmured discussion as his hosts discussed whether a doctor might be required after all. The voices slowly faded as he drifted into a welcome sleep.

Ronan woke in gloom, confused, disorientated, and with no idea of the time or where he was. As before, his memory came seeping back as his brain staggered into life. Unlike before, the pounding was bearable, but a dull ache still radiated from above his left ear. Instead of the bed, he was on the couch, pillow under his head, blanket over his shoulders.

Swinging his feet to the floor, he searched the adjacent table with fingertips for the pain-killers left by Saoirse earlier. While the headache had subsided, and the nausea was in retreat, his mouth was as dry as a desert; he downed the rest of the water. At once, his bladder started complaining. He needed the toilet ... now!

22

THE BOOTMAKER

The room was as black as an undertaker's waistcoat. The bare suggestion of moonlight filtered through curtains, enough to give a hint of the window, no more. Even if Ronan knew where the light switch was, he didn't want to risk waking his hosts, so he set out with hands at arm's length, using the vague window as a guide, easing cautiously toward where he expected to find the front door.

His second tentative shuffle drove his shin into the corner of the coffee table, and although the contact was mild, bone on wood echoed in the silence. Ronan froze, cursing under his breath at both his carelessness and the pain. When there was no stir in the depths of the cottage, he resumed his foot-sliding progress. It took him from the rug and across the cold stone until his outstretched hand contacted a coat, then another, and his toes encountered the collection of shoes. He let out a shallow sigh when his fingers found the door and closed on the large metal handle.

Ronan couldn't recall any latch or hinge noise from the previous day, so he boldly worked the lever. The metallic click was as loud as a gunshot in the night's silence. He held his breath, but once satisfied there was no reaction from his sleeping hosts, he began easing the door open. A dry hinge squealed in protest; he froze, waiting. But his bladder pressure was mounting; he had to move—he'd yank it open, like ripping off a band-aid.

There was only the tiniest squeak as he tugged the door ajar; with a wry grin, he slipped through the small gap. His flapping shirttail caught a projecting umbrella rib, overturning the metal stand onto the threshold with a resounding clatter. Ronan swore as a brolly tangled his feet, sending him sprawling.

An irate growl rumbled from the cottage ... lights popped ... a blinding torch beam hit Ronan square in the eyes.

"Jaysis, lad, what the hell are you doing?" barked a bleary-eyed Darragh.

Ronan stared into the light like a mesmerised kangaroo. "I was going to the toilet," he said feebly. "Sorry."

Sleepy-eyed, dishevelled and bare-footed, Saoirse stumbled from her bedroom into the middle of the apology. At the sight of the wreckage, she halted. "Ronan Ryan," she said, shaking her head, hands on hips, "you certainly are a walking disaster area."

A red-faced Ronan looked from Saoirse to Darragh. "Sorry," he said again, bending to re-right the umbrella stand.

"Leave it, lad," Darragh grunted. "Go and do your business."

Ronan stumbled to the mudroom, face smouldering even harder. In all the commotion, he'd forgotten the stone, but his heart sank when he flicked on the light: in the insipid glow of the single bulb, he saw the wire rack reinstated on the wall, soap and shampoo restored, but no sign of the stone. Last time he'd seen it, it was stuck, barnacle-like, to the rack; Saoirse or Darragh must have it.

Even with this realisation, Ronan was still coiled tight—he had to have that stone in his hand; the jangle of disquiet in his chest told him so.

After relieving his bladder, Ronan sluiced icy water over his face, frowning uncertainly at his undistorted reflection. When he trudged back into the cottage, order had been restored; Saoirse and Darragh were dressed for the day, sitting in the kitchen, waiting for the kettle to boil.

"It's just gone five," Darragh said, nodding at the clock on top of the fridge, "so we may as well have a cuppa and greet the day. Provided you're feeling up to it, lad."

"That'd be good, thanks," Ronan replied. The early morning chill had seeped through his shirt, goose bumping his torso; the cold water hadn't helped.

As he waited for the warm drink, Ronan took in the little kitchen. Everything was worn, but well cared for, which would have impressed his frugal Granddad Doyle. A calendar beside the fridge caught his eye; rather it was the glossy chestnut coat and proud bearing of an aristocratic Arabian stallion—dished face, gracefully curved neck, short back and arched tail. A large, scribble-covered square of yellow notepaper pinned beneath the horse obscured the year and all but the 'er' of the month.

Reluctantly dragging his eyes from the horse, Ronan swept them round the room again. Something was gnawing at his mind, like a dog worrying a bone. Unease crawled up his back; his mind flew straight to the stone—everything weird started with that stone; he had to find it.

"Can you remember your parents' number this morning, lad?"

Darragh's question triggered instant guilt in Ronan. He'd been so fixated on the stone he hadn't spared a thought for his mother; she would be frantic with her son having disappeared without a trace. He could only hope that his bullet-holed shirt would see Masters arrested for murder; from that perspective, it'd be better if it wasn't a dream. Among his churning thoughts, there was one thing he knew for sure, he had to delay giving specific information until he worked out what the heck was happening. Ronan didn't want to be handed over to the guards, or worse, put in a mental hospital.

"I'm ... not sure," he said. The white lies and half-truths he'd told so far, clung to his conscience like the sticky web of a bush spider; however, he needed as much wriggle room as possible with the phone number. "I think it starts with 4664, but I'm not sure."

Darragh raised an eyebrow. "Well, that's more than you remembered last night."

Ronan felt like a suspect in an interrogation room, struggling to stay ahead of a sceptical detective. "My head is much clearer today ... hopefully, I'll be able to remember it all before long." Desperate to change the subject, he turned to Saoirse. "Did you clean up the mudroom? I can't find my stone."

She shook her head, glancing at her father. The kettle began whistling.

"That rack has never fallen before, lad," Darragh said, a glint of mischief in his eyes, "but I guess there's a first time for everything."

"Oh, Dad," Saoirse admonished with a smile, moving to attend to the teapot, "your nose will grow. You're always knocking that old thing off the wall."

"Well, maybe once or twice," he said wryly, gathering cups and spoons, setting them on the table.

Despite his relief at the change of subject, Ronan wasn't in the mood to join their banter. "The stone?"

"Dad, tell him." Saoirse was filling cups.

There was no telltale glimmer of humour in those golden eyes, and Ronan's insides fluttered with panic. "Tell me what?"

"Well, lad, I managed to get the wee pebble off the wire rack ... it was fierce stuck, let me tell you," he said.

"I know," Ronan replied dryly, chuckling in spite of himself. Saoirse smiled.

"Well, I'd just come home from work, hadn't I," Darragh said, "so I dropped it in the pocket of me jacket, and that's where the trouble started."

"Trouble?" Ronan was intrigued, if uneasy.

Darragh grinned. "The jolly thing came out of me pocket looking like a porcupine!" he said, chuckling. "And twice as prickly." He stepped across to the sink and waved a teaspoon above a clump of tiny black quills on the windowsill. The prickly bundle wobbled, then snapped onto the spoon.

Although obscured by a spray of razor-sharp tacks, the stone's lustre was unmistakable. Ronan battled to remain casual in the face of an urgent desire to seize it. "How did that happen?"

"I had a handful of tacks in me pocket, didn't I," Darragh said, seating himself, placing the spoon on a cork mat in the middle of the table.

In response to Ronan's puzzled expression, Saoirse explained,

"Dad's a bootmaker; he's always got tacks in his coat pockets—damn nuisance in the wash—uses them to attach the uppers to the midsoles."

"Huh?"

"Dad is the head bootmaker for Detencin." There was undisguised pride in her voice.

Ronan didn't know what Detencin was, but head bootmaker sounded important.

Darragh had left the room and returned with a worn pair of tan, high-topped boots. "The upper," he said, caressing the soft leather, "is this part that goes over the top of your foot ... the midsole is hidden ... it's what we glue the outsole to." Inverting the boot, he slapped a work-hardened palm onto the worn tread. And, clearly stamped into the side of the inverted boot, was the dT symbol, the same symbol he's seen on Saoirse's boots when he regained consciousness on the shower floor.

"Deetees, the best boots in all of Ireland," said Ronan, parroting his grandfather's words. Saoirse and Darragh stared in surprise, so for good measure, he added, "Better even than Dubarrys."

Both Kellys laughed. "Spoken like a proud local," Darragh said. "And how do you know Deetees, lad?"

"I have a couple of notebooks of my dad's."

"Well, your da must have bought Deetee boots, then," the boot-maker said, winking at his daughter.

"You can only get the notebooks if you buy the boots," Saoirse said, reddening as though realising her words were unnecessary.

"That's what I've been told," Ronan said, causing her face to colour further. But he barely noticed, and he'd lost interest in uppers and midsoles; they wouldn't get him home. If he wasn't in a dream, the living stone was his only hope.

23

THE LIBERATION

The black echidna lay serenely inside the safety of its prickly cocoon. Ronan, Saoirse and Darragh sat round it at the kitchen table drinking hot tea and musing on how to remove the tacks from its magnetic thrall. By the time they finished their drinks, they had settled on a strategy. Darragh fetched two pairs of pliers about the size of household scissors; Saoirse cleared the table; Ronan sat turning the spoon in his hand, looking for a gap between the tacks ... there was none.

The bootmaker sat opposite Ronan and passed a pair of pliers ... not as robust as the ones he used at Doyle Farm to pull wires tight and repair fences, but its slender jaws looked better suited to gripping fine tacks.

"Now get a firm grip on one, lad ... I'll do the same and we'll see which one comes away first."

They gripped and pulled ... and pulled. Ronan was being dragged across the table by the stronger man. Saoirse grabbed Ronan's hands on the pliers, adding her weight to his effort. Her long brown hair hung close to his face, fruity shampoo filling his nostrils. Without warning, his tack popped free, sending him slumping backward in his chair with Saoirse falling half onto his lap. Despite his immediate face warmth, Ronan took comfort from the hint of colour in her cheeks as she apologised and straightened. He relaxed his hand on the pliers, and the tack flew from its jaws, locking back onto the stone where it sat in Darragh's pliers, almost a table width away.

"Well, at this rate," said Darragh dryly, "we'll be here all day and half the night." The absurdity of the statement triggered laughter all round.

"Get a grip, Ronan Ryan," said Saoirse. Ronan reddened further—he didn't know whether she was referring to his pliers or his embarrassment. "And I'll try not to squash you this time," she added impishly.

They tried again. The tack popped free for a second time—her hair smelt of apple. Ronan kept his pliers locked on the tack, holding it well out to the side, dropping it into Saoirse's open hand. She placed it at the extremity of the table, where it quivered and began sliding toward the stone. Almost before astonishment had registered on their faces, it leapt into the air, snapping back into the cluster. The resulting stunned silence morphed into more laughter.

Darragh shook his head. "I've never seen magnetism like this stone of yours, lad. What is it?"

"My parents found it," Ronan said—close to the truth. "I think it's some type of weird magnetite"—assumed true—"but it's really special to me." The last was unambiguous.

"It's certainly different," Saoirse said. "And from now on, Dad, I'll put each tack back in your coat pocket."

When they removed the tack for a third time, Saoirse dropped it into the deep pocket of the largest coat by the front door. One by one, they tugged the tacks from their magnetic captivity; more and more of the lustrous black shape appeared.

"Tell me about your parents." Darragh said as they toiled, catching Ronan unawares.

Relieved at being able to stick to the truth, but still wary of how much he revealed, Ronan told them about his father dying before he was born, his mother marrying, Ruddi coming along, Grandpa Paddy and life on the farm, glossing over the Irish parts, expanding on the Australian ones, and leaving out Masters' abuse.

"And what would you be doing in Ireland, lad?"

It was a casual question, but Ronan sensed its danger. "Visiting friends," he said, mind whirring for a plausible story, finally settling on the truth: "Mum went to uni in Dublin." He left it at that to give himself time to think.

Saoirse paused, halfway to the coat pocket. "Oh, which one?"

"UCD I think she calls it."

"University College Dublin," Saoirse said, a sparkle in her eyes. "That's where I'd like to go." She fell silent, her face colouring.

Ronan enjoyed her discomfort—he liked the colour in her cheeks and was thankful she couldn't read his mind. "What do you want to study?" he asked, missing the opportunity to change the subject.

"Sustainability," she said, shooting a glance at her father.

"You're smart enough to do proper science," Darragh grumbled.

"It *is* proper science, Dad." Saoirse sighed as though they were revisiting a previous disagreement. "It's environmental science *and* engineering—"

"Engineering isn't for girls," Darragh broke in again, squeezing his pliers hard onto another tack.

"You said I could do whatever I wanted to," she snapped, folding her arms.

"What *you* want to do," he said bluntly, "not Caitlin O'Toole."

Ronan squirmed—he'd reignited a simmering family feud, and didn't know how to extinguish it. So, he kept his head down, concentrating on the next tack.

Saoirse dropped her hands. "That's not fair, Dad." Her face took on a deeper hue. "It is what I ... you know what?" She gave a tight sigh. "We're not going to talk about it now."

For the next half-dozen tacks, the loudest sounds in the cottage kitchen were the ticking of the clock and a low hum from the refrigerator. Saoirse was almost snatching each liberated tack from Ronan's hand.

The awkward silence ended when Darragh said, "So, where are you staying, Ronan?"

Ronan hesitated, shaped to speak, then put on his best thinking look, fading it to puzzlement and letting it melt into blankness. "I ... I don't know."

Darragh waved a hand. "Ach, it'll come back to you, lad. Give it time. Until it does, you're welcome under this roof."

Guilt twisted like a knife in Ronan's gut. If they ever found out he'd lied to them, he hoped they would understand, especially Saoirse. The thought of her censure carved a hollow in the centre of his chest. "Thank you, Mr Kelly," was all he felt safe in saying.

By the time the anaemic dawn breeched the curtains, the stone was sitting bare and unblemished in the middle of the table; Saoirse was still radiating annoyance, but Darragh appeared to have moved on. He reached for the stone. Ronan struggled not to snatch it up and clasp it in his own palm, where it belonged. Instead, his eyes followed its every revolution between Darragh's calloused fingers. "It's very heavy for its size, don't you think?" he said, brow creasing. "And it's hard as hobs ... those tacks didn't even leave the slightest scratch ... it's like a mirror. Ever thought of getting it identified, lad?"

Ronan wondered if Darragh's last words were anything more than a passing comment. His muscles twitched and his nerves jangled. While faking composure, he swore to never let it out of his sight again. But Darragh Kelly held it in his large, work-hardened hands.

24

THE INSULT

Ronan's fingers gripped the sides of his chair to control his hands. While he knew he was being paranoid and uncharitable, he craved to have the stone back in his possession; his future depended on it. Saoirse eyes were fixed on the stone as well—perhaps she, too, thought it had value. Instant self-rebuke coloured his face.

To make it worse, Darragh leant across and placed the stone into Ronan's hand. "It's yours, lad ... up to you what you do with it."

Darragh's openness and lack of guile only deepened Ronan's guilt. He sighed to himself as his fingers closed round the stone, hoping the others didn't see its colour lightening on contact. "Thanks for everything," he said, cheeks glowing from ongoing discomfort.

"Ach, wide is the door of this little cottage, lad." Darragh rose and began fussing about the kitchen.

In response to Ronan's blank look, Saoirse explained, "We may not have much, but we're happy to share." Her earlier annoyance with her father appeared to be forgotten.

"Well, I hope I can repay you one day," Ronan said boldly. "If you ever come to Australia, you'll always be welcome at Doyle Farm."

"Doyle Farm is it?" Darragh said. "That's a fine Irish name."

"Mum's family came from Ireland," Ronan said. "Somewhere called Malin Beg."

"Can you believe that?" Darragh said, to no one in particular. "Malin Beg is close by. When did they leave?"

"The 1790s, I think," Ronan replied.

With a theatrical frown, Darragh said, "No, I don't think I knew them." He winked at Ronan, the shadow of a smile crossing his face like a puff of breeze on a pond. "Still, thank you for the kind invitation, but we're not much for travelling."

A glance at the simple furnishings made Ronan wonder whether the lack of taste for travel was more to do with money than desire. Before he could contemplate further, Darragh turned from the open refrigerator and asked, "Who's for breakfast?"

The thought of food started hunger gnawing at Ronan's stomach. "Yes, please," he said eagerly.

Saoirse's eyes darted about his face. "So, when are you going back?"

"I don't know." Ronan said, the living stone warm in his hand. That he might actually, inexplicably, be in Ireland, was like a lead weight in his gut. His mother would be beside herself; he had to call her, but he'd painted himself into a corner with his fake memory loss.

Saoirse must have taken his agitation to be more after-effects of the head knock. "Are you okay?" she asked quickly.

"I'm fine, thanks," he said, mind whirring. "I know my mum will be worried sick, and I was wondering if the rest of the number might come back to me if I try to dial it myself?"

"I suppose it's possible," she said with a frown.

"Can I please use your phone, then?"

Before Ronan finished, Saoirse had it out of her pocket and extended toward him. "Sure," she said.

It had the tiniest screen and no buttons. He tried to open it one way but guessed wrong; his face warmed.

"Don't you have modern technology in Australia?" she said with a mock taunt, taking the phone, flipping it open, poising her thumbs over the buttons in demonstration.

She must think I'm hopeless. "It's just that I've never used an ol ... ah ... phone like this before."

Saoirse stiffened. Her eyes cooled; her tone sharpened. "You mean *old?*"

Ronan's ears ignited, and for once, his quick tongue tangled. "It's ... that's ... I didn't mean it like that." Attempting to recover, he channelled his mother: "It doesn't matter how old it is, as long as it works."

Darragh paused in his tomato slicing, glancing from one to the other, shaking his head with a slight smile before resuming his task.

"Well, you'd better hope it's not *too* old," she said, her words crackling. And with a lift of her chin, she snapped the phone closed, slapping it into his stunned hand. "Work it out yourself. I'm going to feed the horses." She left in a swirl of apple fragrance.

Ronan looked from the phone to Saoirse's departing back, and across to Darragh's quiet smile.

"She can be a wee bit fiery," Darragh said, "like her ma."

"I didn't mean to upset her," Ronan said.

"Ah, but upset her you did, lad. She's been saving a good while for that wee thing ... only had it a few weeks ... as proud as punch, but a bit sensitive that the best she could afford was second hand, and a couple of years old to boot."

Now Ronan understood. "Sorry, Mr Kelly."

"Ach, I should be apologising to you ... I stirred her up earlier." He sighed, shaking his head. "And enough of the 'Mr Kelly', lad, you're good as grown ... call me Darragh."

Ronan didn't know how to respond, so he remained silent.

"But, it's not me who needs your apology, lad," Darragh added. "Now, how about you go help feed the horses while I cook breakfast?" Strips of bacon began sizzling with abandon as he dropped them into the pan. "There's a coat and boots by the door will fit."

Buttressed against the early morning chill, Ronan dragged himself away from the aroma of frying bacon, lugging his hunger across the courtyard toward the stables, dreading further annoyance from Saoirse.

25

THE CALL

The sun seemed as unenthusiastic as Ronan's feet—a mere pale wash marked the eastern sky, while in the west a few hardy stars winked like failing fireflies. The length of the predawn and the shortness of the days was playing havoc with his internal timer—it felt more like four o'clock than six. A square of electric light fell onto the stable forecourt through the wide-open entrance doors. Ronan peered in. Eight horses, necks stretched in anticipation over the half-doors of their stalls, exhaled plumes of fog into the chill air, their ears pricked toward the activity in the feed room. Tentatively, he stepped inside.

Saoirse, head down, face shrouded by hair, was stabbing a large metal dipper into a bag of feed, shooting each measure into a row of buckets with a sound like rain on a tin roof. Before Ronan could speak, she launched into a string of commands. "That's the order for this side —first bucket, first stall," she said, nodding at the row of four buckets half-filled with mixture. "And mind Missy in three; she likes to nip. Check their waters and grab the hay nets ... they'll need to be refilled."

"Saoirse, I didn't—"

She continued as if he hadn't spoken. "I'll do Viking's side. We'll muck out after breakfast."

"Saoirse!"

She stopped, still not lifting her head.

"Saoirse," Ronan repeated, even though he now had her attention. "I didn't mean anything by what I said before. It was just stupid stuff to cover up my confusion and buy time." Saoirse hadn't moved. "I'm sorry." He weighed the phone in his hand, studying its retro design. "There are things that don't make any sense."

Face still set, Saoirse turned, looking up through a veil of hair. "Do you always babble like this?"

Ronan's hope for forgiveness, still only a glimmer, was brighter. "Not usually," he admitted, handing her the phone. "But I've never been this, ah ... frightened." He'd been on the verge of saying 'terrified', but pride changed his mind. However, he needed to confide in someone, and there was no one else. Even if there was, he would rather confide in Saoirse. "Can I talk to you about something?"

"After we've fed the horses." Terse words, but not snapped. Grabbing two buckets in each hand, she led him into the central aisle. Expectant nickers greeted the appearance of the buckets.

Ronan didn't get a chance to talk to Saoirse before breakfast, not that he minded—his grumbling stomach was questioning whether his throat had been severed, so he needed no second bidding to tuck into a generous helping of fried bacon, eggs and tomatoes, topped off with soda bread, and washed down with hot, sweet tea.

On his way to the stables earlier, Ronan had zipped the stone in the pocket of his pants. The whole time they were feeding, a deep, strange warmth soaked into his leg. And now, instead of it sagging in the bottom of his pocket as he sat at the breakfast table, the stone was stuck to the side of his thigh, as if glued.

The meal started well. Darragh appeared satisfied his daughter and their clumsy guest were back on speaking terms, but his mood changed when Saoirse asked if she could take another day off school to exercise the horses; she hadn't got it done the previous day because of Ronan's unexpected appearance and poor physical state. Besides, their guest shouldn't be left alone so soon after a bad head knock, in case he had a delayed reaction.

"You know how I feel about your schooling, lass," he said. "It's the foundation of—"

"My environmental science degree," she said with a cheeky grin.

Darragh shot her a look, the corners of his lips twitching. "—your future."

Saoirse sobered. "Yes, Dad, I know"—she paused as though refining her appeal—"but it's the October holiday next week and I've finished all my exams." She dialled the lustre of her large, pleading eyes up to ten. Ronan sensed Darragh didn't stand a chance. "One more day, Dad. Please?"

With a resigned sigh, he said, "Okay, then. But that's the end of it, hear?"

"Thanks, Dad." She blew him a kiss. "You're the best."

Darragh tried to scowl, but the corner of his mouth twitched again. "The best one you'll ever have."

Ronan kept his eyes on his plate, smothering a rising smile with a forkful of bacon and toast. Darragh was putty in Saoirse's hands.

"Any luck with that number, lad?"

The question caught Ronan unprepared. "What? ... Oh ... sorry ... no, not yet."

Straight after the meal, Darragh donned his big coat and Deetees, and set off for another day of making the finest boots in all of Ireland.

Fearing he might reopen the wound he'd inflicted on her earlier, but seeing no alternative to ease the worry his mother must be going through, Ronan asked to borrow Saoirse's phone again. She handed it across with a neutral expression, leaving him thinking he still had some way to go before his careless remarks were forgiven, or forgotten.

As he thumbed in the number for Doyle Farm, he walked outside for privacy. The connection clicked through; his heart lifted, only to be dashed by a computerised voice telling him the number was not connected. With a tightening in his gut, he punched in Queensland's area code before the main number. This time he got a human voice, but not the one he expected.

"Hello," said a broad Australian accent, "this is The Faulty Rudder. I'm Julie. How can I help?"

Ronan's heart almost missed a beat—must have been a mis-dial—at least it was an Australian number. Unable to disguise his excitement, he said, "G'day Julie. I, ah ... I was just wondering, whereabouts is The Faulty Rudder?"

Julie sounded as pleased as he was by an Australian accent. "Hey, g'day mate, great to hear an Aussie." Before Ronan could puzzle over that, she continued, "We're on Fintra Road, right in the middle of Killybegs. You can't miss us."

Ronan went numb, like he'd been punched in the gut. Killybegs was where the Egan lout was going before he smacked his entitled nose into Ronan's forehead.

"Hello? Hello? Mate, are you there?"

Ronan took a deep breath. "Sorry. Yeah, I'm here. Hey, you might be able to help me. I'm having trouble ringing home in Oz."

"Yeah, no worries, mate," said Julie. "Make sure you put in the area code. Whereabouts you trying to ring?"

"Killarney, in Queensland."

"Fair dinkum? I'm from Longreach."

Ronan thought Longreach was way out west somewhere, but didn't ask. He didn't want to get into a long conversation, he simply wanted to talk to his mother. "So, just the area code?" he asked, knowing how clueless he sounded.

"Zero, zero, six, one, then the area code." Someone in the background called for another beer. "Sorry, got to go, mate ... good luck." The connection cut.

Thumbs trembling, Ronan entered the digits, holding his breath as it started to ring. Eventually, through the distorting echo of connections spanning half the globe, a familiar voice said, "Hello?"

"Mum," Ronan blurted, unable to contain himself.

"Owen?"

Ronan almost dropped the phone. Astonishment left a trail of goose bumps across his skin—Owen was his mother's brother. He had to lean against the wall of the cottage for support as his legs wobbled, threatening to fold. The familiarity of the woman's voice instantly changed from his mother to his grandmother. *How is this possible?* Ronan thought.

"Who is this?" The voice was now, unmistakably, Grandma Doyle, polite but insistent, so like his mother.

Ronan's head was a tornado of confusion and disbelief.

"Hello? Are you there?" said his grandmother's voice.

Ronan's mouth felt full of dust. "Yes," he croaked.

"Who is this, and how can I help?" While annoyance edged the woman's words, they remained unfailingly polite.

"It's, ah, Darragh Kelly," Ronan lied—it was the best he could come up with on the spur of the moment. "And I'm looking for Maureen Doyle."

"This is her mother, Moira ... I'm afraid Maureen is overseas."

The last semblance of internal support disappeared from Ronan's legs; he slid slowly down the rough wall, feeling none of the lumps and bumps scraping the length of his spine. The phone rolled from his slack fingers, the metallic voice of his dead grandmother spilling into the crisp Irish air. "Hello? Hello? Mr Kelly? Are you there? ..." The line went dead.

26

THE REALISATION

When Saoirse joined him, Ronan was slumped on the hard ground beside the mudroom door, staring across the patchwork green of the valley, unseeing. Her eyes clouded as they settled on the goose egg above his ear, before flicking to the vacant stare and chalky face, and on to the open phone beside a slack hand. "Are you okay, Ronan?" She dropped to her knees, gripping his shoulder. "Ronan? Ronan? Can you hear me?" Each word emphasised with a gentle shake of increasing urgency.

Ronan didn't respond; Saoirse probed for a pulse on his neck. Soft fingers on his skin jolted him from the trance. He focused on the eyes ... so close ... golden ... he smelt apples.

"I'm calling the doctor," she said, reaching for the phone, flicking it open.

Ronan's hand closed over hers, forcing the flip top down. "No, please," he said. "I need to tell you something first." As his eyes dropped to her hand beneath his, he released it as if it might scorch him.

Saoirse held his gaze for a moment before slipping the phone into her pocket, propping against the wall beside him and turning her face to the morning sun.

Before either could speak, an electronic burring sounded from her pocket. With a flick of her thumb, the phone was open and at her ear. "Hello?"

"Hello, this is Moira Doyle." Ronan heard his grandmother's voice. "I was talking to a Darragh Kelly on this number a few moments ago and the poor boy sounded unwell ... I just thought I would call back to see if he was alright."

"That's very kind of you, Moira Doyle"—the sun in Saoirse's voice disappeared behind a cloud—"but I can assure you, Darragh is just fine. Thank you so much for checking. Goodbye."

Saoirse immediately did three things in slow motion—closed the phone, stood, and turned a cool eye on Ronan. Her shining hair framed an expression not unlike his mother's when he'd transgressed. "Darragh Kelly are we now?" As she stepped away from him, her hands moved to her hips. "And who was that? You said you were calling your mother. Was it another wrong number? Is your name even Ronan Ryan?" Her breaths came short and fast. "I'm beginning to think you're up to no good, whoever you are."

Each word was a knife-thrust to Ronan's innards. Saoirse stood in front of the sun, hair haloed with gold; he stared at her, shaking his head in denial at the accusation in her eyes. The weight of her suspicion was unbearable. After a tight swallow, he found his voice. "I *am* Ronan Ryan ... that *was* the right number, and"—he searched, but couldn't find the right words—"I'm bloody terrified." That simple admission burst the dam of his surging emotions. Choking back a sob, he laid his head against the wall, closing his eyelids against the embarrassing moisture.

For a while, Saoirse said nothing as she studied his face. Easing closer, she crouched, placing a tentative hand on his shoulder. "Then tell me what's going on, Ronan," she said, tone softening.

He took a deep breath. "That wasn't my mother, it was my grandmother," he said, no longer concerned about dampness in his eyes—it was the least of his worries.

"But why did you say you were Darragh Kelly?" she said, somewhere between admonishment and curiosity.

Anguish etched Ronan's face. "I panicked ..."—a long breath

morphed into something between a shiver and a sigh—"... she died years ago."

Saoirse gaped. At last, she said, "But how's that possible?"

"Only if this is all a dream," Ronan replied, without conviction.

"Well," she said, "I'm not a dream, and neither is Dad, or any of this." She waved her hand vaguely at their surrounds.

"Part of me was hoping you were," he said, his face a field of bewilderment, "because it's the only thing that half makes sense."

"Is this what you wanted to talk to me about?"

Ronan nodded glumly.

Unbidden, his back stiffened. "What year is this?" he asked, a flash of urgency in his voice.

Saoirse hesitated, eyes darting round his face. "2004," she said, as though she might be stepping into quicksand, or unleashing a lunatic.

Ronan couldn't hide his disbelief. Whipping the phone from her pocket, she held it out. "See?"

Fri 22nd Oct stretched like a prison sentence across the bottom of the tiny screen. "Shit," he groaned.

"What is it?" she asked quickly.

"That's the year before I was born!" He shook his head again, although much slower. "Bloody hell," he breathed.

Saoirse squinted at him.

"You think I'm crazy, don't you?" he said with a sigh, thinking she may be right.

She responded with silence, her amber orbs drilling into his core.

"I'm not," he insisted. "I'm just confused"—he gazed into the distance—"and frightened." As much as he tried to order his thoughts, the notebook, the stone, Ireland and 2004 wouldn't fit anywhere. Like additional letters in the alphabet, they were out of place wherever they were put.

As Saoirse's gaze probed his face, a tiny shudder ran through her. "This is spooky."

"You think?" he said, sucking in dollops of the early morning sunshine, trying to calm his jangling heart. As the worst of the shock wore off, 2004 snagged a memory. "That was ... ah ... this is the year my dad died."

"I'm sorry." Saoirse touched his arm as she spoke.

Ronan shrugged. "Like I said, it was before I was born."

"What happened?" Saoirse asked gently.

"They were recovering Viking artefacts from a cliff cave and he fell."

"Oh."

Ronan shrugged again.

"There's lots of Viking history in Ireland," Saoirse said.

"I know," Ronan responded. "Have you ever heard of a place called Sliabh Liag?"

Saoirse spluttered. "You're kidding, right?"

"What? ... Why?"

"Sliabh Liag is only a couple of kilometres"—she hooked her head toward the thick stand of trees at the other end of the cottage—"that way."

Ronan peered at her, feeling a stir of excitement. "They could be round here now," he said. A confusion of thrill and dread danced through his body. Maybe he could meet his father! Or—the excitement shrivelled—perhaps he was already dead.

Saoirse's lilting voice cut through his thoughts. "When was his accident?" She eased to the ground, leaning against the wall beside him.

Ronan sighed. "Mum only told me the details the other day, and I didn't think to ask her the date."

She pursed her lips. Even without speaking, she made him feel inadequate. "Not that it really matters," she responded, "... you can't change the past.

"Mum and Grandpa would never talk about it," he said, trying to justify his ignorance. "I think they decided I didn't need to know ... or they didn't want to relive it." Ronan contemplated for a moment, then frowned. "Actually, it's a wonder Masters didn't tell me just to upset me." Too late, Ronan realised his mistake—he hadn't told Saoirse about Masters' abuse.

"Why would he do that?" she said.

"He likes to hurt me." He left it at that.

"Oh," Saoirse said, then her eyes widened. "The bruises?"

Ronan nodded.

"Oh," she repeated.

They sat in silence. Ronan pushed all thought of Masters from his mind and dwelt on the possible proximity of his parents. Saoirse's thoughts clearly returned to the dig: "Did they find anything interesting?"

Starting with the arrival of David Dalziel, Ronan told her everything, from taking the notebook and stone, to the call to his dead grandmother. With the retelling came his own grudging acceptance that, bewilderingly, he was lost. Even though he now had no doubt he was in 2004 Ireland, he had no idea how to get home to 2021 Australia. While not remotely believable, the only explanation he could find was that he was stuck in some sort of time warp. Regardless, it was utterly linked to the magnetic stone nestled warm against his thigh—one moment he'd been running for his life from Masters' drunken marksmanship, the next, he was on the other side of the world, seventeen years beforehand. The only common thread was the stone.

"What?" Saoirse asked, as alarm flashed across his face.

"Mum will be worried sick. Everyone will be searching for me, and I'll have just ... disappeared."

"I can't imagine how you feel," Saoirse said calmly, "but just think about it for a moment ... there is absolutely nothing you can do ... nothing."

Thankful that she seemed to have forgiven him, and relieved to have finally shared his bizarre tale, Ronan leant his head against the cold stone, closed his eyes, and let out an enormous sigh. Saoirse placed a reassuring hand on his. "It'll be okay, Ronan," she said. "We'll work this out and get you back to your family."

Ronan's breath caught in his throat. He was afraid to move lest he sever the tingling touch. It was as warm as the stone and, like the stone, gave him a much-needed sense of connection, belonging.

The spell shattered. A shiny, gold Range Rover, engine roaring, sped into the yard, skidding to a halt amid crunching gravel. Behind the wheel, a broad strip of white plaster hiding most of his blue and purple nose, sat a leering Fionn Egan.

27

THE FRACAS

"Well, this is a cosy scene, lads?" Fionn Egan turned to two large, smug youths in the car beside him. All three grinned like hungry wolves.

Ronan's pulse quickened. Saoirse stiffened, her fingers tightening on his. "What do you want, Fionn?"

"Well now, me darlin'"—he smirked, elbow crooked out the open window—"we've just come to invite your Aussie friend here for a little drive, to give him a genuine Irish welcome."

Ronan squeezed Saoirse's hand and climbed to his feet, pulling her up with him. Adrenaline started fizzing round his body, readying it for flight. The stables were too far away, the cottage door closer, but there were three of them—bully boys hiding behind collective bravado.

Egan mistook Ronan's move as acceptance of the invitation. "That's the style, Aussie. Jump in the back."

"Thanks for the offer, mate," Ronan said, "but I reckon I'll give it a miss." While his words were offhand, his gut fluttered with indecision —run or stay?

Egan turned to his friends, pointing to his nose. "Ooh, I'm his mate now." They guffawed at his killer humour. He swung back to Ronan, face hardening. "It wasn't an invitation, *mate*," Egan said, almost fracturing the last word.

"Leave us alone, Fionn," Saoirse said disdainfully, fiddling with her phone; Ronan hoped she was calling for help—three against one was dangerously lopsided. Ronan reckoned he could outrun them, but he didn't know how fast Saoirse was, and he wasn't about to desert her.

"Leave us alone, Fionn," Egan parroted; his friends thought him hilarious.

"I think you should leave," Ronan said firmly, moving in front of Saoirse.

Egan bristled. "We'll leave when we're good and ready," he barked. "Now get in the damned car!"

Keeping his tone expressionless, Ronan said, "I'm not going anywhere with you, mate."

"I'm not your damned mate, and you *are* coming with us, like it or not," Egan snarled. He hooked his head at his two companions.

Once they uncoiled from the opposite side of the vehicle, they proved to be at least half-a-head taller than Ronan, and broader in the shoulders. "Go inside," Ronan said to Saoirse from the corner of his mouth.

"No."

"Then stay against the wall ... please." Ronan moved clear of the building, giving himself space. If they called his bluff, he might soon find out if, as he'd been taught, karate stood on the side of justice. He settled in front of the advancing youths, weight balanced, arms loose, ready to move in any direction.

"No need for this to go any further, fellas," he said.

The duo reeked anticipation and confidence; Ronan suddenly wished he'd paid more attention to his karate teacher.

They came at him together, arms relaxed by their sides, smirks plastered across pimply faces. As they approached, Ronan remained still, as though frozen in fear. Their smiles broadened as they reached for an arm each.

Ronan threw his hands up into a defensive guard, dropping beneath their grasping fingers as surprise billowed in their eyes. Without pause, he spun, executing an acceptable spinning back kick into the advancing knee of the larger goon who dropped in a howl of pain, clutching a displaced kneecap. At the sight of his companion's fate, the other hesitated for a split second. Ronan didn't ... he whirled again, driving the stiffened edge of his hand into exposed ribs. The knife-hand strike stopped the second oaf in his tracks; his legs buckled and he collapsed in a moaning heap, gasping for air.

Still in a fighting crouch and with his two larger opponents writhing on the ground, Ronan scanned for further threats, blood running hot. Egan hadn't moved—he was transfixed, jaw slack, clutching the steering wheel. Saoirse, hands shaking and face pale, was tracking the action with her phone's camera. Ronan was ready for Egan if he stepped out of that fancy car, but the door remained protectively closed.

Ronan rose, easing from the auto pilot mode he'd been operating in. It was the first time he'd put his training into practice to defend himself in the real world, and surging confidence chased the adrenaline through his veins. Right now, he had an overwhelming desire to give Egan a taste of his own medicine. Fists clenched, he started toward the car, but the cautioning words of his karate teacher—'never let anger drive your actions'—punctured his burgeoning rage. "Satisfied?" Ronan hurled the question like a hand grenade: Egan recoiled with a startled yelp, fired up the engine and took off in a blur of spinning wheels, peppering his accomplices with flying gravel. Ronan's contemptuous glare pursued the Range Rover down the drive.

Saoirse was still filming, her lens following the departing vehicle before returning to the two thugs groaning in its wake. Puzzled by her diligence in capturing every aspect of the clash, Ronan said, "Are you okay?" Despite her grim nod, he remained baffled. "Why are you filming everything?"

"Fionn is an entitled prat," she said, vehemently. "He's a bully and a coward and a very convincing liar and, if I know him, he'll claim you attacked them."

"Well, keep it up then," he said, moving across to the pair on the ground. They were now sitting, one clutching his right knee, the other his ribs; both threw sullen scowls at Ronan. "You blokes need an ambulance?" he asked.

"Sod off," grimaced Ribs.

"Who *are* you?" moaned Knee.

"Someone who minds his own business, mate," Ronan said in a low tone. "Now, can we call someone for you? ... I don't think your friend's coming back for you."

"He's not our friend," spat Ribs. "He paid us to put you in the car and rough you up a bit."

"I hope it was worth it," said Ronan.

"Sod off," growled Ribs again.

Ronan turned to Saoirse, saying, "I think we should call the police ... ah ... guards." The mention of the Gardai brought the pair of thugs awkwardly to their feet amid howls of pain. With departing glares, they floundered their way out of sight down the driveway, trailing curses.

"Are you hurt?" Saoirse asked as they disappeared.

"No, I'm fine, thanks," Ronan said, warmed by her concern. "They never connected." Her look of relief made him toasty.

"That was savage," she enthused.

Ronan stared. "I didn't have any choice."

After a micro-pause, Saoirse laughed—a tiny cascade of sparkling purity, so similar to his mother's. "No, silly, savage means brilliant."

"Oh." Ronan shuffled his feet, stole a glance at her; his cheeks warmed into the growing silence.

Although clearly enjoying his discomfort, Saoirse didn't make him suffer long. "How do you know all that kung-fu-ey fighty stuff?" she asked.

Ronan was relieved to move on and allow his face time to cool. "It's karate ... I've been taking lessons for years ... started out trying to impress my stepfather ... waste of time." He gave a wry grin. "But I really enjoyed it so I've just kept it up."

"And you're obviously very good at it."

Ronan's cheeks rekindled. "I'm not sure my teacher would agree ... it was pretty sloppy." His mind was wandering in circles around her.

"Do you want to go for a ride?" she asked.

That whiplashing train of thought caught him unawares again, but he recovered quickly. "Sure," he replied. "How about Sliabh Liag?"

"After we muck out the stalls."

Ronan rolled his eyes, letting out an exaggerated sigh. "Of course." But with a sense of satisfaction, he followed her swaying hair toward the stables.

28

THE RIDE

Before long, they were trotting their horses away from the cottage. A small but dense stand of trees extended from the end of the cottage to where the driveway curved from sight. Rounding the corner, they entered a narrow lane. On the left, the trees gave way to a tall, well-trimmed hedge crowding the gravelled surface, on the opposite side, an ancient stone fence pressed close.

Even from the back of his horse, a leggy gelding named Duke, Ronan couldn't see over the greenery. However, as they passed an opening, he saw an indulgent expanse of manicured lawn, a green moat surrounding a sprawling, three-storey mansion. The gravel ended at a strip of asphalt that flowed through the gap, looping into a circular drive in front of the grand house. The way the paved strip dominated the lane announced that the gravelled section to the cottage was unimportant.

"Wow!" said Ronan, "who lives here?"

"Egans." Clearly, Saoirse would much rather be talking about something else.

"Finnegan?"

"Yes"—her eyes sparkled with laughter—"and stop calling him that or you'll have me saying it."

Ronan shrugged. "How do you put up with him as your neighbour?" He slowed his mount to better study the enormous house.

"He's more than a neighbour."

"What do you mean?" Ronan asked quickly. Saoirse hesitated. "Come on, spill it," he added.

"His parents are big landowners ... unfortunately."

"Why's that unfortunate?"

"Can't you guess?" she snapped.

Ronan reined his horse into the shoulder of hers, forcing it to stop. "Why are you cranky with me?"

Saoirse dropped her gaze. "Sorry." Reaching forward to pull a piece of straw from Viking's mane, she said, "Raven's Roost is their farm."

"Oh." There was nothing else to say.

"They own it all—the farm, the cottage, the stables and all the horses, except Viking." She rubbed her horse's neck affectionately.

"So, you rent from the Egans?"

The golden-brown head nodded. "Dad works for them at the Deetee factory; I look after their horses and they charge us rent." Her voice took on a bitter edge that Ronan couldn't fathom.

"So, what's the problem?" he asked cautiously.

Saoirse was silent for so long, Ronan thought she wouldn't answer. "The problem is," she said at last, "there's no fairness to the Egans. They're all take and no give. Dad's been their head bootmaker for almost ten years and they've never once given him a pay rise." She gave a harsh laugh; her tone lifted a pitch. "'We'll have to wait to see what the next quarter's sales look like' or, 'now is not the best time for extra costs'. Meanwhile, our rent goes up every year, while they keep buying new cars and half the real estate in south Donegal." Saoirse regarded him with large, moist eyes. "And all I can afford is an old secondhand phone." Her voice dwindled and she looked away.

Ronan was at a loss for what to say, or do. He didn't understand why the phone was such a big deal—his school laptop was secondhand, although he got a new phone earlier in the year. Leaning across, he grabbed her arm, grinned, and repeated his mother's words, "It doesn't matter if it's old, as long as it works."

Saoirse sniffed, dabbing a cuff at her eyes, attempting a smile. "It seemed to matter earlier."

"I was amazed it still worked," he said in exaggerated banter. "But that was before I found out it was only two years old, not twenty." Ronan released her arm with a quick squeeze and urged Duke into motion. "Come on. Let's change the subject."

As the Egan mansion receded, Ronan made out vehicles on a road ahead. They rode past a shallow recess in the stone fence where a gate gave access, when needed, to the field beyond. On the opposite side of the lane, the thick greenery of the hedge had succumbed to sterile posts and wire, so close that riding side-by-side on the asphalt seemed a tight squeeze. After a few minutes of brisk clip-clopping, the claustrophobia of the quiet laneway yielded to the busy hum of a major thoroughfare.

"This is the Sliabh Liag road," Saoirse said, reining in Viking.

The thoroughfare, not much wider than the lane, was sandwiched between a fence and a ditch. A steady stream of cars, a sprinkling of leisurely campervans, and an occasional bulging mini-bus rumbled by. Most were heading up the incline, toward the rising mountain; a few were coming down, their occupants having viewed the views and hiked the hikes. When opposing vehicles met, they executed well-mannered sidling manoeuvres past each other, like strangers on a gangplank.

As keen as he was to see Sliabh Liag, Ronan wasn't comfortable mixing horses with cars on such a narrow road. While horseback was second nature to him, he'd only ever mingled with the predictable cattle of Doyle Farm. Viking appeared not the least perturbed by the steel monsters rumbling past his muzzle—his ears toggled lazily as he waited for his next instruction. Duke, on the other hand, became more agitated the closer they got to the road. Now up on his toes, he was snorting in fear as each vehicle passed. Ronan rubbed his neck and made soothing sounds.

"What's with this horse and cars?" Ronan asked, continuing to stroke the neck already streaming with nervous sweat.

Saoirse grimaced. "He used to be Fionn's. As a three-year-old, he showed heaps of promise over the jumps ... just low ones but ... Fionn, being Fionn, decided to show off to a bunch of visitors ... put Duke at the water jump ... poor thing baulked at the last second and speared

Fionn straight into the mud. It really was quite funny to watch, and everyone laughed once they knew Fionn was okay"—she smiled at the memory before growing serious—"but he was fuming. When the visitors left, he turned Duke into the big sand yard, took the old farm Land Rover in and hounded him up and down until the poor thing was a quivering mess."

"What a mongrel!" Ronan seethed.

"Poor Duke," Saoirse said, reaching over to give his face a reassuring rub, but he was throwing his head about in increasing agitation. Pointing to a gate on the opposite side of the road, she said, "Listen, I'll go over and open the gate, and when there's a break in the traffic, you come across and ride well into the field ... he'll soon calm down ... I'll lock the gate and catch up with you."

Ronan nodded. "Is that the Egans' field as well?"

Saoirse shook her head. "But I know all the farmers round here, and they're happy for me to ride through if I keep their gates closed, respect their livestock and let them know if anything is amiss."

"Sounds fair," Ronan mused.

They executed their plan without incident, and while Ronan waited in the middle of the field for Saoirse, he felt the tension slowly seep from Duke's steaming body.

With the murmur of traffic fading, they worked their way through several fields deep in lush grass, some with a sprinkling of shaggy, black-faced sheep, others with a handful of toffee-coloured cattle. Saoirse kept up a running commentary on the farmers, their livestock, the grasses and wild animals, pointing out the scratchings of hedgehogs and the gouges of badgers. Ronan was drawn to her genuine interest in the subjects; they were at the heart of people's connection to the countryside.

As the fertile soils of the flatter country yielded to rock-littered foothills, the fences became fewer and, here and there, bleached boulders began mushrooming from the earth. Saoirse led them past a conifer-choked gully before angling up along a jagged ridge, allowing Viking to pick his way between the boulders and scatterings of loose rock. Their trail lifted them through bracken and heather to an open vantage point, high on the southern flank of Sliabh Liag. It was mid-morning by the time they topped the crest, and the horses were sweating freely, blowing from dilated nostrils. Saoirse halted Viking and pushed back in the saddle, face radiant.

"Some view," Ronan breathed, eyes drinking in the panorama.

Off to the southwest, a ribbon of parked cars extended up the edge of the narrow road before ending in a tangle at what Saoirse called the top car park. From there, a sinuous line of hikers snaked upward past their vantage point. Exertion thinned the line as it progressed, and by the time the path twisted its way below where the riders sat, only a scattering of the hardiest individuals remained. These were headed resolutely to the final razor-backed traverse to the summit rising off to the north, their fitful chatter drifting on the breeze.

Beyond the hiking path, the ground disappeared. Down to the right, the relentless ocean had eaten into the side of the mountain; heaving waves, spawned far to the west, crashed against the base of a precipice. Sheets of foam launched up the cliff face with each surge, only to stream from the black rock to be gathered in by the next assault. From there, the deep blue Atlantic stretched beyond the western horizon, to far-off Canada. Overhead, a few wispy clouds provided contrast to a much lighter expanse of blue.

"We're lucky it's a nice day," Saoirse said. "It's a beast when there's a storm."

"I bet," Ronan said, giving Duke's neck a rub of appreciation for the climb. Framed in the valley behind them were the rooftops of a village scattered along the shore of a long, narrow harbour. "Is that Raven's Roost?" he asked, aiming his finger at what he imagined was the green-moated mansion—the distance was distorting.

Saoirse stood and swivelled in the stirrups. "Yep ... and that's Teelin." She nodded at the village before returning her attention to the precipice. "Look!" she cried, pointing to the rock face. "Movement!"

"Where?" Ronan's excitement bubbled, his mind instantly abuzz with cliffs and caves and notebooks.

Saoirse's finger drilled at the lower of two cliffs. It was as if a giant spade had been driven down the side of Sliabh Liag, slicing away an enormous chunk, forming a bay and leaving a monstrous vertical gouge, exposing the innards of the mountain to the unrelenting ocean.

Either side of the scar, the mountainside sloped less precipitously toward the water.

Ronan could see the cliff, and occasional gulls floating on air currents, but nothing else.

"There!" Saoirse's finger stabbed again.

"I can't see anythi—wait. Yes! I saw a glint of something." Certainty gripped Ronan—it could only be his parents down there, edging along the ledge to their dig in the cave, precisely as his mother had told him. If he could only warn his father, then in the future, there would be no Bruno Masters and all he entailed. The germinating idea consumed Ronan. Without hesitation, he said, "I'm going for a closer look."

"Ronan, no! We can't take the horses any further."

"I have to go, Saoirse." He sprang from the saddle, handing her the reins. "You go home; I'll find my way back."

She snatched them from his hand. "If you think I'm leaving you up here, Ronan Ryan, you *are* crazy."

A warm glow radiated through Ronan's chest; their eyes locked and held for a moment before he nodded and started picking his way down through the boulders to the path that he hoped would lead round to the cliff.

"Wait," Saoirse called after him, "you don't even know how to get down there."

Ronan paused and turned. "I'll work it out," he said with a confidence he had no right to entertain. With a half-smile, he jogged off toward the top of the wall of rock rising sheer from the churning ocean.

29

THE FALL

When he crested the first rise in the hiking path, Ronan looked back. Saoirse had dismounted and was sitting on the grass, reins in hand, hugging her knees, watching his every move. He waved and dropped from sight. As he jogged, he pushed thoughts of Saoirse aside, concentrating on finding the track down to the dig site, and wondering if he was totally crazy. Nuts or not, he had no choice but to try to save his father. What else could he possibly do?

Now that he was getting closer, the cliff had disappeared from view, hidden by the brow of the mountain. Ronan visualised the layout and reckoned the way down to the cave was close—it had to descend where the mountainside was steep, but before it became precipitous. The access track *must* be nearby.

With every passing minute, Ronan's anxiety lifted until his head was a cauldron of doubt. Uncertainty slowed him—there had to be other reasons for people to be on that cliff. The thought that he was merely shaping everything to fit his own narrative had crossed his mind, but the warmth in his pocket seemed to dispel his doubts; he picked up his pace.

Around the next bend, a bold triangular sign edged in warning-red, announcing that there was 'Conservation work in progress ... Dangerous drops! ... No Entry!' And skirting the sign was a faint, but fresh, trail of crushed grass angling downward from the hiking path. Right spot, heading in the right direction, it had to be the track to the cliff.

Ronan disobeyed the sign. While the trail before him was unknown, it held no fear, as though his feet knew where they were going.

The track plummeted, and Ronan was thankful for the robust grip on the soles of the Deetees. The mountainside became steeper with every step until, on rounding a corner, he found himself at the cliff proper. And strung between steel pins hammered into the rock face was the safety rope, exactly as his mother had described.

Without hesitation, Ronan started along the narrow ledge. Right hand skimming the rope, he strode across the damp rocks, trusting the Deetees and his inherited balance. The stone in his pocket still clung to the outside of his thigh, and the further he went, the warmer it got, as though it could sense its location. He blanked it from his mind; his parents were close—there were voices ahead.

———

A YOUNG BRUNO MASTERS sat at the cave entrance, his back propped against the wall, three backpacks beside him. Paidin strode into the light, the smooth pebble warming his palm. Dropping his notebook on top of his pack, he stepped out into the crisp breeze, standing nonchalantly above Sliabh Liag's sheer drop, hefting the find, feeling its warmth, pondering its mystery. Plenty of time to tell Bruno about the magnetism later; for now, he was enjoying the sunshine and fresh air after the stale mustiness of the cave.

Bruno picked up Paidin's notebook. The pages whispered across each other as he leafed through the cryptic contents.

"Any insights?" Paidin said without turning.

Bruno, befuddled by the diagrams, drawings and coded notes, couldn't keep the undercurrent of resentment from his voice. "It's all so easy for you, isn't it?"

"What do you mean?" Paidin turned at his friend's tone.

"This," Bruno hissed, brandishing the notebook. "And cricket ... and ..."

With a slow head-shake, Paidin said, "Don't be ridiculous, Bruno."

"I'm not being ridiculous," Bruno snapped, his face reddening. "You walk along that ledge like it's the middle of the damned street ... you read runes like they're road signs ... you're standing there now, right on the edge of the cliff, as if you're waiting for a bloody bus."

Paidin stood stock still. "I didn't know any of that bothered you."

"Well, it does," Bruno shot back, anguish twisting his face. "And I'm sick of pretending it doesn't, and sick of you two rubbing my nose in it every day."

"Rubbing your nose in what?" Paidin's voice remained even, but irritation showed in his eyes. "What the hell are you talking about?"

"You stole her from me," Bruno lamented, almost sobbing.

Paidin frowned, studying his friend. "I didn't know you were keen on Maise," he said, leaning across, dropping a reassuring hand to Bruno's shoulder. "We didn't know, mate ... never meant to hurt you."

Bruno was in no mood for consolation. He tried to shrug the hand off, and when it didn't budge, he flung it away with all his pent-up resentment and frustration.

Paidin stiffened as his foot slipped on the slick surface, and he teetered, back arched, arms spinning. In front of him, the beckoning cave where his Aussie Maise was measuring and photographing; behind him, a several-hundred-metre drop to a boiling ocean; beside him, his friend looking up in horror ... out of reach. His frantic eyes cast about for something to grab, but there was only the warmth in his hand. He clenched it tighter; it was no help. A long, drawn-out 'Maise!' followed him into the abyss.

Bruno's face turned to chalk, eyes widening with horror, body freezing in disbelief. "Paidin," he whimpered. Open mouthed, he stared at the spot where, moments earlier, his friend had stood. With a death-grip on the first span of the safety rope, he leaned out over the void. Far below, turbulent North Atlantic waves smashed onto the foundations of the mountain; in between, nothing but grey rock, swirling air currents and floating gulls. It was as if Paidin had never been there.

Bruno groaned, face contorted. Pulling himself back against the cliff, he gazed about in panic, and froze—not more than forty metres away, a sandy-haired lad stood easy on the ledge, one hand light on the rope. Bruno stared at him long and hard, as though searching for a connection in his memory. The stranger glared at Bruno, eyes brimming with loathing, contempt and accusation.

"Murderer," the lad whispered as he retreated, but it carried, dripping with condemnation and hatred, across the increasing gap between them.

"No," Bruno mouthed, shaking his head. He started toward the stranger but halted at Maureen's call.

"Paidin?"

Bruno gave the youth a final, pleading look before turning back into the cave. He met Maureen as she rounded the last bend.

"Bruno, where's Paidin? I thought I heard him yell."

She froze at Bruno's expression.

"Bruno," she pleaded.

He shook his head. "I'm sorry, Maise ..." The words clogged in Bruno's throat.

The blood left her face. Shaking her head, she tried to push past him. He threw his arms wide to block her at each turn. "No ... no ... no!" It started in a whisper of denial and rose into a scream from the depths of her soul. She beat her fists impotently against his chest, before collapsing, sobbing, into his arms.

———

RONAN WAS CRUSHED. If only he'd run faster! If only he hadn't hesitated before leaving Saoirse with the horses. A scream fought for release—he'd been so close, close enough for a glimpse of the man he never knew. Like a zoomed-in image, Ronan saw the concern as his father put a hand on Masters' shoulder, the surprise as he overbalanced, the raw terror when he realised he was gone, and that final word, the only one Ronan would ever hear his father utter, a drawn-out scream: "Maise!" Every single element of the fleeting encounter was chiselled into Ronan's memory like the runic symbols on the roof of the adjacent cave. He'd failed his father right when he'd needed him most, and all he had left was an image of flailing arms and contorted face disappearing from view.

In front of Ronan was the horrified, ashen-faced man who would become his stepfather. "Murderer," he breathed.

Masters advanced; Ronan backed away. Masters stopped as another voice carried on the breeze. He returned to the cave, and soon after, Ronan heard his mother screaming, a deep, visceral denial of the truth. He took a dozen quick steps toward her before caution stilled his feet. Whether it was a sixth sense or the instant disappearance of the warmth in his pocket, he didn't know, but if he confronted Masters, he might well follow his father off the cliff, and endanger his mother's life.

Ronan continued to hesitate, hand resting on the safety rope, wind buffeting his body. Everything was far too complicated—he couldn't get his head round how different things interacted, and what the potential consequences of any given action might be. If he did something in this time to cause harm to his mother, it might mean that he ceased to exist.

There was no time to ponder further. The priority was to get off the ledge, back to Saoirse, and off the mountain. He was an interloper in that period; he needed time and space to think.

With one last survey of the ledge, Ronan dragged his leaden feet away from his mother's distraught sobbing.

30

THE GLIMPSE

Ronan couldn't shake the overwhelming sense of guilt that he'd failed his father. Fate had delivered this strange journey into the past, and he hadn't capitalised on it. Thoughts churning like an egg-beater, he barely remembered the traverse of the cliff face, or the climb up the vague track to the 'No Entry' sign. Once back on the hiking path, he set off in a blank-stared trot, almost running into two hikers as he bounded down a section of rough, field-stone steps.

"Oi! Look out!" said one.

Ronan blundered on. No matter which way he looked at it, he should have done more, but he didn't know what. Wracked by guilt and adrift in thought, he momentarily lost his connection to the landscape. He halted, staring around. Ahead of him, a group of four adults with a gaggle of children were picking their way through a scatter of bleached rocks, the sharp-edged, shattered remains of an ancient boulder blasted apart by nature's wrath. After a moment of confusion, he thought he recalled this part of the path; Saoirse should be just beyond the next rise.

When he reached the crest, his despondency lifted—on the slope above, Saoirse sat on the grass, still hugging her knees and still gazing at where he'd disappeared almost an hour earlier. An exciting warmth tingled through him. She returned his wave enthusiastically before standing, hair billowing in the breeze as she arched her back, catlike. With a final guilty glance behind, he left the path, climbing to her side.

"Thank God you're okay," she exclaimed, catching herself as she made a quick movement toward him.

"I'm fine," he said, cheered by her greeting despite his consuming sense of failure. There was no escaping the terror on his father's face. He'd been so close ... so close. "Thanks for waiting," he murmured.

"Always." Saoirse flushed, but recovered quickly. "Dad would never forgive me if I lost a good pair of Deetees," she said, with a cheeky flash of teeth.

Ronan knew she saw his pain, and was trying to ease it. "Well, we'd better get these boots home then," he said, taking Duke's reins, brushing her soft fingers in the process, thrilling at the touch. By the spark in her eyes, she felt it too.

"Hang on," she said, ending the fleeting moment. "Aren't you going to tell me what happened down there?"

"I'll tell you as we ride," he said, swinging astride Duke. "Come on."

Side-by-side, they rode back down the valley toward Teelin and Raven's Roost. On the way, Ronan recounted his father's fall, and his guilt and confusion since.

"There's nothing you could've done," Saoirse said with certainty.

Ronan studied her. "How can you be so sure?"

"Think about it for a moment," she said, as if explaining the obvious. "If you could've saved your father, your mother would never have married Masters, Ruddi wouldn't have been born, your grandfather wouldn't have gone to live with you in Australia, and ..." She hesitated.

"And what?" he prompted.

Saoirse lowered her eyes. "We wouldn't have met." The words were soft and warm, and accompanied by a surge of air curling over the mountain, turning her hair into a swirling veil. Through it came a golden gleam as she lifted her eyes to his. It was like a saddle girth had tightened round his chest—he couldn't breathe, he could only stare into those hypnotic orbs. But they disappeared when Duke abruptly stopped, and Viking drew ahead.

They had come upon a patch of jagged rocks; the only way through was the single-file pad Viking followed. Duke fell in behind as Ronan pondered Saoirse's words—all of them—and watched her straight back swaying to the rhythm of her mount. He was amazed at her recall of names she'd only heard a few times, and how she intuitively knew what was important to him.

"I just spent an hour back there thinking about it all," she said, over her shoulder, as though reading his mind.

"Oh. Right."

When they cleared the rocks, he ranged his mount up beside her again. "I haven't told you the full story of the stone," he admitted. "I thought you'd think I was even crazier than you already do."

"That, Ronan Ryan," she said with a playful smile, "would be impossible."

"Look at this," he said, pulling the stone from his pocket and holding it out to her. He gestured. "Take it."

Saoirse tried to pick it up, but it seemed glued to his palm. "I can't." She curled her fingertips under the edge of the polished disk but still couldn't budge it. Ronan let the reins drape across Duke's neck, picking up the stone, pincer-like, between thumb and forefinger. Saoirse's eyes followed as if trying to fathom a magician's deception. "Wow! Good trick."

"It's not a trick," he said. "It just seems to stick to my skin." She searched his face for understanding. "Here, take it," he urged, holding his hand toward her.

With considerable effort, she pulled the stone from his loose grip, curling her fingers securely around it. "It's like it's magnetised to you," she said. "Are you Superman?"

"What?"

Saoirse smiled at his struggle. "Man of Steel?"

"Oh," he said, marvelling at her quick mind. "No. But I first noticed it sticking to me on the way to the stables this morning; I felt it through my pocket, clinging to my leg. But since I went down to the cliff, it's been like a limpet." Ronan gestured to the ink-black disk. "Does it feel warm?"

"No. Wait, probably a bit ... from being in your pocket."

"See its colour? Now keep watching while you place it in my hand."

Saoirse stared at the stone as she dropped it into his palm. "It got lighter," she said, lifting her gaze to his. "What's it mean?"

"I wish I knew," Ronan replied. "But I can't help thinking it's got something to do with me being here."

"Why do you think that?"

"Well, when Masters was shooting at me, I was dressed and carrying the stone and the Deetee notebook. I got this enormous punch in the back, everything went black, then I woke up in your paddock ..."

"Field."

"Huh?

"Field. It's a field." Saoirse grinned.

Ronan realised she was teasing him. "Fine, Miss Kelly," he said in mock indignation, "*field.*"

"Thank you." She clipped the words, barely moving her lips; all the while, her eyes smiled at him. "Now," she said, growing serious, "you arrived in our field with nothing but that wee pebble, which is why you think it's central to your predicament."

"Precisely," Ronan said. "But more adventure than predicament."

"Now there's a positive spin on knocking yourself out, laying waste to our house, and getting set upon by local thugs."

"Yeah, I am a bit of a disaster area at the moment," Ronan acknowledged with a rueful grin. He opened his hand. "I'm blaming the stone."

They laughed. Saoirse urged Viking forward and Ronan followed her down the ridge to the spreading farmland.

At last, the Sliabh Liag road with its payload of scurrying vehicles came into view, and with the traffic, Duke's agitation returned. In a reverse of their outward journey, Ronan hung back with Duke while Saoirse opened the gate. As Ronan approached the road, a phalanx of blue-and-yellow-checked Garda cars, lights flashing, sped past. On the rear seat of the second vehicle, red-rimmed eyes staring unseeing out the window, sat a haunted, youthful Maureen Doyle.

31

THE VANISHING

Duke recoiled at the abrupt appearance of the first Garda car. Ronan had to cling tight with his legs to stay astride—the shallow leisure saddle between his backside and the horse wasn't much more than a patch of leather, nothing at all like the deep-seated Australian stock saddles he was familiar with. For all the security it provided, it may as well not have been there.

When the second Garda car flashed past, blue lights strobing, Duke crabbed away from the blur of colour in a surge of quivering muscles. Ronan didn't notice—his leg grip was reflex, his pressure on the reins automatic—all that registered with his brain was the image of his mother, eyes red and puffy, looking forlorn and alone ... shattered.

"Ronan," Saoirse yelled, "I've called you three times. What's wrong?"

The bite of her words pierced Ronan's numbness, but he ignored her for a moment more while he soothed his agitated mount, before coaxing him toward to the gate. "That was my mother in the back of the guards' car," he said listlessly, eyes following the blue and yellow squares out of sight.

"Oh," she said. After a long pause, she added, "But what I said earlier still applies, so don't you go feeling sorry for yourself now." Saoirse's gentle tone undercut the firm words.

Ronan knew she was only trying to help, and he was grateful, but he couldn't help a good-natured retort. "No, Ma'am." He threw her a mock salute.

"Get yourself across the road," she said in her best school mistress voice.

They navigated the traffic and were soon walking their horses up the Raven's Roost laneway. "Tell me about Finnegan," Ronan said, the sight of the Egan mansion bringing the bully to mind.

"Nothing to tell," she said simply. "You saw what he's like. He's a prat ... never been any different."

"Why did he expect you to go to Killybegs with him?"

Saoirse looked down at her fingers entwining the reins. "I got a lift into town with him earlier in the year, and now he thinks I'm his girl." Her lips twisted. "It was a big mistake. He keeps asking ... telling me to go out with him ... doesn't like to take no for an answer ... says I'll have to say yes sooner or later, or Dad won't have a job ... and we won't have a home." A shudder gripped her; she glanced across at Ronan. "I think I'd rather die."

"Bastard!" Ronan breathed. The revulsion in her eyes triggering a consuming protective instinct.

As they drew level with the recessed gateway in the stone fence, the burble of an engine caught Ronan's attention. Moments later, a gold Range Rover eased from the mansion's driveway, through the gap in the hedge, and into the lane. *Speak of the devil!* Even from the distance, Ronan could make out a small rectangle of white on the driver's face ... his brain filled in Egan's sullen features. Almost immediately, the vehicle surged forward; Ronan's hairs lifted.

"Quick, get in the gateway," he shouted, but Saoirse was already there. Duke shimmied back and forth, fighting the rein.

The golden behemoth continued to gain speed, Egan's smirking face behind the wheel. If he didn't slow soon, he wouldn't be able to stop in time; nevertheless, he accelerated. Duke spun one way, then the other; Ronan fought to control him. Every fibre of the horse was straining to rocket down the lane, away from the approaching danger; his rider knew that nothing but disaster lay in that direction ... the car was still gaining speed; the gate recess was the only survival option.

Ronan finally cajoled Duke into the shallow space, turning him to face the mechanical monster. The roaring vehicle was almost upon them. Ronan tried to soothe his mount, but Duke threw his head about, eyes rolling white with terror; it was too much for him. With the recess hemming him in, the only open route was in front of the two tons of speeding steel. Duke whirled in that direction. Ronan, thighs locked in a death-grip on the saddle, went with him. Even as he turned, Duke must have realised he wouldn't make it; in mid spin, he threw out his forelegs, jinking back toward safety.

Ronan's momentum was too great, his saddle too meagre. With his body weight heading one way, and Duke suddenly heading the other, they parted company.

Ronan catapulted into the path of the barrelling vehicle. In half a heartbeat, the stone's warmth flared in his hand, Saoirse screamed his name, Egan's smirk turned to abject terror, and squealing brakes drowned the engine's roar. A tremendous thump wracked Ronan's body, and darkness claimed him.

————

THE RANGE ROVER skidded to a halt, the acrid stench of burning rubber swirling in the air. An ashen Fionn Egan stumbled from the door, vomiting into the grassy fringe of the lane. While a riderless Duke bolted toward the stables, Viking stood patiently in the gate recess, his toggling ears showing a moderate level of confusion. Saoirse was a wide-eyed, open-mouthed chalk statue, lips still trembling with Ronan's name. Her horror collapsed into a howl of disbelief and anguish.

"It was an accident," Egan cried, raising a beseeching hand toward her. Vomit speckled his chin, tears of terror streamed down his forlorn cheeks. "I only meant to frighten you," he sobbed. With enormous reluctance, his panic-stricken eyes followed Saoirse's to a spot behind his vehicle. Egan's empty stomach heaved again.

There was no splattered blood, no grotesquely broken body. But there was, lying on the still-smoking asphalt, a set of crumpled clothes and a pair of dirty Deetees.

PART III

THE HEARTHING

32

THE VÖLVA

Head-whirling, gut-churning turbulence was Ronan's entire existence. An invisible force wrenched him one way, then the other, taking him to the brink of dismemberment before building into a spin that had his lungs starving and his body at the point of launching into orbit. Without warning, it stopped.

The heavy darkness lifted a fraction. Through his brain-fog, Ronan waited for Saoirse's face to swim into focus—it didn't. The weight eased further, and with it came a fierce chill, burning his skin, as if he was on ice. Fionn Egan had run him down and he was now on a slab in an Irish morgue, zipped up in a body bag—only he wasn't dead. Bile rose in his throat. An attempted scream was little more than a groan by the time it prised past chattering teeth and seeped between parched lips.

Ronan flexed an elbow, expecting to encounter the confines of a bag —nothing; he reached out a hand, but it only found air, icy air. Either side of him was the same, while beneath him, a springy carpet prickled his skin.

The tsunami of relief that he wasn't zipped tight and locked in a freezer, was swamped by waves of furious shivering and an overwhelming conviction that he'd been driven blindfolded through a slalom course, head going one way, stomach the other, breakfast straining to burst from his mouth. He moaned.

Even as Ronan's body shuddered, juddered and churned, he was aware of a familiar and reassuring glow radiating through him from his hand. Yet there was a much stronger warmth off to his left. Expecting a bed of glowing embers, he peered in that direction—there was nothing. In search of comfort, he rolled toward the warmth, only to come up against a smooth, hard surface. But instead of matching the chill air, it was warm, comforting. Ronan snuggled close, ignoring his churning gut.

A flicker, faint enough to be imagined, caressed his eyes. Lethargically, he twisted his head. An anaemic, yellow wash pushed a hole in the darkness, ripples on a pond, spreading, growing brighter, growing ... lapping at Ronan's feet, his waist, his face.

As it approached, the light splayed shadows away from posts either side of Ronan ... posts but nothing between them; a fence without wires. He was outside, same as last time. A disembodied hand holding a crude lamp floated into view, followed by a robed arm and body, and a woman's face ... strong, kind, bracketed by a cascade of the reddest hair he'd ever seen.

"Welcome, traveller." The voice was as soothing as his mother's touch.

"Where ... where am I?" Ronan croaked, teeth chattering.

"You have come home," said the voice. "As I knew you would."

Swimming in the insipid light, the woman's face was blurred, her words nonsensical. Coming home? Ronan shook his head, willing clarity to his vision and brain. Above the face, vague shadows danced across a low wooden roof, barely clear of her head.

"Who are you?" His words were thick, sluggish.

"I am the völva, Freyja. But that is not important now. You need warmth."

A seeress? A teller of the future? Ronan shuddered as renewed spasms wracked his body. His skin was frozen; surely he wasn't naked again. Numb fingers checked. Yep. All at once, it seemed thoroughly hilarious; his attempted guffaw came out as a weak chuckle. He wanted to sleep.

Freyja, the seeress, hoisted Ronan over her shoulder like a sack of grain and bore him off through the brittle night. As if returning from gathering mushrooms, she strode nonchalantly through a pine forest dappled by moonlight falling like feathers, dried needles crunching underfoot. After an icy eternity, the trees gave way to a small patch of frosted grass; on the other side, a stout wooden door was set into a grassy bank from which a shimmering column of grey smoke oozed into the still air.

Once through the door, the abrupt decline in the chill was almost as good as a blanket. A magnificent blaze crackled in a rectangular fire pit in the middle of the floor. It threw its lively flicker round the room with great generosity, but the arms of its warmth were short. Freyja laid him on a deep fur beside the fire, drawing another over his naked body. Returning circulation set his fingers and toes burning in agony, while stinging needles tormented every sliver of skin.

Ronan prised his eyes open, asking again, "Where am I?"

"Shh. There will be time for that later"—the voice was firm—"but first, food." The woman turned her attention to a large pot hanging over the flames.

As the furs wrapped their warmth around him, the shivering ceased, the pain eased from his extremities, his eyelids became leaden, and his memory faded.

The teasing waft of food, accompanied by wet heat on his lips, slowly restarted Ronan's brain. Freyja was sitting on the floor, his head on her lap. With her every movement, red strands trailed across his cheek; they smelt of wood smoke.

She held a spoonful of meaty liquid at the ready. "You must eat, my friend." Freyja rubbed his cheek with a soft forefinger, as a mother might when trying to encourage her toddler's mouth open. "You have become extremely cold ... we must warm you inside as well." The thought of food made his stomach heave, but nothing came up.

"But—" The spoon filled his mouth, and a welcome trickle of hot broth soothed its way down his parched throat. Ronan's nausea eased at once; he felt almost human again, and wondered what was in it.

"Good," Freyja cooed, refilling the spoon.

"—I'm not cold on the inside—" As Ronan belatedly finished his sentence, another spoonful of broth drowned his words.

"Yes, the rune has much power, but never assume it is infinite ... we must help it where we can." As she leant toward the bowl, her hair dragged across his face again. *Smoke,* he thought, *not apples ... apples ... Saoirse. Saoirse! Must get to Saoirse ... make sure she's safe ... can't trust Finnegan.* Ronan tried to sit up; firm hands held him down.

"Relax, my friend. Saoirse is fine," she crooned. He relaxed, taking another mouthful of broth, and another, and another, until the bowl was empty.

With the broth came both warmth and weariness. But Ronan was burdened by the knowledge that he'd left Saoirse, just as he'd left his mother and Ruddi. And now he was lost again, he was sure of it.

The woman with the red mane had him confused. While she sounded Australian, she wasn't dressed like any Aussie he'd ever encountered; the trees he remembered seeing didn't look Australian; and this house was unlike anything he'd seen before. It resembled the upturned hull of a hefty wooden boat. There were ribs and beams and braces and planks and ... his eyelids shuttered the rest of the building. "Where am I?" he slurred.

Freyja eased his head onto the fur, placing her palm, warm and soothing, across his forehead. "You have come home, my friend ... you are safe ... now sleep." She stroked his hair the way his mother did when he had a fever. Ronan relaxed under her touch, welcoming the approaching fog and the peaceful void beyond.

33

THE VÄKTARE

A whispered discussion drifted through the vapour of Ronan's returning awareness. A man's deep voice was saying something about lost lambs. Freyja's tone sharpened when she responded. "They are not lambs, they are travellers, and it is my duty to care for them while they are here."

Ronan lay against the fireplace, soaking up its bounty. He cranked an eye open. Weak sunlight angled through a large hole in the roof, the target of a languid column of smoke, much of which failed to escape, judging by the murky haze in the rafters.

Time was a shapeless blob. The angle of the sun suggested early morning or late afternoon, but his sense of direction was rudderless, and everything about this place seemed foreign, historic, perhaps the set for a medieval movie—extremely realistic. Unlike his Teelin experience, the two voices held no accent, but the unusual phrasing sounded as though it belonged in another time.

The deep voice harrumphed. "Any man who uses seiðr is less than a man."

"If a man has a skill, he should use it to better his world," Freyja retorted.

The man snorted. "Seiðr is not manly."

"Seiðr is a gift, a gift from the gods." Freyja's sharp tone softened as she continued, "Besides, he is only a boy."

They were banging on as if he'd used magic to get to wherever the heck he was. Ronan turned his head toward the gloom at the end of the long room. He could make out Freyja's shape, her tresses now twisted into a knot in the nape of her neck. Beside her stood a solid figure topped with polished copper that tumbled, like a burnished waterfall, over his shoulders and halfway down his back. His luxuriant, neatly combed beard gleamed, a beacon in the shadows. "Close enough to a man to my mind," the man grumbled, pulling on a faded green tunic, snorting his dissent.

"Yes, I know, Sten"—there was a teasing edge to her tone as she straightened the tunic on his broad shoulders—"when you were his age you were raiding Gaelic villages."

Still in Ireland, Ronan thought, as he rolled back and closed his eyes ... so weary.

Sten's whiskered chin jutted. "Well, it is the truth," he insisted, fastening a wide leather belt about his midsection.

"Yes," said Freyja testily, "and you have never stopped regaling anyone who will turn an ear your way." Her voice saddened. "Even after your ramblings lured away two of our daughters, now lost to their mother."

"Don't be dramatic, woman," he said. "They are not lost to you, they simply moved away to fashion their own lives."

"Moved away! Your stories took them over the seas to The Land of the Gaels ... to another time." Freyja's voice rose with every word.

"What does it matter?" Sten asked, pulling his glowing mane from beneath his tunic, securing it into a ponytail with a leather thong. "They are contented ... and you can use your seiðr to commune with them."

"So easy you say that," she retorted, "but you do not have to suffer the umrót ... the older I get, the less I can withstand it."

"How can brief umrót compare to days in the longship tossing on angry seas?"

The gut-churning turmoil Ronan was suffering wasn't brief, and an imagined ocean voyage only made it worse. He expected to lose his broth at any moment; this umrót was every bit as bad as any motion-sickness caused by Granddad Doyle's driving.

Freyja pointed to Ronan. "Look at him to see the lie of your words. Yonder is a well-made lad, but as weak as a kitten from the umrót ... it is fierce on the body ... takes time to recover."

Sten snorted. "I cannot talk all day, woman, I have ships to build."

Heavy footsteps approached. Ronan pushed his eyelids up once more, determined to keep them there; he had to find out where he was. Strangely, he wasn't agitated like when he arrived in Ireland. He now understood the stone in his hand was protecting him, transporting him away from mortal danger; otherwise, he'd be dead—twice.

Drab woollen pants moved past his eyes, the lower legs bound with strips of plain cloth above scuffed leather boots.

Ronan eased himself onto an elbow.

Sten made an exaggerated sidestep at Ronan's movement. "The lamb awakens," he said. He'd split his beard down the middle, tying each side with separate thongs. And he was short—Ronan wondered if he was stunted.

"Hello," he croaked. Ronan's mouth felt similar to his brain, coated with glue.

"Hello yourself, lamb," said Sten, humour sparkling his green eyes.

Freyja knelt and handed Ronan a large, rough-made cup. "Here, friend, drink this." Her voice was a light touch on his skin, the water as sweet as honey ... refreshment and energy in a single swallow. Like the broth, he wondered what was in it.

"I'm Ronan Ryan," he said, holding up his right hand to Sten.

White teeth flashed through the red beard as Sten clamped his work-hardened hand around Ronan's forearm in a vice grip, saying, "Hello, Ronanryan, I am Sten, son of Olaf." Effortlessly, he drew Ronan to his feet, appearing slightly annoyed that he then had to crane his neck upward.

Ronan winced, returning the pressure on Sten's muscular forearm as best he could; his own was numb by the time it was released. "Hello, Sten Olafsson," Ronan heard himself say, wondering how he knew to call the man that.

"What sort of name is Ronanryan?" Sten asked. "I shall call you

Lamb." He chuckled at his own wit, scooping a drab cloak from an adjacent bench, throwing it over his shoulder and striding out the door with a wink at his wife.

Unsure how to respond, Ronan sank back to the floor beside the fire, draping the fur about his shoulders.

"Pay no heed to my husband's banter," Freyja said. "He thinks himself a man of great humour." The bench from where Sten had collected his cloak, doubled as the lid of a long wooden storage trunk; Freyja rummaged for a few moments before coming up with a faded tunic in one hand and a pair of plain woollen pants in the other. The tunic had dark stains across the front, while the pants had holes in both knees and a seat almost worn through. "Sten wore these on his very first víking to The Land of the Gaels, three winters after the death of Ragnar Lothbrok."

The penny finally dropped for Ronan; a thrill of horror swept through him at the prospect he was holding a viking's blood-stained tunic. "You're Vikings?"

Freyja smiled, shaking her head patiently. "Many winters hence, others will give us that name, but in this time, people call us Norse, the people of the north."

"But you just said viking," Ronan insisted.

Freyja gave an indulgent smile and brief nod. "Víking is our word for expedition. Mine are a people of expeditions. Our víkingar travel widely, raiding where they can, trading when they must." The purr of her voice countered the violent images springing to Ronan's mind. "Sten's father, Olaf, was a víkingr of much repute ... he raided The Land of the Gaels many times. But, by the time Sten was of an age, those raids had long since been replaced by peaceful trade. Sten likes to talk strong about raiding and longships, but they are his father's stories. Sten's víkings have always been for trade ... in sturdy cargo ships rather than fleet raiders."

"Now," she said, handing him the clothes, "don these. Then we will sup, after which, your lessons will begin."

"My lessons?"

Freyja looked at him with great seriousness, her eyes the lightest blue, almost grey. "The blóð rún has chosen you as its väktare," she said.

"And you will be a great väktare, but there is much for you to learn before you leave."

Ronan wasn't particularly interested in any blood rune, or being its guardian, great or not, he was only thinking of Saoirse in Freyja's Land of the Gaels, and his mother in Australia. "When am I leaving?" he asked hopefully.

"When either you or the blóð rún chooses."

"What is the blóð rún?" Even as he spoke, Ronan guessed the answer.

Freyja reached out, prising his clenched fingers open. "That is your blóð rún."

Ronan studied the shiny stone warming his palm. "How will I know when it chooses to take me somewhere?"

"The blóð rún only chooses for you if you are in mortal danger and are unable to instruct it," Freyja said. "Otherwise, you will only leave when you instruct it."

"But how do I do that?" Impatience clouded Ronan's thoughts. Twice he'd been in the path of death; twice this blood rune had whisked him to safety, albeit to unlikely places. Now he was caught in the age of Vikings. However, he had no choice but to trust the stone, and Freyja.

"So many questions," Freyja said. "And it is my duty to provide the answers."

34

THE TEACHER

Ronan's head was a bubbling cauldron. His mind boiled with völva, väktare, víkings, umrót, seiðr, Gaels, flaming red hair and more—so much information and so many new things to make sense of. The bedlam in his head was swamped by savage hunger pains woken by the large bowl of steaming meat and vegetable stew placed under his nose. Momentarily forgetting all else, he attacked his stew with a thick spoon and generous chunks of a dark, grainy bread.

"As a novice väktare, you have much to learn," Freyja said solemnly. "And it is my duty to teach you the laws of the blóð rún, and prepare you for your obligations to the Heim Steinn." She had skewered a large grey feather sideways, like a hairpin, through the red roll at the back of her neck; it bobbed with her every move.

Ronan hesitated over a piece of stew-soaked bread—he wasn't sure he liked the sound of laws and obligations, but was curious to know more about this Home Stone. As he ran the last of his bread round the bowl to mop up the juice, he asked, "What is the Heim Steinn?"

"The Heim Steinn is where I found you. Come, I will show you, and explain the others on the way." Freyja passed him a plain cloak, wrapped another about her shoulders, grabbed a long wooden staff polished by much handling, and led the way out the door.

It was a sunny day, but there was an edge to the air when it stirred.

Ronan turned a slow, full circle, taking in the small cleared area, Freyja's sturdy dwelling and the surrounding forest. In daylight, the house was no longer a grassy bank, but a wooden structure covered in sod to guard against midwinter's bite, which was fast approaching, given the russets, reds and yellows peppering the forest.

Closing his eyes, Ronan angled his face into the sun, sucking in its warmth, revelling in his swift recovery from the turmoil, or umrót as Freyja called it. "What was that drink you gave me earlier?" he asked, recalling how he found it so refreshing and energising.

"It is a collection of herbs ... it helps some people with the umrót; others, not."

"I'm guessing it doesn't work for you?"

Freyja nodded. "Very astute, young väktare."

"Is that why you can't visit your daughters?"

She nodded again, eyes distant. "Come," she said, leading him into the autumn colours.

A well-trodden path carpeted with pine needles and fallen leaves meandered through the forest. After a short walk, the track forked; Freyja took the right. It led them down a gentle slope where the trees became thinner and shorter, as if the forest were bowing to whatever lay ahead. Soon after they crossed a narrow brook strewn with boulders, the trees ended in a straggle of stunted shrubs. Before them, in the centre of a small clearing, was a low, nine-sided wooden roof over a shiny black boulder. The structure reminded Ronan of a rotunda in a town park on the other side of the world, in a whole other time. The anxiety billowing in his stomach stilled as he approached the shelter. Weirdly, he sensed he'd entered a protective shield.

The egg-shaped rock, still half buried, was more than a metre long; it bulged up through a thick bed of well-tended pine needles. Despite the mirror finish, its obsidian depths swallowed Ronan's eyes, like trying to see something at midnight through a blindfold. And the closer he came to the shelter, the warmer the stone in his hand became. As bizarre as it seemed, he felt he belonged.

"This is the Heim Steinn," Freyja said, placing a reverent hand on the boulder. "This is where all heim rúnar bring their väktare in times of mortal peril."

Ronan wondered why he wasn't apprehensive that a flake of stone and its parent boulder were now controlling his life. And he was puzzled. "You mentioned earlier about instructions. How do you give a stone, sorry, a rún, instructions?" He placed his empty palm on the polished surface; peace and strength flowed through him like an electric charge. In that moment, he realised he was right where he needed to be, and that he would do whatever he needed to do.

Freyja watched the change in Ronan's face, nodding with quiet satisfaction. "I understand you have many questions ... that is good," she said. "And I have many things to teach you, but I think it best if we approach it like a journey, a well-organised víking, otherwise, entanglements with byways and side roads will delay our arrival."

"What's our destination?" Ronan said, running his gaze over her high cheekbones, wide mouth and resolute jaw—a memorable face, but not beautiful like Saoirse or his mother. The thought of them, and of being stuck where he was forever, stirred a momentary pulse of alarm, but peace, strength and confidence flowed from the boulder. He would learn everything he could from Freyja—she was his only way back.

"We will have reached our journey's end when you can return to your time. But first, we must bed your blóð rún." She propped her staff against one of the roof support posts and drew a short knife from the pouch on her belt.

Ronan flinched, eyes locked on the gleaming blade.

Freyja smiled, placing the knife on the curve of the ebony boulder. It snapped onto the sloping surface. "Do not be afraid, Ronan."

It was the first time she'd said his name; he found it comforting, a reassurance he still existed and wasn't caught in some imaginary netherworld.

"Your blóð rún has bonded to you and it will stick to you no matter what, as long as you obey its laws."

Ronan shaped to ask about the laws, but decided otherwise.

"But," she continued, as though not noticing, "a blóð rún is most truly at one with its väktare when it is held here." She turned and raised her knot of hair. In the indentation at the base of her skull, barely visible through the fiery growth, was a bulge beneath the skin.

"There's a big lump," Ronan said, puzzled.

"That," she said, "is my blóð rún. Now come, we must make a nest for yours." Freyja scooped up the knife as she would from a table top, the force holding it to the rounded surface releasing as if by silent command.

Ronan pulled away. "No way you're cutting my head open to stick a stone inside ... not even the blóð rún." He eyed her defiantly.

The momentary startle in her eyes gave way to a chuckle. "No cutting required." She lifted her hair to again show the lump of her blood rune. "When I was not many winters older than you, my mother shaved a tiny nest there for my blóð rún," she explained, touching a finger to the lump. "Before long, it had burrowed beneath my skin and my hair had grown back."

The image of the rune boring into his skin, like a tick seeking a feast of blood, repulsed Ronan. Before his imagination went further, he realised the skin probably just grew over the top of the blood rune.

"It did not hurt," Freyja assured him. "Now, bow your head." With a sigh, he submitted. She lifted the back of his tangle, wielding the knife like a razor, deftly shaving a tiny circle. "Now, place your blóð rún onto your skin."

He slid his blood rune onto the fresh-shaved patch. Its warmth melted into his body, and he imagined he felt the skin opening in welcome.

"There," Freyja said with satisfaction. "Your blóð rún now has a nest. And if you do not remove it, it will soon burrow beneath your skin, becoming one with you." She pulled his hair down over the stone, dragging her fingers through it to give it shape. With a loud click of her tongue, she screwed up her nose and said, "Your hair is disgusting ... like a thrall." Drawing an antler comb from her belt pouch, she attacked the knots. After a few dozen powerful strokes where Ronan thought his hair was coming out by the roots, she was appeased. "Now you look halfway respectable, and no one will ever know it is there."

Ronan ran his hands over her work, marvelling at the silkiness, even though it hadn't been washed for a couple of days. Or was it? He had no idea how time behaved when the blood rune was bouncing you around the centuries. "Freyja, you said earlier that Sten went to The Land of the

Gaels three years after the death of Ragnar Lothbrok ... when, exactly, did Ragnar Lothbrok die?"

For a moment, she frowned in puzzlement. "Ah, you mean by the Christian calendar?"

Despite having a vague recollection that the modern calendar was Gregorian, Ronan thought 'Christian' made perfect sense to the Norse. "I guess so," he ventured.

"My conclusion," Freyja responded, "from talking to Christian thralls, is that Ragnar Lothbrok died in 856 by their calendar."

"Oh," was all Ronan could say.

Freyja must have read his thoughts, for she said, "When is your time?"

Ronan wasn't sure an honest answer would be wise, but she appeared to know many things already, besides, they had to be able to trust each other. He did a quick calculation. "One thousand, one hundred and sixty-five years after the death of Ragnar Lothbrok," he said, wondering why his head wasn't spinning with more disbelief.

Freyja simply nodded.

"You don't seem surprised," he said, peering at her.

"You suffered much umrót, so I knew you had journeyed far."

"So, what year is this?" Ronan asked, astounded at how calm and unconcerned he was.

"Well, Sten was sixteen winters old on his first víking, and he is now forty-eight. So, that must make it ..."

"Eight ninety-one," Ronan said before she could complete the calculation.

Freyja looked a little miffed. "You have a sharp mind, young väktare."

"And you have a wise mind, Völva Freyja." The source of those flattering words baffled Ronan, but the image of Grandpa Paddy, mixed with the warmth at the back of his head, gave him the answer.

"And you have the tongue of Bragi, god of poetry and music," Freyja added dismissively, but the corners of her mouth lifted. "Come, let us sit ... there is much for you to learn."

35

THE FOREBEAR

They sat on the thick bed of pine needles, backs against separate posts. Each post was an intricately carved column of intertwined birds and animals—bears, horses, wolves, ravens, snakes and ducks, and many Ronan didn't know. There were nine posts, each sending a supporting beam and network of complex interconnecting timbers to the central apex—a square structure with only four posts would've been much easier to build.

"These are amazing," Ronan said, looking from one post to another.

Freyja swelled with pride. "Yes, they are some of Sten's finest work."

Ronan wasn't sure if she was serious. "Sten made this?"

"Yes," she said. "Place wood in his hands and the gods work through him." Freyja ran proud fingers along the post above her head, like a blind person reading braille.

"Did he build your house too?" Ronan asked, mesmerised by her dexterous fingertips.

"Yes. When we married, he was cast from Kaupang, the town of his family, so he built our longhouse in the forest."

"Why was he banished?" Ronan frowned. "Not because he married you?"

Freyja nodded, folding her hands in her lap. "I am a völva, a seeress." She paused, as though it was enough explanation, an adequate reason. Ronan eyed her silently, waiting for her to continue. "I practice seiðr, the weaving of the future. Seiðr is a gift from the gods, from Odin and my namesake, the Goddess Freyja. They were the first practitioners of the mysterious art of foretelling and creating the future.

"It is my gift to see the morrow, and my obligation to prepare people for what is coming. But with this obligation comes great responsibility and considerable danger. As a völva, I have to be very careful what I reveal about the future. If I tell people something they dislike immensely, the consequences may not be pleasant."

Ronan stared in disbelief. "But why?"

"As much as people value a völva's wisdom, we are often viewed with fear, or treated with great suspicion ... even contempt." Freyja shook her head sadly, but with no hint of grievance. "But that is of little concern ... we have a job to do and our work is important."

Ronan leant his head back onto the post, pondering her words, thinking it unfair, but best to change the subject. "Why nine posts?" The structure's unnecessary complexity intrigued him.

Freyja waved an encompassing arm at the roof. "This represents Yggdrasill the World Tree, linking the nine worlds of Ásgarðr, home of the gods of power and war," With each name, she pointed to a post. "Vanaheim, home of the gods of fertility and wisdom; Álfheim, the land of elves; Niðavellir, where the dwarfs live; Jötunheimr, land of Giants; Niflheim, the mist world; Midgard, the land of mortals; Muspelheim, the realm of fire; and Helheim, the underworld."

As Freyja described each of the nine worlds, their names fired Ronan's memory of watching *The Fellowship of the Ring* movie with Ruddi. A pang of longing pawed at the centre of his chest.

"Enough of Yggdrasill," Freyja said, interrupting his thoughts, pointing upward, "... the poem."

Ronan was so caught up in the beauty of the carvings and the story behind them, he hadn't noticed the runic inscription in the roof beams above. To his amazement, the symbols were no longer angular patterns to be puzzled over—he recognised the Norse words his mother had recited to him, their meaning flowing as if he were reading a book. He jerked his gaze to Freyja who was studying him, her face radiating great fulfilment.

"You are the one," she said in a low tone.

Goose bumps skipped across Ronan limbs. "What?" He frowned, excited and apprehensive at the same time.

"You are the one I saw coming."

Before this past week, Ronan would never have entertained the possibility, let alone accepted the reality, of time travel; now, he was prepared to consider that foresight was possible. "How did you see me coming?"

"Ah," Freyja said, touching her temple, "a völva never gives away her secrets." Another smile of sublime satisfaction passed across her face.

Ronan changed tack to the other thing gnawing at the back of his mind. "How come I can read this runic script?"

"Why is it you can understand me?" she asked.

"Because you're speaking ..." Realisation dawned on Ronan. "We're not speaking English, are we?"

With a serene smile, she shook her head.

"But how?"

Freyja tapped the back of her skull.

Ronan's eyes widened. "The blóð rún lets me understand your language? And that's why I can read the inscription?"

She nodded. "Well done, young väktare, but all heim rúnar allow you to understand the local language."

While he wanted to know the difference between blood runes and home runes, Ronan didn't want to be sidetracked from his earlier question, so he tried again. "So, how did you know I was coming?"

Freyja smiled and touched her temple again.

Ronan could see he wouldn't get anywhere with that line, so he returned to the poem, reading aloud, astonished at each word he uttered. "The bearer of the living stone, in solitude is ne'er alone; the gods shall let no ill befall its keeper with eternal thrall." Ronan's brow lined; he glanced at Freyja, who flicked a 'please continue' glance at the beams. "Its power burns if blood enfold the lightening rune, and wealth untold awaits the one who stands apart as true of mind and pure of heart."

Again, he turned to Freyja, her face a picture of bliss.

"What's going on here that you're not telling me?" Ronan cocked his head, then he noticed the tears. "What did I say?" Freyja was simultaneously smiling and teary, much like his mother when her arms were reaching to hug him. He squirmed. "Freyja?"

"There are things I must tell you," she said, "but first, you need to understand why you are here."

"Okay," Ronan said hesitantly. "Why am I here?"

Raising her eyes toward the roof, she said, "Because of this poem."

Ronan spread his hands and shrugged.

"Let me explain the poem, then you can ask any questions you wish."

He gave a single nod.

Freyja closed her eyes and began, "Let us take it one concept at a time.

"*The bearer of the living stone* refers to the väktare to whom the heim rún has bonded, and the living stone is a heim rún, of course.

"*In solitude is ne'er alone* means the heim rún will never leave its bonded väktare.

"*The gods shall let no ill befall its keeper* is a promise from the gods of Ásgarðr to always protect the väktare.

"*With eternal thrall* means the väktare with whom the heim rún has bonded has lifetime command of the rún, unless the väktare voluntarily relinquishes it.

"That first verse was about all heim rúnar; this next verse is specifically about blóð rúnar."

"But what's the difference?"

"Be patient and you will discover," Freya chided, before continuing.

"*Its power burns* means a blóð rún is exceedingly powerful.

"*If blood enfold* states that a heim rún becomes a blóð rún when it bonds to a descendant of The Väktare of the Heim Steinn.

"*The lightening rune* is another name for the blóð rún because it lightens when it comes into contact with a descendant.

"*And wealth untold* refers to the wealth of knowledge, for rune travel enables the gathering of vast knowledge.

"*Awaits the one who stands apart* means that if a väktare ever relinquishes their blóð rún, it will wait an eternity for that special one who can be its new väktare.

"*As true of mind and pure of heart* says that a blóð rún will only bond to one who knows and does what is right." Freyja's eyes remained closed, the lids squeezing a single tear onto each cheek.

Ronan followed the inscription in the roof as she spoke, digesting the explanation, searching for the unspoken. By the end, the hairs on his arms and the back of his neck were as erect as bristles on a brush. Freyja's explanation led him to what he thought was the only conclusion, but he needed her confirmation. "Are you The Väktare of the Heim Steinn?"

Casting her grey eyes over him as if committing every hair, freckle, dimple and line to memory, she nodded slowly. "I am your forebear."

36

THE DECEPTION

While the post was hard in Ronan's back, the pine needles beneath him were soft. He found the polished obsidian boulder comforting, and the proximity of his Norse ancestor remarkably reassuring. While his thoughts should have been a clamour of questions, peace and contentment seeped to his extremities. They sat in silence, Ronan contemplating their connection across the centuries, Freyja inscrutable.

However, Ronan could no longer ignore the question that had been burning in him since he'd realised Ireland wasn't a dream. "Will I ever be able to get back to my time?" Anxiety frayed the edges of the words.

Freyja peered at him before answering. "With practice, a väktare can flytja at will," she said, "but every journey invites the umrót; the further the flytja, the worse the umrót. And, as you have experienced, recovery takes time. If the flytja is to a dangerous time where there is no sanctuary to recover, or if death seeks to claim you, your rún will always heim you here ... to safety."

Ronan's stomach turned at the prospect. "That'd be way too much umrót," he said, reliving the chaotic turbulence of the heimming and the disorientating vulnerability of the recovery. He stared at the inscription, pondering the events of the past week, struggling to make sense of it.

"And the older you get, the more difficult recovery becomes," Freyja said. "'Just go visit your daughters in The Land of the Gaels' Sten says." Exasperation stamped her face. "He has no idea."

Ronan touched the stone at the back of his skull. "This is the blóð rún of one of them, isn't it?"

Freyja dipped her head with a tinge of sadness, and said, "Yes, I believe it was Astryd's."

Ronan felt like an impostor, sitting there with Astryd's blood rune while Freyja ached to see her daughter. But then, Astryd did relinquish the rune, obviously deciding she was better off without it. While this thought made Ronan wonder what burdens or restrictions the blood rune placed on its väktare, he wasn't about to ask—it might be rubbing salt into the wound. However, he was curious why she thought it was Astryd's blood rune. "How can you tell?"

"As Väktare of the Heim Steinn, I recognise the subtle variations in the aura of each heim rún."

"You mean its vibe?"

Freyja looked at him blankly.

"Vibe," he repeated. "... the feeling you get from something."

"Vibe," she mimicked, rolling it around with her tongue, smiling. "What an odd word. But yes, I can recognise each heim rún by its 'vibe'."

Thirsty for more, Ronan followed up with: "How many heim rúnar are there?" His imagination had väktare, all over the world, flitting between times like insects between candles.

"There are nine heim rúnar," Freyja said, quashing the image. "Only five are blóð rúnar."

Ronan wasn't sure why such a low number was a disappointment. "So, where are the others?"

Freyja counted off on her fingers. "There are four heim rúnar on víkingar, two blóð rúnar here, two more are travelling nearby with my other two daughters. The last one has gone to another time; where, I do not know."

"So, it's lost?"

"Temporarily misplaced," she corrected.

"Yeah, lost," Ronan insisted with a grin, before sobering. "So, is that lost person a new väktare?"

"As new as you."

A jolt of revelation electrified him, swamping the last of her words. If he had Astryd's blood rune, and there was another new guardian, then ...? The tingles dancing through him were almost too much to bear; his mind jumped round like a grasshopper in a jar.

"The missing väktare troubles you, Ronan," Freyja said soothingly. "I understand that."

"Was it the rún of your other daughter?" Strands were coming together in Ronan's head; tremors rippled through his body.

"Yes, it was Sigrid's."

Ronan searched her eyes. "You know, don't you?" Raw accusation bubbled to the surface, coating his words. "Why didn't you tell me?"

A fleeting coolness shadowed Freyja's eyes. "Some puzzles are better solved alone," she said enigmatically, "others with help."

Ronan gazed into the forest, not seeing the trees, taking deep breaths to calm his simmering anger. As well as being upset with Freyja, he was annoyed with himself for not thinking of his father earlier. And there was something else that didn't sit right, but it eluded him.

They sat for an age, forebear and descendant, völva and väktare, calmness and anger. Ronan didn't trust himself to speak. While he wasn't entirely sure about Freyja, he knew she was his only way home.

Freyja peered at Ronan as if trying to see his thoughts—he hoped she couldn't. But there was only so long a person could sit still under scrutiny—he began to squirm.

"Being a väktare is more than simply carrying a heim rún," she said evenly. "There are important considerations around what to impart and what to withhold. Living with that responsibility for a long time instils great caution about giving up information that others do not know.

"For a völva, it is more difficult because people pay us to weave the future for them, to foretell its shape. As I said earlier, I have to be very careful what I tell people. A careless word could see me put to death as a norn, as happened several times when I was young."

Having recently been shot—he was now certain his stepfather's drunken aim had been true—and then run down, Ronan was unsurprised by this revelation. But envisioning his forebear being hacked to death for being a witch, not once, but multiple times, troubled him.

Calmly, Freyja continued. "That is why my namesake sent the Heim Steinn and heim rúnar to Earth." If she was aware of Ronan's troubled thoughts, she gave no sign. "With a heim rún to protect us, we völur can go about our work without the fear of death." Freyja placed her palm on the glossy surface of the Home Stone. "But, less extreme retribution, that which does not threaten your life, can be most painful and distressing. Which is why we must be careful in how we tell people things that may be unpleasant to hear. No one wants to go through the umrót, or a severe beating, unnecessarily—both are most disagreeable."

Ronan instantly felt Masters' massive hand locking onto his arm; his gut tightened instinctively. He shook the thoughts away, but couldn't budge his annoyance with Freyja. "But you could've told me my father had been here." The irritation hadn't left his voice.

"Yes," she admitted. "I was only explaining my caution. And now, I have a confession to make. I knew it was another of my blood, and I now see your strong resemblance to him, but I did not know he was your father until you said."

Ronan's anger bubbled. "I don't believe you!"

Freyja's eyes became chips of ice, her words clipped and frosty. "You have much to learn, väktare. Say what you will to me, but ill-advised words to others will have you back here quicker than you would care." She flicked her eyes to the Home Stone. "And," she snapped, lifting her gaze to the inscription above, "may I remind you that the blóð rún does not serve those who are not true of mind and pure of heart. How can I deceive you for no good purpose, and still have my blóð rún in its nest?"

Ronan paled. Freyja was his only friend in the time of the Norse, and he'd insulted her terribly. Then, the blood rushed back in excess as he realised the extent of his stupidity. He would have to control his tongue. "I'm so sorry, Freyja," he said, hoping the grovel in his voice was clear. "It was a stupid thing to say, and you're right, I have a lot to learn. It's just that I thought you knew everything and ..." He stilled his tongue.

Freyja nodded a gracious acceptance of the apology. "As a seer you will come to understand this, but we völur do not see all things. Many times, the future is unclear and we have to lead our subject into revealing things to help fill the gaps. At other times everything is crystal clear, but there must be no difference to others whether we are certain, or stumbling in the dark. Therefore, we must shroud every instance in mystery, and a degree of ambiguity. It is for our own safety."

"So," said Ronan, perplexed by these revelations, "you're saying this whole seeing-the-future business is based on trickery?"

Freyja's head shook. "Not at all. We use all aspects of seiðr and flytja to inform ourselves of what the future holds and how we might shape it in the best light for our benefactor."

Ronan leant his head against the post, unsure how much was real and how much was deception. One thing for certain, the umrót was real, far too real. "I don't want to learn the laws and become a seið-mann," he said at last. "I just want to get back to my family." *And Saoirse!*

"I understand, väktare, but how do you propose to do that?"

Ronan lifted a hand to his blood rune, straightened, and turned to her in realisation.

Freyja's knot of red hair, skewered by the grey feather, bobbed. "That is correct, young väktare, the only way you can return to those times is to learn the laws of the heim rún, the skills of the seiðmann and the art of flytja."

Ronan's shoulders sagged; he sighed. Freyja studied his face. He had no choice—he must learn everything he could. Impatience gnawed at his insides like hunger pains at the end of a day without food.

"When do we start?" he asked.

37

THE RECOUNT

The lessons did not begin at once. First, Freyja took Ronan to the far side of the Home Stone shelter to view a slab of white-grey stone embedded in the ground against one of the carved posts, its flat outer face chiselled with a long runic inscription. Ronan followed the lettering as Freyja read aloud: "The Heim Steinn and the nine heim rúnar are gifts from the gods, hurled to Earth as a fiery ball that split the heavens with thunder and gouged the land with fury. The Vanir goddess, Freyja, the first völva, gave them to those who followed, to aid their work of healing the sick and delivering good fortune to earthly mortals. The power of the stones is eternal, and their unwise use invites ill to the user and their issue."

The shiny, half-buried bulk of the boulder was like a mesmerising eye that had sat there, unblinking, forever. "When did the Goddess Freyja send the Heim Steinn?" Ronan asked.

"Ah, that is said to have been when Yggdrasill had not long sprouted ... before Odin made Askr and Embla, the first man and woman."

The last part had a ring of familiarity to Ronan.

Freyja stepped across to the polished ebony surface, resting a reverent hand on it. "The Heim Steinn lay buried in the earth until the rains of ten thousand winters washed away the soil, exposing its power to an earthly völva."

"Was that you?" Ronan asked.

Freyja dipped her head. "Very perceptive, young väktare. Yes, the Heim Steinn revealed itself to me almost thirty winters ago, after a strong summer storm."

———

EARLY MORNING SUNLIGHT slanted into the forest, leaves sparkled with moisture from the previous day's cloud burst, and the ground was sodden underfoot. Shadows dappled across the back of a young woman stooping to gather mushrooms bursting from the damp layer of rotting leafy debris. A plaited rope of flaming hair hung forward over one shoulder, and with each stoop toward a mushroom, the end brushed her hand. Pine needles caught at the hem of her faded yellow dress, plucking at the woollen fibres. A plain iron brooch fastened each shoulder strap over the top of an undyed linen undergarment with sleeves to her wrists; a string of coloured beads looped between the two brooches; around her waist, a leather belt held a long knife and a large pouch.

The young woman hummed a tune as she filled her basket with the plump fungi, pausing occasionally to listen and cast her eyes about the surrounding forest, checking for danger—it was a land of wolves, bears and outlaws. All she heard was the cheerful call of birds and the contented babbling of a nearby stream swollen from the rain. By the time the basket was full, the steamy morning had drawn sweat to her brow. The water was calling.

As though being guided to a particular spot by an unseen hand, she headed obliquely toward the stream. The closer she got, the shorter the trees became; on the opposite bank, they were even more stunted. After slaking her thirst, the young woman gathered her dress, crossing the energetic current via a log and a couple of boulders. The trees gave way to bushes that soon yielded to a small open area, perhaps a dozen paces across. At its centre, like a gigantic boil festering in the Earth's skin, was a bulge of soil. During the night, the rain had eroded part of the mound, exposing a sliver of black—it was a magnet to her.

The red-haired woman dropped to her knees before the mound,

reaching out to the mesmerising protrusion. Its surface was warmer than the sunshine; she snatched her hand away, looking both frightened and intrigued. As if compelled, she hesitantly laid a palm on it again; as though from an inner power, it warmed to her touch. Fascinated, she began moving the damp earth, working well into the afternoon, intrigued to know the extent of what lay beneath. As she leant across the boulder to push more soil away, her brooches snapped onto the surface.

With a flare of alarm, she tried to free herself, but stopped when she feared her dress might tear. As fast as is appeared, her concern vanished before a wave of serenity. Without thinking, she slid her fingers under one brooch, effortlessly lifting it from the jet-black surface, likewise for the other. Mystified, she took her knife and held it close. It jumped from her hand, yet peeled off as easily as the brooches. While everything about this strange boulder was baffling, the day was getting late; it was wise to be out of the forest before dark—danger lurked in the night, both four-legged and two. In a flash of red, she scooped up the forgotten mushrooms and strode homeward.

Lurid cursing greeted her approach to the clearing the next day. Peering from the shelter of the trees, she saw a well-built lad, both feet planted against the boulder, large hands wrapped round the handle of a woodsman's axe. Back arched, muscles bulging, he strained to separate the iron axe-head from the magnetic bond. He must have been at it for a while and his hands had become sweaty, for they abruptly slid off the end of the handle, sending him sprawling backward into the dirt from yesterday's excavation effort.

Unable to contain herself, the young woman laughed.

The lad spun as he sprang to his feet, face turning as red as his hair. "Who are you?" he blurted.

She tossed her own fiery crop. "I am Freyja." She couldn't keep the chuckle from her voice. "And who are you?"

"I am Sten, son of Olaf," he said, attempting to inject an air of importance into the name as he wiped fresh dirt from his backside with work-hardened hands.

"Well, Sten Olafsson, what do you think you are doing here?" Freyja's voice lost its laughter. While she was certain she'd never seen this lad before, people like him had made life difficult for Freyja and her völva mother, Estrid. Even though she had been shunned by those uneducated in seiðr, and fearful of what they didn't understand, Estrid trained her talented daughter in the craft. As Freyja was learning, the life of a völva was a life of wariness.

"This is not your forest"—Sten snorted—"I have as much right to be here as you." The lack of hostility in the green eyes belied the jut of the chin.

"Perhaps you have," Freyja said, her own antagonism draining away, replaced by a mischievous gleam in her eyes. "It seems, Sten Olafsson, your axe is too heavy for you."

"It is not too heavy," Sten growled, puffing out his chest, "it is stuck to this stone ..." He shaped to say more but thought better of it.

Freyja completed the sentence for him in her most innocent voice. "And you are too feeble to remove it."

Scowling, Sten shook his head. "This rock is a powerful magnet."

"Here, let me see," Freyja said angelically. She stepped forward, slipped her fingers under the iron blade and lifted it free.

Sten gaped. "By Odin," he breathed, face turning a deeper red. "How did you do that?"

"This is my stone," Freyja said, tossing her head as she passed him the axe. "It obeys my command."

Sten frowned, rubbing a calloused palm across the wispy copper fuzz sprouting from his chin, and staring from Freyja to the boulder to the axe, and back again. "Humph!" he said, hefting the heavy blade in one hand, like a feather, easing it closer to the black surface. It started to pendulum before wrenching from his grasp and locking on with a loud, metallic clunk. "By Odin, it has much power," he said, trying to wrestle the axe free for the second time.

Freyja stood, watching with a smile as Sten tried to replicate her method, but the axe wouldn't budge. The more he grunted, wriggled, heaved and puffed, the redder his face became. Finally, his shoulders sagged, and he stood back, barrel chest sucking in deep breaths.

Peering at her from beneath suspicious brows, Sten asked, "Can you show me your trick again?"

This time, Freyja peeled the axe-head away with one hand.

"How do you do that?" Sten was flummoxed.

"I told you, this is my stone and it obeys my command," Freyja repeated. Instead of passing the axe to Sten's outstretched hand, she playfully allowed it to snap back onto the boulder.

Sten sighed, shaking his head. "Please command your stone to release my axe? I must cut a mast for my boat."

"First, you must help me dig."

"So, DID STEN HELP YOU?" Ronan asked as she paused the recount.

Freyja chuckled at the memory. "It was the only way he was going to walk away with his axe."

"But you would've given it to him if he'd refused to help, wouldn't you?"

Freyja smiled serenely, stroking the hard surface like she would a favourite cat. "The Heim Steinn drew me to its side, and asked me to free it from the earth. The soil was soft, but I found Sten amusing ... I did not want him to leave ... I wanted to tease him further." Her playful smile made Ronan like her more.

"Well, it obviously worked," he said.

"Yes, we married before the next winter."

38

THE GUIDANCE

R onan and Freyja stood on either side of the Home Stone, bound by blood and the pull of the gleaming obsidian bulk between them. As Ronan pondered his Norse ancestor, he couldn't help thinking how dissimilar they were.

Freyja, with her knot of red hair, faded woollen dress, metal brooches, leather belt and sturdy frame, looked exactly like the middle-aged Norse woman she was. But Ronan's tallness, ill-fitting clothes and unruly mop gave him away. While his hair hung long over his ears and down the back of his neck, it stopped well short of his shoulders. His wasn't the proud mane of a Norseman—it either shouted slave, or whispered foreigner.

That his homeland was almost twelve centuries away was enough to challenge Ronan's sanity, or at least stretch his belief in the possible. Yet there he was, sucked back through time from twenty-first century Australia, a land that wouldn't bear the footprint of a European for another seven centuries. Home had never felt so distant, had never *been* so distant.

Ronan laid his palm on the sleek surface, absorbing the warmth, sensing the power, the connection. "So," he said, "where did you find the heim rúnar?"

"They were stuck to the Heim Steinn like sheep ticks," Freyja told him, also laying her hand on the boulder. "Sten and I found them as we cleared the soil but, try as he might, he could not budge a one." She smiled at the memory. "They came away easily for me. And neither could he remove the fine grains of earth from the surface, yet I did it with ease. We keep this deep bed of pine needles around the Heim Steinn to keep it clean ... control the dust."

Ronan wanted to backtrack. "Then there are only seven völur?"

"Oh, no," Freyja replied, "there are many more völur wandering the lands of the Norse, but most are charlatans, pretenders with no genuine power. Calling yourself a völva does not make it so.

"Because there are only nine heim rúnar, only seven völur may truly call themselves so, and you are a seiðmann, regardless of your preference, as is your father."

Mention of his father threw Ronan's mind into disorder—it jumped from Paidin, to Maureen and Ruddi, then on to Saoirse and the two fleeting days spent with her, days now floating on a cloud of memory. And while desperate to make sure she was okay, if he was being honest, he craved to tumble into those amber eyes, drink in the lilt of her voice, and revel in her proximity.

Freyja snapped him from the reverie. "Ronan!"

"Huh? Sorry ... just thinking about my mother and brother, and a girl I met in The Land of the Gaels."

"Saoirse?"

Ronan gawked—that one word convinced him the powers of the völva were real, and substantial. "How could you possibly know that?" he blurted.

Freyja raised an eyebrow. "Do you doubt my gift?"

"Not anymore," he said.

Freyja laughed.

"What?"

"This is the perfect example"—her smile lingered—"of how a völva, or seiðmann, must use all the information at their disposal to emphasise their ability to know the present and weave the future."

"What?" Ronan still didn't have a clue what she was talking about.

Freyja leant forward, lowering her voice. "I will only speak of this to another trusted väktare, but you mentioned Saoirse's name when you were delirious from the umrót."

Ronan's lips compressed. Freyja was a powerful völva who could travel through time, yet much of her magical ability appeared to be smoke and mirrors.

"I vaguely remember now," he said. "And you said she was safe. How ...?"

"That," she replied. "I cannot say until you learn to flytja with precision."

Ronan almost asked her if that was true, or merely another ploy, but recalling her earlier reaction, he turned and stared into the forest instead. Not only did he need her, she was family, albeit extremely distant. Besides, he liked her ... a lot. And thinking of family brought him back to his father.

"You said you didn't know where my father went," he began, speaking toward the trees, "so how can I find him?"

Moving to his side, Freyja laid a tender hand on his shoulder. "You cannot, Ronan ... he must come to you."

"But how?" Ronan continued staring into the forest.

"Your father was a man in a hurry. I had barely advised him how to instruct his rún, and off he went ... it was not even bedded ..." Freyja gave him a regretful glance. "It is my fault. I should have recognised his impetuous nature and withheld the information until he was ready. There is no doubt he was trying to return to your mother, but only the gods know where he set down. I expect he will heim again, before long." Freyja paused, gazing into Ronan's eyes. "This is why I have not told you how to instruct your rún yet ... I want you fully prepared so you arrive where you intend." She dropped her hand to his arm. "Now, tell me about him ... your father."

Ronan shrugged. "He died before I was born. I only know him from Mum's stories and what Grandpa told me, and photos."

"What are photos?"

Oh, shit, Ronan thought, brain going into overdrive, *how am I going to explain this?* "It's like a drawing on a small square of sheepskin," he said after a pause, holding up splayed fingers to show the size.

Freyja nodded slowly, but her face remained puzzled. When he'd finished telling her about the dig and seeing his father fall, she said, "It is understandable that you wish to meet your father, but it will only happen if the Heim Steinn and your blóð rún allow it."

"And how will I know that?" Ronan asked, unable to hide his annoyance.

"When it happens." Freyja's eyes flicked round his face. "I see your father's impatience in you, young väktare."

"I'm not impatient," Ronan insisted testily. "I just want to get home."

"And get home you will, my Ronan, but first, you must learn everything necessary ... including patience."

39

THE FLYTJA

Ronan didn't speak—he was still simmering from Freyja's inference that he was impatient as, by extension, was his father. And with Paidin foremost in his mind, the niggling thought that he was missing something returned. Eventually, it crystallised—the time-line was wrong. It was so obvious, how could he have missed it? Unwelcome, suspicious thoughts intruded once more. But hadn't Freyja said her blóð rún would desert her if she wasn't true of mind and pure of heart? Ronan suddenly didn't know what to believe.

"How long was my father here for?" he said at last, trying to sound offhand.

"Mmm, several days."

Ronan swallowed a gulp of disbelief. "And when did he leave?"

"One ... no, almost two moons before you came." Freyja shot him a glance. "What vexes you, my Ronan?"

Two months! Ronan was on the verge of asking her what she was hiding but, uncharacteristically, caution stilled his tongue; the memory of her earlier reaction remained fresh. "It doesn't make sense," he said at, shaking his head. "I saw my father fall off a cliff, then later the same day, I was heimmed here, so how"—misery enveloped him—"can we have missed each other?"

"That is a troublesome question," Freyja said, squeezing his shoulder, "and one I do not have a precise answer for." After some thought, she continued, "All I can suggest is that the Heim Steinn did not wish for the two of you to meet. Perhaps there is some version of trufla of which I am not aware."

"So, my blóð rún brought me back to the Heim Steinn at a later time so I wouldn't meet my father?" Ronan's agitation lifted. "Because it would create some sort of interference with the past?"

"That is my best assumption, my Ronan." Freyja frowned. "Trufla usually only causes a short heim, to another place in the same time. It is the rún's way of preventing meddling with the past."

"I'll never be able to find my father," Ronan lamented. That one glimpse had given him a flesh and blood memory, and his newfound knowledge of the Home Stone and its runes gave him hope he might finally fill that gap in his life. But now, it appeared the Home Stone had other ideas. That brief sighting had become a cruel encounter that would haunt him forever.

"That is up to the Heim Steinn," Freyja said solemnly, "and the gods."

Well, they shouldn't torment. Ronan pushed his festering resentment aside. There was no point blaming his father's impatience either; if Ronan knew how to instruct his rune, nothing would hold him back. Perhaps Freyja was, by far, the wisest of them all.

"But you are different," she stated.

"How?" Ronan couldn't even bother being chuffed.

"Because your blóð rún has bound to you like no other I have seen. And I think I know why."

Ronan said nothing. In his mind, he'd been building a full head of steam to connect with his father, to find him somewhere in time ... somehow. But that was now dashed; helplessness was choking him. And whatever Freyja thought she knew, she would tell him when she was good and ready, so why waste breath asking.

"I consulted the gods while you slept last night," she said. "I believe your mother is descended from Astryd, and your father from Sigrid ... you have my blood on both sides."

"Fair enough," Ronan said, too emotionally spent to even begin to be curious about how she'd come to that conclusion. What difference would it make now? As long as he could still get back to Saoirse and his mother, he didn't care what blood was where. If the Home Stone wouldn't allow him to meet his father, that was the end of that.

Without warning, Freyja cuffed him over the ear—not hard, but he winced anyway. "Do not become the lamb that Sten has named you," she said sharply. "If you are to retain the allegiance of the blóð rún and return to your time, you must remain true ... you must not lose your spirit."

"Why are you so damned cranky?" Ronan whined, rubbing his ear.

"Because you have the opportunity to be a great väktare, a seiðmann of note," Freyja shot back, "but you are pouting like a child."

Ronan remained silent, thoughts churning as he drew a deep breath, letting it out in a whoosh. "I know you're trying to help," he said, "and I'm sorry, but I just feel so ..."—the correct word eluded him—"... upset that I might never meet my father."

"There is an alternative way to view it," Freyja said, her annoyance ebbing. "You have at least seen your father. Who else, whose father died before they were born, can say as much?"

The pine needles beneath Ronan's feet held particular interest while he mulled her words. "You're right," he said, reluctantly meeting her eye. "I'm sorry." Then, as his mind replayed their conversation, he added, "Why your blood?"

"Not actually mine, young väktare," Freyja said, "but the blood of the Goddess Freyja."

Awareness spread like a sunrise across Ronan's face. "You're ...?" The words caught on the sides of his throat.

With a serene nod, Freyja said, "Yes, I am descended from the Goddess Freyja. That is why it is only me, or my blood, who can remove anything from the Heim Steinn." She smiled. "The local lads like to think they might have väktare blood, so they place something metallic on the Heim Steinn to test their worth. Sometimes, when I arrive, it is festooned with swords and knives and axes." The feather skewering her hair bobbed in time with her brief chuckle.

Ronan grinned at the conjured image.

Freyja frowned. "The first time was amusing, but now, removing the misguided efforts of wishful youth is simply tedious."

Ronan's memory of the echidna of bootmaker's tacks lit up, and while his recount of the experience made her smile, it was fleeting. "What?" he asked, frowning.

"That is where Astryd and Sigrid chose to live." Freyja sighed.

"Right, but can't you flytja to them just once?"

"You sound like your grandfather," she said with an exaggerated pout.

Ronan went still. "Have you met Grandpa Paddy?"

Freyja laughed, feather jiggling again. "No, I speak of Sten Olafsson."

"Oh," Ronan said, boggled by the magnitude of the generations separating them. "But seriously, why don't you visit your daughters?"

Freyja's face sobered. "You are young and hale, Ronan, and it took you more than a day to overcome the umrót ... imagine what it is like for one of my age?"

"You're not *that* old," Ronan responded quickly.

"And what a smooth tongue you have." Freyja's smile reflected her pleasure. "But this winter will be my forty-seventh."

"Oh, that *is* old," Ronan deadpanned.

Freyja snorted, giving him a stern gaze. "Smooth *and* sharp," she said with a chuckle, before sobering. "A long flytja is purgatory, but a short one is no burden." Her eyes blanked as her mind turned elsewhere and, with a sound like a quick intake of breath, the air itself seemed to slice open, her extremities folding inward as if sucked through the gash ... and she was gone.

40

THE HUNTERS

Ronan gaped; Freyja's body had simply curled inward until there was nothing. It happened so fast he almost missed it, but not the grey feather floating to the ground, settling into the indentation her weight had left in the thick bed of pine needles. Suddenly alone, he swivelled his head, scanning the surrounding forest, half expecting to see her step from behind a tree. His eyes had seen her disappear, but his brain was resisting the concept, convinced it was trickery.

Without warning, the space Freyja had vacated a moment earlier gave a sharp sigh; she reappeared, folding outward from a slit in the air, until she was all there—faded woollen dress, flaming hair, firm jaw, grey eyes regaining their focus.

"That was only to the longhouse and back," Freyja explained, when the air settled and she'd re-skewered her feather.

"Cool," Ronan said, managing to close his mouth.

Freyja frowned. "You speak of the weather?"

Ronan chuckled. "No, cool means ... I don't know ... good ... or amazing, yes, amazing."

"Cool," she repeated, shaking her head as if wondering what was becoming of the younger generation.

Ronan enjoyed the consternation his twenty-first century word caused, but he had to ask, "How come you've still got your clothes?"

Freyja smiled. "Clothes or belongings cannot flytja to a time where they should not be. For example, if you do not wish to arrive naked when you flytja to the past, you must wear a plain robe that would fit the time you are going to."

Ronan's nodded response morphed into puzzlement. "And the feather?"

"Ah, the feather," Freyja said with a half-smile. "It is said that when a völva disappears, she has used her seiðr to turn into a falcon and fly off ... and when a feather is seen after she disappears, it reinforces the legend."

"So," Ronan said, "another piece of deception."

"Deception, reality or the wishful thinking of the ignorant, young väktare, all are part of practising seiðr."

Ronan sighed. "What about the true of mind and pure of heart business?"

"You have much to learn, väktare," Freyja said. "Where is it written that the world is black and white?"

"What's that supposed to mean?"

"Simply this ... sometimes, to achieve that which is both good and just, you must do something that, in itself, may not seem true or pure."

"Sounds like a convenient excuse to me," he said dismissively.

"It sounds exactly what it is ... a reason, not an excuse."

Before Ronan could respond, the drift of voices from the forest caught their attention. Freyja held up a hand. "Could be outlaws," she breathed. There was a flash of movement.

Hairs lifted on the back of Ronan's neck—the Home Stone was out in the open, and the voices were heading straight toward it. There was time for him to make the trees, but not Freyja. Instantly, he chided himself for thinking like a farm boy rather than a väktare. "Flytja to your house," he murmured. "I can outrun them."

Freyja shook her head. "But can you outrun their arrows?"

The voices were closer, louder. An occasional higher-pitched melody danced across the top of the dominant bass rumble—it sounded like a couple of women with several more men. The murmurs grew louder and more distinct, and intermittent laughter carried with fleeting clarity on the still air.

Freyja exhaled with relief. "I think it may be a hunting party." She gathered her staff as vague shapes began emerging from the concealing forest. "And a successful one," she added.

There were five stout lads and two muscular girls, all about Ronan's age or slightly older, all with weapons, and all but one with slaughtered game. The girls carried bows that stirred the envy in Ronan's chest— one was a beautifully made yew longbow with a rawhide string, the other shorter, an exquisite curved weapon. His hands ached to hold it. Four of the lads held spears, long wooden shafts topped with broad iron points. The fifth lad, better dressed, taller and much broader than the others, had a longbow in one hand, spear in the other and a quiver of arrows on his belt. Each wrist sported a thick metal band etched in flowing designs that caught the light with every movement. He was the only one not carrying game; his spear tip flashed clean in the noonday sun, his hands showed no stains from gutting a kill.

Ronan and Freyja stood together beside the Home Stone as the party threaded from the trees. "Looks like Halfdan has not blooded his spear," Freyja whispered, eyes never leaving the group.

The taller girl had a serious face and a braid of jet-black hair hanging down her back. Blood from her kill smeared the hand carrying the elegant recurve bow, while a smudge of red decorated one cheek, like a careless swipe of war paint. She carried three rabbits and a squirrel skewered on a stick over one shoulder. The other girl wore a lengthy braid as well, but hers glowed brown, not dissimilar to Saoirse's. She had laughing eyes and shouldered one end of a long pole threaded through the tied legs of a dressed deer carcass. A sandy-haired lad with near identical facial features carried the other end.

Another two lads laboured under a large black boar, similarly gutted and trussed. The fourth had a deer carcass draped over his shoulders; blood matted his long dark hair, and had dried like a maroon cowl around the neck and shoulders of his beige tunic.

The one called Halfdan walked in the lead, aloof from the banter of the successful hunters in his wake. Dark fuzz sprouted like weeds across a broad, youthful face twisted into a scowl. He halted at the sight of Ronan and Freyja watching him. Resentment settled heavy on his features, as if his lean day was the fault of others.

"What are you looking at, norn?" he growled at Freyja, before turning his irate gaze to Ronan. "And do not dare to meet my eye, thrall," he barked.

Freyja placed a warning hand on Ronan's arm. "Insulting me and my guest will not hide your failure on the hunt, Halfdan," she said in the calm voice a mother might use to admonish an errant child.

The rest of the hunters froze, watching their leader in anticipation. Halfdan's eyes narrowed, lips tightening, ruddy complexion darkening.

"You know I am no norn," Freyja continued, "so why bother throwing insults?" She tilted her head at Ronan. "And do not judge my friend by the shortness of his hair or the state of his dress ... he is a traveller from a distant land with different customs, and no more a thrall than you."

Halfdan snorted, curling his lip. "If you are no thrall, traveller, why do you not carry weapons? Are you unmanly?" He chuckled at his own wit ... a deferential titter ran through his companions. For a Norse youth like Halfdan, being a man was all about fighting and hunting; returning empty handed from a hunt must be galling when his companions were laden with game.

"It's not the weapon that makes the man," Ronan said, repeating one of the favourite mantras of his karate teacher, "but the man that makes the weapon."

Freyja, hand wrapped round her staff, glanced sideways at him with a faint but knowing smile.

Halfdan glowered, expanding his broad chest, stepping closer. Barely more than shoulder high to Ronan, he was well muscled and moved like a lumbering bear. His demeanour reminded Ronan of his stepfather.

"What is that supposed to mean, traveller?" Halfdan's words were pure disdain wrapped in naked challenge. Having failed in his hunt, he appeared set on belittling Ronan, perhaps to regain stature in the eyes of his band.

Briefly, Ronan wondered why bullies gravitated to him—Masters, Egan, and now, Halfdan. Whether they saw opportunity or sport, or were simply like wild animals sensing weakness, he didn't know. Regardless, he couldn't help but push back, and he did it with his most ready weapon, his tongue. "It means," he said, as though explaining a simple concept to a small child, "that the bow does not make you a man, and neither is it a good weapon if the hands holding it are unmanly."

It was instantly clear that throwing the youth's taunt back at him was a poor choice. Halfdan darkened—his weapons were still falling as he charged at Ronan like an enraged bull, eager for contact, no finesse, all bulk and brute force.

With adrenaline zinging through him, demanding flight, Ronan stood rooted. At the last moment, he feigned toward Freyja, and when he saw Halfdan adjust, he propelled himself the other way, swaying out of reach of the grappling arms, like a matador. To Ronan's surprise, the bottom of Freyja's staff flicked out as Halfdan shot between them, clipping his ankles, sending him sprawling, headlong. His momentum carried him into the immobile bulk of the Home Stone.

Ronan raised an eyebrow at Freyja; she shrugged.

While Halfdan's arms cushioned his fall, they couldn't stop his cheek crunching into the boulder with a meaty thwack. His companions stood gaping. Halfdan moaned, rolling onto his side, touching his temple, fingers coming away red and sticky. As his eyes regained focus, they flamed with raw malevolence.

The hunters lowered their kills and formed a rough semicircle facing the Home Stone, but Ronan ignored them. He turned his ear to Freyja, who was leaning close.

"Be ready to move," she warned. "He means to hurt you."

A chill of fear did a tiny tap-dance up Ronan's spine, his mind jumping to karate. The wash of heat from the blóð rún at the base of his skull sent confidence surging through his body. And with it came the certainty that he wouldn't allow this oaf to hurt him ... or Freyja.

Halfdan glared from one to the other, as if undecided who caused his predicament. His scowl settled on Ronan.

41

THE CHALLENGE

Ronan looked down at the dishevelled youth. Despite Freyja's cautioning words, and the inner voice warning him not to make matters worse, he had to ensure he remained the focus of Halfdan's ire. "Well," he said nonchalantly, "if that's the way you blunder about the forest, it's no wonder you've come back empty-handed."

An unsympathetic snicker lifted from the band. Shooting a murderous glare at Ronan, Halfdan rose to his haunches against the Home Stone, coiling his massive legs, reaching behind to push off the boulder and propel himself at his tormentor. With almost simultaneous metallic snaps, the Home Stone snared his bracelets, shackling him like a slave.

No matter how he reefed, wriggled, squirmed and cursed, Halfdan remained trapped. Ronan's lips twitched; Freyja's eyes twinkled; the hunters guffawed. Halfdan twisted and heaved, spitting curses in every direction; all he accomplished was bloodied wrists and the increased mirth of his companions. Arms quivering from exertion, body shaking with fury, he finally slumped, defeated.

Freyja stepped forward, stooping to place a cautioning hand on his shoulder. "Be wary of meddling with powers you do not understand, my friend."

"I am not your friend," Halfdan hissed at her. "Now set me free."

"Your quarrel is not with me, it is with the traveller." She inclined her head in Ronan's direction. "You will need to seek his help."

Freyja could have peeled Halfdan's wristbands from the stone, but she clearly had other ideas. Ronan glanced at the group—they were absorbed by their leader's predicament. The hunters appeared unmoved by Halfdan's circumstances, yet fascinated by how he would react to grovelling to the one he sought to humiliate. He didn't keep them waiting long.

In an eye-popping frenzy, Halfdan launched into renewed thrashing, roaring like a caged bear. Sweat streamed from his brow; spittle flew from his lips. He whipped his shoulders alternately, heaved them in time, and even tried lifting his bracelets free by driving upward with his weightlifter's legs. The air crackled with his curses—he cursed Ronan; he cursed Freyja; he cursed his companions, together and separately; he cursed the gods; and finally, he cursed himself. All he achieved were deep gashes to his wrists and deeper lacerations to his pride. With a loud groan, Halfdan surrendered, slumping, a manacled prisoner, chin on chest, breathing in ragged gasps, blood dripping from his fingers.

A hush fell across the tiny clearing. The hunters exchanged apprehensive looks. While unperturbed to see their leader trapped, they remained indecisive. None of them possessed Halfdan's arrogant carriage, and although armed and capable of retaliation, they clearly respected the seiðr shackling him to the mystical boulder.

Ronan moved forward, glancing at Freyja for a hint of what he should do. His instinct was to release the hapless bully, hoping he'd learnt his lesson. Freyja produced the slightest head shake. Ronan halted, straining his ears for any sign that Halfdan's companions might move against him, but there was silence from behind.

Slowly, whether from reluctance or fatigue, the slumped figure stirred. "Free me," he moaned.

Ronan glanced again at Freyja and lifted an eyebrow—her shoulders gave the ghost of a noncommittal shrug, but her head moved as before. Ronan had no clue what it meant, so he took a wild stab. "I didn't hear you," he said. "You'll need to speak up. And, while you're at it, apologise to Freyja for your insult."

A murmur swelled from the watching semicircle. Ronan wondered if he'd gone too far; he resisted the urge to turn, instead, forced a nonchalant stance. While the words were his, he sensed that Freyja, through her subtle signals, was guiding him down this path of antagonising Halfdan further.

The lad lifted his head. His eyes held surrender and hatred in equal measure, but he had no choice. "Free me, traveller," he croaked. Transferring his dejected gaze to Freyja, Halfdan mumbled, "I withdraw my insult."

Freyja dipped her head graciously as if he'd complimented her choice of dress. "Then all is good, Halfdan," she said.

"And I will free you," Ronan said, squatting beside the stone, easing the bloody bracelets from its surface. He stood, extending a hand down to the dispirited youth. Halfdan's arrogance flooded back, eyes turning to chips of granite as he glared up at Ronan. "I do not need your help, traveller," he said, slapping the offered hand aside, pushing himself to his feet.

"Interesting," said Ronan, rubbing his chin, "you seemed to need it a moment ago."

Halfdan's chest swelled, his face darkening. "Do not mock me," he spat, shouldering past Ronan, wincing as he eased the bracelets clear of the bleeding wounds, jamming them up onto meaty forearms.

The hunter who had carried the deer over his shoulders stepped forward, gathered Halfdan's spear, bow, and belt with its quiver of arrows, and held them out to his leader.

"That is Birger, Halfdan's attendant," Freyja whispered from the side of her mouth. "The jarl pays him to make sure Halfdan does not create too much havoc."

"I'm not sure Birger is earning his money," Ronan murmured as Halfdan, without a word, snatched his weapons from Birger.

Fastening his belt, Halfdan turned his livid face to Ronan, spear in one hand, bow in the other. "You have insulted me," he snarled, raising the spear and driving it into the ground at Ronan's feet.

Ronan didn't flinch. His confidence in the blood rune's protection was absolute. "Funny," he mused, "but I thought it was the other way round."

"I demand satisfaction," he roared, spittle flying again.

"Do not meddle with that which is beyond your understanding," Freyja warned before Ronan could respond.

Halfdan ignored her, gesturing at Ronan with his bow. "Hólmganga," he growled. "In the town square on the third day, when the sun is at its peak"—his voice lowered and lips curled—"unless you are a coward."

Ronan raised a quizzical eyebrow at Freyja before he remembered he was somewhere in late ninth-century Scandinavia—Halfdan called it a duel, so Ronan knew that's exactly what it would be. Despite his blood rune, he shivered with apprehension.

"You have thrown down the gauntlet," Freyja said to Halfdan, "therefore, my friend has the choice of weapon."

The challenger's chest expanded like a barrel. "It matters not what he chooses, I will have his heart."

"You can try," Ronan taunted with hollow conviction. While he was almost a head taller than Halfdan, the latter was much broader, heavier and more muscular, with arms the size of Ronan's legs. Ronan knew nothing of swords and spears and, in a test of strength, he'd be lucky to survive a minute.

Halfdan's eyes burned; he poked the bow at Ronan again. "You will rue this day," he seethed. "But not for long because soon, your blood will stain the earth."

Ronan returned the gaze with a calmness he did not feel.

"And you," Halfdan barked, stabbing a beefy forefinger at Freyja, "you, I will have driven from your hovel, and from the lands of my father."

"The jarl will be interested to hear of this," said Freyja coolly. "Your father depends on my foresight to guide decisions of great importance." She lifted her staff at a tentative Halfdan, warning him in a low voice, "I can see that particular endeavour not ending well for you."

As the son of an earl, Halfdan was not used to being challenged, but Freyja's words made him pause. After a moment in which he appeared to subdue his hostility toward her, he strode forward, wrenching his spear from the ground, jabbing the point at Ronan. "On the third day, in the town square—"

"Yeah, yeah," Ronan interrupted, as if tired of boring repetition. "When the sun is at its peak. Unless I'm a coward. Oh, and"—he gave his best impression of a careless smirk—"something about having my heart, I think."

Cursing, Halfdan dropped into a half crouch, cocking his spear arm.

"Enough!" Freyja barked, knocking the spear tip down with a flash of her staff. "You have issued your challenge. Now go before I turn you into a goat."

A titter escaped the knot of hunters. Halfdan snarled, first at Freyja, then at Ronan, before spinning on his heel, shouldering his way through the group and stalking off. The others exchanged uncertain looks before gathering their game and trudging off in their leader's wake.

Ronan and Freyja watched them disappear into the trees.

"You have made an enemy there, young väktare," Freyja said.

"And you did your best to make it happen," he replied.

"You did not need help."

42

THE PREPARATION

A restive silence settled across the Home Stone's clearing. Noonday sunlight slanted through the trees, casting dapples on a scatter of dropped pine needles. Autumn leaves, long since shed and curled like ageing russet parchment, were snagged on tussock, rock or fallen limb. In places, the winds had dammed them in a hollow or behind a stick, creating a reservoir of decay that fed a field of mushrooms and an army of bugs. The sharp tang of the pine trees drowned the musty waft of decomposition. An occasional bird flitted through the edge of the forest and, off in the distance, a raven cawed mournfully.

The angle of the midday sun played havoc with Ronan's internal clock—he had to keep reminding himself that in those high northern latitudes, the autumn sun arced low in the southern sky.

"Could you really have turned him into a goat?" he asked after a while.

Freyja grinned. "It does not matter what I *can* do, only what they *think* I can do."

Ronan returned her grin. Freyja pulled a couple of pieces of dried beef from her pouch, passed one to him, and started munching on her own. The texture reminded Ronan of beef jerky, but without the spicy flavour; it knocked the rough edges off his hunger, but it kindled a thirst.

"You showed compassion earlier," Freyja said, as they strolled to the stream.

Ronan frowned. "When?"

"Before you told Halfdan to apologise to me, you made a move to release him. They will see that as a sign of weakness."

"Do you?"

"You are from a different time," was all she said.

She's got that right. Saoirse, his mum and Ruddi were waiting, more than a thousand years in the future; all he could think of was their safety. And, in response to his rising concern, came the reassuring warmth at the back of his skull.

Saoirse was smart, which made it easy to convince himself she was safe, and using her video of the assault to keep Egan in line. He discussed it—minus the recording—with Freyja as they slaked their thirsts in the chill, sweet water rushing between the boulders.

"If this Finnegan talks of your disappearance," she said, "his words will be dismissed as ramblings. And they may also add another layer to the local myths of mysterious happenings."

As they returned to the Home Stone, Ronan's thoughts flew to Doyle Farm. Fergal Gallagher would be settled in by now, and keeping Masters in check; why, then, could he not shake his mounting dread? Halfdan's challenge jumped back to his mind—how could he have forgotten that, even for a moment? Looking across at Freyja, he asked, "Why did you manoeuvre me into humiliating Halfdan?"

"You must establish a reputation so they do not treat you as a thrall," Freyja insisted.

"I don't give a damn what they think."

"Well, I do," Freyja snapped. "You are my blood, and I will not have them disrespecting you."

Taken aback by her passion, it was a moment before Ronan understood—she'd escalated the confrontation, silently manipulating him into shaming Halfdan in front of his companions, all for reputation. "Why does it matter?" he retorted.

"In my culture, personal reputation is everything," Freyja said, "which is why Halfdan challenged you to a duel."

But, in manoeuvring Ronan into creating a reputation, she'd unwittingly forced Halfdan down the path where he had no choice but to throw down a challenge. Ronan's flare of resentment dissolved into silence as he realised that his smart mouth was as much to blame as Freyja's signals and actions. "Can you help me prepare to meet Halfdan?"

Freyja shook her head. "If you use seiðr in a duel for honour, you invite the wrath of all."

"But I don't know any seiðr."

"Your blóð rún does," she said, "and when it whisks you from before his blade, all will see. You will be declared an outlaw to be hunted and hounded; you may never have the peace to learn what you need to know to return to your time. And, because of our association, I may also fare poorly in such a scenario ..." She stared at where the band of hunters had disappeared through the trees earlier.

"Why didn't you foresee all this when you manipulated me?" Ronan said, not bothering to hide his annoyance.

"I am not the Goddess," Freyja said, "merely her namesake."

Ronan's exasperation mounted. "So, I have to beat him fair and square?"

Freyja nodded, hair glowing in the sun as they settled back against the Home Stone's posts.

With the hólmganga filling Ronan's thoughts, there was no space for continuing discontent. "What's his weakest weapon, then?" he finally asked.

Freyja gave an exaggerated laugh. "He is a Norse aristocrat; he does not have a weak weapon."

"Well, how do I stop him defeating me?"

"Defeating?" she said, as if surprised by the word. "Halfdan will not aim to defeat you, my Ronan, he wants you dead at his feet."

Ronan knew his blood rune would protect him—it had already saved him from certain death, twice—but he still didn't fancy being skewered by a spear or sword. Freyja studied his face as he sat there, staring unseeing at the black boulder, searching for a solution. "Maybe it'll be best if I just apologise to him."

She scoffed. "If you deny Halfdan his opportunity to restore his reputation, you will be branded a coward and beaten ... much worse than being." There was no doubt what she thought of the idea, but she wasn't finished. "Your blóð rún will only heim you to prevent death, not serious harm." Freyja fixed him with a sober stare, then added wryly, "The gods have a mischievous bent, and they do not want you to lose touch with your mortality."

Digesting her words, Ronan stared up at the runic inscription on the beam. "So, it's better to be killed than badly injured?"

Freyja gave a single nod, saying, "Fear not, young väktare, Halfdan wants to see you dead."

"But I don't even want to hurt him, let alone kill him." Ronan's stomach churned at the thought.

"Then you are doomed," Freyja said, lips firm. "Halfdan has no such qualms ... he will kill you, or die trying, and greet Valhalla with open arms if he wins honour in death. We Norse welcome death in battle; we know a place in Valhalla awaits those who die with honour."

"Is that what you believe?"

Freyja placed a palm on her breast. "It is what I know."

Ronan let that declaration hang while considering a sequence of potential responses, dismissing them one by one. Finally, and as neutrally as possible, he asked, "How does true of mind and pure of heart fit with murder?"

Freyja sighed. "Sending a foe to Valhalla is not murder when done in battle, and the hólmganga is a battle ... for honour ... think like a Norseman."

"I'm not Norse," said Ronan testily, "and I'm not a fighter."

As if unsure whether to chastise or soothe, Freyja considered him in silence, then said, "The power of the blóð rún is great; trust in it and there is nothing you cannot do."

Even if that were the case, he still needed a plan. "What happens if I choose the bow?"

Freyja dipped her head, eyes glinting. "That is the obvious choice for an archer."

Ronan fought to stop his jaw dropping. "How do you know that?"

She winked, tapping her temple with a forefinger.

After several seconds of fruitless whirring, his mind settled on the fingertips of his right hand, calloused from the bowstring. "You saw my fingers," he accused.

Freyja smiled serenely.

"I'm a bowyer and fletcher as well," Ronan said, pride creeping into his voice.

"Are you?" Freyja's eyebrows lifted.

With a quick nod, Ronan said, "My stepfather smashed the bow and arrows I bought, so I made my own."

"You are full of surprises, young väktare."

While he smiled at the compliment, Ronan had more important things on his mind. "So, what is the process for a hólmganga with bows?"

"Well, the jarl will set the rules, but it is customary for the hólmganga to continue until one cedes, is incapacitated, or blood touches the ground."

Ronan swallowed, craving to be anywhere but where he was.

"It is also customary," Freyja said, "for participants to get five arrows to fire at each other, in turns. Then, if they are still standing, they can use their opponent's arrows until one prevails."

Taking a deep breath, Ronan closed his eyes, concentrating on his rune's warmth. Despite Freyja's efforts, he did not have a good feeling about the duel. "If he kills me, my blóð rún will heim me back here to the Heim Steinn, won't it?"

Freyja nodded, eyes narrowing. "What happened to the confident väktare who humbled that rascal?"

"I was high on the power of my blóð rún," Ronan admitted, "... in a different place."

"Go there again and you will prevail," Freyja told him. "Now, let us indulge tomorrow with tomorrow's concerns ... today you need to learn."

43

THE LESSONS

There were still several hours of daylight remaining. The sun cast a halo around the Home Stone, bathing Ronan's face with warmth that drooped his eyelids and seeped through his skull, merging with that of the blood rune. The post was hard on his back, and the pine needles soft beneath him as peace and contentment duelled with trepidation and anxiety, backward and forward across the town square of his mind. He didn't want to fight Halfdan; neither did he fancy the prospect of being grievously beaten. He'd much rather be killed—quicker, cleaner, almost painless. But he also didn't want to make life difficult or dangerous for Freyja, or damage his chances of learning everything he needed to get safely back to his own time. Ronan was caught between a rock and a hard place—an image of the Home Stone in front and the post behind, slowly squeezing together, made him laugh.

"It is good to have pleasant thoughts, Ronan."

Freyja's use of his name was like a warm coat, yet, despite her proximity, he felt alone. While they shared a blood connection, they were strangers in so many ways—customs, beliefs, values. He longed to hear his mother's voice, and he ached for the sparkle of Saoirse's liquid eyes through that veil of hair, and the tingle of her touch. And he missed slumping on the couch with Ruddi, battling video-game monsters and sharing brotherly jokes.

"Have you left me, young väktare?"

Ronan snapped from his brief reverie. "What? Oh, sorry. What did you say?"

"I said it is good to have pleasant thoughts."

"What? Oh, yes, I was thinking of Mum and Ruddi, and Saoirse."

"Well," she scolded mildly, "if you pay attention, you can return to them sooner than if your mind takes to wandering. We have much to cover."

"Can we start with how I ended up in The Land of the Gaels when my stepfather shot me?"

"Very well," Freyja said. "It will help explain a key part of what is needed to flytja to a place and time of your choosing."

Ronan leant forward.

"But be warned," she said sternly, "because I will only tell you some of what is required; if you try to flytja before you learn the last step properly, you will not arrive where you wish."

"Like my father?"

"Exactly. Now, from what you have told me, you were running with this little book when you fell into mortal peril."

Ronan nodded.

"Well," Freyja continued, "at the instant your blóð rún snatched you from death, your thoughts must have been filled with the book, which is why it heimmed you to where the book was made."

"But," Ronan said with a frown, "I was only thinking of escaping, and the notebook wasn't made in the field where I woke up."

"Then you must have a connection to the notebook that I do not understand"—she frowned—"but the field makes sense, because the blóð rún will always set you down in a safe place where you can recover from the umrót. And did not the daughter of the little book's maker assist you?"

"Saoirse? Yes." Saying her name triggered a fresh wave of loneliness and longing.

Freyja smiled knowingly. "You will see her soon enough."

"How can you be so sure?"

"Because your lineage from me on both sides gives you great affinity with your blóð rún and, through it, the Heim Steinn. Never has a rún bonded with such speed and strength, and you, my Ronan, have the potential to build that into great power and do much good in the world. The question is, are you willing?"

Freyja gazed deep into Ronan's eyes as she spoke, as if peering into the hidden recesses of his mind. He squirmed.

"What's the difference between a heim and a flytja?" he asked at once, wanting to feel less vulnerable.

"A heim is when the rún initiates the travel, *usually* bringing you here to the Heim Steinn, which is why it is called a heim." Freyja's tone became more businesslike, distant. "A flytja is when the väktare initiates travel to a particular place and time of their choosing. Generally, both cause the umrót in equal measure."

"Did I say something wrong?" Ronan said.

"Why do you ask?"

"Because your vibe changed."

Freyja's face softened; she gave a throaty chuckle. "What a strange word ... vibe."

"I'm serious," Ronan insisted.

"I can see that," she said, sobering. "I was trying to see the seiðmann you will become, but I could not, and it troubled me."

"Why?"

"Why could I not see, or why did it trouble me?"

Ronan clicked his tongue and gave her side-eye. "Both."

"You have a powerful mind, Ronan, very much like Astryd. And it troubles me because I like to see ... it is my duty."

Silence stretched between them; Ronan was determined not to break it.

Eventually, Freyja said, "I saw you close your mind to me ... I was annoyed."

"It's my mind," Ronan snapped, stronger than he intended.

Freyja reached out, dropping a placating hand on his forearm. "I am sorry, I should not have intruded. Next time, I will seek your invitation."

"Okay," Ronan said, appeased, but unsure if he would say yes.

After another brief silence, Freya said, "Before we start homeward, I shall run through the laws of the Heim Steinn and its rúnar."

"Can we go back to heimming first?" he asked. Without waiting for permission, he continued, "You said that both a heim and a flytja will usually cause similar umrót. When don't they?" Ronan's stomach was already somersaulting—if there was a chance of going through even worse umrót, he must know what to avoid.

"There are three circumstances in which a rún will heim," Freyja began. "Haetta, you have experienced twice already."

Ronan's body twinged as he relived the impact of both the bullet and the vehicle.

"The second circumstance is fundur, which is encountering your younger self if you flytja to an earlier time in your life. The rún will not allow fundur, and will heim you a short distance, but still within the same time."

"Like your flytja before?" Everything appeared to involve umrót; his stomach tumbled.

"Yes. In which case, the umrót is nothing, the journey is too short." Freyja finished with a knowing smile.

"Phew," Ronan said with a lopsided grin, "I thought you couldn't read my mind."

Freyja tapped the side of her head and winked.

Ronan was immediately serious again. As anxious as he was to leave as soon as possible, there was so much to learn. "And what's the third circumstance?"

"Trufla," she said solemnly, "we spoke of it earlier. You must not meddle with the past; the rún will not permit it."

Squinting at her, Ronan said, "What, exactly, constitutes meddling?"

Freyja gazed into the depths of the Home Stone. "Only the gods decide that." Glancing at Ronan, she added, "In essence, do not try to change the course of history."

"So," Ronan said, "no trufla."

"Correct. However, should you journey beyond your own time, you may shape events as your heart desires and your head allows."

As Ronan mulled all she'd told him, a great weight lifted from him —it was now clear that he couldn't have saved his father; had he tried, the rune would've whisked him elsewhere to prevent meddling. But would meeting his mother with his foetal self in her womb have constituted fundur? He doubted it, but wasn't sure.

"So, if there's no haetta, I don't trufla, and there's no risk of fundur, can I stay in any time for as long as I like?"

"You are a curious one, young väktare, and it is good that you wish to know," Freyja said. "How long you can stay in a time is determined by how you travelled to that time. If the rún heims you, there is no time limit; however, if you flytja, you may stay no longer than nine days in any time other than your own."

"Why nine?"

Freyja shrugged. "Why are there nine realms? ... and nine rúnar?"

"What if I want to stay longer?"

"Then you must relinquish your blóð rún."

The sadness that crept into Freyja's eyes reminded Ronan of her own connection to Ireland. "Why did Astryd and Sigrid choose to live in The Land of the Gaels?" he asked quietly.

Freyja sighed. "After hearing their father's stories of the beauty of the land, they decided to flytja there to see for themselves." The smallest of tears gathered in the corner of her eye. "They met two brothers, fell in love, and ..." Her eyes grew distant. "They came home briefly to tell me of their intentions ... I have not seen them since." She stared at her hands fiddling absently with her pouch.

Her loss hollowed out his gut, and he could find no words to comfort her. To divert her thoughts, Ronan said, "What are the laws of the Heim Steinn you were going to teach me?"

Freyja met his eyes, face brightening. "But you already know them, young väktare."

Ronan couldn't recall her stating any laws. He frowned, searching the inscription above him for a clue, replaying their conversations in his mind.

After a long silence, Freyja said, "What do you think they might be?"

Eyes locked on the last line of the poem, Ronan said hesitantly, "The rún only bonds to the worthy?"

Freyja gave a tiny inclination of her head.

Having got one right, Ronan's confidence grew. "The rún will heim if there's haetta, trufla, or fundur because it will not permit them. The umrót is the same for both a heim and a flytja." He pondered a moment before continuing, "And while you must remain true of mind and pure of heart, it's in the sense of Norse laws and traditions."

Freyja nodded, clearly pleased. "What you said about the umrót is only my advice to you, not part of the law. And the last one is an expansion on the first one you mentioned. But you have learnt well, my Ronan."

They sat in silence, weak sunlight slanting into their faces, Ronan thinking of umrót, Freyja looking contented. As soon as the thought struck him, Ronan blurted, "I can deliver a message to your daughters."

Freyja searched his eyes, shaking her head. "You offer much, my Ronan. Not only will there be strong umrót, it will take considerable knowledge and skill to flytja to the correct place and time."

"Then teach me and I'll practise."

44

THE ATTENDANT

The sun was low when they finally left the black boulder. Apart from occasional short walks to the stream to quench thirst, or into the surrounding forest to relieve themselves—'rustle some leaves', as Freyja put it—they had sat there all afternoon.

It seemed an age since Ronan had stirred from the umrót to catch his first glimpse of the burnished locks of his great-grandfather, many times removed, but it was only that morning. In the meantime, Ronan and Freyja had two lengthy sessions at the shelter, punctuated by the run-in with Halfdan and his band of hunters. Besides the chunky breakfast stew, he'd only eaten a single piece of dried beef; hunger gnawed at his hollow stomach.

Although a long day, it had been a productive one. Piece by piece, the mystery of the Home Stone and its blood runes unravelled. Layer by layer, Freyja unwrapped the secrets of how to harness the tremendous power they held. Yet, Ronan felt they had only scratched the surface; he needed to learn much more than he had so far, and said so.

"Most of the knowledge that makes a great seiðmann comes from experience," Freyja told him as he followed her across the stream and through the forest toward the longhouse. "And being able to flytja with precision is central to everything, so we shall concentrate on that tomorrow."

"I have to practise for the hólmganga," Ronan reminded her.

"If you are not already a proficient archer, I fear it is too late."

"But your bows are different to what I'm used to ... I have to practise with what I'm going to use, so I know its ... vibe." Ronan liked the way the word kindled a smile on Freyja's face.

"Perhaps Sten will allow you to practise with his hunting bow. I shall ask. However, you cannot take your own weapon to the hólm-ganga. You must use what is provided."

"That hardly sounds fair ... they could give me anything."

"In theory, yes ... in practice, both combatants choose from the weapons in an allotted space, usually a pile in the area chosen for the hólmganga."

The sunset glow came early to the forest as the sun dipped toward a mountain in the southwest. While golden light still spangled the tree-tops, at path level, shadows gathered, the air grew chill. From the corner of his eye, Ronan caught the hairy flit of a squirrel's tail. When he turned his head for a better look, he thudded into Freyja's stationary back, jolting her forward. Before he could apologise, she held up a silencing hand.

Through the thinning trees ahead, he saw the longhouse, its lazy spiral of smoke rising into the sun's last rays. An armed man approached the dwelling from the direction of the town, the spear tip's lustre catching the soft light. "It's Birger," Ronan said as Freyja squinted beside him. He sensed the tension drain from her.

"You have the eyes of a hawk," she whispered. "I wonder what he wants?" With that, she strode into the clearing. "Heill, Birger," she called, acknowledging him with a short lift of her staff.

The lad halted, eyes darting. "Heill, Freyja ... traveller."

After Ronan politely returned the wish for health, he eyed Birger with suspicion.

Drawing up in front of the newcomer, Freyja gave him a gracious smile. "How may I assist you, my friend?"

"I come to speak with the traveller," Birger replied, visibly surprised by the friendly greetings. He planted the butt of his spear on the ground by his right foot and turned to Ronan. "The jarl wishes to know your choice of weapon."

Ronan pursed his lips as though giving the matter considerable thought. "That's a tough question ... I'll need to consult the völva"—he hooked his head toward Freyja—"and I may not decide until the hólm-ganga." Ronan wanted to keep Halfdan in the dark for as long as possible. "But if I chose the spear, who'll provide the weapon?"

Interest flickered in Birger's eyes. "The spear is a good choice," he said, hefting his own. "The jarl will provide a selection from which to choose."

"Good," said Ronan. "And he'll get my decision at the town square."

Birger made as if to respond, but stopped.

"What is it, Birger?" Freyja prompted in a firm, school-teacher tone.

"But that is in three days! The jarl must make preparations ..."

A sardonic smile played on Ronan's lips. "And I'm sure Halfdan would love to know too, so he can prepare."

Birger's face coloured.

Ronan gave a single, unyielding shake of his head. "Once I've consulted, and made my choice, the jarl will know ... at the hólmganga."

"Very well," Birger responded. He looked from one to the other, shifting his weight from foot to foot.

Freyja's patience evaporated. "Spit it out, Birger!"

"I should not be telling you this," he said to Ronan, "but I do not agree"—he dropped his voice—"Halfdan means to kill you."

A frisson of apprehension danced across Ronan's skin. "Now that's a surprise," he responded with heavy irony. Silently, he considered the lad. Birger was about his own age and build, but shorter. Unlike Halfdan, he appeared to have a few scruples.

"Be wary"—Birger gave Ronan a hard stare—"he has henbane in his veins."

Ronan shrugged, feigning disinterest.

Birger's bewilderment was clear. "I have said as much as I can, and more than I should." With a curt bow to Freyja, he added, "Remember this." She dipped her head in acknowledgement. Birger grasped his spear, and with a final glance to Ronan, turned and strode toward Kaupang.

"What's henbane?" Ronan asked as they watched the shadows engulf Halfdan's attendant.

Freyja reached into her pouch, bringing out a pinch of small, shrivelled, brown seeds. "Too much kills, but a tiny amount helps healing, while larger amounts induce a fearful fighting rage. And grim sickness, I might add. It makes warriors bear-strong and fearless ... Berserkers."

"I know what Birger means," Ronan said. "Did you see Halfdan's eyes when he couldn't free himself?"

Freyja nodded, contemplating the point where Birger disappeared. "That was a fair warning," she said at last, before turning to the door of her longhouse. "Come, my Ronan, there is a bow to find."

45

THE PRACTICE

Beyond the longhouse door, they found Sten standing over the stew pot above an indifferent fire. A large white carrot disappeared before his flashing blade until only a tuft of green remained in his beefy hand. That, too, went into the pot. Further dexterous strokes demolished a small cabbage in much the same way.

Closing the door and setting her staff aside, Freyja called through the smoky air, "Hello, husband."

"Hello, wife," he returned, assailing the contents of the pot with a broad wooden spoon, splatters of thick, brown liquid sizzling into the coals and catching in his fiery beard. Fierce concentration etched his face as he slurped a taste.

Ronan wasn't sure whether interrupting this particular chef was wise, but for the sake of exercising his smart mouth, he took the risk. "Hello, Grandfather."

Sten spluttered into the spoon, spraying its contents across the pot and into the fire, setting the coals hissing again. The utensil landed in the stew with a heavy plop, sending more droplets into the beard. Freyja clamped her lips and turned away, but the quivering of her body couldn't be hidden.

"What did you call me, Lamb?" Sten's chin jutted pugnaciously.

"Grandfather," Ronan repeated, suppressing a smirk.

Sten puffed out his chest, saying, "I'm still young enough to best you."

Ronan spread his hands. "But you're my grandfather."

Sten chewed on air. By this time, Freyja was chortling.

"What?" Sten sputtered.

Tears streamed down Freyja's cheeks. "Oh, husband, the look on your face is worth a piece of silver." Still shaking, she sat, pressing hands to her sides.

Sten's eyes darted from one to the other like a cornered forest cat.

"My mother is descended from Astryd," Ronan explained, deadpan, "and my father from Sigrid."

Between tremors, Freyja managed to nod. "It is true, husband," she gasped.

"Humph!" he said to the stew pot as he regathered the spoon, licking first the handle, then his fingers, before resuming the stirring. "Well, you don't favour either of them." His tone was curt, but the beard at the corner of his mouth twitched as he added, "Although you do have Astryd's clever tongue."

"He will need more than Astryd's tongue," Freyja said. "He needs a good bow to practise with." She related the encounter with the hunters, from Halfdan's capture by the Home Stone to his hólmganga challenge and, finally, Birger's warning.

The threat of Halfdan drove an instant embrace of grandfatherhood by Sten—Ronan soon had in front of him an elegant recurve hunting bow of yew, antler and sinew. Curled beside it was a sturdy, three-ply string of waxed hemp. The weapon was a twin to the one carried by the black-haired girl in the hunting party, and she had bagged several rabbits and a squirrel. Not only was she an excellent archer, she possessed a great bow.

Hefting the exquisite instrument stirred an itch to string it and loose arrows—it was a bird coiled for flight, balanced and alive. "Wow," he breathed. "I'd love to meet the bowyer who made this beauty."

Sten looked chuffed. Freyja raised an eyebrow at him and said to Ronan, "He also builds boats."

Absorbed by the craftsmanship in his hand, Ronan took a while to register the words. "I'd like to meet hi—" He flicked a quick glance at

Freyja before turning widening eyes to Sten, who gave a snort and hurried into the gloom at the end of the longhouse, mumbling something about arrows.

Boats, the house, the Home Stone shelter, and now this bow. Ronan was awed by the talent in Sten's compact frame and the dexterity and skill in those stubby fingers.

"Wow!" Ronan said again. "This is a real beauty." He caressed the sweep of antler along the bow's belly, fondled the sinew-covered back, and sensed the power in the core of dark yew sandwiched between. As he rotated it, he marvelled at the elegance of the design, the strength and precision of construction, and the quality of the finish.

Sten returned from the shadows with a cylindrical leather bag full of arrows. "Here," he said gruffly, handing the quiver to Ronan, "you can use these to practise."

"And I suggest you do your practising in here, away from the prying eyes of Halfdan's spies," advised Freyja. "The less he knows, the better."

"But this room isn't long enough," Ronan complained, judging the space barely a dozen metres long and five wide.

"Bah!" Sten's bellow gave Ronan a start. "If Halfdan means to kill you, he will be closer than that," he said, stretching his arms wide, indicating the length of his home.

Before Ronan could respond, Sten scooped up a blackened stone dish, small, chunky and brimming with thin oil reeking of fish, wick sagging over one corner. After lighting the lamp from the fire's rim, he bore it purposefully down the room, setting it on a chest-high sill, its determined flickering taking the edge off the gloom.

On his return, Sten scrutinised Ronan as the latter tensioned the bow between his lower legs, dropping the string's loop into its notch. "You do know your way around a bow," he said. Freyja merely smiled.

Ronan remained silent and selected an arrow. "I'll try not to spill your lamp," he said.

"My lamp is safe," Sten declared. "I vouch you will not make the flame tremble."

The bow was light in Ronan's hands, and he was warming to his host's humour. "I'll make it more than tremble," he said, fitting an arrow, drawing the string to his chin. Exhaling the last of his breath, he made a minute adjustment to his aim, and relaxed his fingers. The taut string zinged away, sending the arrow humming the length of the longhouse and thunking into the wall near the lamp. A little low and to the right. The wick burned steadily.

"Hah!" cried Sten, raising a fist in delight as the flame maintained its steady flicker. "Try again, Lamb."

"I will, Grandfather," Ronan quipped, reaching for a second arrow. Freyja's contented smile broadened.

"But, not bad for a first attempt," Sten admitted, stroking his beard. "And likely good enough," he added with a chuckle, "for Halfdan is a sizable target."

"That," said Ronan, fitting the arrow, "was nowhere near good enough." He aimed for the head of the previous arrow. Zing, hum and thunk! The flame remained unmoved, but the second arrow lay close along the shaft of the first.

Sten clapped with delight. "You missed again, young Lamb."

"We shall see, old Grandfather." Ronan selected another arrow. This time, he changed his target. The arrow blurred through the air, plunging the extremity of the room into darkness.

"By Odin," breathed Sten, eyes wide. Freyja smiled knowingly; Ronan grinned with satisfaction.

"This is the perfect bow for hunting rabbits and squirrels," said Ronan, rotating the weapon in admiration and thinking of the huntress with the black hair.

"Her name is Frida," Freyja said as if reading his mind, "and yes, Sten made her bow as well. My husband is a talented man and a good provider." She wrapped Sten in an affectionate gaze.

Sten harrumphed and strode down the room with a second guttering lamp. Its yellow glow revealed the third arrow laying across the top of the extinguished wick. He wriggled all three arrows from the wall, re-lit the first lamp, placing the second beside it on the sill. Handing two arrows to Ronan, he said, "Darken the longhouse with these and the bow is yours."

Zing, thunk! One lamp out. The bow was part of Ronan's arm, the arrow an extension of his eyes. Zing, thunk! Again, darkness.

Sten huffed. "I have never seen such mastery, Lamb."

Ronan dipped his head in acknowledgement. "Thank you, Grandfather. And I have never drawn such a fine bow."

"Humph."

"And I practise a lot."

"Practice is one thing"—Sten scratched his cheek—"the artistry of the gods is another."

"My ability must have come down through the generations."

Sten's chest swelled. "If you lose the hólmganga, Lamb, it will not be from lack of skill."

"From what I've been told, I can't take this bow with me ... the bow the jarl provides may not be as good."

"Lamb, it does not matter what bow they give you." He placed a hand on Ronan's shoulder. "Now, we must plan how to use your skills wisely."

46

THE TRAINING

For the next two days, Ronan was drilled without break—by day, it was Freyja; by night, Sten. Each morning, when Sten went off to build his boats, Freyja took Ronan to the Home Stone for instruction on the foundation of flytja; each evening, after Ronan had sent a volley of arrows the length of the longhouse, he and Sten would sit round the fire, heads together, discussing strategies for the hólmganga.

On the first morning of the hólmganga countdown, Ronan realised the enormity of his task. He and Freyja were at the Home Stone with Freyja drilling him mercilessly. "The primary skill for flytja," she instructed, "is emptying the mind."

Training his mind to block out the cacophony of cluttering thoughts seemed an impossibility to Ronan—his head boiled with flashes of Saoirse, his mother, Ruddi and Grandpa Paddy, all swirling around Masters, Finnegan and Halfdan. The harder he tried, the greater his exasperated sweat.

"You must be able to enter ró," Freyja said patiently. "You cannot flytja without mastering the empty mind."

Contemplating the required tranquillity, Ronan sat, legs crossed, eyes closed, back against the reassurance of the Home Stone, absorbing the calmness of Freyja's voice.

"Block out your surroundings ... empty your mind ..." Fresh

thoughts kept breaking across her words like waves on a reef. "Focus on the warmth of your blóð rún," she crooned. "Feel it soaking up those thoughts you do not need. Feel the ró ... surrender to it. Focus on the warmth ..."

On the verge of nodding off, Ronan's head jerked, his mind opened, and all the clutter rushed back in. After an age, he threw his hands in the air. "It's no use," he said despondently, "I can't do it."

"Relax, my Ronan," Freyja soothed, "ró comes easily to no one; it takes concerted effort and much practice."

Again, Ronan closed his eyes, concentrating on Freyja's purr. Eventually, the intrusive thoughts lost their shape, seeping from his mind, merging with the vapour of her murmur, floating him into tranquillity.

Excitement exploded like fireworks into a tangle of thoughts. Ronan sighed, opened his eyes and said, "I think I might've done it, but only for a moment."

"That is good," Freyja said, inclining her head in acknowledgement. "You progress well, but you must learn to stay in ró to flytja accurately."

Ronan leant forward. "How do I do that?"

"The same way you became a great archer."

"Huh?"

"Practice, my Ronan. Practice."

By the beginning of the second day, Ronan was repeatedly slipping into the required trance-like state of beguiling calm, although he had trouble maintaining it—his date with Halfdan in the Kaupang town square the next day was dominating his thoughts.

Both he and Sten agreed, as did Freyja, that banking on his bowmanship was a fair strategy, for Halfdan appeared a poor shot—or a lazy hunter. Their strategy, however, was very thin on detail because Sten said only the jarl knew what the rules of engagement would be, and wouldn't announce them until the hólmganga.

"There is no purpose to your worry, young väktare," Freyja said when Ronan shared his troubled thoughts. "What will happen, will happen ... the gods will take care of it."

They were munching on a handful of juicy berries and a couple of tiny, tart apples, Ronan with his back to the Home Stone, Freyja leaning against a post.

"Right," Ronan said slowly, demolishing half an apple in a single bite, then regarding her through narrowed eyes. "Have you seen it?"

Freyja shook her head. "It is fine to foretell the future of others, and call me unwise if you want, but I do not wish to know my own destiny. Whether I am soon to be banished is a matter for the gods. However, I am confident you will prevail if you enter the hólmganga with a clear head."

Ronan popped the last morsel of apple into his mouth, searching her face as he chewed. He laid his head back against the comfort of the Home Stone and stared unseeing at the inscription under the roof. "But how can you be sure?" he asked, letting his eyelids droop.

Freyja considered him for a moment. "I have a feel for these things," she said.

Silence embraced them: Ronan was weary, Freyja content. But Ronan's mind wouldn't rest. Without opening his eyes, he said, "When I lean against the Heim Steinn, why doesn't it capture my blóð rún?"

Freyja smiled. "Because the Heim Steinn knows that blóð rún is now bound to you. Even though they do not snap together, they remain connected. Fear not, should you encounter haetta, you will be brought here."

Ronan opened an eye. "Are you reassuring me for tomorrow?"

"You will not need it tomorrow," Freyja responded with certainty. "Now, we must resume the training. While you have learnt much, you do not yet have the required grasp on ró."

Ronan dragged his other eye open and made a slight bow. "As you wish, Sensei."

"What is 'sen-sigh'?" she asked, frowning.

"Sorry ... 'teacher' ... karate teacher, to be precise."

Freyja remained puzzled. "What is 'k-rah-tay'?"

"Sorry," Ronan repeated, "my brain is a bit foggy at the moment. Karate is a form of unarmed combat."

"Interesting," Freyja said, stroking her chin. She glanced at the shadow thrown by the post and became animated and businesslike. "Sharpen your mind, young väktare, we still have an afternoon of training."

For several hours, Ronan practised entering ró and holding it for as long as possible. By the time the sun was halfway to the southwest mountain, he was maintaining ró for many minutes at a time.

"You have progressed remarkably, my Ronan." Pride garnished Freyja's words. "As I have said before, you will make a great seiðmann, but"—she wagged a finger—"do not get a swollen head."

Regardless, Ronan glowed.

"You will be able to flytja accurately far sooner than I expected; I have never seen anyone learn so quickly." In an exaggerated whisper, she added, "It must be the double lineage of my blood."

"And the quality of the teacher," Ronan said, poker faced.

"Of course," she said, and they both smiled. "Come"—she climbed to her feet—"it is time for your first attempt."

Ronan hesitated. "Are you sure?" he said, thinking of his father lost somewhere in time.

"It will be a short, easy flytja," she assured him. "Come," she repeated, and set off through the trees to the nearby stream.

Freyja halted by the gurgle of water swirling round rocks. "Now," she said, anticipation sparkling, "picture the Heim Steinn shelter"—she pointed—"relax and enter ró with that image firmly in your mind."

"But how do I get the time right?" Again, Ronan thought of his father.

"Unless you instruct otherwise, a flytja will not leave your current time. Now, exclude all other thoughts ... allow your destination to fill your mind."

Ronan shook his arms loose, closed his eyes, used the image of the Home Stone shelter, like a trowel, to push everything else from his mind. He became lighter, drifting into ró with his only thought the Home Stone shelter. The air gave a quick intake of breath, and he was gone.

Freyja clapped with delight and marched off toward the clearing. As she emerged from the trees, she froze. There was no Ronan. She spun, eyes desperately probing every shadow. She was alone.

"Ronan, oh, Ronan!" she cried. "No!"

47

THE INTRUDERS

Nothing stirred round the small clearing: the trees were silent, the birds still. The polished obsidian of the Home Stone lay like the freshly deposited egg of a gigantic, prehistoric creature.

Freyja cast about wildly. "I thought you were ready," she lamented. "I have failed you, my Ronan, just as I failed your father. Oh, Ronan! Where have you gone? What have I done?"

At the sound of her mounting distress, Ronan sprang up from behind the Home Stone where he'd been lying flat.

Freyja spun; her shoulders dropped as she sighed with relief. Then her eyes flamed and her chest swelled. "Do not ever do that to me again," she blazed, stomping toward him, thumping her staff into the ground with each stride.

Ronan's face fell as he stepped backward, the elation of his first flytja evaporating under the implosion of his backfired prank. "I'm sorry, Freyja." he said, voice shrinking.

"As you should be." His apology had not softened her stony features. "You caused me immense alarm."

"I'm sorry," he repeated, eyes downcast. "I didn't think it would frighten you."

"You simply did not think!" Freyja snapped. Her expression collapsed and she dropped her staff, wrapping him in a fierce embrace.

"I feared I had lost you," she groaned, sudden tears sliding down her cheeks.

Staring across the top of her head, Ronan returned her hug, thankful she couldn't see his burning shame.

"Having you here has been"—she sniffed into his chest—"like having a fragment of Astryd and Sigrid around."

Freyja's distress was heavy on Ronan, and he was only going to add to it when he left. For a moment, he wondered whether she might scheme to prevent him leaving, but as soon as the thought formed, he banished it, feeling even more guilt. He tightened his arms, as much to ease remorse as to convey sincerity.

"I know you must leave when the time is right," Freyja sobbed, "but I wish to bid you a proper farewell. Please promise me that, my Ronan."

"I promise, Grandmother," Ronan said past a lump in his throat. The barriers of time, distance and cultures melted away; in that moment, Freyja was his grandmother.

Pushing him to arm's length, she scrutinised him. Her tear-tracked face twisted the knife of repentance in his heart. "Now," she said, flicking back to teacher mode, but with an edge of retribution to her voice, "you are going to flytja to our fireside, count the number of onions hanging from the rafter, then flytja back here and tell me."

The abrupt change made Ronan think of Saoirse. How he longed for the smiling curve of her lips, the playful sparkle in those amber eyes, the waft of apple from her hair.

"Ronan."

Freyja's voice cut through his thoughts like an echo. "Sorry" he said. "What was that about onions?"

"Where is your mind, young väktare?" She frowned. "Perhaps you are not ready for this."

"No! I'm ready ... I just got a bit distracted ... it won't happen again ... the onions?"

Freyja considered him for a moment, before repeating her instructions.

"Right," he said, checking off his to-do list, "fireside, onions, rafter, return."

Freyja eyed him doubtfully. Ronan shut her out, turning his mind inward, feeling himself drifting into ró. The air inhaled, drawing him inward to nothing.

Next moment, he was standing in Freyja's home, beside the fire pit where this morning's logs had burnt down to dull embers. Even though the turbulence was longer and stronger than his first flytja, it was minute—a few tumbles and spins and it was done.

Ronan found the onions at the opposite end of the longhouse to his target lamps, dangling from a rafter like a bunch of enormous papery grapes. Halfway through counting, he froze at a furtive noise outside the building. Padding through the gloom, he flattened himself behind the bulky wooden door fashioned with the same skill as the rest of the dwelling.

"Are you sure there is no one?" a deep voice whispered.

"I checked every corner just now," insisted another male voice.

Ronan braced his feet. Clandestine footfalls floated beneath the door; the lifted latch clicked like steel on flint. Pulse quickening, Ronan coiled his legs. The door—a solid structure made to thwart chill winds and shameless vagabonds—swung slowly. As a broad, dark-fuzzed face poked through the gap to peer round, Ronan threw his shoulder against the timber, driving forward with all his leg power, crunching the intruder's head into the door frame.

As Ronan stepped clear, a dead weight fell against the door, flinging it wide, and the unconscious bulk of Halfdan collapsed into the room. Beyond the threshold, a wide-eyed Birger gaped from his companion's body to the shape in the shadows.

"You're not doing such a good job of keeping him out of trouble," Ronan said wryly as he emerged.

Birger jumped back, dropping a bundle of dried grass and twigs, holding up his palms. He glanced from Ronan's set face to the kindling at his feet. His guilty cringe was the only confirmation Ronan needed that the pair had come intent on arson.

Ronan took another pace forward. Birger spread his fingers wider. "I could not turn his mind from this course." He shook his head in desperation. "And the jarl has me pledged to remain by his side."

"Lay down with dogs, you get up with fleas," Ronan said impassively, nudging Halfdan's inert form with a toe. "Now get this worthless piece of shit out of here."

Birger stared at his charge. "But how ...?"

"I don't care, Birger"—Ronan's fury bubbled—"but do it now! Drag him all the way back to Kaupang for all I care, but get him out of here so I can shut out your treachery."

Wordlessly, Birger grasped Halfdan's ankles, dragging him like a sack of potatoes from the hard-packed earth of the entrance.

"Find another job, Birger, and never enter this longhouse again."

Head down, Birger pulled Halfdan, bit-by-bit, away from the door.

"Do you hear me?" Ronan's voice was low, sodden with fury.

Birger struggled to meet Ronan's eye. "Yes, traveller."

48

THE SEIÐR

Ronan threw the door closed, slumping against it, breathing heavily, limbs shaking. Whether from fury, fear or reaction, he wasn't sure, but he hoped he hadn't just made life harder for Freyja and Sten.

Thinking of Freyja, Ronan knew she would be worrying that he'd failed the longer flytja, or was playing another prank. He tried to relax and empty his mind, but there was too much charge in his veins. While he'd bluffed his way through the confrontation, it had left him shaken. This assertive, assured and fearless person he now seemed to become when facing adversity felt like a stranger. It was as if there were two Ronans—the one who spent years copping whatever his stepfather threw at him, and the one who was now väktare and seiðmann. As well as changing his life, the blóð rún had transformed his character and enhanced his skills—until a few days ago, he could never shoot out a lamp wick at will.

Pushing away from the door, he shook his limbs, trying to ease the tension for another attempt at ró. But before he could take his second deep breath, the air near the fire pit gave a sharp sigh as Freyja unfolded fluidly from a vertical slit in the fabric of the moment. She was walking toward him before her legs had fully formed, as though emerging from a thick ground mist.

"I feared, again, that I had misjudged—" She froze at the look on his face. "What has happened?"

After listening to a quick recount of the confrontation, Freyja pondered for a moment, before saying, "Flytja into the edge of the forest. Come out when you hear my voice, then follow my lead."

Without question, Ronan nodded, trying to blank his racing mind.

A loud finger-click in his face snapped his focus to Freyja. "Ronan, you must learn to enter ró amid great distraction. Now close your eyes, breathe deeply, merge your mind with your blóð rún and picture the trees. Go!"

It felt like an age before he became weightless ... thistledown floating on the breeze. A brief agitation and he was surrounded by trees, the longhouse visible between rough-barked trunks. From a nearby branch, a small drab bird scolded him for the intrusion, but he wasn't worried about its chatter, for a straining Birger was immersed in his task. With a boot in either hand, the lad dragged Halfdan's unconscious bulk in short, slow bursts across uneven grass to the Kaupang path. With each spurt of motion, Halfdan's head bobbled over the tussocks. Birger had slung the incriminating bundle of kindling over his shoulder, but every time he leant into his next effort, it slid under his arm. At every pause, he hitched the bundle—he clearly didn't dare leave incriminating evidence.

"Heill, Birger," Freyja called cheerfully, stepping from the longhouse.

Birger froze in mid heave. He gawked at Freyja, the longhouse, down at his charge, then back to Freyja. The way the deserted building continued to disgorge people was causing him immense bewilderment.

"Your friend has encountered misfortune, I see," Freyja said conversationally.

Birger's eyes flicked to the open door, expecting Ronan to appear. He threw a desperate glance toward the town, but there was no help from that direction.

"Have you lost something, my friend?"

The lad opened his mouth to speak, but words deserted him. Thrashing his head in confusion, he searched in vain for an avenue of escape. Then Ronan stepped from the trees with a casual, "Heill, Birger".

Halfdan's boots thunked onto the ground. Birger retreated from Ronan's approach, hands lifting defensively. "What ... but ... how?" he sputtered. "... you were in there." He turned, pointing to the door. Freyja was gone.

"Have you lost something, Birger?" Ronan couldn't bring himself to call him 'friend'.

Huffing, he spun to Ronan.

"What is it you have lost, Birger?" It was Freyja, walking serenely from the woods fringing the path to Kaupang.

Face chalky, Birger dropped the bundle of kindling beside an inert Halfdan, and backed from Freyja.

Birger pivoted to Ronan, but he was gone.

"Poor Birger," said Freyja, her tone silken. "You are looking every-where ... what have you lost?"

"I ... I ..." he stammered, retreating toward the door. "Nothing!" he finally managed.

"Then why are you searching?" came a voice from behind.

Whirling, he caught Ronan striding out the door, mere metres away. Birger's knees wobbled as he reversed direction, looking for Freyja; she was gone. Yet, when he turned to Ronan, the völva walked from the longhouse door.

"Perhaps we can help you find it," Freyja said.

Birger moaned, took another step backward, then turned to run. His first stride encountered Halfdan's inert form, and he went sprawling across the top of the body, the side of his face scrunching into the ground between a pair of massive thighs.

Ronan and Freyja shared a satisfied smirk, straightening their faces as Birger rolled off Halfdan's barrel chest, landing beside him with a graceless 'oof'.

Impassively, they stood over him as he began crabbing backward with a panting whimper. Freyja strode after him, raising her staff. Birger shrieked, cringing behind raised hands as the staff slammed down, pinning a fold of his tunic to the grass. When the staff remained anchored, Birger's hands eased downward. "Wh ... wha ... what do you want?"

"What I want," Freyja began, "is for you to say what it is you have lost."

"I ... I ... do not know what you mean?"

A soft intake of breath dragged Birger's eyes to Ronan, but he was gone.

"Perhaps this is what he's lost," Ronan said, folding from the air behind Birger, bending to retrieve the abandoned bundle of kindling.

Quicker than his neck could twist, Birger's mind spiralled. "What is this seiðr you bring upon my head?" he moaned, blood leaving his face.

"This seiðr," Ronan said, jaw tight, "is nothing compared to what's in store if you don't answer Völva Freyja's question."

"What you mean?" Birger wailed. "I have lost nothing."

Freyja's eyes hardened. "Perhaps you should begin with your integrity ... your self-respect ... your family's reputation?"

"Wh ... what are you talking about?"

"What were you doing with the kindling?" Freyja's words dripped ice.

Birger's frenetic eyes flicked from the bundle to Ronan, and to Freyja looming above him. "What?"

"Does this refresh your memory?" Ronan said through gritted teeth, flinging the kindling onto Birger's unsuspecting chest.

Air whooshed from the lad as his last shred of resistance evaporated. "I could not dissuade him," he lamented. "Halfdan wanted to burn your longhouse to avenge his humiliation at the stone."

"Which was his own doing," Freyja said.

Birger nodded with reluctance. "But the way he sees it, you could have released him from the stone's seiðr, but you left it to the traveller, and he humiliated Halfdan further."

"It was the traveller who was wronged," Freyja said, "so it was only just that the traveller should dispense retribution."

"That is not how Halfdan sees it," Birger replied, the quaver settling from his voice. "He sees you, and the seiðr of the stone, as complicit in his humiliation."

"But he sought satisfaction through the hólmganga," Ronan pointed out.

"This is not about honour," Birger muttered, "it is revenge ... he hates with zeal. Defeating you at the hólmganga will never be enough. Halfdan aims to see you dead."

Ronan nudged Halfdan's ribs with a toe. "So you say, but we can see how that's going."

The brute stirred; Birger remained silent.

"Think about what shape you wish for your life, Birger," said Freyja, lifting her staff.

Throwing the kindling bundle from his chest and rolling to his feet, he dusted himself off, regarding them both sourly. Halfdan groaned and levered open a glassy eye. One side of his head sported a large goose egg, the other, something of which a small hen would be proud. He cranked up the second eyelid. There was no focus in either eye, and no reaction to Ronan's and Freyja's presence.

"And that goes for you as well, Halfdan," Freyja added.

Halfdan struggled onto an elbow, his head bobbling. He tried to follow the voice by squinting, but failed. "Huh?" was all he managed.

"Think about what shape you wish for your life," Freyja said. Halfdan stared into space. "Because, another shambles like this"—she prodded his ribs with her staff—"and I will weave a future for you where there will be no peace."

"What hit me?" Halfdan slurred. He was struggling into a sitting position; no one moved to help.

"I did," said Ronan, "but you deserved worse." He continued to be surprised by the authority and assurance with which he spoke.

The swaying Halfdan blinked, and blinked again. "Help me, Birger." Head still wobbling, words stumbling across sluggish lips, he raised an appealing hand to his companion.

Freyja pushed the arm down with her staff. "Can you hear me, Halfdan?"

"Corsh I can." The hen's egg straddled a vertical crease near the corner of his left eye, where his head had thumped into the door jamb. A spreading purple tide was laying siege to the eye. On the opposite side, the goose egg reigned supreme. It was further back, abutting the ear, courtesy of the collision with Sten's well-made door.

Freyja turned to Birger. "You will get him up ... you will get him home ... and you will do a better job of keeping him out of trouble." She poked the end of her staff at his face.

Birger bobbed his head sourly, took a fistful of Halfdan's tunic and threw the oaf's arm across his shoulder.

"I will know if you follow him into error," Freyja cautioned, "and I will find you."

"If Freyja doesn't, I will," added Ronan.

The völva and väktare stood watching Birger man-handle Halfdan onto rubbery legs. As the intruders staggered off toward Kaupang, Birger glanced over his shoulder. "He will make you pay for this, traveller."

49

THE JARL

The morning of day three dawned crisp and clear. Birds sang in the forest, a pot of stew bubbled fitfully at the edge of the fire, and Sten tramped off to build his boats, leaving with a brusque farewell and a vague undertaking to meet them at the square, to 'see Halfdan get his dues'.

Sleep had come reluctantly to Ronan the previous night. Even though Halfdan was knocked senseless earlier that day, Ronan had seen the brute's iron-hard toughness at close quarters and knew recovery would be swift. Despite the confidence he projected, Ronan's head festered with doubt—how could a twenty-first century farm boy match it with a beefy Norse lad who had trained for battle his entire life?

Ronan had often fired arrows between the trees at Masters, but only in dreams. Apart from pinning the man's sleeve to the hat rack, Ronan had never loosed an arrow in the general direction of a person, let alone with the intent to draw blood. The thought of deliberately wounding was alien to him—dispatching a sick animal on the farm was a struggle. How would he fare against a fighting machine with henbane in his veins? One thing for sure, Halfdan's approach would be hard, fast and ruthless.

In searching for a winning strategy, Ronan and Sten had arrived at a single imperative—do not miss. And because Ronan didn't want to inflict grievous injury, his target area would be tiny, his margin for error minuscule. On the other hand, Halfdan would have the freedom to aim at the centre of Ronan's body, and not worry if he was a bit off target.

Ronan's goal was simple—make sure his shield caught all of Halfdan's arrows, while putting all of his own into his opponent's extremities. Freyja had said the duel would end when blood touched the ground. Ronan was pinning his hopes on that happening quickly or, if it didn't, that blood loss would weaken Halfdan enough to stop the contest. Perhaps the henbane might drain out with the blood, but Ronan doubted it.

By the time he woke to the sound of Sten's raspy, pre-dawn snoring, Ronan's gut was hollowed from hunger and dread. He lay on his fur, prickly woollen blanket under his chin, gazing up at the dull reflection of embers on the rafters. Win, lose or draw, he wanted it done. But to win, he had to wound Halfdan seriously; a draw seemed an impossibility; a loss meant he would be back at the Home Stone in a heartbeat. All three scenarios turned his stomach.

As well as the churning, his gut held a solid knot of apprehension for Freyja and Sten. If the jarl felt his son had been cheated by seiðr, then ...? Ronan knew he *must* prevail.

In the wake of Sten's noisy departure, Ronan rolled from his bed, pulled on the tunic, and stepped up to the fire. Freyja, flaming hair not yet restrained, greeted him with a smile and the usual large bowl of stew and knob of bread.

"It is a fine day for the hólmganga," she said cheerfully.

Ronan was nonplussed. "Pardon me if I don't share your enthusiasm."

"Ronan, Ronan, Ronan," she said, touching his shoulder. "Trust yourself. Even without your blóð rún, you are capable of much more than you realise." Freyja lifted his chin with a curled forefinger, forcing him to meet her eye. "Stop trying to second-guess everything. Do what you did with Halfdan at the Heim Steinn, and when he tried to set a fire, and what you did with me to frighten Birger. Go with your instinct, rely on your skills, embrace your blóð rún. None of them will abandon you."

Freyja's eyes drew Ronan in, absorbing him into her calmness. He nodded.

At mid-morning, they set out through the woods to Kaupang. Before long, the trees succumbed to a narrow valley of farmland—on one side, a rugged ridge of slate-grey rock frowned through a cloak of birch, spruce and pine; on the other, a low rise carried an arm of the woodland toward the southeast. The sprinkling of autumn leaves among the dark evergreens held a different beauty to the drab foliage and stark cream trunks of an Australian eucalypt forest.

The valley was a patchwork of fields, with crops and grass hugging the fertile grey soil around a scattering of rocks and boulders.

"Where are the longhouses?" Ronan enquired, curious at the absence of farm buildings.

"There is one in that copse yonder," Freyja said, indicating a column of smoke rising from a clump of trees on the opposite side of a small stream, "another over that hill, but most are on the outskirts of the town."

"Which must be close," Ronan surmised, sniffing wood smoke from the breeze. Before long, the whiff of cooking fires was joined by the faint hum of the settlement, the tang of salty moisture and the distant squawking of gulls. They rounded a low knoll—a lump of flattened dough stuck to the landscape—to be greeted by an expanse of water to the south.

"Viksfjord," Freyja said.

After the knoll, the path split. The left headed toward a similar, but much larger rise from which the assorted buildings of Kaupang sprouted. The right fork led them across a meadow sandwiched between the town and a marshland of reeds, sedges and gaggling waterfowl, to the shore of Viksfjord. As they descended the final slope of the well-used track, the skeletons of several boats in various stages of completion rose to meet them. Beyond the boat yard, the grey-glass surface of the fjord stretched southward.

Everything about the day was grey—the rocks, the soil, the water, the sky. Ronan hoped it wasn't an omen.

They found Sten, covered in sweat, sawdust and wood shavings, fitting out the hold of a trading vessel. It was an elegant fusion of graceful curves, with overlapping planks sweeping from a high post at the stern to another at the bow, making it difficult to tell one end from the other.

"I thought we would collect you in case you forget the time," Freyja told him as he clambered from the hull, wiping dirty hands down the front of his tunic. Freyja frowned, shaking her head.

Sten gave the bulwark an affectionate pat. "This beauty will earn its master much wealth," he said.

"It's a splendid boat," Ronan agreed, but he had no idea; it felt the right thing to say to such a fine craftsman.

The boat builder gave a modest snort of approval as they turned their backs on the fjord and ambled toward the centre of Kaupang. Their approach to the square was along a street of sorts but, to Ronan, the town had been thrown together in a haphazard manner—few of the buildings lined up with either the thoroughfare or each other. Perhaps the owners had rolled dice to see which way they would face, and no two managed the same number. Nonetheless, they were sturdy houses —wood and stone topped with sod, thatch or shingle, built to withstand harsh winters.

It appeared all the locals, and others as well, had gathered in antici-pation. In the absence of a defined thoroughfare, the buzz of excitement guided Ronan, Freyja and Sten to their destination. As they drew near, the sharp spine of a massive longhouse rose above the surrounding roof tops. By the time the street spilled them into the square, the longhouse swelled to its full importance, looking down its nose on its lesser neigh-bours, imposing itself on the centre of the town.

A carnival atmosphere prevailed—the music of flute and lyre swirled; people chatted and laughed, swayed and danced. The excited locals had come for entertainment, to enjoy themselves and have time away from the usual workday drudgery. Many carried a favourite sword, axe, spear or bow; shields were everywhere. Ronan wondered if it was only for show, or whether the duel might descend into a widespread brawl if the outcome was disputed, similar to a twenty-first century soccer match where passions ran high.

He tried to ignore the hubbub, but failed. Like the bow wave of a boat, it lifted with their approach, before swirling and subsiding in their wake. The familiar flutter of pre-game nerves had his body tingling and tightening. Ronan chided himself—it wasn't a cricket match; blood would be spilt—he only hoped there wasn't too much of his.

In an open space roped off in the centre of the square, a small group of burly men were stacking an array of weapons, ferrying them from an unseen storage. "They are making the hrúga," Sten said, indicating the growing pile. Ronan saw a couple of old bows, two quivers—he couldn't see how many arrows—swords, knives, axes, spears, hammers and shields. While desperately wanting to rifle through them to check the quality, he sought any slim advantage there might be from appearing nonchalant about the coming contest.

Sten nudged him with an elbow and jutted his bronze beard at the corner of the square. Under the edge of a grand marquee in front of the longhouse, stood Halfdan, surrounded by a motley collection of supporters who, by the look of them, preferred a fight to most other things. The jarl's son looked to have been run over by a wagon—both wrists were bandaged, his right eye a mere slit, the adjacent skin stretched and hued like the ominous underbelly of an approaching storm; the other glared at Ronan, a hot shimmer of hatred bubbling through the separating air. Beyond Halfdan, there was a flash of orange, and a dark head rose from the centre of a knot of men.

"Thorald Ottarrson," Sten said, "the jarl."

50

THE STEINKAST

J arl Ottarrson was a solid man. With a son built like Halfdan, that was unsurprising. While he appeared taller than his son, he was still short of Ronan's sprouting figure. His coal-black hair was pulled back like Sten's, apparently the Kaupang fashion. And his beard, although not as long as Sten's, was every bit as luxuriant and well-tended. As befitted a nobleman, his clothes were the finest wool and linen, embroidered and trimmed. No other man in the gathering sported the burnt orange of his tunic, or the sea blue of his pants, and there were no boots—apart from his son's—as carefully crafted, or adorned with carved straps and bone toggles.

Beside him stood a stern woman of similar build. Her hair was also long and dark, but shot with grey and gathered in a series of twists that melted into braids above her ears, before merging into a single, smoky rope hanging between her shoulder blades. Bands on her fingers and wrists glinted as she moved, as did the string of wealth round her neck. Her flowing dress oozed expense and exclusivity with every thread and stitch. While a similar blue to the jarl's pants, and hemmed and embroidered with his tunic's orange, it went one step further with a splash of scarlet—a short cowl barely covering the points of her shoulders and reaching the flare of her breasts. But it was the face that caught Ronan's attention—cold eyes and thin-lips curled into permanent disdain.

"Idonea the Dane," whispered Sten from the side of his mouth, "the jarl's wife. It is no wonder he takes concubines." He chuckled at his own wit, ignoring the frowns turned toward him, but not his wife's cautioning touch.

The jarl raised his hand; silence floated across the crowd, smothering the revelry. But it didn't reach a clamour of young children playing in the background, or a couple of distant, yapping dogs, probably scrapping over a morsel.

"This hólmganga was called by Halfdan Thoraldson to satisfy his honour," the jarl began earnestly, "after he was humiliated by this traveller three days since."

A murmur rippled through the gathering, but Ronan couldn't tell if it was protest or support—it rekindled his doubt.

The jarl waited for the buzz to die before continuing. "Because Halfdan challenged, the traveller has the choice of weapons."

All eyes turned to the pile of assorted fighting hardware in the middle of the square.

Dipping his head to the jarl, Ronan said, "Jarl Ottarrson ... forgive me, I'm not familiar with your customs, but may I speak?"

The jarl's gleaming black head inclined in acknowledgement.

Ronan felt the assurance radiating from his blóð rún, coursing through his body, quenching his apprehension, boosting his confidence. "First," he said, voice carrying across the gathering, "Halfdan humbled *himself*, both at the Heim Steinn and at the longhouse of Völva Freyja yesterday."

"Liar!" Halfdan roared.

Jarl Ottarrson held up an imperious hand, thick fingered and hairy. "Let the traveller speak."

Ronan took a breath. "Unprovoked, Halfdan insulted both Freyja and me. His lack of self-control led to his wristbands being captured by the Heim Steinn. And I refused to free him until he apologised to Freyja for his harsh words. So, yes, my lord, he was humbled, but by his own actions."

Halfdan surged toward Ronan but, before he took two paces, large hands clamped around his arms, halting his progress. A couple of powerful men held him as easily as a spoilt child.

"Yesterday," Ronan continued, "Halfdan entered Völva Freyja's long-house uninvited, no knock, no greeting ... nothing. I happened to be there and, fearing an outlaw, I slammed the door in his face without checking who it was." Ronan stared at Birger standing with the brother and sister hunters, a distance apart from Halfdan's group. The lad couldn't meet Ronan's gaze, but it looked like he was already distancing himself from his toxic charge.

Halfdan glared at Ronan with his one good eye, thrashing about, but unable to break free.

"Is this true?" The jarl was looking not at Halfdan, but at his trusted source of advice, Völva Freyja.

Freyja dipped her head. The jarl dropped a hard glare on his son, who glowered, unrepentant. Anger hummed through the throng.

"So, it was not a drunken impact with a door?" the jarl said. There was no answer. The man was not accustomed to being ignored—he glowered. "Why did you enter the völva's longhouse without invitation?"

"To teach a lesson," Halfdan hissed in Ronan's direction.

"Was the hólmganga not enough?" growled the jarl.

"Never," Halfdan spat at Ronan as if he'd asked the question.

"It *will* be enough, do you hear?" Ottarrson barked, drawing a line under the subject.

There was silence from his son. Even the crowd stilled, not wanting to miss any of the exchange.

Across the quiet, Ronan said, "With respect, my lord, what if the weapon I wish to choose isn't in the hrúga?"

The jarl chuckled. "Then you may choose whatever you can find within a steinkast of where you stand."

A stone's throw? Ronan liked it. "And how far is that?"

"How strong is your arm?" quipped the jarl. A pulse of laughter greeted the question. Halfdan had stopped his struggling, and he shrugged off the restraining hands with a sullen scowl.

A surge of relief coursed through Ronan. He'd seen the dark-haired hunter, Frida, in the opposite corner of the gathering, the bow Sten made dangling from her back. She was about fifteen metres away. If the stone was a similar weight to a cricket ball, that bow was his.

"So, anything within the radius of where the stone lands?"

The gleaming head inclined again.

"And does Halfdan select from the same steinkast?"

"Halfdan must make his own," the jarl replied with a smile, holding a hand out to the side. An attendant placed a stone, larger than a cricket ball, into the upturned palm.

The jarl's hand dropped with the weight; Ronan's heart went with it; Frida's bow flew from his reach. Despite the man's displeasure at his son's conduct, Ronan wondered whether the jarl may have ordered a heavy stone to restrict the weapon choice to the hrúga.

"Come, traveller, your stone awaits," said the jarl. A collective murmur ran through the crowd—their familiarity with the stone's weight was clearly colouring their assessment of Ronan's chances. "You must cast from the hrúga." The pile of weapons was seven or eight metres from Frida.

Halfdan smirked. He couldn't know about the bow, but Ronan's dissatisfaction with the pile was obvious, as were his slim arms.

Reluctantly, Ronan approached the stone. His whole strategy depended on pinpoint archery; if he couldn't get Frida's bow, everything fell apart, and he'd have to settle for a battle-scarred relic from the pile. There was no telling how true it would be; he'd need multiple sighting shots to be sure of his aim. His energy drained away as he took the stone, but he was surprised that it wasn't as heavy as he'd feared. An idea fizzed into his head. "Are there any rules on how to throw?"

In answer, the jarl strode to the hrúga and scratched his heel across the grass. "You must cast from behind this line," he said. "Your steinkast will be measured from here to where the stone lands."

Ronan hefted the dull grey stone as he approached the pile of weapons, rolling it from hand to hand, getting a feel for it. While lighter than the shot he used at school, the rock was several times the weight of the cricket balls he could throw so well. And, even though he bordered on hopeless at shot put, he knew the technique. A ghost of optimism stirred. He needed nine metres, at least—his personal best in athletics was six point eight. The optimism faded.

Freyja gave him an encouraging smile; Sten looked concerned, no, gloomy.

The chatter hushed as Ronan walked up to the mark. From the corner of his eye, he imagined he saw Frida shrinking away. The stone seemed to gain weight.

'Your body simply isn't built for shot put,' Ronan's high school athletics coach had finally told him after three years of fruitless training, '... stick to cricket; you have real talent there.'

Ronan turned his back on the target, took three long strides from the line, gave his limbs a shake, cleared his mind. As never before, he needed good technique.

A buzz of curiosity hummed through the square. Halfdan's derisive laugh drew dutiful mimicry from his cronies. Ronan ignored them. He shut everything out, even the spreading warmth from the rune, concentrating entirely on technique—shot at the base of the fingers, nestled against the neck; elbow high; left arm high, aiming the shot. Deep breath ... balance ... steady ... skip, stretch, pivot, leg drive, arm power, wrist flick, roar. The reluctant rock lumbered into the air.

51

THE CHOOSING

F ace scarlet, neck rigid, Ronan teetered, toes within millimetres of the line. With windmilling arms, and a couple of bounces on the balls of his feet, he regained balance. His eyes followed the rock, urging it higher, willing it past eight metres. Scores of faces arced skyward, glued to the path of the graceless projectile. It sailed ponderously above the crowd, landing with a sullen thud on the street beyond.

For a moment, Ronan was immobile. A full-throated roar from Sten swelled as most of the gathering joined in, thrusting shields and spears into the air. He looked round in disbelief—they were cheering *him* and his enormous throw. If only his coach could see him now.

From the corner of his eye, he caught an unsmiling Frida turning to leave, only to collide with the determined shape of Freyja and her staff. With a satisfied sigh, he turned to the impassive whiskers of the jarl.

"My lord, I choose the bow ... Frida's bow."

The features behind the beard gave nothing away. Ronan got no sense of whether it displeased the man to be out-manoeuvred, or if the entertainment of an unconventional steinkast delighted him. From his earlier conversations with Sten, Ronan knew the nobleman must be seen as an unbiased arbiter of the contest. Regardless of the outcome he desired, he couldn't risk the discontent of his people.

Meanwhile, what was visible of Halfdan's face, past all the bruising, was a reddening collage of puzzlement, fury and disbelief. For the first time, Ronan sensed doubt stirring in his opponent.

The burly youth hefted the retrieved stone and toed the line. He swung his arm backward and forward a few times before releasing the projectile in a powerful underarm hurl. It bullied its way through the air, arcing toward a knot of onlookers who fled left and right as it thudded into the ground.

Ronan wanted to gape—Halfdan, as strong as a bull, and with the temperament to match, would've made a great shot putter.

The jarl stepped it out with his short legs and pronounced that Halfdan had thrown fourteen paces and a foot—he hadn't bothered measuring Ronan's throw; it was obviously much further than required. Watching the man measure his son's cast with care made Ronan suspect two things: whatever Halfdan now wanted—to counter Frida's bow— was close to the limit of his distance; and his father knew what that weapon was. The subtly longer strides the man took as he paced toward his entourage confirmed Ronan's suspicions. His glance to Freyja drew a lifted eyebrow.

"… eight, nine, ten …" the jarl counted as his group parted for him. With a final long stride, he passed a high-backed chair, called 'fourteen', and halted. It was the ornate, carved chair he'd occupied when Ronan, Freyja and Sten arrived—leaning against its back was every weapon a Norse nobleman could desire. Any doubts Ronan still harboured evaporated; the jarl had his finger firmly on the scales of the contest.

"I choose your warbow, my lord," Halfdan crowed. Turning to face the crowd, and throwing a one-eyed smirk at Ronan, he raised a monstrous longbow of polished yew in a victory gesture. There was an enthusiastic roar from the jarl's group, but a far more muted response from elsewhere.

When Halfdan lowered the bow and rested an end on his foot, the opposite end reached far above his head. It would take tremendous strength to draw it, let alone hold it long enough to aim accurately, but it would be lethal at close range. Fear billowed in Ronan's heart; he swallowed, then swallowed again … the harsh taste remained. His strategy was in tatters.

Under Freyja's watchful eye, a sour Frida delivered her bow and quiver to Ronan. As exquisitely crafted as it was, and coiled with elegant power, it barely came to the middle of his chest—he was taking a knife to a sword fight.

A hand touched his arm, and Freyja leant close. "You have the advantage," she murmured, "... you do not miss." While those few words of encouragement gave his spirits buoyancy, her next ones sunk them. "Now choose Sturla's war shield ... you will need it."

Ronan threw her a questioning look. "Do not ask," she hissed in his ear, "just choose it."

"And I choose Sturla's war shield." Ronan spoke with a strong, confident voice that belied his apprehension. The jarl's bow was massive, with power to match; the shield would need to be exceptional.

A rumble of uncertainty rolled through the gathering. The jarl's eyes narrowed as he inclined his head in acknowledgement. Halfdan scowled.

Eyes turned to a stir in the crowd as blonde hair bobbed through, red-painted shield held high. Sturla was tall and skinny by Norse standards, almost as tall as Ronan, and of similar build. Like Sten, he'd split beard in two; unlike Sten, he'd shaved the sides of his head, leaving a long narrow strip of leather-bound hair hanging down his back. With a slight head dip, he presented his shield to Ronan. "Looks are deceiving," he said. Ronan was unsure whether the man was referring to himself, the shield, Ronan, or all three.

Sturla's shield was thin, perhaps two centimetres. "How's this going to stop an arrow?" he whispered to Freyja. Stretched across its face was a thick layer of ox hide; in the centre, a domed metal boss covered a hand grip; several layers of linen coated the rear surface. It was unlike any of the other shields sprinkled throughout the gathering.

"Sturla's new design," she murmured. "Sten swears it's arrow-proof ... hunting arrows."

Ronan swallowed—the jarl's mammoth warbow likely had twice the power of Frida's dainty weapon.

"I choose your war shield, my lord," said Halfdan with a fresh smirk.

The embers of Ronan's anxiety glowed bright; he must starve them of oxygen, so he closed his mind to Halfdan's swaggering bulk and fearless face, and revisited his new strategy. He needed two arrows—one to calibrate his aim, another to carry out his plan. Sten had told him that with bows, the challenged person shot first, then they took turns until either combatant fell, or there were no arrows left. If that held true, he had to survive only one arrow from the warbow, but could Sturla's shield withstand such a missile?

"Each combatant shall have five arrows," the jarl was saying. "If there is no result with five arrows, they shall progress to the second, and final, weapon."

The buzz of surprise swept through the gathering. Sten hadn't mentioned a second weapon choice. Ronan glanced to Freyja for guidance; she shrugged. The jarl's face gave almost nothing away, but Ronan detected a vague twist of satisfaction on the lips, and the faint glint of challenge in the eyes.

Heart thumping, Ronan stood motionless, as if gravely considering his options. His mind spun suicidally from spear to sword to knife, and even axe. And then he felt it, the warmth and calmness emanating from his blood rune.

"I choose bare hands, my lord."

52

THE HÓLMGANGA

Thorald Ottarrson was motionless in the midst of a collective breath catching. Then Halfdan threw his head back, guffawing; his companions followed, and chortles rippled round the square. Even Sten appeared to think it a joke until he saw Ronan's set jaw and flinty gaze. Freyja nodded in silent satisfaction.

Finally, Ronan sensed a path to victory. As the mist clouding his mind lifted, the words of his karate teacher floated clear—'wait until your opponent commits, then attack their weakness'. He would do it with the shield, with the bow, and with his hands.

The jarl raised a hand; the laughter died in fits and starts. "It is settled," he announced. "Five arrows, then wrestling."

"My lord, I didn't stipulate wrestling," Ronan interrupted with a respectful dip of his head. "I choose bare hands as the weapon."

Annoyance flitted across the jarl's face. "Very well, the second weapon is bare hands to be used however the combatants choose."

Halfdan was almost dancing with glee. He chuckled, cracked his fingers, flexed his massive shoulders and fixed his open eye on Ronan. "I will happily forgo the first weapon and move straight to the second," he declared.

"Don't you trust your aim?" Ronan taunted. "Or do you doubt your ability to draw your father's bow?"

There was a scattering of half-suppressed chuckles. Halfdan's vanity popped; his face darkened and he threw himself at Ronan, but the same large men as before held him back.

"Enough!" the jarl snapped, eyes boring at Ronan. Then, in a dispassionate voice, he said, "The hólmganga will begin with bows at fifteen paces."

"You wish to keep your son safe, Jarl," Sten protested, his tone accusing.

"He won't be safe at twenty," Ronan stated. The warmth at the back of his skull imbued him with confidence and composure, and a certainty that he would punch Halfdan where it hurt most, squarely in the centre of his self-esteem.

At Ronan's words, Halfdan became an enraged bull—spittle flew, shoulders thrashed, massive legs pumped. He broke free and made two paces toward Ronan before several more burly bodies joined the vortex of action.

"Enough!" Thorald Ottarrson bellowed, his face the colour of his wife's cowl. "Fifteen paces," he growled, dropping a hard stare on Sten. After a settling breath, he commanded, "Clear the field." The pile of weapons disappeared in a flurry.

Dragging his heel through the grass, the jarl scored a vague line, walked fifteen short steps, drew another, and retired to the margins. "The combatants will not cross their line until my word," he instructed. "The fight will continue until blood touches the ground."

Ronan and Halfdan took their weapons to their respective lines, the people behind them parting like combed hair, leaving clear passage for errant arrows.

"Let the hólmganga begin," the jarl intoned, theatrically dropping his right arm.

"Be true, my bow," Ronan breathed, fitting his first arrow. Halfdan held his shield nonchalantly in front of his body, ready to move as required. It was patterned in tan and blue quadrants, and only lightly scuffed and nicked. The lack of major battle scars spoke either to the jarl's fighting skill or the quality of his opponents. Such was the shield's size, Ronan could only see Halfdan's head and below his knees.

Regardless, Ronan took careful aim. The arrow zinged off his string, embedding itself with a wooden thunk, about two arrowheads to the left of a small scuff in a tan-coloured section. It wasn't what the crowd expected, for a puzzled murmur arose.

As soon as Ronan noted where his arrow struck, he snatched up Sturla's hide-covered shield, holding it loosely at arm's-length, trusting in Freyja's judgement.

Halfdan lifted his father's warbow. Shoulders rippling and neck corded, he drew the monster weapon, and his aim caused no puzzlement.

The arrow strike was a hammer blow. Sturla's shield bucked in Ronan's hand, absorbing most of the arrow's force. With a scraping, splintering tear, the arrowhead bludgeoned its way through the ox hide, burst through the wooden centre and sliced out through the linen backing before halting. Ronan looked down; the glittering point was only a finger's length from his chest.

He swallowed, glancing across at Freyja. While a formidable shield, Ronan doubted it could withstand more than a couple of similar strikes, especially if Halfdan could hit the same spot. After snapping the arrow off front and back, he exchanged the shield for his bow and second arrow. At one with the warmth of his rune, Ronan drew the bowstring to his chin, adjusted two arrowheads to the right. He lifted his aim to his opponent's head, and when the shield rose to cover, he dropped to his true target ... zing, thunk!

The warbow twisted in Halfdan's beefy hand, Ronan's arrow embedded in its back, about a foot from the end. A jumble of oohs, aahs, chuckles and titters bounced across the gathering. "Yes," breathed Sten. The jarl's face was stone. Halfdan dropped his shield, flicked the arrow from the back of his bow like it was an annoying insect, and grabbed his second arrow.

Again, Halfdan strained to draw the weapon to its fullest extent, but the arrow, when it struck Sturla's shield, reverberated a shock-wave up Ronan's arm. Halfdan was either a much better shot than his recent hunt indicated, or he'd been very lucky—his second arrow struck beside the first, penetrating even further through the weakened barrier.

Ronan felt a bee sting and looked down to see his tunic pinned to his chest, and warm blood ooze into the fabric. Failure, and all that went with it, ignited a prickle of fear. Expecting to be heimmed, he was relieved when the tip dislodged. While only a shallow wound, the ooze became a trickle.

Sturla's shield had done as much protecting as it could; now, all that stood between Ronan and the might warbow, was a single arrow. He gripped Frida's elegant, accurate, but far less powerful weapon, and reached for his third arrow.

Neither the disbelief on Sten's face, nor the total lack of concern on Freyja's disturbed his focus. He stilled his mind, concentrating on the only thing he could control—his next shot. Shutting out the murmur of anticipation from the crowd, he peered at the spine of the warbow, searching for the wound from his previous arrow. There it was, peeking below the rim of Halfdan's shield. Ronan drew the bow, sighting two arrowheads to the right, releasing his breath, lifting his aim to the head, then dropping it quickly. Zing, thunk!

Halfdan laughed, swatting Ronan's arrow from the same place as the previous one, only this time it took extra effort—the arrow was more deeply lodged in the heart of the mighty bow. But it appeared not to concern Halfdan, for his eyes were fixed on the blood on his opponent's tunic, a triumphant smirk twisting his lips. Muscles straining, he drew his weapon to full stretch, dropping it into line with Ronan's shield. Crack! The warbow exploded! Its spine severed where Ronan's strikes had weakened it. Halfdan's arrow plopped lifelessly onto the grass at his feet.

A mutual 'aah' escaped the onlookers. Whether from disappointment or approval, Ronan wasn't sure, but he didn't have time to contemplate—Halfdan threw the tangle of wood, sinew and string aside, and charged, roaring, a berserker entering battle.

While Halfdan's circle cheered; the rest of the crowd booed in unison—rules were being flouted.

Dropping his shield, Ronan fitted, drew and fired his fourth arrow in one fluid motion. It embedded in Halfdan's massive, pumping thigh, but he didn't break stride. In a blur, Ronan's fifth arrow buried in the other thigh ... same result. Ronan was out of arrows and out of time— the roaring bundle of rage was almost upon him. With Halfdan's grasping hands reaching for him, Ronan cast the beautiful hunting bow aside, throwing himself backward. As his shoulders hit the ground, he drove one foot into his opponent's stomach, the other to his chest, stiffening his legs, allowing Halfdan's momentum to send him cartwheeling through the air. With an almighty thud, he landed on the flat of his back, breath punched from his lungs, arrows protruding from his thighs like miniature flagpoles.

Most of the gathering roared; Halfdan's supporters were silent, open-mouthed. Ronan sprang to his feet, facing the prone form, hoping the jarl called an end. His son needed attention—blood flowed freely from around each arrow shaft.

A man beside the jarl pointed an accusing finger at Ronan and called, "Cheat!" Others from Halfdan's circle joined in, but the accusation rang hollow. In a lone dissenting voice, Sten started chanting, "Cheat, cheat, cheat ...", stabbing his forefinger at Halfdan with each word. The chorus was picked up by others, little fragments of resistance spreading, joining, running like a contagion through the onlookers. It swelled into full-throated protest, harsh slaps of sound drowning the efforts of the jarl's group.

Halfdan pushed himself into a sitting position, shaking his head, gazing about at the wall of noise. He saw the arrows buried in his legs and, with a roar that was more anger than pain, reefed them from his flesh, casting them aside as though they were minor irritants. The crowd fell into awed silence. Blood bubbled from the wounds, soaking through his pants, staining the grass.

"My lord," Freyja called, "blood has touched the ground. The hólm-ganga is decided."

Jarl Ottarrson ignored her; he glared at Ronan, who had dropped into his fighting stance and heard nothing, so fierce was his focus.

Halfdan was rising. Freyja strode in front of the jarl. "My lord," she repeated, "blood has touched the ground."

Waving dismissively, he said, "It only touches the grass."

Before Freyja could respond, the air reverberated with Halfdan's blood-curdling roar. He charged, going low, looking for a wrestler's grapple. Ronan knew that if those limbs entwined him, they would crush the life from his body.

He waited and, at the last moment, sidestepped, but stayed close to deliver a passing blow to the back of the neck. Halfdan changed direction as much as his momentum allowed, flinging his massive right arm up and out.

Too late, Ronan realised he'd been impatient, perhaps arrogant—he hadn't waited for his opponent to fully commit. He desperately threw up a block, but Halfdan's swinging limb was a battering ram, smashing past Ronan's forearm, bouncing off his temple. His vision exploded into pinpoints of dancing light at the centre of crowding darkness.

53

THE DEFEAT

Halfdan roared in triumph. Ronan staggered backward, eyes unfocused, falling hard as his heel caught in the grass. The crowd's hush breathed into a disappointed 'ooh' as Ronan's supporters--most of the gathering--sensed the imminent end to his plucky resistance. Now that Halfdan had landed a blow, it would be quick, but not painless, for the traveller. The jarl's group found their voice, spurring their man to victory. Sten winced; Freyja chewed her lip.

The ringing in Ronan's ears drowned out the rising din from Halfdan's outnumbered backers. While his eyes were open, all he saw was throbbing light surrounded by grey shadow. Halfdan's glancing impact was as solid as the stone floor at Raven's Roost, only on this occasion, there was no time for recovery; he had to move--if Halfdan caught him on the ground, he was done. Ronan blinked hard, shaking his head, trying to clear his vision and brain simultaneously.

Meanwhile, Halfdan had come to a lumbering halt and turned, pausing to gloat, basking in the sweetness of his followers' cheers. But the waiting victory clearly held too much allure, for he threw himself at Ronan's prone form.

Sensing rather than seeing, Ronan tried to spin away, but could only manage a slow roll, almost too slow. While he avoided Halfdan's flopping bulk, the brute's flailing forearm cracked a nasty blow above

Ronan's left elbow. A blaze of agony brought tears to his eyes; the limb felt broken.

Instead of a soft body to cushion his landing, Halfdan encountered the unforgiving ground. Air exploded from his lungs for the second time; he lay like a stunned fish. A loud groan escaped the jarl's entourage; the rest of the throng thundered approval that their man, and therefore the contest, still had life.

Ronan lurched to his feet, left arm dead, hanging limp--limp, not dangling; numb, not broken. He shook his head against his hazy senses--another miscalculation meant death.

When Halfdan pulled himself upright, the two large blood stains he left behind triggered much finger pointing and murmuring of dissent among the onlookers. Like his opponent, the young warrior was unsteady, struggling to gather his wits.

Making the most of the respite, Ronan worked his left hand, flexing his elbow, easing feeling and function back into the limb. By the time Halfdan moved, Ronan could lift his arm again, although it was far from useful.

Fortunately, some of the battle lust and impatience appeared to have been knocked from Halfdan by his latest heavy encounter with the ground. Despite Ronan's obvious handicap, uncharacteristic caution now guided Halfdan's movements. He advanced slowly, feigning, retreating, feigning again, trying to draw his quarry within grasp.

Ronan refused to take the bait, allowing strength to return to his legs, and clarity to his thoughts. While Halfdan was still probing, Ronan was back on his toes, a boxer, dancing out of reach of his opponent's every advance.

The jarl's followers saw what was happening and yelled encouragement, urging Halfdan to attack, to finish the contest. At last, he responded--instead of bluffing, he kept coming, seeking, once again, to grapple. Ronan rocked back on his right foot, kicking out and up into the approaching jaw with his left. It was like hitting a tree trunk--shock ran along his leg, dissipating through his hips.

The blow checked Halfdan's momentum, yet he remained standing, head rotating as if trying to work out what had happened. Before he could recover, Ronan spun full circle, driving a lifting right foot in a blurring swing to his opponent's unguarded head, the same spot that was crushed into the door jamb the previous day.

It landed with a resounding meaty smack, like a lump of dough being walloped with the flat of an axe. Halfdan's head snapped sideways, rebounding off his shoulder into a stupefied bobble. He tottered backward--one, two, three, four ragged steps--before regaining partial balance. There followed a couple of slow circles, where he peered hard in all directions, as though searching for a mooring for his swirling world. The crowd was hushed.

At last, Halfdan's unfocused gaze fell on Ronan, his purpose, his target. The bruised and disfigured face contorted even further as he attacked. It wasn't fast, or stable, but it was powerful.

Again, Ronan waited. He waited until the hands were almost at his throat, then feigned right. When Halfdan steered his bulk in that direction, Ronan stepped nimbly back to the left, cocking his rigid right hand over his opposite shoulder. As his opponent rumbled past, Ronan chopped a short, sharp strike to the exposed side of the brute's neck.

Halfdan's body went rigid, his good eye glazed, his legs folded, and he hit the ground with a heavy thud.

54

THE APOLOGY

Silence sucked the air from the centre of Kaupang. Ronan stood, legs splayed, panting, staring at the prone form at his feet. There was no euphoria, only disbelief, then fear bordering on panic—too hard, and the knife-hand strike could kill; too soft and Halfdan would pick himself up again. The steady cadence of the barrel chest soothed Ronan's concern, but he continued to tingle with adrenaline, not yet prepared to acknowledge that Halfdan would stay down. Seeking reassurance, he gazed unsteadily across the disbelieving hush to Freyja, who gave him a satisfied smile and congratulatory dip of the head.

Sten punched the air with a guttural, "Oogh, oogh, oogh," victory chant. It swelled, billowing like smoke, reverberating up through Ronan's feet as hundreds of boots began stomping in unison. Only those around the jarl were silent, awaiting guidance. Thorald Ottarrson was a statue, gaze flinty, lips tight. At last, and with obvious reluctance and a sardonic smile, he half-heartedly added to the din.

With their jarl hailing the traveller's unexpected triumph, his entourage dutifully swelled the hubbub. Sten and Sturla emerged from the crowd, hoisted a hesitant Ronan onto their shoulders, and paraded him on a victory lap about the square. The clamour followed them, a wave, swelling as they approached, subsiding in their wake.

Ronan was momentarily beguiled by the acclaim, even raising a victorious fist. Regardless of whether the adulation was genuine, or driven by dislike of the vanquished, he soon became uncomfortable with it, sliding from the shoulders before they'd completed a single circuit of the square.

All eyes were on him as he walked across the battlefield, collecting Frida's bow, Sturla's shield, and the broken warbow, before approaching the jarl. Determined to mend bridges and ensure there was no ill will harboured toward Freyja and Sten, Ronan showed his respect with a deep inclination of his head. "Jarl Ottarrson," he said, "I'm honoured to have met such a worthy opponent in the hólmganga." A surge of warmth explained his eloquence.

Despite a slight head dip of acknowledgement, the jarl's lips remained set, his eyes hard. They flicked to his prone son, but displayed no apparent concern. Halfdan lay unattended, massive chest rising and falling with reassuring regularity. Ronan suspected the jarl was trying to restore some of his son's reputation by allowing him to recover and leave the arena on his own.

While Ronan had no respect for Halfdan the person, Halfdan the fighter was another matter. "His throat will be sore and his voice hoarse, my lord, but he'll recover fine," he said, shaking his head in exaggerated wonder. "Those two arrows would've stopped a bull, but he pulled them out and fought on like they were only scratches."

While remaining expressionless, the jarl couldn't hide a faint swell of pride. He gave another short nod.

"And may I commend Sturla's shield to you, my lord?" Ronan held up the red disk of hide, wood and linen. "I've never held another that could withstand such assault." It wasn't a lie—the only real shield he'd ever held was Sten's, when they'd been discussing tactics.

After studying Ronan for a moment, the man said, "You are, indeed, blessed by the gods, traveller."

It was Ronan's turn to give a head dip of acknowledgement. "I would also commend the master bow-maker, Sten Olafsson, my lord." He thrust Frida's weapon aloft; a small cheer rose from the gathering. "This is, by far, the finest bow I've ever used." He'd never spoken a truer word. "With a bow such as this, it's no wonder Frida is such a great hunter of rabbit and squirrel." There was another muted ovation. It reminded

Ronan of a post-match interview of a victorious sports captain—at every mention of a hot button word, the clamour of the crowd would lift.

Thorald Ottarrson took the offered bow, hefting it, turning it, caressing it with his eyes. He drew it to its fullest extent, holding it effortlessly, before easing the string forward. "Bah," he said at last, handing it back to Ronan, "it is a woman's bow. There is no power in it." There was a murmur of agreement from behind him.

"My lord, why use a mighty rock to crack the acorn if a well-aimed stone will do the job?" Ronan said, no longer surprised by his artful tongue. As he spoke, he fitted an arrow, gesturing with its tip toward the top of a building opposite, about thirty metres away. "Suppose that knot in the roof beam was the only chink in your enemy's shield wall." Ronan drew the bow, settled, adjusted, then allowed the string to caress from his fingers, launching the arrow like a missile. Heads panned to follow its arcing flight which ended with a thunk in the centre of the whorl, and another muted cheer. "It has its place," Ronan insisted.

"Traveller," said the jarl, "I think you have deceived us into thinking you are one thing when, in truth, you are something else entirely." There was much murmuring and head nodding.

"I can't control what people think, Jarl Ottarrson—"

"Oh, but I think you can," the jarl interrupted with a wry smile.

Ronan shrugged as he gathered the broken warbow. "I can only control what I do, my lord, which brings me to your warbow ... it had awesome power and struck fear into my heart." A murmur of bewilderment rippled through the onlookers, as though they'd never heard anyone admit to fear. Ronan touched his hand to the still seeping wound in his chest. "One more strike and I wouldn't be standing here." He held the broken bow in two hands to the jarl. "I'm truly sorry to have broken such a fine weapon," he said, dipping his head in respect. "Please accept my humble apology."

A rumble of animated discussion greeted Ronan's words. Gestures and puzzled looks came at him from every direction; he feared the apology was the wrong choice, but the jarl gave a mirthless chuckle. "You are a strange one, traveller," he said, "apologising for my broken bow instead of boasting your victory." His eyes held a touch of disbelief. "Are you going to apologise for that as well?"

Ronan shrugged. "I didn't want to fight your son, but he's an arrogant bully who brought this upon himself."

As if on cue, Halfdan moaned. Ronan shaped to walk to him, but a couple of men blocked his path. He looked down at the hand against his chest, then back at the jarl, who frowned momentarily before waving them aside.

Ronan bent to the stirring Halfdan, grasping his hand, pulling him into a sitting position, then squatted and dropped a solid grip onto the meaty shoulder. Slowly, Halfdan lifted pain-filled eyes. Ronan leant in close so others couldn't hear. "I didn't ask for this fight," he said.

"You have shamed me," Halfdan mumbled. "You should have sent me to Valhalla." Bitterness seemed to solidify the words in the air.

Ronan disregarded them. "You don't deserve to die, Halfdan." He paused; the battered youth looked at him sourly. "You're not your father; allow yourself to be Halfdan. And remember, a truly powerful man does not need to speak of his power."

Pondering his own words, Ronan rose, nodded to the jarl and the crowd in turn, then strode resolutely toward Freyja's longhouse.

55

THE GOODBYE

The evening's gloom shrouded the longhouse by the time Freyja and Sten returned from the town. Freyja had tended to Halfdan's wounds before being called into council with Jarl Ottarrson. His longships would be ready to sail from the fjord in one moon, and he sought the latest portents. The real reason, Freyja said later, was the jarl wanted Ronan to join his víking; he saw in Ronan, a secret weapon for his arsenal, and asked Freyja to make representations on his behalf.

Sten, on the other hand, had spent the afternoon with Sturla, celebrating with anyone who would buy them drinks to hear the inside story on the traveller with the lethal skills and strange ways, the making of the hunting bow with the amazing accuracy, and reasons the shield withstood the warbow as well as it did—none appeared to have thought it possible.

Freyja entered the longhouse, broad shoulders draped with her drunken husband's arm, her own about his waist. Sten slurred the chorus of a boat-builders' song, making up for quality with volume; Freyja grimaced at each tuneless crescendo.

Ronan, hair still damp from bathing, sat on the bench opposite the fire, staring into the glow, barely raising his eyes when they staggered through the door.

"Heill, Lamb," Sten called when he sighted Ronan. A loud hiccup punctuated his high-pitched giggle.

Freyja sighed, releasing her husband, who promptly teetered sideways, hooked his toe on the smooth floor and collapsed, in another burst of giggles, onto the bench beside Ronan. Freyja sighed again, then smiled at Ronan with a shrug. His lack of response drew a frown.

"What troubles you, my Ronan?" She sat beside him, a concerned grandmother. "You have just had a great victory. You are the toast of Kaupang, and all the land around." Still no response. "Everyone wants a Sten bow and a Sturla shield. Thorald Ottarrson wants you on his next víking. Sten and I are safe. And I am proud of your hólmganga, especially the aftermath. You have them puzzled and impressed." Her hand gripped his knee.

Gratitude and emotion overcame Ronan, and he fought welling tears. Without looking up, he said, "I need to go home." The words rang in his ears like desertion, or worse, betrayal.

Sten broke into another disjointed chorus; Freyja's fingers squeezed reassurance. "It is right that you wish to leave," she said. "Your mother and brother need you ... and Saoirse."

Her words crystallised the dilemma Ronan had been wrestling with all afternoon. Both his mother and Saoirse were home stones to his heart; both were calling. "They're in two different times," he lamented, "and I don't know what to do."

"Every problem has a solution," said Freyja, "but it is not always as we wish."

Ronan found no comfort in her words. But he had to go; his mother and Saoirse were waiting. Thinking of Saoirse lifted his pulse and lightened his mood. But what if she wasn't keen? Drawing hope from the recollection of their brief time together, he decided to flytja home, check that his mother and Ruddi were safe with Fergal Gallagher, then return to Ireland. The umrót would be worth it, if for nothing else than the music of Saoirse's voice and the spell of those eyes.

A spreading glow from his rune told Ronan his decision was the right one, and having made it, relief swept his anxiety aside, replacing it with quiet determination.

Freyja, who had been studying his face, smiled with contentment. Sten was snoring with gusto, vibrating the walls.

"Grandmother," Ronan began, "please teach me what I need to know?"

Freyja sighed. "You are ready. But first, food."

Over bowls of the endless stew, Ronan and Freyja discussed the day's events, particularly how the blood rune may have influenced things. "And if it did," Freyja mused, "was that any different to how Jarl Ottarrson favoured his son?"

"I guess not," Ronan replied. "But the blóð rún was a huge advantage."

"And as well it was," Freyja said with certainty.

Ronan studied her before nodding agreement. For a moment, he gazed over her shoulder, searching for the best way to express his thoughts. "It seems when there's a threat, I become this other person," he said. "While I'm still me, the blóð rún makes me different ... harder, more confident."

"The blóð rún can only strengthen what is already there," Freyja said.

He relived the exhilaration of the bow being part of him and the arrows going exactly where he wanted. He revelled in the precision of his hand-strike, and marvelled at the memory of that lump of stone sailing through the air. "I still can't believe it," he said, shaking his head, struggling to comprehend what happened.

"As I said," Freyja began, "you already had those skills, your blóð rún simply amplified them."

"Yeah, Grandpa always said I'd kissed the Blarney Stone"—Ronan grinned—"but now I'm amazed by what comes out of my mouth."

"They are now you, as is your blóð rún." Freyja put a hand on his shoulder. "And you are väktare and seiðmann."

Suddenly serious, Ronan set his empty bowl aside. "How do I get home?" he said.

"As you have so capably learnt, enter ró with your only thought an image of where you wish to go."

"That gets me to the place," Ronan said, "but what about the correct time?"

"Time takes care of itself," she responded cryptically, "unless you choose otherwise."

"What's that supposed to mean?" The words came out more harshly than Ronan intended.

Freyja ignored his demeanour. "Unless you instruct your blóð rún otherwise, it will set you down a heartbeat after you left that particular time."

Ronan considered it for a moment before glancing at her sharply. "That's why you've been so insistent they're all safe. You didn't actually know they were safe"—disapproval crept into his voice, accusation to his stare—"all you knew was that I'd be going back to the instant after I left."

Freyja shrugged, holding up her palms. "What is the difference?"

"You know," he insisted.

Her shoulders sagged. "I know, I have deceived you yet again," she admitted, "but for good cause. Look at how readily and accurately you can flytja now." Freyja paused, gazing at him—Ronan returned her stare, refusing to waver. "I was not going to lose you as I lost your father," she said, underlining her words with a head shake. "It is a fool who repeats the same blunder ..."

Surprised by her brimming eyes, Ronan instantly regretted his tone.

"I had to be sure you were ready," she murmured.

Ronan pretended he hadn't seen the tear, but gave a nod of understanding before moving on. "So, how do I go beyond my own time?"

"That is very uncertain," she replied, "and entirely reliant on good fortune, for you must visualise a place as you think it will be in the future. If you get it close, you may flytja; if not, you may go nowhere."

Ronan was only half listening, his excitement building, or was it anticipation? If he returned to Doyle Farm right after Masters shot him, his mother and Ruddi weren't in danger, because they would still be in Warwick for Ruddi's guitar lesson. A horrible thought occurred to him: Masters could immediately shoot him again! He said as much to Freyja.

She shook her head. "Your blóð rún will not allow it. Remember I told you that it will always set you down in a safe place so you can recover from the umrót?"

"Okay," he said slowly, beginning to tremble. "So, I could go to

Saoirse first, before I return home?" The question ended with an involuntary, hopeful lift.

Freyja beamed. "The Goddess Freyja has indeed woven her magic around your heart."

Ronan's confusion was clear.

Freyja chuckled with delight. "Not only is Freyja the goddess of seiðr, she is the goddess of love."

Ronan's cheeks reddened. His mind searched for another subject, but it was locked on Saoirse—his face burned hotter. "So, travelling beyond your own time," he said, jumping back to an earlier question, "is completely random?"

"Not entirely," Freyja said, still chuckling, "but it is easier to flytja a few moons beyond your own time, or even a winter or two ... much more difficult beyond that."

A quiver started at the core of Ronan's body, spreading outward; surely it would be noticed and invite more mirth.

But Freyja sobered, gazing at him. "I know you must go, my Ronan, but I will miss you ... and your strange ways."

Ronan's excitement faded—part of him wasn't ready to leave. In their few short days together, he'd become very fond of his Norse grandmother, as far removed as she was.

Recognising his tumult, Freyja turned away, shaking Sten's shoulder. The snoring abated, but that was the only response. "Sten. Sten. Wake up." She highlighted each word with a vigorous shake.

"Wha ...?" He opened a reluctant, bloodshot eye.

"Your grandson is leaving."

The finality to her words added to Ronan's misery. He blinked hard.

Sten's second eye was redder than the first. He swung stubby legs over the side of the bench and sat swaying, squinting and blinking.

"Bless, Grandfather," Ronan said, gripping Sten's forearm.

"Bless, Lamb," Sten returned, locking his craftsman's fingers around Ronan's arm. Sten's other hand went to Ronan's shoulder. They remained locked together while Sten continued struggling with his eyes and balance ... he finally gave up. "Smooth may be your entry to Valhalla, Ronanryan." With that, his hands fell away, he toppled back with a thud, and recommenced his snoring.

Ronan's throat constricted at Sten's words—he wasn't interested in his own death, but the sentiment moved him, along with the man's use of his name.

Freyja sighed. "He will remember nothing in the morning."

Ronan turned to her and, without thinking, drew her to his chest, chin on her head. "Bless, Grandmother," he said, the goodbye catching in his throat.

Freyja's arms clamped around him, her shoulders shook. "Bless, my Ronan," she sobbed.

"I'll be back," he said, voice fraying.

"I know," she murmured.

Ronan kissed her forehead, pushed her to arm's length. "Thank you, Grandmother."

"May the gods smooth your path," she breathed as he turned and strode into the gloom at the end of the longhouse.

It took him a few moments to compose himself, to rein in his emotions, blank his mind. Eventually, he floated into ró; the smoky air sliced open with a breath.

And he was gone.

PART IV

THE RECKONING

56

THE REUNION

Despite preparing himself, the agitation still came as a shock to Ronan. Abrupt, unpredictable changes left his stomach going in one direction, everything else in another, and, when it became a tornado spin, Ronan thought his head might fly off. Eventually, glorious calm descended.

But not for long. Ronan's world soon started swirling and his gut churning; he wanted to puke. At least there was no shaking. Sten's coarse-woven tunic and pants against his skin, and the supple leather boots encasing his feet, were reassuring. And the ground was soft, dry and ... smelly. One eyelid eased open, a wisp of straw caught in the lash. As Ronan blinked it free, he saw movement—flies were buzzing round a green-brown mound in front of his nose. When he opened the other eye, all he could see was the same colour.

At last, the odour found the right memory connection—horse dung! Ronan was lying on his right side and using a pile of equine excreta as a pillow. The smell clogged his nostrils; he wanted to laugh and vomit at the same time. Instead, he simply lay there, breathing in the aroma of stale horse poo.

The clatter of panicked hoof beats penetrated his stupor, drawing closer, becoming muffled, then stopping altogether. In their place, the heaving breaths of a terrified animal.

Ronan willed himself alert—part of his mind was registering the animal's distress. He rolled off his horse-poo pillow, rising onto his backside. The horse snorted at the movement, blowing moisture across Ronan's back. Gingerly, he turned. It worked! He was at Raven's Roost! Before him stood Duke, eyes rolling, coat running with sweat, flanks quivering. Distended nostrils sucked in barrels of air as he pawed at the sawdust, snorting.

And there was the empty saddle Ronan had catapulted from four days ago ... no, only minutes ago ... everything was so damned confusing.

Remnants of the pillow were stuck to the side of Ronan's face; most came away with a procession of feeble swipes. Head still spinning from the umrót, he pulled himself upright on the stall door, sagged over the top, vomiting into the straw, immediately feeling better.

The memories of Kaupang swirling in his head were displaced by an earlier one of a horrified girl watching him die.

When he'd entered ró after Freyja's and Sten's farewells, Ronan was clutching his last image of Saoirse, face white with terror as she screamed his name. Consequently, he'd expected to be set down in the laneway near where Egan hit him—behind the hedge, or stone fence. But the rune had set him down in the stables, in a safe place, just as Freyja said it would.

There was more of the clinging stench on his face, and matted in his hair. With the door frame for support, Ronan straightened, crooning to the horse as he tottered toward it. "Steady boy, steady," he crooned, holding out a dung-stained hand to the flared nostrils. *It should smell horsey,* he thought, almost laughing. Duke snorted distress, blowing wetness everywhere. "Easy. Easy, boy." Ronan rubbed the velvet muzzle, murmuring, soothing, edging fingers to the bridle.

Rein in hand, he led the trembling animal into the stall, but hadn't even shut the door when the steady clip-clop of trotting hooves echoed through the building. *Saoirse!* He wanted to run to greet her, but his umrót-weakened legs saw him leaning against the front wall of Duke's stall as Viking entered the stables. The big grey gelding's head lifted and ears pricked, but Ronan only saw Saoirse—dishevelled hair; puffy, red-rimmed eyes; ashen, tear-tracked face. She gasped when she sighted Ronan, leapt from Viking's back, running before her feet touched the ground.

Ronan smiled as he pushed off the wall.

Saoirse slammed into him with a shriek, driving him against the stall. "Ronan!" she cried. "I thought you were dead! What happened?" She clung to him, sobbing into his chest.

Wrapping his arms about her, Ronan whispered into her hair, "I'm fine, Saoirse, I'm fine." While far from true, at the moment, he was floating, face buried in her scent.

Saoirse pulled away, nose wrinkled, cheeks glowing. "You stink," she said, fanning the air.

The old Ronan would've been embarrassed, both by the extended embrace and the clinging horse poo, but the new one didn't give a damn. Instead, he grimaced and said, "Yeah, I woke up in Duke's dung heap." He gave a wry smile. "You wouldn't happen to have a shower and a change of clothes, by any chance?"

Squinting and rubbing her chin, Saoirse said, "Can you be trusted now, Ronan Ryan?" Her face had been working up to a teasing smile, but it evaporated.

"What's wrong?" Ronan asked, instinctively reaching for her, wobbling as he did.

Saoirse put a palm against his chest. "I said, you stink." But as she spoke, her eyes filled.

"No," Ronan said, searching his mind for what he'd said or done, "there's something more."

Saoirse dropped her eyes. "I was just picturing your clothes lying in the lane," she said, lips trembling. "You just disappeared!"—fresh tears tracked down her cheeks—"I thought I'd never see you again." She sobbed, falling into his embrace once more. "And next minute you're back here as if nothing happened ... it's impossible." Her voice muffled against his chest. "What's happening?"

They clung to each other until even Ronan couldn't stand the stink. Easing her away, he hooked a curtain of hair behind an ear, gently thumbing the tears from her eyes.

"I'll tell you everything," he said, "but after a shower. And would you have any ginger beer?"

"What?" She looked at him blankly.

"I need something for the umrót." Ronan grimaced, rubbing his belly.

Saoirse frowned. "The what?"

"Sorry. The turmoil ... er, like travel-sickness?"

Her frown deepened.

"I'll explain later," he said. "Do you have anything for a queasy tummy?"

"Dad has ginger ale in the fridge"—she grinned—"but *you* can tell him where it's gone."

"Deal," Ronan said, easing from the wall, welcoming Saoirse's steadying hand on his arm. Viking, who had been standing patiently the whole time, nickered a reminder that he was there.

"Sorry, boy." Saoirse gathered the reins as they passed, and the horse plodded obediently behind, across the yard to the mudroom. "You know where everything is; just don't put that wee pebble on the soap rack ... don't want you destroying the place."

They both chuckled, then Ronan said, "Don't worry, it won't happen again." He turned, lifting his hair.

"Ugh, it looks like it's burrowing into your head." Saoirse touched a tentative fingertip to the fresh skin expanding over the edges of the blood rune. "Ooh." She shivered, snatching her hand away. "Does it hurt?"

"Nah, feels great. Very warm ... reassuring."

"It's weird."

Ronan shrugged, dropping the hair into place, wondering how repulsed Saoirse really was. Before he could dwell further, she rolled her eyes, turning him toward the door, and with a gentle prod, saying, "Off you go, then. I'll go down and get your clothes ... be back in a few minutes."

"Wait"—Ronan caught her arm—"what about Finnegan?"

Saoirse laughed. "Will you stop calling him that?"

Ronan gave a non-committal shrug, but didn't release his grip.

Still smiling, Saoirse said, "He claimed it was an accident, spewed a couple of times, and drove off towards Teelin in an absolute blue funk." Her lips curled. "Fionn will be shitting bricks. He knows he hit you, and he won't know what to make of no body ... it'll drive him spare." She chuckled. "Fionn will think he's gone round the twist."

Reluctantly, Ronan released her. "Do you think anyone saw?"

Saoirse shook her head. "Those big oak trees shield that spot from the house, and no one would see much from the road."

Ronan wondered if Egan would even be game to tell his mother about it; probably not. "Off you go, then," he said, boomeranging her words with a half grin. Saoirse sprang astride Viking and trotted off.

57

THE KISS

By the time Saoirse returned, the bench had grown warm under Ronan's backside. Wrapped in a towel, he was contemplating the glow emanating from the centre of his chest, rather than from the base of his skull. Ten minutes under the hot shower had sluiced the horse dung from his face, the longhouse smoke from his hair, and some of the umrót from his body, or so it seemed.

At last, there was a business-like rap on the door. "Are you decent?" Saoirse called.

"As decent as I can be." Ronan replied, and she pushed into the room, bundle of clothes in one hand, frosted bottle of Poachers Premium Irish Ginger Ale in the other. The tear tracks had been washed from her face, and the disorder combed from her hair. Even beforehand, she was the prettiest girl Ronan had ever seen.

"Sorry I took a while," she said, "but I tended to Viking and Duke.

"I thought you'd got lost," he quipped with a grin.

Saoirse gave him an exaggerated eye-roll and continued as if he hadn't spoken, "Duke is an absolute mess ... what a murdering gobshite."

Ronan sobered; he would've used a more vehement word for Egan —the horse was scarred for life. "The poor bugger will never get over it."

As Saoirse dropped the clothes on the bench, her eyes flitted from his face to his naked chest. "What have you done?" she said. Handing him the bottle of Poachers, she squatted in front of him, fingertips feathering around the seeping wound. At her tingling touch, his skin quivered and muscles twitched. She snapped her hand away. "Sorry."

"It didn't hurt," he said. "It was just a ... a ..." He wanted to say thrill, but settled for, " ... an unexpected shiver."

Saoirse's cheeks coloured regardless.

Again, fingers whispered across Ronan's skin; his breath caught. An invisible band tightened round his ribs, more consuming and more urgent than pre-match nerves. Ronan's whole body was buzzing with a restrained, yet uncertain, energy. He gazed into Saoirse's liquid eyes, damp and sparkling. Long lashes drooped as she lifted her face to his. A strange current surged through him. He bent; their lips met hesitantly, unsure but compelled. Hers were moist, soft and sweet. And electric!

Next instant they were in a tangle of arms, lips mashed together, trying to climb inside the other's mouth, each striving to outdo the other. Finally, they broke apart, panting and flushed, and simply held each other. All Ronan smelt was apple; all he felt was connection; all he desired was that Saoirse felt it as well. His head was spinning, from Saoirse he hoped, not the umrót. But his stomach rumbled ominously.

Easing her away, he reached for the Poachers; a loud protest came from somewhere behind his bellybutton.

"We shouldn't do that again," she teased.

"Umrót," he said, taking a good slug of ginger ale, embracing its soothing effect. "And it was the flytja, not you," he added with a grin.

"Will you speak English?" she said with mock censure.

"Sorry," he said, "umrót is the turmoil, ah, motion-sickness, caused by flytja. And flytja is the travel to another time ... or the same time."

Saoirse stared blankly, a tiny frown reshaping her eyebrows. "Have you been on drugs again?"

Ronan laughed, feeling better despite the rumbling in his gut—it wasn't the Poachers. He drew her close. "We should try it again to make sure."

"Mm, I'm not sure about you," she murmured before their lips met with a sweetness that stole his breath. Blood pounded in his ears; he never wanted to let her go.

Saoirse disentangled and eased to arm's length, dropping her eyes to his chest, becoming serious. "You haven't answered."

"What?"

Saoirse's fingertips produced another electric charge around his arrow wound.

Ronan looked down, wanting that touch to never leave his skin. "Long story," he replied.

Saoirse heaved a sigh. "Always is with you."

"It was an arrow."

Saoirse froze, gawking at the wound. "An arrow?"

Ronan nodded, and took a swig of the ginger ale, revelling in the spicy bite fizzing into his stomach.

"Jaysis, Ronan Ryan, what have you been up to?"

"It's a long ..." he began, before they both chuckled. "Look," he said, dropping his free hand to the clothes, "how about I get these on, then I'll tell you everything?"

"Deal," she said with a brisk nod, gathering his Norse garb, sweeping from the room in a swirl of hair.

As he dressed, Ronan kept sipping ginger ale and belching deep, from-the-bottom-of-the-stomach burps, each one lessening the discomfort—he sensed the worst of the umrót was behind him. When he joined Saoirse in the cottage, she was running Sten's tunic through her hands. "Wow, this looks homemade."

"It is. All of it is, tunic, pants, boots."

"Where did you get them?" There was genuine interest in her face.

"From my grandmother."

"Your grandmother?"

"Yeah," he said dryly, "about fifty times removed."

Saoirse was halfway through another eye-roll when her fingers found the blood-stained slit. The animation fled her face, her lips tightened, eyes clouded. "What happened, Ronan?" she asked in a small voice.

And so, Ronan related all that took place in, what was to Saoirse, the handful of minutes between when Fionn Egan ran him down, and she'd ridden, distraught, into the stables. During the telling, he had a second bottle of Darragh's ginger ale, Saoirse dressed his wound, and they shared a cup of tea and a slice of bread and jam—he revelled in the light, modern bread melting in his mouth.

The last light of day was slanting through the curtains by the time Ronan finished his tale, but they remained nestled together on the couch, touching, talking, holding hands, enjoying the closeness.

The crunch of tyres on gravel heralded Darragh's return. They looked at each other, Saoirse frowned and, wordlessly, they slid to opposite ends of the couch.

Darragh stamped his boots clean on the outside mat, and clomped through the door with an unnecessary, "I'm home." After shedding his hat and coat, he walked into the lounge, beaming. If he noticed the deep indentations in the cushions between them, he gave no sign. "Well, you two haven't moved far," he said cheerily.

58

THE REVELATIONS

By the following morning, Ronan was almost normal, amazed at the speed of his recovery. He decided it was a combination— Poacher's for his body; Saoirse for his spirits. Being in her presence was the most exciting, all-consuming, and sometimes confusing feeling he'd ever experienced. And for the hundredth time, he marvelled at the way his blood rune was changing him.

Masters' bullet struck the back of a sixteen-year-old boy who, a few short days later, and on the other side of the world, was more a man— mature, self-assured, eloquent and even a little wise, at least to his own ears. It was a Norse rune, after all, and the Norse considered a male of sixteen a man, Halfdan being a prime example.

But the morning brought with it an immediate and major problem. Darragh was insistent that today was the day they tracked down Ronan's parents. "We'll discuss it over breakfast," he called after them, as they walked into the chilly dawn to feed the horses.

Darragh's adamant tone sent Ronan and Saoirse into a huddle as soon as they were in the feed room. Hungry nickers and impatient hoof-stomping went unanswered as every option was examined. At last, Ronan said, "We'll have to tell him everything; there's no way round it." Saoirse nodded.

After completing the feeding, they dragged their feet back to the cottage for breakfast—Saoirse's uncertainty about how her father would react heightened Ronan's nervousness.

Surprisingly, Darragh's restraint held for most of the meal. At first, he appeared not to notice the furtive glances, but by his second piece of toast, his patience ran out. "All right, you pair, what's going on?" He pushed his mug aside, leaning his forearms on the edge of the table, locking a firm gaze on his daughter. "Saoirse?"

"Dad, you won't believe this ..." she began.

"Try me," he responded, peering at Ronan.

Ronan swallowed, then calmed as the rune's power washed through him. He held firm under Darragh's scrutiny; he knew exactly how to convince the man.

"Mr Kelly ... Darragh," Ronan began, his voice steady, "I'm going to show you something that's not possible, but you'll see it with your own eyes. Then I'll tell you something that I can't know, unless what I show you is true."

Darragh raised his eyebrows. "You're not making much sense, lad." His tone was terse; he glanced toward his daughter. "And the only reason I'm listening is because Saoirse puts great store in you"—he folded his arms, pushing back in his chair—"so this better be good."

"Oh, it's better than good, Dad ... it's weird, bizarre, and absolutely fantastical."

Darragh was unmoved.

While Ronan appreciated the support, he thought she was over-doing it. He stood, pointing to Saoirse's bedroom. "If I shut myself in that room, how long do you reckon it would take to open the window, climb out, run round and into the stables?"

Darragh chortled. Ronan turned to Saoirse with a puzzled frown.

"That window's been jammed for years," she said with a smile. She must have guessed what he was up to, for she gave a tiny nod.

"All the better," Ronan said, moving to Saoirse's room. As he closed the door, he said, "Now, please go out the front and check the stables."

Darragh looked from the door to his daughter, but didn't move.

"Please, Dad?"

Eyes never leaving Saoirse, he reluctantly rose. The scrapping of their chairs hid the intake of air behind the bedroom door.

Saoirse ran ahead; her father followed sedately. As he exited the cottage, he halted, took an involuntary backward step and breathed, "Bejaysis!" Ronan was strolling from the stables.

Darragh gawked from one to the other. "How did you get that window open and round there so fast?" Turning, he strode through the door toward Saoirse's room, but a muted sigh from the kitchen caught his attention. There stood Ronan; Darragh blanched.

"Come on, Dad, let's sit you down." She took an arm, but it was like his Deetees had sent tap-roots into the floor.

The man gaped at his daughter, then spun to Ronan as if trying to catch him in the middle of some trick or illusion. Dumbfounded, he let Saoirse guide him to a chair.

For the next half hour, Ronan told Darragh the gist of what had happened since he'd run for the creek at Doyle Farm, notebook in one hand, stone in the other, including the fact that his initial bruises were from his stepfather, not a mugging. Ronan showed the arrow wound in his chest and the blood rune at the base of his skull. At the end, Darragh was still shaking his head. "I saw it with me own eyes ... still don't believe it."

Ronan leant across the table. "Have you heard about the accident at Sliabh Liag?"

Darragh nodded. "It was on the radio ... some poor soul fell off the cliff yesterday ... no name until they notify relatives."

"That was my father," Ronan said sombrely, "Paidin Ryan, twenty-seven. The others present were Maureen Doyle, his fiancé, twenty-six, and Bruno Masters, twenty-eight. Maureen is my mother, and she's only just pregnant with me ... I'll be born on the first of July ... next year."

"Jaysis, lad, what more is there?" Darragh's head shook as though clearing a fog, and Saoirse squeezed his arm—she hadn't left his side. "I think I need to have a wee lie down," he said, patting his daughter's hand, leaving the kitchen in a daze.

"I'm not sure how that went," Ronan said when the bedroom door closed.

Saoirse offered a weak smile. "He'll be fine once he's had a chance to mull it over."

Ronan flopped onto the couch, exhausted; not from the two short flytjas, but from trying to convince Darragh—his entire future depended on it. Not only did he want to stay the full nine days, he was desperate to keep coming back.

Saoirse seemed to have taken it in her stride. Although she'd seen him disappear when he should have died, and then reappear when logic said he couldn't, she didn't turn a hair when he flitted from bedroom to stables to kitchen like a hyperactive moth. She sank onto the cushion beside him, taking his hand, dropping her head to his shoulder.

Six days ago—two for Saoirse—he'd lain in that same spot, recovering from umrót and a head-knock. Six days? Or was it seven?

"What are you thinking about?" she murmured, as if sensing his distraction.

"Huh? Oh, I was trying to work out how time fits together ... I was away for days, but it was only a few minutes for you ... How can that even work?" All that flitting around the world and back through time defied sense; applying logic to any aspect of it was futile.

"Caitlin will know; she's a whizz at maths."

Ronan stiffened. "You can't tell her."

Saoirse was smirking when she lifted her face to peck him on the cheek. "Gotcha!"

He smiled, revelling in the lingering sensation of soft lips on his skin. As it faded, the family portrait above the television caught his attention. A potentially perilous question—one he couldn't ignore—floated to the top of his consciousness. "What happened to your mum and brother?"

It was Saoirse's turn to stiffen, and Ronan held his breath. With a long sigh, she said, "They left when I was eight." There were no tears, only resignation.

"I'm sorry." There was nothing else to say.

A short silence was followed by a cascade of words: Niamh O'Brien was a city girl working at the Teelin pub when she met Darragh; they married, had two kids and all was great, then things lost their lustre. Saoirse came home from school one day to find the house empty—they lived in Killybegs then. Niamh took her youngest to Dublin, eventually remarrying. Niall and Saoirse exchange visits occasionally.

"When I got over my anger at her for leaving, and the heartbreak at being left behind, I realised she'd done the best thing in the circumstances ... I was always a daddy's girl, and Dad would've died if he lost all of us ... I think it's all turned out okay. Not the best, but okay."

"At least you still get to see each other," Ronan said.

"Yes, it's not like she died, although ... sorry, I wasn't thinking."

Ronan squeezed her hand. "It's fine. Besides, I know he's alive now. I have to find him ... if the rune will allow it."

"What do you mean?"

Before Ronan could answer, the bedroom door opened and a perplexed Darragh emerged. This time, Ronan and Saoirse remained together, hands clasped. Darragh took it all in, looking from his daughter to Ronan. "You've got me flummoxed, lad." He shook his head in disbelief. "I have no idea how you did that. As for the other, you may as well hang about until they release the names ... just to see whether you know as much as you say."

Saoirse shot to her feet, throwing her arms round her father. "Oh, Dad, thank you."

Darragh contemplated Ronan across her shoulder, his usually cheery face stuck in a morphing loop—confusion, unease, concern, suspicion, and back to confusion.

"And Dad," Saoirse said, releasing him, "you mustn't breathe a word of this to anyone. Promise?"

"Don't worry, I won't be saying a word ... they'd take me away."

"Cup of tea, anyone?" Saoirse said, moving to the kettle.

Ronan felt the mental whiplash; even Darragh looked surprised. He threw a resigned wink at Ronan, who smiled in return, as much from relief as at their shared moment—it was short lived.

With his daughter's back turned, Darragh stepped into Ronan's face and whispered with protective ferocity, "Don't you go breaking her heart now."

59

THE WARNING

The rest of that day, and the ones that followed, passed in the dreamy blur of Saoirse's company. It was weightlessness, like being in ró. Except his head was far from empty, and his heart pounded and pulsed in all directions. Seeing his feelings reflected in Saoirse's face only drove it faster.

Day nine rocketed toward them; they needed a plan.

"What're we going to do?" he asked Saoirse after he'd explained the nine-day rule. They were sitting, thighs and shoulders touching, on a low stone wall at the back of the stables, faces tilted to the sun's warmth. Ronan gathered a delicate hand as he spoke, and as those huge, liquid eyes turned to him, he tumbled into their depths.

"I don't want you to go, Ronan Ryan."

"And I don't want to go, Saoirse Kelly." Her name was honey on his tongue, while his name came from her lips like music. "Why do you always call me that?" he wondered aloud.

Saoirse jolted her weight against his shoulder. "It's your name, isn't it?"

Ronan pushed back. "You know what I mean."

"I don't know," she said, shrugging, kicking her heels absently against the wall. "I suppose, to start with, I was being a bit aloof."

"A bit?" Ronan teased.

"I didn't know you from Adam, did I now?" Saoirse's voice rose in mock defence as she threw a free hand into the air. "This naked boy just appears in the stables."

Ronan laughed at the memory. "That *was* pretty funny."

Saoirse smiled, then sobered. "I really don't know. Maybe I'm being a bit cheeky ... I just like the sound of it."

"And I love the way you say it," he murmured.

She squeezed his hand. Ronan's gaze flitted about her face—those eyes, the cute nose, moist lips with permanently upturned corners, the faintest dusting of freckles. Saoirse's eyes softened. They leant in, noses caressed, lips met. Flies buzzed, horses stamped and nickered, but none rose above the pounding of their hearts. At last, they separated and sat, foreheads touching.

"I wish you didn't have to go," she purred.

"So do I."

That was day six, the day the papers carried the full details of the accident at Sliabh Liag. And, with Ronan's words confirmed, Darragh reluctantly acknowledged the whole fantastical tale.

The following day, Ronan and Saoirse paid a visit to the Egan household. A small, straight-backed woman with fine features and cold eyes answered their knock. The sprinkling of age through her wavy auburn hair was eye-catching; an errant twist hung across the side of her face, like a blinker—too precise to be accidental—while the rest nestled above her collar in regimented order.

"Ah, Saoirse," the woman said, "how lovely to see you."

"Hello, Mrs Egan. Erm, this is my friend, Ronan. May we see Fionn?"

Mrs Egan arched an eyebrow toward Saoirse and peered at Ronan, extending a veiny hand with blood-red nails. "How very nice to meet you, Ronan," she said silkily.

Ronan took the hand, as cool and limp as a dead fish. "The pleasure is mine, Mrs Egan." If it wasn't for the reptilian eyes, she would be a striking woman. Fionn's looks and build must come from his father, but his character from her. The eyes remained calculating as she chuckled with delight, holding on way longer than etiquette required. Saoirse shot him a sideways glance.

"You're lucky to catch Fionn; he's been away in Dublin for the week, and I think he's off to Letterkenny this afternoon. I struggle to keep up with young people today." A mild head shake sent the wavy hair rebounding like a shampoo ad—the dangle beside her eye held firm.

Ronan got the impression that she didn't struggle with—or miss —anything.

The woman stepped aside and, with a flourish, ushered them into a sitting room. "I'll let Fionn know you're here, Saoirse," she called over her shoulder as she breezed away.

"Finnegan hasn't told her," Ronan whispered, gazing at the empty doorway.

"I think you're right," Saoirse said.

"Anyway," Ronan added innocently, "she seems like a lovely lady."

Saoirse's glare melted when she saw his smirk. "Watch her, she's a manipulative witch. She's had me married off to Fionn for years."

Before Ronan could respond, heavy footsteps sounded from the hall. The blocky form of Fionn Egan strode imperiously into the room, slamming to a halt as if hitting a brick wall. The blood drained from his face, the rigid bearing melting like midsummer ice cream. "But ... but you ... how?" he stammered, spittle collecting on slack lips.

"I know," Ronan began sardonically, "it's not fair, is it, Finnegan? I shouldn't be here."

Egan's eyes rolled, and his head bobbled as though on a spring, neither nodding nor shaking. Backing toward the door, he threw a pleading look at Saoirse, but got a cold, hard stare in return.

Ronan stepped into Egan's face, grabbing a fist-full of shirtfront, twisting tight. "I will always come back," he growled. "If you so much as look sideways at Saoirse or Darragh, I'll know, and I'll come. Do you hear me?"

Egan was mute, trembling, knees on the verge of folding. Ronan gave him a shake, and hissed, "Do you hear me?" Egan's head bobbed frantically between sobbing breaths. Releasing the shirt, Ronan pushed him aside, saying to Saoirse, "I need clean air." She shot a withering look at Egan before following Ronan from the house.

"That was fun," Saoirse said without humour, as she caught him at the bottom step.

"That's exactly what I meant about becoming this more assertive, self-assured person." His breathing was slowly returning to normal. "I would never have acted with that confidence before the blood rune, or been so flattering to Mrs Egan."

Saoirse took his hand. "Well, I've only known the blood-rune you, and it's what I love."

Her tone was so conversational, Ronan wondered if he'd heard correctly. He stopped. "What did you say?" He needed time to think.

"You heard me." Saoirse tugged him onward, leaning her head onto his shoulder as they walked through the opening in the hedge. A familiar flush of warmth spread from the centre of Ronan's chest.

Neither saw red nails draw the second-floor curtain aside; neither noticed the cool stare through the silent window pane.

60

THE PLAN

R onan and Saoirse strolled up the laneway, cocooned in their thoughts and emotions. On rounding the corner into the cottage yard, Ronan stopped, turning Saoirse to face him, taking both her hands in his. She raised an expectant eyebrow—her perfection engulfed him. With his tongue dry, on the verge of paralysis, his eloquence disappeared. "I ... um, I was ... um, waiting for the right time." Saoirse frowned, but before she could speak, Ronan continued, with a nervous laugh, "Sorry ... just struggling with my newfound grasp of language."

Saoirse ignored his droll humour. "What are you trying to say, Ronan?"

After a pause and several tight swallows, his words tumbled out. "I was waiting for the perfect moment to tell you that I love you, and when you told me back there, it threw all my plans into chaos ..." Ronan waited, unable to believe what he'd said.

"You eejit," she said, throwing her arms around him, pressing her lips to his.

When they finally parted and set off again, Ronan drew her close, their steps synchronised, hips swaying in time. Saoirse dropped her head to his shoulder once more. "I hadn't intended to tell you just yet either," she admitted, "but once it was out ..."

Back in the cottage, the sight of the calendar on the kitchen wall snapped Ronan out of his dreamy state, deflating him. "I have to leave the day after tomorrow," he said, the words weighing on his heart.

Saoirse was in the middle of filling the jug for yet another cup of tea when she twisted. "When will you be back?"

"As soon as I can," he said, "... promise."

"Will it be straight after you leave, like last time?" she asked hopefully.

Ronan hesitated, trying to recall everything Freyja had told him. "It'll be a flytja, not a heim," he said, "so it'll be up to me to set the time, I think." Saoirse's face brightened. "But," Ronan added, quelling her swelling optimism, "I don't really understand the connections between the different times and directions of travel." An edge of frustration crept into his voice. "There's so much I don't know ... I thought I was prepared ... Freyja said I was, but ..." He took a couple of settling breaths. "Maybe my dad wasn't impetuous at all; maybe he honestly thought he *was* ready."

Water cascading into the sink snapped Saoirse's attention to the overflowing jug. The sunlight streaming through the window caught a few strands hanging loose from her ponytail, painting them gold. Ronan noticed her hand quake as she switched the kettle on, so he stepped closer, hooking the errant strands behind her ear, cupping her face. "Hey," he said, "I didn't mean I mightn't be able to get back here. I can flytja accurately, I'm just not sure how times interact with each other, that's all." She clung to him with a fierce desperation, as though trying to jettison her disquiet. "Nothing," he said, "will keep me from you."

"Now," Ronan said, easing her away and throwing a theatrical forefinger into the air, "I have a brilliant plan." He led her to the couch and flopped down, head propped on one end, feet overhanging the other. Pulling her down beside him, he held her close.

"So, this is your brilliant plan?" Saoirse said with a throaty chuckle.

"Don't you like it?" he asked with exaggerated bewilderment.

"I like it very much," she said, snuggling into his neck.

"But wait, there's more!" Ronan said, imitating a television infomercial host hawking the latest kitchen gadget or weight-loss machine.

"Mmm?" she nuzzled.

"It's a two-part plan ... ahh, maybe it's got three parts."

"Do tell." Saoirse's words hummed against the skin in the crook of his neck.

Ronan stared, unseeing, at the ceiling, formulating the plan as he spoke. "Okay, so I think I may have found a way to overcome the umrót."

"Mmm."

"You're not listening, are you?"

"Yes, I am," she murmured, her fingernails lightly tracing the curve of his jaw.

"I need the strongest travel-sickness tablets I can get."

She propped herself onto an elbow, the loose strands falling into Ronan's face. "We can catch the morning bus to Killybegs and get some at the pharmacy." She tapped a playful forefinger on the tip of his nose. "See, I *am* paying attention."

"Good," he said, craning up, pecking her on the lips.

"What else?"

"School."

Saoirse wrinkled her nose. Ronan drew in a breath to argue his case, but she put a finger to his lips and gave an impish smile. "Only kidding. I'm just lucky this last week has been holidays, otherwise I'd have a lot of catching up to do."

"But *I* won't."

"That's not fair," she snorted in mock indignation.

Ronan gave an exaggerated shrug and a wry grin. "Them's the breaks."

Again, Saoirse screwed up her nose, this time poking her tongue. He feigned to bite; the tongue disappeared.

"Anyway," he said, "as long as the motion-sickness medicine works, I can come back as often as I like. But I reckon it should only be on weekends."

The corners of Saoirse's mouth dropped as she made puppy eyes.

"You ... are ... beautiful," he said, pulling her head down, kissing her tenderly. While her expression melted, it became a fake scowl as they separated, prompting Ronan to give a gentle push. Saoirse gasped as she toppled, but at the last second, Ronan caught her with a cheeky smile, ducking against her velvet retaliation.

Even though her lips were compressed, her eyes sparkled with laughter. "I'm not sure I want you back every weekend, Ronan Ryan."

"Ouch!" he said. "What happened to, 'I don't want you to go'?"

"You," she said, poking a benign finger in his chest, grinning at his injured expression. "Of course I want you back," she cooed. After a moment, she added, "What's the third part of your devious plan?"

"We need a story to explain why I turn up on weekends."

"Well, Dad's no problem now, so who is?"

"Caitlin for one," Ronan replied. Saoirse had told him about her best friend who had kindled her interest in environmental science.

"Dad thinks I just want to share uni classes with Caitlin," Saoirse had said, shaking her head. "But I really want to do ES because"—her voice had risen with passion—"I know this sounds pretentious, but ... I want to do something that helps solve the world's problems."

Snapping back to the present, Ronan said, "Then there's the Egans ... visitors to Raven's Roost and"—he shrugged—"maybe any other school friends we run into. I assume you'll show me the local sights, or are you going to hide me?" He made an exaggerated pout.

"I'm going to keep you locked up"—she smiled impishly, tapping his nose, giving him a peck—"all to myself."

"Can't wait," Ronan said with a smile, easing her face away so he could focus on her dreamy eyes. "Be serious," he said at last, "we need a good story, and sooner rather than later."

"Because you love me," she suggested, "and you can't bear for us to be apart."

"Why didn't I think of that?" he said, bumping the heel of his hand to his forehead. "Seriously, where am I supposed to be all week, and how do I get from there to here?"

They studied each other, then Saoirse shrugged, saying, "No idea at the moment, but I'm sure we'll think of something."

After a long silence during which he watched her brow furrow, smooth, and furrow some more, Saoirse said, "I have a confession to make."

"What? You're secretly married with three kids?" Ronan said in mock horror.

"Don't be an eejit," she said, unsmiling.

Ronan felt a small tug of apprehension. Rolling onto his side to better study her, he waited, wondering what she could possibly have to confess.

"I didn't believe you at first," Saoirse said. "I just played along to keep you calm until you recovered, and all your memories unscrambled." She held up a hand as Ronan shaped to speak, to console her. "Then, when we rode up the mountain and you saw your mum and dad, I thought I was catching whatever you had."

The corners of Saoirse's lips ticked upward as she swallowed. "I don't think I really believed you until you reappeared with the arrow wound. I thought I did, but it was ... is ... all so impossible. There was still a part of my brain that wouldn't accept it, even after you disappeared ..."—her words slowed; her gaze dropped—"I'm sorry."

A tear swam along Saoirse's bottom eyelid; he thumbed it away, holding her cheek in his palm. "It doesn't matter." Ronan shook his head. "You were only a few days behind me in accepting it all ... and I was living it. And you're right, it's absolutely unbelievable, so please, apart from your dad, not a word to anyone else, not even Caitlin. Okay?"

Saoirse nodded absently, as though still scolding herself.

"Now I have a confession," he said, studying her face.

Saoirse gave him a doubtful look, as if expecting flippancy, a bit of humour to balance her own disclosure, make her feel better.

"I don't have any way to pay for a bus ticket or tablets."

Saoirse narrowed her eyes. "Ah, so you're a freeloader, then?"

"I'll repay you as soon as I can ... promise."

"Sure, and I've heard that before, Ronan Ryan." She made a crooked smile.

Saoirse's readiness to share what little money she had, sent a shaft of guilt through him, but he was also puzzled—she hadn't mentioned any job. "How do you earn your money?" Ronan asked bluntly.

"Well," she responded without hesitation, "I make a few euros each week from looking after the Egan's horses ... after I've paid for Viking's feed and board."

"You must do something else."

"Why?"

"You've just bought a phone." Ronan held his breath.

While she appeared to have forgotten his earlier insult, Saoirse propped herself on an elbow again, arching an eyebrow at him. "Just because we're a couple now, you expect me to share all my secrets?"

Ronan flung his eyes wide. "You're a hooker?" It was the most outlandish thing he could come up with in that split second. Concerned his wacky sense of humour had gone too far, he grinned up at her.

Saoirse threw him a withering look—momentarily rattling him—then she smirked. "Only on weekends."

Relieved, Ronan mused, "That's going to present problems then, isn't it?" They grinned at each other. "Seriously, what else do you do?"

"Oh, I do a bit of leather work," she replied cryptically.

"Like father, like daughter," he said and, when she didn't respond, "Do I have to drag it out of you? What do you make?"

"Notebooks."

"Like your dad?"

"No, he makes boots."

"Okay. Well, like Deetee notebooks?"

"No, not *like* them."

Ronan missed the emphasis. He was revelling in their to-and-fro, lost in the golden sparkle of her eyes. "Okay, like what then? Can I see one?"

"You already have."

"When? What ...?"

Saoirse chuckled at his confusion.

With an almost-audible clunk, the penny dropped. "*You* make Deetee notebooks?"

By now, she was laughing with gusto. "That was like drawing teeth, Ronan Ryan."

Ronan made a face; she told him the story of the Deetee notebooks. Saoirse shared her father's love of the soft texture and sweet tannin scent of leather, and he would bring home scraps for her to play with. When she created a notebook cover adorned with the dT symbol,

Darragh showed his boss, who was so impressed he ordered as many as she could make—charged her for the waste leather, of course.

One of Ronan's mysteries was making more sense. "Does anyone else make them?"

"Only me at first, but I can only do it on weekends ... pretty soon I couldn't keep up, so they put on another person. But we still struggle."

"So, demand is growing?"

"Yeah, they're trying to find someone else who does quality leather work."

"That'll work," he said with instant satisfaction.

It was Saoirse's turn for confusion. "What?"

"I'm going to come over here each weekend to make notebooks with you." Ronan tingled with anticipation. "I'll be your extra person; I love working with leather."

Saoirse gave a tiny clap. "Perfect!"

"But I can't put my initials in the logo."

"Oh, you noticed that?"

Ronan nodded, soaring with satisfaction as that piece of the puzzle dropped into place. "It's what brought me here, to you."

Saoirse raised a quizzical eyebrow, then beamed. "You were carrying one of my notebooks when that beast shot you! That's why the rune brought you to Raven's Roost!"

Ronan nodded again. "Thank you," he whispered, drawing her head down for a kiss that he never wanted to end.

61

THE SEPARATION

By sundown the next day, they were back in the cottage, having taken a good chop at Saoirse's savings. Earlier, they had made the thirty-minute run into Killybegs with Darragh hunched over the steering wheel, peering at the road, eyeing oncoming traffic with great suspicion. He hummed away, shooting occasional rear-view-mirror glances at Ronan and Saoirse, strapped in adjacent seats, hands clasped, shoulders rubbing to the swaying as the little car followed the curves in the road.

Darragh said he needed to attend to a few chores at the factory, unfinished ones from the previous day—Ronan suspected it resulted from a request from Saoirse, but he wasn't complaining. However, considering how little money they appeared to have, their generosity distressed him. In the quiet moments of the drive, he contemplated how to repay them, but didn't come up with anything better than helping Saoirse make notebooks. With each doing the parts they were quickest at, they should be able to churn out a good few each weekend while enjoying each other's company, and still have plenty of free time. At all costs, he must avoid anything the rune might consider meddling in the past. The prospect of committing trufla and being whisked to the Home Stone in a heartbeat was disconcerting—it hung over Ronan's head like a suspended prison sentence.

A double row of cheek-by-jowl houses, pressing tight against the narrow street, escorted them into the town. Most were two-storey, well maintained and presenting cheerful, flat facades to passers-by. A foot-path, barely wide enough for two people abreast, was all that separated their front walls from traffic gliding past. Ronan imagined the forlorn faces of children with nowhere to play, pressed hard against breath-smudged window panes ... he hoped the houses had backyards.

Almost before it registered, they eased past The Faulty Rudder with its round Guinness Draught sign swinging in the breeze. Ronan nudged Saoirse and pointed behind them with his head. She spun, then frowned a question at him. 'Faulty Rudder', he mouthed.

Killybegs was a bustling little town. As well as hosting the Detencin boot factory, it was, according to Darragh, 'the biggest fishing port in all of Ireland'. Given the harbour full of trawlers that swept into view as they turned down the hill at the first crossroad, Ronan believed it.

Before disappearing around the waterfront toward the boot factory, their driver dropped them in the tiny car park beside the visitor infor-mation centre, with an agreement to collect them from the same spot in two hours.

After buying a packet of Kwells—recommended by the pharmacist—they shared relaxing fish and chips in a grassy park overlooking the Sunday inactivity of the harbour. The sun's warmth was heavy on Ronan's eyelids and, combined with calling gulls, salt-tanged air, and even-saltier chips, pushed the next day's departure from his mind. He sprawled back on the hard wooden bench, revelling in the tug-of-war across his face between the sunshine and the fresh breeze coming off the water. It was so different to Doyle Farm where the air was hot, the sun hotter, and water scarce. For a moment, he forgot about Saoirse until she pressed against him while reaching across for another handful of chips.

That morning, she'd drawn her hair into a separate plait along each side of her head, joining them into a single golden-brown rope that hung between her shoulder blades. It looked familiar, but Ronan's fleeting attempt couldn't place where he'd seen it. How she did it baffled him, but he liked it ... a lot.

Drawing Saoirse closer, he kissed her tenderly. "There is nothing," he said when they separated, "that will stop me coming back to you."

Saoirse lifted her hand, cupping his cheek, holding it close, liquid eyes locked on his. "Good," she murmured as their lips met again.

On the way back to the information centre, they bought a six-pack of Poacher's ginger ale, and as Ronan watched the euros leaving Saoirse's hand, a fresh wave of guilt engulfed him.

The morning of the ninth day saw them both subdued—Ronan more so than Saoirse—and staying close. When Ronan was with Freyja, he never doubted his ability to flytja to wherever he wanted; now, without her reassuring presence, uncertainty stirred in his gut. Gnawing at his confidence was the fear that he may not be able to return to Saoirse, or that he mightn't even get home to Doyle Farm. Then, he felt the warmth of his blood rune. As they returned to the cottage after exercising the horses, he was buoyant, determined for their last hours together to be as cheerful as possible.

Earlier, he'd bidden farewell to Darragh, thanking him for his hospitality, but with no mention of an imminent return. After a warm handshake and an invitation to come any time, Darragh waved a cordial goodbye as he headed out for his regular Sunday game of cards at the pub in Teelin. "He'll be there all day," Saoirse said. "Never drinks much, but loves catching up with his mates and playing Twenty-Five."

Now, lying in each other's arms on the couch, they chatted about the events of the past week and a half, and planned their following weekend. Already Ronan was aching to be back with her. He still couldn't believe he had, by total chance, met such an amazing, beautiful person who understood him so well.

When he'd briefly gone out with Chloe Stuart at the beginning of the year, his mother warned him of puppy love and teenage romances; she needn't have worried—Chloe was too serious and clingy, although she did teach him how to kiss. Saoirse was different. Without her, he seemed incomplete, like they were two parts of a single whole. At the same time, she was a bottomless well, one he was still falling into. He only hoped he was the same for her.

As if in answer Saoirse said, voice brittle, "Promise you'll come back?"

Ronan drew her close, hoping the intensity of his embrace would be her answer.

"Promise me," she whispered into his shoulder.

Ronan eased her away so he could commit every pore, curve and freckle into his memory. Everything about her was perfection, invading every cell in his body, stretching each one to breaking point. "I'll always come back to you, Saoirse ... I promise."

With mounting disquiet, they watched the kitchen clock tick toward noon. Neither of them was sure of the exact time he'd arrived from Kaupang, and while Ronan thought he may be able to wait until closer to one o'clock, he wouldn't risk going over the nine-day limit and being heimmed away. He swallowed two Kwells, trusting they'd dampen the worst of the umrót.

The closer the long hand got to the top of the clock, the louder the ticking became. Hardly daring to breathe, Ronan willed the sweeping second hand to slow its insistent ticking—it ploughed on regardless. And, before it should have been, it was time.

Ronan rose, pulling Saoirse up, holding her close. *By Odin, I love this girl.* He almost laughed—his rune's Norse origin was even infusing his thoughts.

"I'll be back on Friday," he said, easing her to arm's length. "But not before you've finished your homework." Ronan wagged a finger under her nose.

Saoirse poked her tongue before snuggling her cheek into his shirt-front. The scent of apples filled his nostrils.

The long hand ticked through the vertical without pause.

"I love you, Ronan," Saoirse sighed into his chest.

"And I love you more than I can ever say," he responded. "Now, I really have to go."

Trying to ignore her pleading eyes, he peeled her away, gave her a quick, final kiss, took a deep breath, steeled himself, and walked toward the next room.

"Ronan! No! I need to see you leave ... please?"

Ronan stopped before the doorway. "I'll try. But you've got to be quiet." His tone was firmer than intended; he immediately felt bad. But he wasn't game to turn; it would only create further delay. The long hand ticked on, gathering pace as it began its descent. "Saoirse," he said tenderly, "I have to blank my mind to do this, and my time will run out at any moment."

"I understand." After a distraught sob, she added softly, "Ronan Ryan."

The possibility Saoirse was saying goodbye forever was like an arrow to Ronan's heart. It was all he could do not to turn and embrace her, but the clock was ticking, ticking. Instead, he inhaled and focused. Sobbing breaths filled his ears; it was no use, he couldn't do it. *Freyja, Freyja, what would you do? Please tell me, Grandmother?* Close your eyes ... empty your mind ... picture your destination ... float into ró.

With a quick intake of breath, the air sliced open, sucking his extremities inward through the gash ... and he was gone.

Ronan missed Saoirse's shocked gasp and the choked sob that followed.

62

THE GHOST

The agitation on Ronan's body was much less severe than his previous flytja, and nothing compared to his two violent heims. It was more like Darragh Kelly's sweeping turns and feathering brakes, rather than Granddad Doyle's jabbing turns and stabbing stops. But, best of all, he was in the shed at Doyle Farm! There was no mistaking the huge, round poles soaring to support the vaulted roof, or the protesting squeak from loose iron flapping in the breeze. The cocktail of old hay mustiness combined with the sweet freshness of the new, along with subtle undertones of horse dung, was the scent of home. He bounced to his feet, pumping a fist—there was no sign of umrót.

The cavernous building was gloomy, with only a seep of evening glow coming through a small gap in the wall. Barely a year earlier, Ronan had crouched with his eye pressed to that same hole, watching Grandpa Paddy put Masters in his place; that now seemed half a lifetime ago.

Sidling across to the loose sheet of iron, he peered through the gap. Masters was lurking out there somewhere, in a drunken fog, casting about with the rabbit-shooting rifle, searching for a target. While Freyja had assured Ronan the blood rune would always return him to the instant after he was heimmed, the prospect of being shot again—and all it entailed—was utterly unappealing.

The tinge of pink thrown up by the recently retired sun was performing a final curtsy to the sullen heat of the day. Soon, it would dissolve as the star-punctured blanket of night crept across the heavens, bringing a welcome drop in temperature.

Amid wondering where Masters could be, Ronan threw a mental hand against his forehead. Mere seconds ago, he'd set down, which meant it was only a pulse longer since Masters had shot him. Right now, the man would be approaching the creek bank, concentrating on where his quarry had disappeared. Ronan had plenty of time to enter the house from the opposite side; he must be close when Masters put down the gun—it was his best chance.

As he craned his neck round the corner of the shed door, Ronan saw a dull reflection from the shaved dome bob from sight as the man negotiated the slope toward the watercourse. Ronan knew there wasn't much time, so he sprinted to the front fence, vaulting it without breaking stride, and was halfway up the steps before noticing the wagging tail in the shadows. "Hey, Smoke," he said, bending to rub a grizzled shoulder. "Hang in there, old fella; tomorrow will be a better day." With a final pat, he ghosted across the verandah and into the interior gloom.

No sooner had Ronan entered the hallway than he paused in disbelief, the urge to laugh almost irresistible. After a deep breath, he blanked his mind, and the air disgorged him into the shadows of his recently violated bedroom with its sagging door and splintered frame. In some respects, the ability to flytja had made life much less complicated; he settled on the familiar edge of the bed with a contented sigh.

Without thinking, Ronan grabbed his phone from the bedside table, and with his thumb about to wake it, he froze—any light, no matter how dim, would be a beacon. Snorting annoyance at himself, he slipped the phone into his pocket and waited.

Masters' curses drifted up from the creek. Perhaps the man had found the bullet-holed shirt, maybe the notebook. But there were two things Ronan knew his stepfather wouldn't find: the stone, and him.

The grumbling and cursing grew louder. Ronan tensed, uncertain how to proceed. A sudden, comforting warmth spread from the base of his skull—he'd leave it to the rune.

The hinge on the back gate let out a dry squeal. Ronan visualised the overweight shape gliding past the vegetable patch, past the lemon tree where Ruddi once played golf with the fallen fruit, past the flower garden—his mother's pride and joy. Guilt stirred: he'd landed among the gerberas when he'd jumped from the bedroom window earlier. Was it only a few minutes ago? Or every bit of two weeks? Blóð rún, Heim Steinn, haetta, trufla, fundur, flytja and ró—none of it made sense. Yet all of it did, but only ... only because he'd lived it.

A deep-throated growl rumbled up through the floorboards. Swearing at the dog, Masters clomped up the back steps, across the verandah, and into the hallway. Ronan edged to the open window, body quivering from the man's proximity. When an electric blaze burst through the doorway, rupturing the shadows, he dropped into the garden bed, grimacing again at the muted crunch of broken stems. The hall light pursued him, laying a yellow, out-of-whack rectangle over the lawn. Ears straining, he hunkered in the gloom beneath the edge of the house.

Above Ronan, the footsteps stopped. A shadow interrupted the rhomboid illumination on the grass; Ronan pictured Masters' bulk filling the bedroom door. If the man came to the window, he'd surely see the indentations in the flower bed. Ronan waited, immobile, legs coiled, ready to bolt. Once again, in the pressure of the moment, he'd forgotten about flytja. And that's when the calmness, certainty and warmth washed through him.

"Bastard!" Masters growled from above. The curse was still reverberating as the man's boots clomped a well-worn, drunken course into the office, crunching through the broken glass and morphing into a squeal of protest from the swivel chair. Urgent riffling followed the familiar scrape of the drawer runner. A barked 'damn!' and a furious slam came soon after, two more exclamation points on an over-done day.

A wet nose pressed against the back of Ronan's hand, and his head almost struck the floor's underside as he sucked in a quick breath. Afraid he'd given himself away, he paused, ears straining toward the office; all that filtered past the floorboards were a few lingering squeaks of grievance from the chair. "Oh, Smoke," Ronan breathed, exhaling with relief and scratching the old dog's ear, "you frightened the shit out of me."

Then came the sounds Ronan had been waiting for—the clink of bottle on glass, the gurgle of escaping whiskey, the smack of satisfied lips.

Ronan recalled the torment of Birger, and how the rune had always set him down where Birger couldn't see him. He chuckled mirthlessly, fiddled with his phone, and emptied his mind.

When Ronan unfolded into the room, Masters was sitting at his desk, tumbler of scotch in one hand, open notebook in the other. He whirled at the soft sigh behind him, blanching, immobile, eyes thrown wide.

"What's the matter, Bruno," said Ronan silkily, "seen a ghost?"

63

THE CONFRONTATION

Bruno Masters sat transfixed, light glistening off his sweating dome. He swallowed like he was in a desert; blood abandoned his face. "Where ... how ... what ...?"

The notebook fell from slack hands; Ronan scooped it up before the man could react. Contact with the leather cover was almost like the touch of Saoirse's fingers—there was immediate connection, a sense of belonging. He was certain that, were he to check, he'd find a tiny SK carved into a swirl of the dT symbol. But there were more urgent things to worry about.

Masters' normal bluster was returning, indignation bringing the colour rushing to his face, the aura of menace once again radiating from the large body.

The sudden clamour in Ronan's gut forced an involuntary backward movement, a reflex built on years of never knowing whether a scathing look would morph into an assault. Even though a surge of familiar warmth stilled the fear as soon as it raised its ugly head, the damage was done—Masters smirked with satisfaction.

Ronan chided himself for continuing to think and react like a helpless victim instead of the empowered survivor he'd become. A rising tide of confidence quelled the uneasiness; his stepfather would never again lay a hand on him. He gave the man a mocking half-smile and stepped closer. Masters didn't flinch, but Ronan sensed indecision in the loathing gaze.

"I thought you were smarter than this," Masters scoffed.

Ronan knew the man was trying to get inside his head, so he sneered, enjoying the uncertainty on the flabby face.

As if trying to gain the upper hand, Masters growled, "Where's my rune?"

"Where you'll never find it ... ever." Ronan was still sneering, oozing self-belief, and his distinct lack of fear obviously gave Masters pause, for his eyes darted, searching for an opening. Ronan revelled in the man's uncharacteristic caution.

"You stole my damn notebook," Masters snapped.

"And you shot me in the back!" Ronan gestured from the nearby rabbit gun to the bullet-holed shirt on the desk.

Masters glowered. Ronan could feel the man's coiled strength, but was unconcerned.

"There's an interesting story behind these, you know," Ronan said, conversationally, hefting the notebook. As though of its own volition, it fell open to a double-page spread: the left held the meticulous recording of a cluster of runic symbols, the right, row upon row of slanted, spiky handwriting. In the margins, like ranks of soldiers on parade, were clusters of notes.

In half a heartbeat, everything made perfect sense. "You lying, thieving, murdering bastard," Ronan snarled, stabbing a finger at Masters' face. "This is Dad's." He held up the journal. It hadn't gone to the bottom of the Atlantic, Masters had stolen it! No wonder he wouldn't let anyone see it, especially his wife.

"You don't know what you're talking about." Masters' words were brittle with crumbling confidence.

"Oh, but I do," Ronan stated. "I have three others full of his writing—"

"You're a liar!"

Ronan continued as if Masters hadn't spoken, "Which you would have known if you'd stayed around to see what that lawyer gave us."

The man had no immediate response, doubt infused his alcohol-reddened eyes.

Shooting contempt at Masters, and without referencing the notes, Ronan recited in fluent Norse, "The bearer of the living stone, in solitude is ne'er alone; the gods shall let no ill befall its keeper with eternal thrall. Its power burns if blood enfold the lightening rune, and wealth untold awaits the one who stands apart as true of mind and pure of heart."

The whole time Ronan spoke, Masters gazed, uncomprehending.

Reverting to English, Ronan said, "All the years you've spent trying to decipher the meaning of that verse were a total waste of time." His lips curled. "You were never getting your grubby hands on the promised riches. In short, *stepfather*"—Ronan's sarcasm dripped from the word—"you're unworthy, and the rune knows it."

"Who the hell do you think you are?" Masters demanded, uncertainty undermining the ferocity of his words.

"Someone you can no longer bully," Ronan responded with satisfaction.

Masters' eyes flicked to the rifle propped against the end of the desk.

"Make one move for that and I'll lay you out like a slab of meat," Ronan said through clenched teeth, surprising even himself.

A switch flipped in Masters; his eyes flamed. "Don't you dare threaten me, you ungrateful little mongrel," he roared. With his usual blustering arrogance and hostility taking control, he launched at Ronan.

64

THE CONFESSION

Masters shot from the chair like a raging bull, a beefy bundle of raw menace. Ronan dropped into a karate crouch, hands stiffening. In a blur of pumping fists, he jabbed at his stepfather with a left before uncoiling a cocked right with an explosive 'hyah!'. The curled knuckles sunk deep into the man's ample paunch; the crack of shattered bone punctuated the air whooshing from Masters' lungs. Ronan had aimed below the ribs, but went a fraction high; he didn't care.

With an animal howl, Masters flew backward, clearing the desk top on the way, crashing to the floorboards with a thump that shook the room. The laptop clattered into one corner, the whiskey glass shattering across the floor toward the other. A swirl of loose paper circled like graceless butterflies before settling onto the disarray.

"Ungrateful?" Ronan hissed, stepping round the desk, panting from pent-up emotion rather than the effort of the single blow. Masters moaned, holding his chest. "Am I supposed to be grateful," Ronan ground through clenched teeth, "that you killed my father? That you stole his notebook and rune ...?" He couldn't go on.

Masters glared at Ronan. "I didn't kill him"—he winced, gasped and groaned in rapid succession—"he fell. It was an accident. And it was my rune. I found it ..."

Ronan ignored him. "Oh, I know," he said, oozing sarcasm, "I should be damned grateful for all those thrashings, all the bruises, all the threats"—despite his heaving chest, he was surprisingly calm—"I should be thankful for your generosity ... thank my lucky stars that you came into my life."

"You deserved it all," Masters said, voice brittle.

"Like I deserved a bullet in the back?" Ronan yelled, control vanishing. "The only thing you've ever done that I'm grateful for, is fathering Ruddi." Panting with fury, Ronan turned away; he couldn't bear looking at the man. Trying to get his emotions under control, he paced about the room, past the bookshelves, past the open window, past the low cupboard behind the desk, obligatory family photo conspicuous in its solitude.

Still agitated, Ronan lifted the studio portrait mimicking a bygone era—his mother sat in a high-backed chair, one arm holding toddler Ruddi on her lap, the other around Ronan's seven-year-old self, Masters standing arrogant and aloof, possessive hand on her shoulder, the family patriarch. All four faces showed teeth, but only three sets of eyes were smiling. Despite the familiarity of the image, it had never before spoken to Ronan like that.

"You have your father's smart mouth," Masters said, gasping as he squirmed into a sitting position, propped against the front of the desk.

Ronan ignored him, studying the photograph instead, hefting it. "Why *did* you marry Mum?"

"No one else would have her," Masters sneered. "Not with you by her side."

A red mist blurred Ronan's vision. He shot round the desk, fists clenched, foot cocked, but caught himself before he could drive a savage kick into damaged ribs. "Don't you dare speak about her like that!" he screamed.

"If she'd chosen me in the first place," Masters began bitterly, "you wouldn't even be here ... a daily, walking reminder of that irritating mick she left me for."

"Left you? Mum was never *with* you to start with." Many times, Ronan had heard the story of how his mother and Masters met in the Brisbane airport, excited young students flying to Ireland for education and adventure.

"We went to Dublin together," he insisted, grimacing and gasping.

"You happened to be on the same plane," Ronan pointed out, "... an entirely different thing."

"Well, we would have been together if mister high-and-mighty Paidin bloody Ryan hadn't come along."

Ronan's fists bunched again. "Is that why you killed him?" He was needling Masters, keeping him off balance; Ronan knew the man wouldn't hesitate if given an opportunity to turn the tables.

Masters' head shook repeatedly. "I didn't kill him! How many times do I have to tell you?"

"But you were happy to see him gone," Ronan shot back.

"For the same reason I'd be happy to see you gone. You're just like him ... everything comes easy." Masters' pasty face contorted into a sneer, his words jealous and mocking. "Paidin Ryan sets one-day cricket on fire; Paidin Ryan wins President's Medal for academic achievement; Paidin Ryan engaged to most sought-after beauty at university; Paidin Ryan's brilliant archaeological mind sheds new light on Norse history; Paidin Ryan dances along cliff without holding safety rope ..." The sarcastic tirade descended into an impotent whimper.

Filled with contempt, Ronan looked down at the man his mother married, and wondered why. "So you pushed him off the cliff, wormed your way into Mum's heart like a parasite"—his voice grew ragged—"and made my life a misery. If it hadn't been for Grandpa—"

"Paddy Ryan?" Masters' jowls quivered with emotion and pain. Bordering on hysteria, he continued, "That interfering old bastard got what he deserved."

With a flinty glower, Ronan dropped a vise grip onto his stepfather's neck. Fear jumped into the man's eyes as Ronan shook hard. "Don't say another word."

Masters gasped, clutching a hand to his chest. "You've broken my ribs, you little mongrel." His head hit the desk-front with a loud thunk.

Ronan's lip curled. "What's the matter, Masters? Feel like you've fallen off a cliff? Or been shot in the back?"

"I didn't kill him." Masters head shaking had become constant. "I didn't kill your father," he repeated.

"But you wanted it ... you caused it."

"You can't say that." Masters' indignation was as hollow as an echo. The sweat beaded across his shaved skull was collecting and giving in to gravity, tracking down the flabby jowls.

"I can, because it's the truth."

Masters started, glowering up at Ronan, beady black eyes narrowing as if trying to dredge up an old memory, then stretching wide. "It was you," he breathed. "Impossible! But there was someone who looked like you on the cliff the day your father fell."

"Me?" Ronan said with a frosty smirk. "Now, how would that be possible?"

Masters huffed in pain, his face awash with sweat, his mind wandering. "But I shot you ... saw you fall," he said in desperation. "There's a bullet hole in the back of your shirt." Moaning, he edged away. "What are you? Some sort of hallucination? A ghost?"

"I'm your worst nightmare," Ronan snarled, walking out the door.

Ronan sensed Masters' beady, pain-wracked gaze following him, heard a sob of relief. There was a sharp intake of breath in the hallway, followed by a sigh behind Masters, and Ronan's voice: "Don't relax, Bruno, I'm not finished with you yet." Masters' head whipped as Ronan walked round the desk. He gawped at Ronan, the door, and back at Ronan. He whimpered, bewildered and fearful.

Strangely, Ronan no longer had any problem using the man's first name. With his newfound confidence, the fear of his stepfather had evaporated; in its place were loathing and contempt. And he saw the beginnings of the same disintegration he'd seen in Birger.

Ronan picked up his shirt, poking a finger through the hole between where his shoulder blades would've been. The quivering form at his feet had lost its threat, its nightmare-inducing power drained like a lanced boil. In its place, just another pathetic bully, or worse, a cowardly murderer. "You killed me," Ronan accused.

Masters' shoulders slumped, head still shaking. "I didn't," he insisted. "You're here, alive."

"Am I?" Ronan smiled frostily, gathering the rifle from the end of the desk.

Masters threw his arms up in front of his face, immediately crying out, dropping a hand to his cracked ribs, sobbing. Fear or pain? Ronan didn't care.

"No, no, I didn't mean it," Masters cried. "I didn't mean to shoot you ... I'm sorry. All those times I hit you, I never set out to hurt you ... ever. It was my temper ... and the drink." It was as though a dam had burst, a plug removed. Masters' words gushed like water from a burst main. "And I would never have hurt your mother or brother ... those threats were just to keep you quiet ... cover up what I'd done ... I'm sorry, Ronan, I'm so sorry ..."

"You expect me to swallow that?" Ronan scoffed.

Snick, snick. He worked the bolt; a bullet spun lazily through the air; his hand flashed, snaring it nonchalantly, mid-spin. "What's this?" he said, holding it up. "After shooting me in the back, you reloaded, ready to shoot again? You really are a murdering swine." Ronan's lips curled; Masters had to go. He'd shown himself capable of killing; none of them were safe with him around. Ronan had no choice. While the rune would keep *him* safe, he couldn't risk his mother or Ruddi. By taking his father's notebook and the rune, he had unwittingly unleashed a blatant murderer, and he had no doubt Masters would kill again, either in anger, or as part of a cold calculation. He knew what must be done.

Face granite, eyes overflowing with loathing, he drove the rifle bolt home, locking it down.

"Please ... please don't kill me, Ronan," Masters begged. "Think of your mother."

"I am," Ronan said, lifting the weapon.

65

THE RETRIBUTION

For years, Masters had pounded away at Ronan. Now, standing over the man, rabbit-shooting rifle raised, he felt nothing but relief. Never again would Masters hurt him, never again would the man threaten his family. It would all stop now.

"No, Ronan, no," Masters pleaded, hand reaching imploringly toward the stepson he loathed. "Please don't shoot me. No, no, no ..."

Anger bubbled through Ronan; pent-up rage fizzed from brain to muscles as his hands tightened on the gun. He slammed it down in a sweeping arc onto the edge of the desk with a loud thunk. The barrel punched a deep gouge in the soft wood, and bent under the force of impact. Ronan threw it aside ... it would never fire another bullet.

Masters' cringing scream gurgled into a single relieved sob, then silence.

"Now," Ronan said through gritted teeth, "you are going to leave Doyle Farm and never return."

The man glared up at him with a shadow of returning arrogance. "I'm not going anywhere ... you can't make me ... this is my home, too."

"Only when it's convenient," Ronan shot back, his fury subsiding. "We both know that."

Masters tried to puff out his chest in defiance, but the movement ground bones together, stealing his breath. He winced, shaking his head. "I'm not going anywhere," he repeated stubbornly, a weak imitation of his former self.

"Oh, I think you are," Ronan said, pulling his mobile phone from his pocket, swiping, tapping, and tapping again. Master's distorted voice filled the room: '… all those times I hit you, I never intended to hurt you … and I would never have hurt your mother or brother … those threats were just to keep you quiet … '. He tapped the phone into silence, slipping it away.

Masters glared, hatred distorting his face.

"You'll leave and never come back," Ronan ordered. "If you do"—he tapped his pocket—"I'll release this recording. Likewise, if anything happens to Mum, Ruddi or me, or the farm, or anything else we own, value, or are associated with in any way …" Ronan ran out of conditions. "Do you understand?"

Masters glowered. "You arrogant little smart-mouthed shit," he snarled.

Ronan smirked. "Call me whatever you want," he said, "but for the rest of your miserable life, I'll be your worst nightmare." His fingers tap-danced on the end of the desk. "Before you go"—he pulled a sheet of paper and pen from a drawer—"write a lovely note to your wife explaining how you've gone off to make your fortune … or not. Write whatever the hell you like, but make it damn clear that you're never, ever, coming back. Right?"

"Go to hell!" Masters spat. "You can't make me do anything."

"Are you sure about that?" Ronan gripped the base of the man's neck, digging a thumb into the nerve above the collarbone. Masters howled, trying to twist his body away, but rib bones scraped, and he moaned, collapsing, face chalky. Ronan increased the pressure; Masters nodded with a whimper.

When the man finished writing, Ronan scanned the page. 'Maureen, I've had enough, I'm leaving. I've taken my laptop, passport and the Nissan. I'll arrange someone to collect the rest of my stuff, not sure when, BM.' Ronan set the letter on the desk, pen on top. "You really are a heartless, unloving bastard, aren't you?"

Masters tried to glare past the pain, but failed.

The laptop, obscured by an unpaid telephone bill with a semicircular coffee stain, lay against the wall among the debris from the desk. Beside it, still curled from being confined to an envelope, was a printed page emblazoned with the now-familiar *Dempsey, Darcy and Dalziel* legal letterhead. Without qualms, Ronan lifted it and read:

Dear Sir

Please be advised that in accordance with the wishes of the late Padraig Ryan, one Fergal Seamus Gallagher will soon be arriving to take up residence at Doyle Farm. You are further advised that Mr Gallagher was a trusted confidant of Mr Ryan and, as such, will continue Mr Ryan's role in maintaining a harmonious household. Mr Gallagher will remain at Doyle Farm until Ronan Padraig Ryan reaches majority on 1st July 2023.

Yours faithfully

David Dalziel

Ronan wondered if there was time to stop Fergal Gallagher from embarking on the long flight from Ireland; the man was certainly no longer needed, Ronan and his blood rune were seeing to that. Dusting off the laptop, he dropped it onto the desk with a thud. "Where's your passport?" he asked impassively. Masters' head was slumped, his face almost as pallid as the paper he'd just written on. If it were anyone else, Ronan may have felt sympathy; as it was, he nudged Masters with his foot. "Where's your passport?"

"At the back of the drawer." The words appeared to suck the last resistance from him.

A short rummage later, Ronan's hand emerged with the small, blue booklet, an etched kangaroo and emu supporting a shield on the cover. He tossed it on the laptop and jerked his head at the door. "Now, get lost."

"I don't think I can drive," Masters moaned.

"You'll drive if it's the last thing you do," Ronan said. "But to prove I'm not heartless, I'll take these out to the Nissan, then come back for you." He shaped to leave, but spun, catching Masters' eyes on the yawning gun cabinet. Sitting in its rack was a polished shotgun, on the shelf above, a box of cartridges. Ronan smiled, locked the cabinet and left the room, whistling, key in one hand, laptop and passport in the other.

Masters immediately struggled to his feet, clutching his ribs, scowling. He moved round the desk, hunching over the open drawer, scratching through the contents. The air behind him sighed, and he whirled, gasping in agony.

"Looking for these?" Ronan jiggled the spare gun-cabinet key he'd grabbed when fetching the passport.

Masters seemed not to notice the keys as the last colour drained from his face. Pupils dilating with fear, he backed away. "How ... what?" he stammered.

"You shot me in the back like a dog, so now I'll be snapping at your heels if you dare come anywhere near here again." With a bleak glare, Ronan flicked his hand, and said, "Now go."

Clutching his ribs, Masters shuffled through the door and along the hallway, shooting agitated glances over his shoulder; dread drove his feet faster, agony slowed them down. Ronan followed, eyes fixed, through the lounge, the kitchen, across the verandah.

Masters lurched down the steps, panting and groaning, past a growling Smoky, hackles raised, and out the garden gate to his waiting vehicle. As he pulled the door open, he couldn't stifle a sharp cry; another escaped as he eased himself behind the steering wheel. After settling, he glowered at Ronan, who was now propped against a verandah post. When the engine rumbled into life, Masters gave the dials an automatic glance before throwing a final, apprehensive peek toward the verandah—it was empty.

A sigh from the rear seat turned him to stone. Seemingly against his will, his eyes were drawn to the mirror. An involuntary yelp of terror rolled into one of pain as he recoiled.

"Remember," Ronan said from behind, "never come back."

Masters wrenched the vehicle into gear, stomping the accelerator to the floor, spraying gravel and dirt into the warm evening. Ronan had already stepped lithely from the vehicle, before it lurched into a tight, sliding turn, straightened and sped away.

With the dust settling round him, Ronan visualised the entrance to Doyle Farm. Next instant, he was behind a huge bluegum tree about fifty metres from the closed gate. Almost immediately, he heard the deep-throated growl of the Nissan; soon after, headlights came bounding along the track, slicing the young night, carving shadows that quickly melted into the darkness that spawned them.

Masters was cursing as he got out to open the gate; Ronan set down on the rear seat for the second time. Still swearing, Masters gingerly climbed back into the cabin, and Ronan tapped on his shoulder. The man's terrified scream merged with a yowl of pain, becoming a single rolling clamour, only cut short when he collapsed against the steering wheel. A long, mournful horn-blast echoed through the trees.

With a fistful of shirt collar, Ronan yanked his stepfather's head off the horn button. A couple of slaps across the face and Masters stirred. As the man gathered his senses, Ronan alighted and stood, relaxed and casual, elbows on the driver's window sill. When Masters regained focus, he cringed away; bones scrapped, and he groaned. Huffing in misery, he peered sideways at Ronan. "You're not real," he whimpered.

"I was when you shot me."

Masters looked as if he was trying to swallow a cotton ball. "But ... but ... you just keep appearing out of nowhere ... like a ghost." His eyes became saucers, he puffed and snorted simultaneously, spittle flew from his lips.

Ronan stepped back, his task almost complete. "Come near Doyle Farm or any of this family again, and you will have no peace," Ronan promised him. "I will haunt you for the rest of your life."

Masters squawked and stood on the throttle. The Nissan catapulted through the gateway, drifted into a right-hand slide before disappearing in a cloud of dust toward Deadman's Gap.

66

THE SHOCK

A quick flytja and Ronan was back in the office ... no longer Masters'. It looked like Vikings had raided. Leaving everything as in place, he went to his room, immediately deleting the first part of Masters' recorded confession—Ronan didn't want to have to explain the shooting to anyone.

Although desperate to talk to Saoirse about it all, he had to settle for sitting on the edge of the bed and reading through his father's notebook from the desk. There was only a single day of entries, his last. It was the notebook Paidin had started when Maureen convinced him to take more legible notes. While scanning the notations on the runic inscriptions, Ronan realised how intelligent his father was; it almost read like Paidin had heimmed to the Viking Age and learnt Norse language and culture. Ronan swelled with pride at his father's insights, and he revelled in reading the poem in Norse again, tasting the words as they flowed from his tongue, recalling the scent of pine forest, the smokiness of the longhouse, the glow of Freyja's and Sten's fiery hair, and the aura of the Home Stone.

Movement in the window caught his attention. A wash of moving light swept across the garden fence, picking out the posts. Smoky barked from beneath the floor—not the hackles-raised warning reserved for Masters, or strangers, but an airy woof of welcome. The murmur of his mother's mellow driving drifted through the walls, so like her character—placid, smooth and gentle, coaxing rather than forcing, a sharp contrast to Masters' aggressive acceleration and combative gear changes. Smoky recognised the difference as well, for he gave another greeting bark, this time from out near the gate. Ronan could picture him standing there, tail wagging, so close you had to prod him out of the way to get through.

Shadows stretched along the fence wires, pivoting across the ground from the bottom of each post as the vehicle followed the twists and turns of the road to the house.

Amid his rising excitement at seeing his mother and brother again, he reminded himself to stay calm and casual. While only a few hours since they'd seen him, it was more than two weeks since he'd seen them. For a moment, he wondered if maybe it was all a dream. *Impossible! Saoirse was real!* The weightlessness of being in her arms, her electric touch, the sweetness of her breath in his nostrils, the exhilaration of her tender lips on his, all as undeniable as his heartache and anguish at parting. His fingertips traced the lump of the blood rune at the base of his skull, then moved to his chest, where he touched the fresh arrow scar, embracing its tenderness, drawing comfort from its presence.

But what to tell his mother?

The twist of trepidation in Ronan's stomach tempered the jangle of emotion at being back with family. While unsure how she would react to a banished husband, he knew he had to tell her everything—apart from the unexplainable bits, like blood runes, Saoirse, Kaupang and quite a bit more. To prevent tripping up, he must stay sharp. And, as he focused his mind in preparation, he realised he still wore Raven's Roost clothes.

They were almost home! Ronan ripped off his Irish gear, flinging it into the bottom of the wardrobe, pulling his cricket kit-bag over the top. The car purred like a contented cat as it glided up to the garden gate. Ronan jumped into a pair of shorts, snatched up a tee-shirt, tugging it on while rushing down the hall.

By the time the dusty vehicle came to rest in the pool of brightness cast by the outdoor lights, Ronan was propped nonchalantly against a verandah post. As he ambled down the steps, his shadow stretched out to where Smoky stood at the gate, nose pressed to the opening, tail whipping to and fro, wagging his whole body. The instant Ronan lifted the latch, Smoky forced it open with his muzzle, sliding through and darting across to stand, whining and wiggling, below the driver's window.

As soon as the door cracked, the dog's head was inside, demanding attention. "Hello, boy," Maureen said, patting the grizzled face, pushing it aside so she could exit.

"Hey, Mum," Ronan said casually, pulling the door wide, holding himself in check.

Maureen straightened, pecking him on the cheek. "Hello, love."

Ronan so desperately wanted to give her the biggest, longest hug.

"Thought I'd grab a few things while I had the chance," she explained, opening the rear door to a seat laden with overflowing grocery bags.

"Looks like you bought the whole shop," he said with a wry smile. As he reached in for a clutch of bags, he gave Ruddi a playful push on the shoulder. "Earth to Ruddi."

"Hey, Ro," Ruddi called absently from the front, his disembodied face levitating in the light thrown up from the gaming console on his lap.

"Hey, Ruddi," Ronan returned. His brother's voice was worth a dose of umrót.

Maureen frowned. "He bought that new Pokemon game he's been wanting," she said with exasperation. "He's barely lifted his head since … the world could end and he wouldn't notice."

A distracted 'would too' drifted from the front seat.

Ronan smiled at his mother, filled both hands and trailed her into the kitchen.

After lifting a leg to irrigate clinging dust from a tyre, Smoky followed as far as the bottom step with a wagging whine of content-ment; he sat, panting, cocked head and pricked ears following voices and footsteps. "Good boy," Ronan said, scratching the dog's ear in pass-ing, making a final trip to the car for the remaining groceries. Ruddi shadowed him up the steps on autopilot, thumbs and fingers dancing on buttons, face buried in the rising glow. He peeled away from Ronan's wake, carrying his beeping and flickering device toward the lounge room, his preferred gaming location.

When Ronan entered the kitchen, his mother was packing the last of the cold goods into the fridge. He dropped the bags on the table with a rattle of jars and cans. Maureen turned, pausing as she played her eyes over him. "You've changed," she said.

"Yeah, I put a hole in the other shirt," Ronan replied, trying to sound offhand, but panicking—his bullet-pierced tee-shirt was somewhere among the office debris. He must get it before his mother found it!

"I can see you changed your tee-shirt"—she chuckled—"you've got it on back-to-front."

Looking down, Ronan laughed. "Oh, I hadn't noticed."

His mother smiled; the room brightened; it was magic. But not as magical as Saoirse's.

"I didn't mean your clothes," she said, "you look different ... taller ..."

"Mum, you've only been gone a few hours." He wanted to deflect the examination. Inwardly squirming, he shrugged. "Same old me."

Maureen peered at him. "I know, love, but ... even your voice sounds"—she gave her head a slight shake of disbelief—"different ... more mature. I don't know ..."

His mother was seeing and hearing the changes wrought by the blood rune and all that had happened since. But the hidden power that, when needed, flowed through his veins, bolstering muscles, sharpening skills and strengthening character, seemed to desert him when he inhaled to begin his story. Ronan felt the weight of his mother's gaze. "Mum," he said, licking instantly dry lips, "I have something to tell you."

Maureen stiffened. "Did you take Bruno's notebook again?"

The mixture of reprimand and accusation in her tone stung Ronan. "No!" he responded, too sharply. Her hands flew to her hips, and his shoulders drooped in immediate apology. "I didn't take his notebook," he said, before continuing to himself, "It's Dad's notebook." He held his breath, hoping the hair-splitting was acceptable to the gods. Nothing happened apart from his mother's hardening stare. "But," he continued, his confidence returning, "Masters has left." With a sense of satisfaction and finality, he added, "For good."

Maureen grasped the back of the nearest chair. Blood draining from her face, she stared at Ronan as though recognising the undeniable truth in his tone and demeanour. Still, she appeared to fight it, seeking an alternative. "What are you talking about, Ronan?" she asked, voice shrinking, uncertain.

"You need to sit down, Mum."

67

THE WEAVING

For almost an hour, the story flowed from Ronan's lips. Piece by piece, Maureen's reality of the past sixteen years was dismantled. And with each revelation, she shrank further, until she was hunched over her elbows, clinging to a damp handkerchief as the marriage she thought she had, crumbled round her.

"He came home drunk, as usual," Ronan began. "I was in my room, reading Dad's notebooks, and when he went into the office, I thought I'd try again ..."

During the telling, Ronan ignored the needles to his conscience whenever he twisted the truth to alleviate undue stress to her, or grief to himself. Where necessary, he left out bits—even huge chunks—as he meticulously wove an alternative version of events that was least traumatic and most believable to his mother. And whispering in his ear the whole time was Grandmother Freyja—'it is the seiðmann's role to weave the future ... use your powers to do good in the world'.

"Masters was sitting at the desk with the notebook open ... it was Dad's handwriting, not his."

Head shaking, face haggard, Maureen lifted red-rimmed eyes, seeking understanding.

"I lost it," Ronan admitted. "... accused him of stealing the notebook."

Eyes swimming afresh, Maureen said, "But Bruno said Paidin was holding it when he fell. I don't understand."

"Mum, it's simple, Masters lied. And it wasn't the only thing."

Maureen's head jolted. "What are you talking about?"

"Well ..." Ronan hesitated, searching for the best way forward. A minefield of half-truths and selective fabrications lay before him, but they were necessary to minimise his mother's shredded feelings, and to protect the secret of the blood rune. He could never tell his mother the truth of the twin runes discovered in the cave on that fatal dig. At least, not with her supposedly dead fiancé caught somewhere in the web of time. "... when I accused Masters of stealing Dad's notebook, he got really aggressive and, as he jumped up, I hit him with a full chudan tzuki." It was the first karate straight-punch Ronan had ever thrown with intent. Driving up from his legs, through his hips and chest, putting his full body behind it, he'd tried to drive his knuckles clean through his nemesis.

Maureen's hand flew to her mouth. "Ronan!"

"Mum, he was going to wallop me." Masters' eyes always gave him away; Ronan had so much practice in recognising it, he knew when a blow was coming even before the man himself.

"Ronan, Bruno would never hit you."

"What about the time with Ruddi and the golf clubs?"

Maureen swallowed. "Yes, but that was the drink. And Bruno didn't hit you, he choked ..." Her voice faded as if recognising the absurdity of what she'd said.

"Mum," Ronan said, exasperation showing, "hello?"

Maureen lowered her eyes. "Bruno would never deliberately hit you." It was a hopeful statement devoid of conviction.

Ronan reached across the table, clasping his mother's hands, peering past her tears. "Mum, for years I've been too afraid to tell you this ..." He sucked in a breath. The familiar bowel loosening he always felt whenever he imagined the consequences of confiding in his mother, failed to materialise.

Maureen frowned. "Love, what is it?"

A fragment of that banished dread returned to do a little jig, deep beneath his belly button. It was a reflex, and now that he was trying to break free, it wasn't giving up without a fight. Ronan cursed himself. Closing his eyes, he embraced the warmth and strength flowing from the rune, rippling through his body, stilling his gut, quelling the dread.

"Masters has been hurting me." The barriers collapsed. Years of pent-up fear, rage, helplessness and shame leapt to freedom from the centre of his chest like caged animals, and as they did, a torrent of words fled his mouth even faster. During the breakout, Ronan's tears welled, mirroring his mother's. While his sprang from liberation and relief, hers started as denial before morphing to disbelief, then horror.

Without detailing individual instances, Ronan outlined how the rough words had turned into arm twisting, progressing to whacks, pinches, cuffs across the ears, and the occasional fist, becoming worse as time passed. Nothing Ronan did was good enough, and most of what he said was smart-mouthed, even when it wasn't. But it all stopped when Grandpa Paddy came, only to start again after he died.

Maureen stared, unseeing, shoulders slumped, face streaked with tears. The denial lasted until Ronan lifted his shirt to show the fading yellow mottling on his back. As the damning evidence sank in, disbelief succumbed to horror as she laid the blame at her own feet. "Oh, Ronan, my poor darling," she sobbed, clutching his hands. "How could I have been such a blind fool?"

"It's not your fault, Mum," he said, covering the bruises, fetching her a glass of water.

"But I should have known."

"Mum," Ronan said, more sharply than he intended, "how could you have known? It was only just rough talk in front of you ... or anyone else." While he was no longer afraid of Masters, the thought of the man triggered a reflexive shiver. Deep loathing replaced it in an instant, settling in the top of his chest, writhing like a dying snake. "Besides," Ronan continued with a heavy scowl, "Masters said it wouldn't be pretty for you and Ruddi if I blabbed."

Maureen's gasp sucked the air from the room. The usual, healthy glow of her skin was gone, so too the sparkle from her eyes; even her hair looked dull, lacking its customary sheen. It had been obvious for years that her husband would never love his stepson, but hearing her husband's threats of violence to herself and Ruddi—his own son— seemed like a punch to her stomach.

"But I loved him," Maureen declared, her misery thick enough to touch. "At least, I loved the person I thought he was."

"Well, I don't think Masters was ever that man," Ronan said. Regretting his tone at once, he reached out, squeezing her hand. "I don't think he ever loved you, Mum," he said gently. It was a harsh thing to say, but if she was to have any chance of moving on from that loathsome man, she had to hear the truth.

Maureen choked back a sob. "Then why did he marry me?"

"He wanted to prove to himself, and the rest of the world, that he beat Dad after all ... even though Dad was gone." Ronan couldn't bring himself to say 'dead', it might tempt fate. "Masters made it very clear to me he couldn't stand Dad ... resented his talent at cricket and with his work ... reckoned Dad stole you from him."

Struggling to make sense of his words, Maureen stared, denial shaking her head. "But they were friends ..."

"He never loved any of us," Ronan said with finality.

68

THE TELLING

Maureen's body shuddered with surging waves of misery. Ronan circled the table and hugged her. Her howling must have cut through the electronic beeping of Ruddi's gaming console, for he materialised with a puzzled expression that instantly turned to concern. "Mum, what's wrong?" he said, embracing her.

"Your dad has left," Ronan said simply.

Ruddi stared from Ronan to his sobbing mother, frowning at her distress. "Something else is wrong?" After no response, he added, "When will he be back?"

"Never." Ronan relished the sweet finality of the word long after it left his tongue.

"Has he died ... like Grandpa?"

"No."

"But he isn't coming back?"

"Nope."

Suspicion tightened Ruddi's face. "Are you sure?"

If Maureen heard the hope threaded through her younger son's words, she gave no sign. She sat, head bowed, shoulders shaking.

"He left a letter on his desk saying he was never coming back, and he told me so himself," Ronan said.

"And you believed him?" Ruddi gawped at his brother.

Lips compressed, Ronan gave a single nod; Ruddi mouthed, "Oh."

At last, Maureen spoke. "Ruddi, did your father ever hurt you?"

"Plenty of times." There was no hesitation.

Two heads jerked toward him.

"When?" said Ronan, taken aback.

"How?" Maureen asked, as if afraid of the answer.

"I copped the strap heaps, and cuffs over the ear, and smacks on the bum," Ruddi admitted. "But nothing like Ro."

Maureen considered him. "What do you mean?"

Ruddi swallowed. "I ..." He paused, eyes darting. "Are you sure he's not coming back?"

"Positive," Ronan assured him.

"It's okay, love," Maureen said. "Just tell me."

Ruddi swallowed again. "Well, I made this fort once, on top of the hay bales in the shed, and"—he drew a ragged breath—"one day I was up there playing and I heard Dad growling ... he was furious ... and he dragged Ro in ... by the arm ... Dad's neck was so red ... I was petrified ... I just hid." The colour drained from his face, and he cast a fearful glance toward the front door. "Never?" he asked his brother.

"Nev-er," Ronan replied, emphasising each syllable, shaking his head in time.

Regardless, Ruddi kept an uneasy watch on the door; it remained resolutely closed. Reassured, he continued, "Dad was twisting your arm, remember?"

That day returned to Ronan, as fresh as yesterday. He nodded grimly. The crushing, vise-grip on his biceps, the screaming tendons in his shoulder, the fire in his flesh as that length of polythene water pipe rained down with a hollow, echoing thwock, thwock, thwock.

"I thought he was going to break your arm." Ruddi looked sickened. "But you never made a sound." Admiration crept into his voice. "He grabbed a piece of poly pipe and flogged you until you collapsed. I thought he'd killed you." Ruddi's tormented voice trailed away as the relived fear became too much. Ronan's gut twisted. Maureen, eyes widening in horror, gave a strangled, moaning gasp.

But there was no holding Ruddi back now. The walls of silence toppled—words, so long imprisoned by fear, jostled for freedom.

"You were lying there ... not moving ... and Dad yanked your head up ... by your hair. I'll never forget the way your eyes ... rolled"—Ruddi choked on a sob—"and I'll never forget what he said ..."

Unbidden, a brief, irrational sense of guilt flashed through Ronan at the thought of Ruddi overhearing what Masters had hissed that day. Despite the flow of energy and confidence from the rune, he struggled as Ruddi's words ripped the scabs off half-healed wounds. He wanted to close his ears, yet he also felt the load lifting, and wanted the relief and freedom of having it gone. But, hearing someone else tell of that first beating was like having a hessian sack dragged across fresh sunburn.

That day in the hay-shed had been an epic battle of dogged determination against brute force, of savagery versus innocence; Ronan's mind had long sealed those recollections in a deep recess, hidden from even himself. Occasionally they were let out into the daylight of his recall to fuel resistance to yet another assault and, with their purpose served, the guardians of his sanity would, once again, cast them into that unacknowledged dungeon.

"He said," Ruddi continued, "'if you ever breathe even one word of this to anyone, your mother and brother will cop it', and ..." Face crumpling, tears welling, his words turned into sobs. "I ... wet ... my ... pants."

Maureen howled harder, great keening sobs wracking her body.

Ronan, arm still wrapped round her, drew Ruddi in with the other, holding them both close, two sobbing, shaking bodies, each confronting their own horrors. "So did I," he lied. He didn't know what else to say, but wanted to ease Ruddi's torment.

But it had no impact on Ruddi's misery or wailing. "I was so scared ... I thought you were dead ... and I was so ... ashamed."

The distress of her youngest, her baby, cut through Maureen's anguish. She blew her nose in a genteel snort of determination, wiped her eyes, took a deep breath, and pulled Ruddi onto her lap. Cradling his head to her breast, she crooned and rocked. "I should've helped you, Ro," he sobbed into her bosom.

Ronan shook his head. "He'd only have hurt you"—he squeezed Ruddi's shoulder—"but he can't anymore, 'cause he's never coming back."

"But how can you be so sure?" Ruddi gave an enormous, shuddering sigh.

"Because I showed him he couldn't bully me anymore," Ronan said, face bleak. "Actually, I knocked him off his feet." The memory brought a grim smile. "And I think I broke his ribs."

Ruddi gawked; Maureen gasped.

"He was going to hit me," Ronan said impassively, "and I wasn't ever going to let him do that again."

Instance after instance, Ronan recounted the abuses he had suffered at the hands of his stepfather, right through a piecemeal dinner and late into the night. While every occasion was tattooed across his memory, the worst were only dredged up by the retelling of the lesser ones. And playing on his mind was the bullet-holed tee-shirt lying among the debris from Masters' desk.

Making an excuse to duck to the toilet, Ronan darted into the office, snatching the holed garment from the disarray, and throwing it into his wardrobe with his Irish clothes. Soon afterwards, Maureen sobbed her way through the mess, howling afresh as she read the cold, detached note on the desk. Ruddi stayed close, unable to relax despite Ronan's assurances.

It was after ten o'clock when an unexpected bark from beneath the floorboards made them all jump. Smoky's warning bark was unmistakable—a strange car was coming. Maureen chewed her lip, Ruddi blanched, and Ronan's heart gave a quick flutter before his ears told him it wasn't Masters' Nissan. He glanced at the clock and frowned. When he got to the verandah, the approaching lights were playing over the garden fence, spraying shadows across the house walls.

Maureen and Ruddi joined him in time to catch the full blaze of the headlights as the vehicle rumbled up to the front gate. Despite dazzled eyes, Ronan recognised the stripe of blue checks along the side of the white four-wheel-drive, and the bar of unlit blue lights on its roof. "It's a copper," he said unnecessarily.

69

THE CLOSURE

Constable Ted Reynolds was a barrel on legs, rather stubby legs. The pressure from his enormous girth turned his blue uniform shirt into a loaded weapon: the straining buttons were a row of high-tensioned projectiles on the verge of exploding free, a danger to any unshielded eye within ricochet range. It always fascinated Ronan how those tiny disks with their flimsy anchoring threads held back such a weight, especially when the man laughed. And he laughed often, but not tonight. Tonight, as he rolled from the vehicle, his normally cheerful face was sombre.

"G'day, Maureen," he wheezed, sweat glistening across his brow, damp stains spreading from his armpits. It was a warm night, the warmest of the summer so far, and it made every movement by the policeman appear to come with great effort. He pushed open the gate, dropped a hand to absently scratch Smoky's head, and puffed, "G'day, boys."

Although Ronan couldn't recall a time when the man wasn't a candidate for a weight-loss program, his mother often told stories of how a young, lithe Edward Reynolds dominated tennis courts from Warwick to Toowoomba, danced all night, and would show up the local lads at sports days by pole vaulting higher than them, even in his police boots. But that was many years and many meals ago.

Ronan nodded a greeting in response. He was expecting admonishment from his mother for saying copper instead of policeman, but none came—she was off her game. Ruddi's 'g'day', Smoky's wagging tail, and Maureen's 'good evening, Edward' rounded out the greetings. Ronan marvelled at his mother: it didn't matter how she was feeling, she never lost her manners—so like Grandma Moira.

Constable Reynolds looked from one cheerless face to another. "Is something wrong, Maureen?" Despite his jovial nature, he missed nothing. He often brought a drunken Bruno Masters home, or delivered a friendly warning about the previous night's conduct. Ronan always got the impression it was the policeman's friendship with his mother that stopped more serious fallout from her husband's troublesome behaviour. Ronan also suspected that, like every other man in the district his mother's age, Ted Reynolds was under her spell. He saw it all the time.

"I was about to ask you the same thing," Maureen replied. Before he could respond, she added, "But come in and have a cuppa." Without waiting for a reply, she returned to the kitchen.

The loaded shirt followed her; Ronan and Ruddi brought up the rear.

"Is this about Bruno?" she said, turning from setting the kettle to boil.

The man's salt and pepper beard hid most of his face, but not his eyes. They sharpened. "Why do you say that?"

"He left this evening," she told him wearily. "There was a note on his desk, said he wouldn't be back."

Ronan and Ruddi edged to her side; the policeman's eyes followed them. "Why did he leave?" Reynolds asked.

They were harmless questions, but to Ronan's ears, they carried subtle interrogation.

"I told him to," Ronan said, without expression, jumping in before his mother could say anything to make things sound better than they were. "Actually, I told him to leave and never come back."

If Ronan's admission surprised Ted Reynolds, he didn't show it. "And why was that?" the policeman asked, as if wanting to know something mundane, like why the hens preferred to lay their eggs under the house.

The prospect of laying out all the details, yet again, left Ronan numb, so he turned, lifting his shirt, holding up an arm.

"Bloody hell," the policeman breathed. "Did Bruno do that?"

Reynolds aimed the question at Maureen, who nodded, pressing her lips against the shame. While Ronan sensed her body tremble, preparing for another bout of tears, he was smiling inside—there was perverse justice in Masters being blamed for the remnant bruises from the hólmganga. *Karma.*

"When?" Reynolds eyes were like tiny radars pinging at each word, verifying whether truth or lie.

"Pick a time," Ronan replied. As soon as the bitter words slid past his lips, he heard their insolence. He flashed a glance at his mother, but she was studying the policeman.

"So, you just told him to leave?" Reynolds asked—ping ... ping. "And he did?"

"No. He shaped to hit me, so I let fly with a karate punch ... knocked him over the desk ... think I broke his ribs."

"Is that right?" A shadow of incredulity crept into the constable's words.

Ronan ignored it, he just wanted it done, wanted to slam the door on all memories of his stepfather. "And I smashed the rifle across the desk ... bent the barrel."

"Did you now? And why was that?"

"Edward, is this really necessary now?" Even her words were slump-shouldered and haggard.

"It's all right, Mum," Ronan injected before the policeman could respond. With his attention returned to his inquisitor, he said, "Because he kept looking at it ... it was propped on the end of the desk ... I didn't trust him."

"So, what did you do?"

"After I wrecked the gun? That's when I told him to clear out." Ronan pulled his phone from his pocket, tapped play, and set it on the table. When Masters' recorded admissions ended, Maureen was wailing afresh, Ruddi was ashen-faced but resolute, and Constable Reynolds was mute as a stone.

The radars fell silent. "What a cowardly bastard," he said to no one in particular.

A heavy silence settled, each of them lost in their own thoughts, memories and emotions.

Constable Ted Reynolds studied Ronan. "I don't know how," he said at last, "but you put the fear of God into him. He drove like a maniac down Deadman's Gap Road. By the looks of the tracks, he took every corner so fast, he drifted sideways on the gravel ... every corner bar one."

Expectant silence embraced the kitchen. Ted Reynolds tugged at his beard. "I'm sorry to have to tell you this, Maureen, but we've found his burnt-out Nissan at the bottom of the gorge at Deadman's Gap."

———

FOUR DAYS LATER, Fergal Gallagher limped his way into their lives. Having completed his Covid quarantine, he hitched a ride on a truck to Killarney, then caught a lift with the mail lady to the Doyle Farm front gate. From there, he hobbled the half-kilometre up to the house, lugging a huge backpack of belongings and an assortment of envelopes from the mailbox.

The family resemblance to Grandpa Paddy was unmistakable around his right eye and, perhaps, his nose, but whatever else he shared with the cousin of his father was hidden behind hair and an enormous burn scar. The luxuriant growth sprouting from his head swept in a sandy curtain across his ears, through a leather thong, and well down his back. A short, darkish beard carpeted the right side of his face, while the left side was an upheaval of scar-tissue, a discordant Play-Doh creation. It dragged his eye downward, tugged at his nose, and lifted the corner of his mouth into a Halloween smile. The disfigurement ran from his temple to his collarbone, and whatever the accident was must have damaged his throat, for he spoke with a husky rasp. Fergal Gallagher wasn't particularly tall, but you wouldn't lose him in a crowd.

The scar intrigued Ronan and fascinated Ruddi, while Maureen acted as if it wasn't there, as did Fergal himself.

Despite Ronan's insistence that he was no longer needed, Fergal said he was duty-bound to honour his undertaking to Paddy Ryan. He promptly unpacked his belongings into the cottage where Grandpa Paddy had lived, and proceeded to make himself useful round the farm.

———

THREE DAYS after the arrival of Doyle Farm's latest Irishman, they buried a bundle of charred remains as far away from Grandpa Paddy as the tiny Killarney cemetery allowed. When the four of them returned home, Maureen and Ruddi went straight to bed, exhausted by yet another funeral and all it entailed; Fergal retired to his room; and Ronan tried to manage his mounting excitement. When the last light blinked out, he downed a couple of his Australian supply of Kwells, slipped into his Irish clothes, and sat on the edge of the bed to wait. The instructions on the packet said two tablets, thirty minutes before travel.

Ronan looked at his phone for the hundredth time ... only twenty-one minutes. But he could wait no longer; he blanked his mind, pictured Saoirse's cottage, set the date to Friday, fifth of November 2004, and floated into ró.

OLD NORSE WORDS

FOR THE FEW words attributed as Norse in this book, I have tried to use genuine Old Norse words; however, where the relevant Old Norse word was either unknown, or visually or phonetically unsuitable, Icelandic was used—Icelandic being the closest modern language to Old Norse. In one instance—väktare—Swedish was used. I humbly seek your indulgence in embracing them as part of the story.

The following pronunciation guide is not intended to be definitive, but is an earnest attempt to provide a close approximation of authentic diction using Icelandic as a guide where Old Norse was not available. Without exception, the first syllable of an Old Norse word is stressed, and where there is an accent over a vowel—as in Víking—it is a long vowel sound, although not necessarily the same sound as in English.

I hope you have as much fun with the words as I did, and thank you for your leniency.

Bless (BLAIRsss) - **goodbye** (Icelandic)

Blóð (BLOW-th) - **blood** (Old Norse)

Flytja (FLEE-t-ya) - **relocate** (Icelandic)

Fundur (FN-derr) - **encounter** (Icelandic)

Haetta (HIGH-ta) - **danger** (Icelandic)

Heill (HI-l) - **health**; luck (Old Norse)

Heim (HEY-m) - **home** (Old Norse)

Hólmganga (HOLE-m-gung-ka) - **duel** (Old Norse)

Hrúga (HRROO-ka) - **heap** (Icelandic)

Jarl (YAR-l) - **earl** (Old Norse)

Norn (NORR-n) - **witch** (Icelandic)

Ró (RRO) - **tranquillity** (Icelandic)

Rún (RROO-n) - **rune** (Old Norse)

Rúnar (RROO-nar) - **runes** (Old Norse)

Seiðmann (SAY-th-mun) - **male practitioner of seiðr** (Old Norse)

Seiðr (SAY-ther) - **enchantment; spell**; the art of shaping and foretelling the future (Old Norse)

Steinn (STEY-n) - **stone** (Old Norse)

Trufla (TROO-f-la) - **interfere** (Icelandic)

Umrót (OOM-rote) - **turbulence** (Icelandic)

Väktare (VEK-tar-ray) - **guardian**; custodian (Swedish)

Víking (VEE-king) - **expedition**; raiding or trading trip (Old Norse)

Víkingar (VEE-king-arr) - plural of **víking** (Old Norse)

Víkingr (VEE-king-rr) - **expeditioner**; víking participant (Old Norse)

Völva (VURL-va) - **of the staff; staff woman**; female practitioner of seiðr; seeress (Old Norse)

Völur (VUR-lure) - plural of **völva** (Old Norse)

Yggdrasill (IG-dra-sil) - **an immense tree** connecting the tangible world with the mythological (Old Norse)

ACKNOWLEDGEMENTS

WRITING A BOOK is a solo endeavour, but getting it into the hands of you, the reader, takes a group of talented and dedicated people.

My heartfelt thanks to sounding board, initial reader, fearless critic and general task master, my beautiful wife, Delia. Also, much gratitude to mentor and inspiration, Bruce Honeywill; early readers, Iaman Petrie, Roelie Hartwig, Helen Avery and Naomi Scott for their insightful feedback; editorial adviser, Evelyn Quinlan; Kit Carstairs and the fantastic team at The Manuscript Appraisal Agency; and cover design wizard, Hannah Maddock.

To everyone else who provided encouragement, friendship and space to work during this process, my sincere gratitude.

And to you, precious reader, thank you for accompanying my characters on their journey ... they look forward to having you with them on their next adventure. And to whet your appetite, a snippet of *The Fire Rune* begins over the page ... enjoy!

THE FIRE RUNE

THE SMALL COTTAGE was deathly quiet; the air held its musty breath. The last of the dying day fought a hopeless rear-guard against the advancing dusk. Nothing moved.

With an almost resigned sigh, the air split open like a torn curtain, and through it, a shadowy figure folded outward into the room. The sight would have made a watcher question their sanity, but there was no one else.

The shadow froze, melting into the gloom—something was wrong, very wrong. As the head eased round, the failing light caught probing eyes. But there was no danger to detect, only emptiness and silence where there shouldn't have been.

With a sigh, the figure stirred, only to freeze again as the curved picture tube of an old television set reflected the movement. Then, with a faint smile and shake of the head, the shadow strode across the room, stepping round a low couch and shin-biting coffee table, reaching out, flicking an unseen switch.

Light burst across the darkness, throwing the shape of a strapping sixteen-year-old lad into sharp relief. "Saoirse?" he called, blinking away the sudden brightness. There was no answer. Ronan Ryan strode to an adjacent doorway, poking his sandy mop into the girl's bedroom. The pastel bedspread was rumpled, drawers sagged open, some with clothes draping out. It looked like she had packed in a hurry, or someone had gone through her things—he much preferred the first possibility. And, try as he might, he struggled to suck a trace of her apple-scented hair conditioner from the stale air.

Anxiety clutched at Ronan's heart— only a disaster could have stopped Saoirse from being here to meet him as arranged. Last Sunday, he'd left her to return home, promising to be back the following Friday evening— now.

For a moment, he wondered if his flytja had been inaccurate, whether he'd overshot in his excitement to see her again. But no, he'd taken extra care in visualising the fifth of November 2004, emptying his head of all other thoughts, and floating into the weightlessness of ró.

Still, uncertainty squirmed in his gut, and he had no way to quell it —no phone, and no one to call. Of their own accord, his fingers found the lump at the base of his skull—his gut calmed. But it was short-lived.

The rumble of an approaching vehicle ruptured the silence. Ronan's heart tumbled at the thought of seeing Saoirse again, wrapping his arms around her lithe body, burying his nose in the scent of her long, brown hair. But it wasn't the contented purr of the Kelly family car, it was the impatient growl of pent-up power. The sound was familiar, the memories it triggered, unpleasant.

Twin beams of insistent light stabbed into the kitchen as the vehicle approached. Ronan shrank from the window. Gravel crunched, the engine stilled, headlights blazing against the front of the building, threatening to blister paint. Ronan retreated further into the house. At the other end of those beams, a gold-coloured Range Rover crouched— a tiger ready to pounce.

Doors slammed, and two sets of footsteps clomped toward the front door. "I tell you, there's someone in there," said the familiar griping voice of Fionn Egan.

"Are you sure the light wasn't left on?" It was a woman's voice, much older than Egan, but with clear kinship.

"Of course I'm sure, woman," was the arrogant response. "I was here last night ... it wasn't on then."

"Do not speak to me like that." Despite the menacing tone, Ronan now recognised the voice of Egan's mother. Even though they'd only met once, Fionella Egan left an impression—everything about her was unforgettable, especially the calculating reptilian eyes and the silky voice.

What were Egan and his mother doing at the Kelly's empty cottage?

"I'll speak how I damn-well want."

Ronan could picture Fionn Egan's pale blue eyes cold with disdain, even for his mother. And he could imagine the woman's own eyes flashing an icy warning to her son.

But that wasn't his concern. Saoirse had been desperate for him to return, and knew he was coming at this time. So where was she? Ronan's fluttering gut told him to flytja to the stables, but his brain said staying close was the best way to discover more.

"Do not forget," the woman hissed, each syllable dripping with threat, "what I am doing for you."

"You mean for yourself." The harsh slap of an open palm on a flabby jowl cut Fionn Egan's words short. There was a long silence before a churlish, "What was that for?"

"To teach you some manners," Fionella responded, her words brittle with arrogance and restrained rage.

The apple never falls far from the tree, Ronan thought, channelling his Irish grandfather.

"Now, do you have the key?" she asked, simmering.

"Of course," Fionn Egan snapped, his earlier insolence returning.

"Well, what are you waiting for? Open the damned door."

Good sense told Ronan to leave, but he was worried about Saoirse and Darragh. Rather than a short flytja to the nearby stables, he stayed, hoping to overhear some hint of the Kelly's whereabouts. For an absurd moment, he considered asking the Egans, but how could he explain his presence in the locked house? Instead, he slipped beneath Saoirse's bed, under cover of aggressive key rattling in the front door.

Squealing hinges gave way to Fionn Egan's born-to-rule whine: "I tell you, the light wasn't on yesterday."

"Well, let's see if anyone's here, shall we?" Subtle double snicks punctuated Fionella's response, and the icy hand of fear clamped around Ronan's throat—there was no mistaking the sound of a shot-gun's hammer being thumbed back through half to full cock, ready for firing. Either both Egans had a single-barrel gun, or one held a double-barrel killing machine. At close quarters, there was nothing more deadly.

Ronan bellied further into the bed's shadows, the stone floor as cold as death through his shirt. Despite the Egans' belated attempt at silence, the scrape and click of soles on stone whispered into the stillness.

Peering from his sanctuary, Ronan saw two pairs of legs creep past the open doorway, heading for the back of the small building. His nostrils twitched at disturbed dust.

"We know you're in here." A quaver of uncertainty edged Fionn Egan's voice. "Come out so we can talk. We won't hurt you."

With the pretence of stealth dropped, the searchers opened and closed doors, searching potential hiding places. The younger Egan, patience clearly spent, whined, "What's it matter if someone's been here, anyway? It's not like they're going to find anything."

"You will learn"—Fionella's voice left Ronan with no doubt where her son got his sneer—"that when you play for high stakes, you leave nothing to chance. Now, check this last room."

Ronan's nose twitched again, then decided the dust had to go. He pinched his nostrils in desperation, striving to swallow the sneeze, almost succeeding. An involuntary convulsion gripped his body, only a tiny one, but enough to tap the back of his head on the underside of the mattress slats.

In panic, Ronan tried to blank his mind, to flytja away, but before he could, booming double explosions shattered the night. Twin barrels sent screaming pellets skipping off the stone floor, filling the space beneath the bed with a swarm of deadly lead hornets. A thousand excruciating stings engulfed Ronan. His world went black.

————

To be notified of the release date of *The Fire Rune,* scan the QR code on the back cover.

www.ingramcontent.com/pod-product-compliance
Lightning Source LLC
Chambersburg PA
CBHW030522120726
47904CB00005B/1579